In the great tradition of hard-boiled detective fiction, Scott [illegible] written a noir tale that casts shadows on a sunny place. *Kona Winds* is a moody, thrilling novel about scandal and corruption in 1950s Hawai'i, where war veteran and homicide detective Francis Yoshikawa takes us through a Hawai'i version of Dante's *Inferno*. It's a rare, fascinating look at the underbelly of O'ahu.

—Steph Cha, author of *Follow Her Home*, *Beware Beware*, and *Dead Soon Enough*

Homicide detective Francis "Sheik" Yoshikawa imbibes bourbon every chance he gets, but it's Scott Kikkawa's readers who will be intoxicated by the intricate plot and the whirlwind ride. This noir thriller is notable for its remarkable verisimilitude, its sumptuous reconjuring of Honolulu in the early 1950s.

—Rodney Morales, author of *For a Song* and *When the Shark Bites*

Evocative and riveting, *Kona Winds* grabs the reader from the first page and does not let go until the end. Even then, prepare to be haunted by author Scott Kikkawa's scarred characters, gritty 1950s Honolulu, and layered tale in this elegant noir. I loved it!

—Pamela Rotner Sakamoto, author of *Midnight in Broad Daylight*

Scott Kikkawa's *Kona Winds* is a blast of fresh air that lets Hawai'i's people—both good and bad—speak for themselves in a crime narrative. Homicide detective Frankie Yoshikawa is a revelation. Only he can lead the reader through a harrowing world that is at turns tougher and more multihued than expired SPAM. *Kona Winds* blows past *Hawaii 5-O*. It goes all the way to 11!

—Ed Lin, author of the Robert Chow mystery series and the Taipei Night Market Mystery series

Kona Winds

ISBN 978-1-943756-02-5

This is issue #116 of *Bamboo Ridge, Journal of Hawai'i Literature and Arts*
(ISSN # 0733-0308).

Published by Bamboo Ridge Press
Printed in the United States of America

Bamboo Ridge Press is a member of the Community of Literary Magazines and Presses (CLMP).

Typesetting and design: Jui-Lien Sanderson
Cover art: *Yoshikawa Meets Ellen Park*, 2019, by Tommy Hite, oil on wood panel, 19"w x 24"h

Bamboo Ridge Press is a nonprofit, tax-exempt corporation formed in 1978 to foster the appreciation, understanding, and creation of literary, visual, and performing arts by, for, or about Hawai'i's people. The organization is funded by book sales and individual donors and supplemented in part by support from the National Endowment for the Arts; the Hawai'i State Foundation on Culture and the Arts (through appropriations from the Legislature of the State of Hawai'i and grants from the National Endowment for the Arts); and the Hawai'i Community Foundation's Baciu Cultural Fund and Robert Emens Black Fund.

NATIONAL ENDOWMENT for the ARTS arts.gov

HAWAI'I STATE FOUNDATION on CULTURE and the ARTS

HAWAI'I COMMUNITY FOUNDATION

Bamboo Ridge is published twice a year. For orders, subscription information, and back issues contact:

Bamboo Ridge Press
P.O. Box 61781
Honolulu, Hawai'i 96839-1781

808.626.1481
brinfo@bambooridge.com
www.bambooridge.com

5 4 3 2 1   19 20 21 22 23

Kona Winds

SCOTT KIKKAWA

BAMBOO RIDGE PRESS

For my mother, who endured the challenges of a different time and emerged the strongest person I know.

Prologue

Each of us bears his own hell. I remember that from between naps in a classical lit lecture.

Virgil. Dante's tour guide in the netherworld. In the space of a few days in a single week I was to play Virgil to a handful of doomed souls, lighting the way to their personal hells with a big fat neon parking-garage arrow.

I'm a homicide detective in Honolulu, a pretty place that can feel like one of the burning rivers of Dante's *Inferno* when the kona winds announce their presence. I ka 'ōlelo no ke ola, i ka 'ōlelo no ka make. *In words there is life, in words there is death.* The old Hawaiians knew what they were talking about and they must've known something about the shit that comes out of the mouths of homicide detectives. Life and death. *Paradiso* and *Inferno*. The endless *Purgatorio* in between. Reports with carbons. The stink of cigars to mask the stink of corpses. Bad testimony or worse, bad coffee. It feels medieval, but it isn't. It's 1953. *Anno Domini.*

I got my first taste of the *Inferno* overseas, in the broken streets and scorched fields of Italy and France. I crossed over the River Styx into the fire with a lot of other Japanese boys from Kakaako; we were ferried by Charon, Dante's pilot of the damned, from Oahu to Camp Shelby to the far shore of Anzio. One of the lucky few who cheated the ferryman, I crossed over and returned. Most of those Kakaako boys ended up being planted in the black soil of Europe, their last taste of chicken hekka coming from out of a soon-to-be-fallen comrade's helmet. I went back to my mother's hekka, with a healthy side of monku and shibai served up by my older sisters. I devoured it all and, for the first time, did so gratefully. I hung around for a few weeks until the novelty of having survived wore off and used the G.I. Bill to head for New York. There, I traded in tales of Momotaro and Chushingura for Dante, Chaucer, Shakespeare, and Milton. If I wax poetic, it's only because the only good my course of study ever did me was to put all those dead bodies and dead feelings into context.

I killed people in the war. I had first-hand experience in producing corpses while avoiding becoming one. After four years of reading stanzas as to why and how corpses came to be, Dante taught me that death is a farce, that eschatology is a grand joke, a satire of gluttonous living for sellout crowds. A *Divine Comedy* indeed. It certainly didn't help me professionally; I'm a cop, not a Nobel Laureate.

My Honolulu is choked with corpses, most of them made because of their hard lives, labor, luck, and drinking, and eventually bad arteries. In that respect, the cane-cutting immigrant and his haole exploiter have been the same. We all have to go sometime. Every now and then, though, a corpse is made by the deliberate hand of someone else, and that is when I earn my paycheck.

Artillery smoke hung in the cold stale air over the expanse of ruined bodies in my time on the battlefields. These sooty little death clouds followed me home and became the smoke of cheap cigars over the chalk outlines of discarded lives in the forgotten corners of Honolulu; always there, it got into my eyes and hair and reminded me that Hell or Paradise was just around the corner from Purgatory. I slogged through and, if I wasn't careful, I could turn that corner before I wanted to.

Editors' note: In the story that follows, Hawaiian place names and the names of royalty do not include diacritical marks and appear as they would have been printed in English language newspapers in 1953.

1

It began with a corpse. A flaccid, bloated, waterlogged corpse late on a Sunday morning. When you sought refuge in a bottle of whiskey on a Saturday night, Sunday mornings were your time to crawl out of it slowly and cautiously, but I was dragged into Sunday suddenly and rudely by the telephone. Too soon to leave the past for the present.

Make no mistake, for a homicide dick, corpses were the present. The past was something you started hunting down the moment the corpse made its presence known. The future was something that was in the hands of lawyers and out of yours. I stared the present in its puffy, crab-ridden face after it had been pulled up out of Honolulu Harbor. The heavy and damp air around Pier 23 reeked of the sea and old cardboard boxes. Above the tin gables of the rusting warehouses the green peaks of the Koolau Mountains jutted up against the sky. By the time I got there I was working on my third Lucky Strike. That's what happens when you smoke in a convertible; your cigarettes burn fast in the artificial breeze.

I stopped staring at the bloated face for a moment to look about. Rusting maritime junk, the kind that looked like it belonged in the muck at the bottom of Pearl Harbor, littered Pier 23. Industry's graveyard. One old tug with a black hull and near-empty ballast bobbed on the sluggish ripples of the harbor like a balloon. Above its stern, Aloha Tower rose skyward across the water, the water of Honolulu Harbor like dark green glass. Striped manini and other more colorful reef fish made an occasional appearance near the surface then drifted back down into the hazy abyss.

"Sheik. Did you bring 'em?" Gid Hanohano had shambled up from behind me and I nearly jumped off the pier into the still murk, his movements remarkably silent for someone his size. I pulled the cigars out of my jacket and handed one to him. Gid bit the end cap off and spit it into the harbor, then ignited the other end with his chrome Zippo. A small fog billowed about him in his brown suit. He handed me his lighter and I did likewise, adding to the general cloud he created. The smoke hung in the hot, still air like cobwebs.

"Whoa! This is really good! What is this, anyway?" Gid asked. He took another draw off the stick.

"Partagas, Gid. From Havana."

"You mean to tell me that the old Pake at your place sells these?"

"Chang? Hell no. He'd shit if he knew how much one of these sticks sold for. I picked these up at the Moana last Thursday when I was interviewing the housekeeper who found that tourist's body."

"Well, remind me to send you into Waikiki more often."

"No thanks. Steel guitars make my fillings ache."

Gid stood there squinting and puffing on his cigar and looking content in the shade of his brown fedora. For such a big man he never seemed to sweat. Watching him look so cool only seemed to make me stickier. I took another drag and expelled smoke which hung around our heads until the sun burned it away.

"It's a good smoke. Thanks, Sheik."

The Sheik. That's what all the rest of the Homicide Detail called me. One of the haole dicks, Jack Morris, thought Yoshikawa was too long for him to pronounce or remember, so he shortened it to "Sheik." Not *Shaykh*, the way it's properly pronounced in Arabia, but *Sheek,* as in Yo*shik*awa, or "The Sheik," as in Rudolph Valentino. The irony is, Jack married a girl whose last name was Kaumeheiwa.

Francis Hideyuki Yoshikawa. That's what was typed on my birth certificate. My Japanese parents couldn't even pronounce the Christian name they gave me, so they called me Hide-kun. Most people who knew me well called me Frankie, as in the bow-tied Sinatra when he had Ava Gardner and a full head of hair. But not the cops I worked with. Having a nickname meant you were a colorful part of their colorful family, like the New York Yankees. Or the Mafia. So Sheik it was.

Gid was the father of that family, or at least its big brother. Detective Lieutenant Gideon Hanohano of the Honolulu Police Department's Homicide Detail was a dormant volcano. He stood about six foot two and weighed in close to three hundred pounds. Once upon a time, he played tackle at Kamehameha and was damn good at it. He was someone who could trace his lineage back to the islands' monarchs. A lot of good it did him. His family's land on the windward side, a consolation prize awarded to them in the Great Mahele, was sold to a haole-owned company that bled its water supply for sugarcane on the leeward side; all Gid's family got out of the deal was enough to build a house on a patch of land near an old fishpond. During the monarchy, the Mahele, or "division" as it's roughly translated, was supposed to introduce the concept of modern property ownership to a society unfamiliar with it. It ended up being a means for white men to take away land from brown men without having to shoot them to get it.

If Gid was bitter about losing his birthright, he never showed it. In fact, Gid never showed much of anything. He had two facial expressions: irony and fatigue. He was an intelligent man who managed to get his point across with a wonderfully stingy economy of syllables. The lieutenant walked with a limp, the souvenir of an arrest gone south when he walked the beat in Chinatown as a young cop. He was my teacher and sometime chaperone.

I moved up into Homicide after just two years in Patrol, partly because of my college degree and partly because Homicide needed a

Japanese speaker. We comprised a good forty percent of the Territory, each one of us a former agent of the Emperor of Japan if the haole elite of the islands were to be believed. Now we were Stalin's agents. Gid took me under his wing because I appreciated his theories and tolerated his moments of deep thought. "We need more *thinking men* like you," he once told me. He might well have changed his mind if he really knew what I thought about most of the time.

It was hot. The weather report on the radio said kona winds. Winds out of the southeast up to fifteen miles per hour. Sometimes, the kona winds brought rain. Sometimes, if you were lucky.

Kona winds. What a misnomer. Most of the time they weren't winds at all—just a lot of wet, dead air that got under your shirt and into your psyche and made your manners really bad. Sometimes they'd last up to a week before the tradewinds came back to cool things down. It was another one of those Turkish bath days; a day to make you drown by filling your lungs with the dampness in the air; a day to make you put your fist in the face of the first person who looks at you the wrong way; a day to take a look at a body and wonder how it turned into a rotting corpse and ask yourself why the hell you do what you do for a living.

Gid let more smoke out of his mouth. He was enjoying the taste. This made up for the last time when I forgot to bring the cigars. The cardinal sin for any homicide dick was to forget the cigars; the dense smoke covers some of the stench of decaying flesh and blood. If you didn't smoke cigars before getting into Homicide, you learned to take up the habit quickly. We stood side by side puffing and staring at the mess on the pier.

Our smokescreens did little good that morning. The cloudless sky was bleached white by the burning sun; the heat released the aroma of the corpse, a heady mix of sea salt, kelp, and buckets full of wet, nauseating death. The bloated face looked like a round loaf of pao doce, the puffy panned bread from the new Portuguese bakery in Kapahulu, but a hell of a lot less appetizing. Black a'ama crabs skittered sideways across the forehead and over the body like overgrown ants. I choked a little and loosened my tie, my collar as wet as the corpse. It had been a woman, but whether she had been pretty or not was impossible to tell. She wore what looked like a once ritzy black velvet cocktail dress and patent leather pumps. The whole body was a sickening mess like soggy Saloon Pilot crackers from Hilo Macaroni Factory, the kind that came in a giant tin.

The heat became oppressive and everybody on the pier sweated profusely except Gid. I took my coat off and threw it in the backseat of my car, rolling up my shirtsleeves and loosening my tie. Why the hell did we wear coats and ties like dicks on the mainland? Were we stupid? I kept the front brim of my porkpie hat snapped down for scant shade.

The uniforms started cordoning off the scene in a fairly generous perimeter, bringing the line all the way up to the bow of the tug where I had parked my car. The medical examiner entered the corral, as comfortable in the damp heat as a shell-less turtle. His observations were general: the body had been in the water for some time, she had been Oriental based on her hair. *Shit, I could have guessed that on my own.* Beyond that, we'd need to wait for the autopsy for more.

An hour or so later, after combing the pier and squatting to examine every little errant speck, the patrol boys packed up and left. Before Gid got into his maroon Ford Crestline, he turned to me and said, "Sheik. Use your na'au. When somebody dumps a girl into the harbor, we're dealing with a different kind of mind." Na'au. Guts. Gid told me it's where everything comes from. Sure, the head and the heart were sources of inspiration, but how else can you explain the butterflies when you're nervous or have the urge to shit when you're scared? The head misleads, the heart deceives, but the na'au never fails to tell you something is amiss. I wish I knew this before I got shipped off to Europe in 1944. It might have saved a friend's limb.

Gid got into his car and started the engine. I tapped the ragtop of the Ford Crestline a couple of times with the palm of my hand and stepped back. Gid waved and drove away, his car turning and disappearing behind the rusted hull of a small vessel dry-docked for repairs that never happened.

When the last of the uniforms had left, I stood alone on the pier. I pulled my hip flask out of my pocket and took a long, caustic swig. The edges of the world softened around me and I stopped hearing the hammering of my heart in my head. It had been that way with me since the war. The bottle was the only place I felt safe from myself, from the guilt and despair. And the shame. The shame was back again, the same shame that burned my insides for managing to stand there breathing while other boys from Kakaako were torn apart by German lead. I thought about the drowned girl, whoever the hell she was, spending her last moments in the murky green of the harbor. Dante's Fifth Circle of the *Inferno*. The Sullen are submerged beneath the fetid waters of the River Styx, choking on the mud at the bottom for all eternity.

It seemed that was all my degree in Medieval Literature was good for—conjuring up grotesque images like the gargoyles on the Cathedral of Chartres, the kind of crap that gave kids nightmares. God knows what attracted me to such an obscure course of study. Maybe it was because there was a certain Gothic bent to my samurai-like upbringing, but probably more likely because the stark, vivid imagery was so like the blood-soaked passion play that was the war in Europe. A poor kotonk kid from Fresno left me with his copy of King Arthur stories before he was riddled with bullets on a hill in the Vosges woods. That book set me down a path of useless knowledge. All that illuminated manuscript stuff never taught me to see life in literature; it made me see literature in life. The whiskey made those pictures of a medieval hell sharper, cantos resonating in bright crimson gore. But it also made those images tolerable in a strange way, like sitting through some macabre performance where you always had box seats, safely high above the stage.

It was then when my mind was lurking under the naves and buttresses of *The Divine Comedy* that had sprung up in my bourbon-hazed view of Pier 23 that I felt the eyes watching me from the shadows under the dry-docked hull.

The eyes were filmy and dull milky gray with a veneer of mucus stretched over them. They belonged to an old haole guy with faded maritime tattoos on his wrinkled bare chest and forearms. He was barefoot in dirty dungarees, and scabs crisscrossed his bare flesh where he had raked himself with his filth-encrusted fingernails. His scraggly hair was yellow-gray like the crotch of an unwashed dog. The charmer was also missing most of his teeth.

Gid had told me about this wino when I first arrived at the pier. I didn't pay much attention at the time because I was too busy sucking cold black coffee out of a paper cup and wishing it were Four Roses. Besides, Gid had already interviewed him. This was the stellar citizen who brought the body to our attention.

I motioned to the old drunk to join me at the cleat at the bow of the tug, mooring lines wound taut about it. He staggered along behind me and sat cross-legged right on the pier while I pulled a pad and pen out of my pocket. I guess in some places like the movies, dicks get to interview beautiful starlets or arrogant millionaires in their dining rooms with long tables with sixteen chairs around them. They eventually make accusations in a sunken living room with gorgeous people all around, all dressed up and waiting to hear their brilliant deduction. The butler did it. Yeah, right. I got to talk to a piss-smelling wino on a pier on a kona winds day. So much for *The Thin Man*.

"What's your name?" I asked.

"Jacob," the man said. He sullenly picked his nose.

"You have a last name, Jacob?"

"Mooney."

"Occupation?"

"What?"

"Never mind. How'd you come to find the deceased . . . uh, the body?"

Jacob Mooney pulled his knees up to his chest and started rocking frantically on his ass. Most of his "statement" was incoherent mumbling and croaking, but the gist of it was that he was trying to fetch the remainder of a fifth of gin he had inadvertently knocked into the water. My guess was that everything he did was inadvertent. He saw the dark spot in the water just below the surface near his precious bottle. When he realized he was looking at a human head, he ran for Route 92 and nearly ended up under the front wheels of a prowler. All this I knew from Gid's synopsis of his own short interview with the character.

Something was missing. What didn't they ask this citizen of the pier?

I asked him if any cars or trucks ever came to the pier after dark over the last couple of weeks. On this point Mooney was surprisingly clear and firm: no vehicles ever came at night, and certainly not over the last two weeks or so. The swinging chain-link gate allowing access to Pier 23 was always chained and locked at sundown. Mooney knew where to sleep and drink so he couldn't be found and chased out during those early morning and early evening times when the harbormaster's truck came to the gate. When I asked him if boats came during the night, he told me that sometimes they do, including the tug; sometimes they tie up for a while and sometimes only briefly, mostly to fuel.

I chewed on this then I tossed Jacob Mooney a nickel. He greedily tucked the coin away in his dungarees and continued to stare at me, swaying like a palm trunk. I realized then that his eyes were locked on my hip flask, which I had carelessly tucked into my waistband before interviewing him.

"Sorry, Jacob," I told him. I genuinely felt bad. "You may not believe it, but I need it more than you do."

He gave the flask one last longing look and staggered off into the shade of a nearby warehouse where he lay down on the concrete. He was snoring in seconds. At that moment, I truly envied him. They say a man's home is his castle; Pier 23 was Jacob Mooney's very own Iolani Palace. I left him to his nap.

I looked up at the hull of the old tug. In rusted letters that were once white, I could make out the name, *Hinalea*. The patrol guys checked out the vessel but found nobody aboard. There wasn't a soul around Pier 23 except Jacob Mooney and me, and he was out cold. I looked back at the end of the pier where we had laid out the body that was chained to a small anchor, the type used on small fishing crafts berthed at the piers near 23. The chain was about thirty feet to forty feet in length, the draft of the Harbor about forty feet and probably between thirty-five and forty where it met Pier 23. Our perpetrator didn't intend for the body to be discovered. But someone did a sloppy job with the chain, winding it around the body like a spool after initially fastening it. Once the body was dumped, the chain eventually unraveled to its near full length when the gases that built up in the corpse started floating it upward like a buoy. I looked at the tug. I felt something like heartburn.

I turned back to the tug and hopped aboard. The *Hinalea* was a little worse for wear and looked quite frankly as if she may have already been put out to pasture. Her deck was poorly maintained and loose lines lay about like so many earthworms at the bottom of a tin can. I carefully moved my way aft, trying not to scuff my new wingtips when I saw it. The midday sun caught something small but brilliant on the deck. The sharp flash nearly blinded me. Gingerly, I tiptoed between the strewn lines and pulled a handkerchief out of my pocket. It wasn't fire that caught my eye. It was ice. A whole string of it. I squatted near the stern and picked up a king's ransom in diamonds in the form of a bracelet.

Pinched between my fingers through the handkerchief, I could feel the hardness and heft of the thing. I'm no jeweler, but I could tell it was real—as real as my fatigue and the growing sinking feeling that I had many more sleepless nights ahead, and not just because of kona weather.

I folded the handkerchief with its staggering contents and secured them in my pocket. Then I got the hell off the tug. Something about the *Hinalea* gave me the creeps. It had the feeling of every victim's bedroom I ever searched—a lonely place that had seen the last of its former occupant. A place where dust motes swirled in the scant light and whispers of an insignificant life echoed off its walls unheard. All of those places seemed to have a chill that wouldn't go away. As soon as I hopped back on the pier, the cold dissipated as quickly as it overwhelmed me and I was once more standing in the hot, muggy, dockside air.

I stumbled back to my car and sat down behind the wheel. I took a couple of long drinks from my flask and beat down the urge to weep or shout or throw myself into the harbor. The last swallow brought back the warm, hazy light that always framed the grotesque images I imagined Dante had in his head as he wrote. Devils in sooty gray-black or maggot-white hides, angels resplendent in tempera scarlet and cobalt trimmed with antique gold. Another big sip took me even further back, before my college dreams of a Gothic afterworld were fueled by weak-lipped poets in baggy hats. The fuzz around the edges of memory grew thicker and the images were impressions of a different kind of verse from deep in my consciousness. Bold black strokes on delicate white paper, kanji characters done by To-san's hand—virtue, enlightenment, power, void—all of them hanging on the tongue-and-groove walls from red-orange or purple silk cords in our steamy Kakaako parlor.

Then, inevitably, pictures of the war. Bleak, gray skies over red tiled roofs and white plaster walls torn asunder by mortar fire, exposing the broken timber bones of villas. Narrow cobblestone streets littered with rubble and spent brass shells. Children in torn clothing with grubby faces and desperate eyes. All of it edged with that glowing, pulsating frame of gentle light that tasted of haupia and blood at the same time.

I pulled my handkerchief out to wipe the sweat off my face and realized there were diamonds in it. That brought me back from the shadowy little chamber of memory to Pier 23. I tucked the handkerchief back into my pocket with that exaggerated caution that drinkers often employ and looked toward the shade of the warehouse where Jacob Mooney lay snoring. Sometimes I felt just like that, when the guilt and the self-pity threatened to swallow me up before the booze did.

I shoved some Sen-Sen in my mouth to mask the scent of the liquor. Lately, I had been chewing more and more of the stuff. I was still at the stage where I could successfully hide my drinking from the world, but only barely so. I hit the starter and swung the car around, away from the *Hinalea* and the pier, out through the chain-link gate and between the warehouses back to Route 92.

2

I headed to my mother's place in Kakaako. It was almost as if my Cadillac Eldorado drove itself. For the amount of the monthly payment, it damn well should have.

Kakaako was a hot, crowded, mostly Japanese neighborhood just Diamond Head of downtown across Punchbowl Street. Like children in mismatched clothes and dirty faces who played in the streets, the houses, sitting on rickety wooden stilts or masonry bases, had tin or shingled roofs and walls of tongue-and-groove pine with the newfangled aluminum siding in green, white, gray, or pale yellow that had been quickly covered with grime. Some of those houses had little yards with ti leaves and stunted coconut palms. All were interspersed with industrial businesses like automobile mechanic shops or sheet metal contractors; on the lanais, the matrons could be seen peeling daikon, and in the yards, old men pruning the hedges. Most of the houses were grouped into "camps" and slept multiple families under the same roof. Kakaako was perpetually hot and noisy until sundown, when it became hot and quiet save for the tinhorn and cry of the tofu man. It was Purgatory for the Japanese on Oahu, but it wasn't as bad as the Inferno of the sugar plantations. Yet, it was still far from being the haole paradise of Manoa or Kahala.

My mother and father moved to the neighborhood after To-san was able to leave the cane fields when he found a job as a mechanic. By the time I was four years old he had his own shop that, like so many other Kakaako industrial businesses, was run out of the garage attached to the house. Ka-san was everything, from To-san's bookkeeper to his mechanic's helper. Not living in a "camp" made us something of Kakaako royalty, which meant I only had to vie for hot bath water with my own sisters and not every other male in the communal bath.

The only pink house on Kawaiahao Street with its enormous lychee tree in the small front yard was something of a Kakaako landmark. I grew up in this house, along with my four sisters. After we had become adults, only Ka-san lived there but insisted on having us all come back on Sundays for dinner, without fail. My sisters, churchgoers all, would come with their families right after services and have lunch, which included Ka-san's own tsukemono and pickled mango when it was in season. Their kids would run around out front, playing catch or climbing the lychee tree while my sisters sat in the parlor gossiping with their Doris Day hairdos bobbing in nods of agreement. Their husbands would start a card game in the old shop and open a few beers from the icebox Ka-san had outside for extra produce. They'd all carry on in this fashion until dinner.

My family attended services at the Makiki Christian Church on Pensacola Street. It looked like some daimyo's castle from Tokugawa Japan, decorated with gold crosses under the awnings. I used to go as a kid at Ka-san's insistence but stopped as soon as I was old enough to figure out that all of Reverend Takaki's life-changing sermons were the same story with different characters. Religion was a fluid concept in my family. We were Shinto when a baby was born, offering prayers at the shrine in Moiliili for the kid's good health, then turned Christian, going to church every Sunday and making wedding vows in front of an altar. When someone died, we suddenly became Buddhist. Jack Morris once asked me why I didn't just choose one faith and stick to it. I told him, "None of them seemed to have all the answers and all of them made your ass sore by making you sit still for long periods of time."

I usually wouldn't make my appearance at Ka-san's until just before dinner, which gave me an opportunity to sleep in and maybe have a quick whiskey or two at a neighborhood bar and grill on Waialae, the kind of place that'll usually play the ballgame loud enough for those sitting at the bar to hear. The guys who sat in the booths would ask what the score was and what inning when they got back from taking a leak in the stainless-steel trough in the men's room. I could usually chew on the complimentary fried aku bone with shoyu for my lunch or get the "Neptune's Platter," which was just their leftover sashimi battered and deep fried and laid on a bed of cabbage with a cute little cup of tartar sauce and a lemon wedge. This is the kind of shit that most of those old Japanese men would slap their wives silly over if they served it to them for dinner, but they'd gladly pay fifty cents for it in a dark Kaimuki bar and grill and marvel over the fantastic deal they just got.

I could have had the fried fish lunch with the Four Roses chaser, but this particular Sunday I decided instead to head to the pink house and some of Ka-san's pickles and the old furo. I liked taking a soak after dealing with initial scene investigations. The hot water seemed to cleanse the mind and soul as well as wash away the stench of death—sometimes old, cold death—in a way that a lukewarm shower in my apartment at Old Chang's building somehow would not. Like To-san, I did all of my best thinking in the old furo. Before he passed, To-san converted the water heating method from burning kiawe logs to a heater fueled by a huge gray propane tank just outside the bathhouse.

I pulled up in front of a furniture warehouse a couple of doors down from the pink house. Because all four of my sisters were there with their families, there was no available parking in front of the house. A white Mercury Coupe that I didn't recognize was also parked in front of the pink house. When I got to the front gate, my sister Iris was walking out from the house with a slim, pale brunette in a white sheath dress with white gloves and a white hat with a lily in its band. Pretty damn continental, even for church. The brunette was elegant looking and somewhat familiar to me, though I was fairly certain I would've remembered meeting her before. Her large, dark eyes met mine as I held the gate open for them. She blinked a few times then smiled, slightly. Her hair was the color of good scotch with the fluid glow to match. She was haole with maybe a touch of something else or maybe not and she stuck out like a sore thumb in Kakaako, like someone had cut her out of the pages of *Harper's Bazaar* and pasted her onto a plumbing supply ad.

"Someone's early," said Iris. She slapped me lightly on the chest with a small envelope.

"Yeah," I replied, "I couldn't wait to see all of you."

"Oh, shut up, Frankie. This is Ruth Prentiss. Ruth was kind enough to stop by Ka-san's on a Sunday to drop off this donation check for our organizing efforts."

"Pleased to meet you," said Ruth Prentiss as she shook my hand.

"Likewise," I said.

"You must be very proud of your sister. She's doing something new and daring but very much needed. I admire her a great deal."

"Sure," I said. "We're all very proud of her." I shot my sister a questioning look.

Ruth Prentiss nodded at me then made her way to the Mercury Coupe in front of the house. She turned and gave me a final demure smile that sent an electric thrill through me. She got into the coupe and drove away down Kawaiahao Street toward downtown in a cloud of dust.

"She single?" I asked my sister. I watched the white car disappear in the afternoon heat.

"Dream on, Frankie. She's out of your league."

"Well, pardon me. And what 'organizing efforts' are you talking about?"

"We need a teachers union. Look at what the stevedores and the sugar workers and pineapple workers managed to accomplish. We have to schedule parent meetings on non-school days. We don't have a paid lunch period. I'm looking at the stevedore model and I'm trying to drum up some support here."

"Since when did you become so politically active?"

"I've always supported the cause," said Iris with an air of saintliness, "and you should, too, you know. Things are going to change around here soon, Frankie."

"Better be careful or the HUAC will make a set of new hearings just for you."

"Shut up." She hit me again with the envelope. "You're so ignorant, Frankie."

The HUAC. The House Un-American Activities Committee. It was still fresh in the collective consciousness of Honolulu. Just three years earlier, the Committee took their show on the road and came all the way the hell out to Hawaii to investigate the growing Red Menace here. That and to lie out on the sand at Waikiki and watch the hula dancers and sip rum out of coconut shells. The hearings convened at Iolani Palace. What they found were a handful of petrified haole businessmen hanging onto their colonial lush life by the fingernails and scores of angry, brown-skinned dockworkers and cane-cutters who managed to shut the Territory down in a months-long strike. After all the drama of turncoat union guys pointing the red finger at their former compatriots and haole moneymen whining about a new Jap conspiracy, the HUAC concluded that communism was rampant in our little tropical Eden then packed up their hundred-dollar suits and went back to Washington. They didn't stomp out any red threat, real or perceived. They only managed to make the likes of my smart-mouthed sister angrier and more defiant than ever.

"You're trying to change the world single-handedly and *I'm* the one who's ignorant?" I smiled and shook my head. Iris never knew when to shut up, but maybe that was her gift. She was at it again because I provoked her.

"The world is seeing more stevedores and sugar workers willing to bite the hand that feeds them crumbs. You should be grateful and help them instead of just being a parasite benefiting from their efforts." She made her self-righteous face, the one with the skinny lips and sullen half-closed eyes.

"I'm no parasite, Iris. If anything, *they* are. I didn't see any of your clever labor friends next to me in the war-torn fields of Europe getting shot at. Our sacrifice gave your activism credibility."

"What an ignorant, ungrateful thing to say. It's the effort of those willing to push back that make it possible for you to drive that Cadillac."

"I *earned* that car with my blood. Your goons didn't hand it to me."

Iris sighed. "One day you'll grow up and see." Then she chuckled and adjusted the hat on my head. She dashed up the steps with her envelope and into the house. I shook my head once more and walked through the front gate. My sisters' boys were out front chasing each other with old broomsticks under the lychee tree; their girls were playing jacks on the lanai. I traversed the front yard, climbed the stairs up to the lanai and made my way to the front screen door to a chorus of "Hi, Uncle Frankie!" I stopped to muss the hair of one of my nieces, removed my wingtips and set them next to the rest of the shoes and opened the screen door.

"Tadaima," I announced out of habit. The pink house wasn't really home for me anymore, but I think Ka-san liked it when I did that. To her, it would always be home for me.

My sisters were all named after flowers. Violet, the oldest, was in the kitchen helping Ka-san with dinner while Daisy, Iris, and Pansy sat around the living room with the television on, fanning themselves with Ka-san's paper fans. They had all changed out of their church clothes into sleeveless blouses and baggy camp shorts with their hair held back by broad ribbons. Though my sisters were all older than me they weren't older by much. Yet they never stopped talking to me in that patronizing tone reserved for children and house pets.

I often wondered what would possess my folks to name their kids after English flowers they couldn't even pronounce, which came out like *Baioret* or *Deiji*. They named me after some kindly Portuguese luna who had To-san help him fix the old trucks on the plantation.

"Look who's here," said Daisy, who always sat ramrod-straight, even in To-san's soft, old chair. "You're a little late for lunch but there's still some rice and lots of tsukemono and kamaboko."

"Thanks," I said, "I'll get some after my bath."

"Bath? Looks like somebody has a new case," said Iris. She was still clutching her prized envelope. "What's this one about, Frankie?"

"Some girl chained to an anchor in the harbor. She was all bloated and crawling with a'ama crabs."

"Eww," said Pansy.

"She looked like wet Saloon Pilot crackers in a black dress," I quipped over my shoulder as I headed for the kitchen.

"Eww!" they all yelled, save Violet, who was sitting at the kitchen table slicing tofu while Ka-san was bent over a large pot on the stove, moving things around in it with a long pair of hashi.

"Oh, hi," Ka-san said. She looked up for a moment, her wire-rimmed spectacles fogged up. "Violet, make him a chawan of rice."

"No, that's okay." I motioned for Violet to stay seated. "I'm going to the furo first."

"You must have a new case," said Violet, taking the knife up once again. Old Grouchy Face. Ka-san, Jr. "That's the only time you come early. And you take a bath first."

Right. My family really had me pegged. The one good thing about being predictable was that if people knew what you were up to and you did them no harm, they pretty much left you alone. Nothing fascinated my family less than the same old song-and-dance. That suited me fine. I was tired of talking.

I made my way back to my old bedroom, which Ka-san preserved like a museum. The bed was neatly made and all of my high school football and baseball trophies crowded the headboard shelf. Even the threadbare teddy bear I slept with as a kid was still resting neatly on the pillow. My Army commendations and my Columbia diploma all in Latin hung on the wall. Ka-san had my Purple Heart framed in a shadow box. I earned it in my time with the 442nd in Europe for getting grazed by a German bullet on my right shoulder. A lot of other guys I knew in that outfit with Purple Hearts didn't get off that easy; many of them lost limbs and a whole lot more. My best friend, Wally Yoshida, came home without a leg. I got lucky and returned in one piece, and for that I got my country's thanks, a medal, and a good amount of government cash to study Medieval and Renaissance Literature at an Ivy League university. What was left of the cash after school was done was parked out front.

The Cadillac was more than just an affectation. It was a survivor's prize. I waited until my promotion in the department to sergeant and had some time in Homicide to finally get up the nerve to ink the agreement at Schuman Carriage. I told Wally when we were in the midst of bullets flying over our heads in our first action that if I lived to get back home, I was going to get myself a Cadillac and marry Millie Miyasaki. At least I got the car. Millie had broken up with me before we shipped out. She was always a little distant and her mind was somewhere else, even when she let me have her in To-san's old truck or after sneaking into her bedroom through the window. There were no tears or apologies when the end came—just a shrug and my school ring returned without ceremony. It was for the better. The car was warmer and it responded to my touch.

Still, Millie remained the memory I clung to in the foxholes, though I Technicolored her liberally. When I got back to Hawaii, I never saw her except for a brief encounter when I ran into her and her folks at the airport the day I started the long series of flights to New York for my first term at Columbia. She gave me a blank look and a cardboard smile and waved her little white hand at me. It was in that moment that I realized she wasn't what kept me longing for home all those dark, dingy days of the war. It was the idea of her. I hadn't seen her since. When I was at Columbia I briefly dated a Jewish Barnard coed from Canarsie named Rachel Levinsky and that was the end of my ersatz dreams of Millie. Young romance. Heavy breathing, broken hearts, and another round of the same over and over until you grew up and realized that a good movie and a shot of whiskey gave you the same thing without the resentment when it was all over.

Ka-san always wanted me to be more with all my fancy education. I told her all my degree was really worth along with a driver's license might be a bus driver's job. And that's only if I could get myself a union card. A cop's paycheck seemed a little fatter, though not by much. There weren't a lot of Japanese boys at recruit school; the Honolulu Police Department had a height and weight requirement. You had to be at least five foot nine and 160 pounds. At a hair less than six feet and tipping the scales at 190, I was a rare specimen for a Japanese boy. Besides, most Japanese boys were busy becoming teachers or accountants, like my sisters' husbands, and a few of the brighter ones aspired to law or medical school, which was Ka-san's not-so-secret hope for me. But me being me, I figured with a batting average of just under .300 and being a decent pistol shot, I had a choice of doubling as an English teacher and baseball coach at one of the Territory's high schools or continuing to protect and serve in a different uniform. Sometimes I wondered if I made the right choice.

I took off my suit and put on a cotton yukata from the top dresser drawer. I sniffed it. Camphor. I tucked the handkerchief with the bracelet in it in the same drawer under another yukata and slid the drawer shut.

The old bathhouse smelled the same as always: slightly damp with the light perfume of soap and a trace of the earthy smell of old kiawe smoke, lingering like the ghost of my father. The furo of the pink house was a modest affair, basically a small but deep pine box of hot water with a couple of board covers. I shed the yukata and washed myself outside the tub with furo water poured from an enameled basin, then I eased myself into the deep box for a relaxing soak. I shut my eyes tight, held my breath, and dipped my head below the surface then came up after a few seconds. I wiped my face with my hands and went limp, eyes still shut but with slack lids.

I thought of the girl in the harbor and the string of rock candy I found on the deck of the *Hinalea*. Were they hers? The M.E. said she was Oriental. The daughter of a filthy rich Chinese family might have a bauble like that, but they'd have to be really big money—landowner money—not just Pake shopkeeper money. Japanese and Koreans were a little too austere for something as eye-catching as that, but I could be wrong. One thing was certain, though—the clasp was broken, not undone. Things get broken under duress, and I'd say you're under duress when you're getting fitted with a chain girdle to maximize your dive time. I couldn't see any of the scruffy deckhands who worked the vessel in possession of that kind of wealth. Even if they "happened" upon something like that, they sure as hell wouldn't have been careless enough to lay it on the deck. This was all I was certain of.

One of the first things Gid Hanohano taught me was maka'ala ke kanaka kāhea manu. *A man who calls birds should always be alert*. It was a reference to the guy who called the colorful birds whose feathers were used to make the capes for the ali'i. When the birds finally arrived, he had to be up to the task of capturing them. Seize opportunities. Be alert to the facts. The "what" and the "where" are obvious, the "how" and the "who" become apparent after time and effort, but the "why" is the prize—the most elusive of them all. Find the "why," and you find the rest. I barely had "what" at this point and only had a vague idea as to "where." Shit. It was going to be a long week.

The bracelet was almost certainly not stolen; Honolulu was getting to be a bigger town, but it wasn't that big. When a string of diamonds gets pinched, the whole department practically knows about it in seconds. The rightful owner of said property, usually a sunburned haole lady in golf clothes with martini breath, would generally harangue any uniformed cop in eyeshot at the receiving desk, demanding a progress report on the hunt for her precious anniversary gift. She'd do so at the top of her lungs, louder than all the pickpockets, winos, and hookers waiting to be booked. We'd had no such incident in recent memory, but I'd double check in the morning just to make sure. It didn't seem likely that what we had was stolen property. Maybe this would make my job easier. How many Oriental girls could there be with a bracelet like that? Maybe we'd find out tomorrow and maybe the case would be closed in a matter of hours. Maybe I'd sprout a pair of wings and just fly off somewhere so I wouldn't have to make monthly payments on a brand-new Cadillac. Maybe I should stop thinking about it for now. If I weren't careful, I'd grow up to be Gid Hanohano.

After my soak, I got dressed and played a couple of hands of hanafuda out in the shop with my brothers-in-law, going through a beer and a couple of cigarettes. It was nasty hot and muggy in the corrugated tin shed that To-san labored in for so many years; no wonder I never saw him wear anything but an undershirt. The toolboxes and workbenches were still there, but now they were only places to rest an open beer. Ancient oil stains still graced the concrete floor, though fading a little every time I looked at them. It was all that was left as a testament to To-san's years of backbreaking work. Sometimes, I felt like just that—a stain on the floor—a nuisance at first, but getting a little smaller and less significant with every passing moment. I lost both hands I played, and I made small talk about recent National League trades until dinner.

The evening meal was the usual assortment of Ka-san's pickles, rice, something hot with tofu and watercress in it, fried SPAM and shoyu. SPAM had become the most ubiquitous meat in the mostly Japanese neighborhood since the war. Ka-san even made it tempura-style. That night there was a special treat. Mr. Fujita across the street caught a couple of uhu and gave one to Ka-san. Pansy and her husband brought a coconut cake for dessert from the bakery in Liliha. The cake prolonged my stay. I could usually pass on the German chocolate if I wasn't in the mood, but I could never turn down the coconut.

I took all of the kids for a spin around Kakaako in the Eldorado with the top down. Ever since I bought the car, it had been the highlight of my nephews' and nieces' Sunday to go for a ride. I knew just how they felt every time I got behind the wheel. It was also the easiest way to cool off when kona weather settled in; a fake breeze was better than none at all. Kakaako by night had the charm of a foul-mouthed short order cook. We drove by the corrugated tin walls of the warehouses and camp houses radiating dully in the streetlights. After our little joy ride, I had one last cigarette on the lanai before heading back to Kaimuki.

The lights had come up along Waialae Avenue. I put the Eldorado back where I usually parked it. I dragged my wingtips up the concrete stairs and let myself into the box Old Chang called an apartment. I pulled the cork on a bottle of Haig and Haig Pinch and grabbed a tumbler from the cupboard. I poured myself a double and inhaled it and poured myself another and took it into the shower with me. When I dried off, I poured myself another.

The world took on the warm haze that was the magic of scotch. My bones hummed in my skin and my sweltering cinderblock box of an apartment and all of Kaimuki drifted away. I floated into bed and sunk a thousand fathoms down into the mattress. My descent into the Circles of Hell had only just begun, and I knew it even in my medicated state. It was time to get a little rest.

3

The telephone brought an abrupt end to my dreamless sleep. I rolled over and tugged the daisy chain on my nightstand lamp, knocking over an empty fifth of Haig and Haig.

The telephone rang again. It wasn't a bad dream. It was a bad reality.

I looked at the telephone. It kept ringing. So much for staring it down. Against my wishes and my better judgment, I lifted the receiver. As I guessed, Gid Hanohano was the voice at the other end, like it had been the morning before.

"Hello," I said, not really meaning it.

"Sheik?" the familiar voice rasped.

"It's Audrey Hepburn. The Sheik's still asleep. Shall I wake him for you or would you like to call back at a more polite hour?" A dry, barely audible wheeze of a laugh drifted through the receiver.

"It's Gideon Hanohano, Sheik."

"I know. What can I do for you, Lieutenant?" My mouth was dry and my eyes were crusted over and a headache was waiting like Mickey Mantle watching a fastball coming.

"Did I wake you?" Gid asked. I could almost hear the contemptuous smile at the other end. Early risers. Where the hell did they come from?

"Yeah, you woke me. I know how considerate you are, so I'm guessing there's a pretty good reason for calling at . . . Jesus, Gid!

Four-thirty!" I looked at the face of the red clock with sore eyes. The little brass bells weren't scheduled to make noise for another three hours.

"I need you down at the M.E.'s right away. He's going to start opening the stiff up."

"It's four-thirty, Gid."

"No it isn't. It's four thirty-two now. I know how much time it takes you to make yourself pretty, so I'm expecting you here in an hour."

"It's four-thirty, Gid."

"You're welcome, Sheik."

I tossed the receiver back into the cradle. I turned the radio on, hoping to get some Sinatra tune about regret. It was a morning for regret. I regretted a lot of things that morning, but probably none more than answering the telephone. I searched in vain for one of those songs that went so well with my 92-proof-refuge from the ghosts of all the ruined people I dredged up in my search for their violent final stories. Instead I got the weather. Another muggy day. Swell.

Outside my window, Waialae Avenue, Kaimuki's main drag, was silent save for the clicks of the traffic signal at the corner and the faint hum of the wires overhead.

A gang of mynahs bunched together on a sagging utility line jerked their heads back and forth. The birds probably just got through shitting on Old Chang's Packard. The car was the one thing my miserly landlord obsessed over. He had all the flamboyance of a nun in a two-dollar pair of shoes so he predictably picked the one jet-black car out of the entire Schuman Carriage inventory. He could have had something these days, in mint green, sky blue, or even screaming fire truck red. He should've picked white. Bird shit looked awful on the hood of a black Packard.

When I was showered, shaved, and dressed, I picked up the half-gone pack of Lucky Strikes on my nightstand and stuck one in my mouth. I lit it up and dropped the rest of the sorry pack into the same pocket with the extra .38 rounds. I grabbed my porkpie hat off the dining table, put it on, snapped the brim down over my eyes, and yanked the door shut behind me.

Downstairs, Old Chang's niece Vivian was minding the store. She was up frightfully early. Vivian Chang managed the counter from five in the morning until eight while her uncle went down to Oahu Market for the day, mostly to haggle over roast pork and ong choy for his dinner. Vivian was also her uncle's bookkeeper.

Vivian, a drum majorette in high school and at UH, had the legs to prove it. She sported her shiny black hair in a beehive like the Kaimuki prom queen she once was and sat with her legs crossed on an old wooden stool next to the register, reading an old book. She was wearing light blue pedal pushers and a crisp white blouse; she peered up at me over her spectacles. I stood over her and tried to give her a winning smile. It probably only made me look more tired.

"What's that you're reading, Viv?" I asked. I didn't have much real interest one way or another. It was one of those things you ask when you're too tired to say anything but you don't want to appear rude. Sometimes you're too tired to even care about *that*, but I wasn't there yet. That's me—ever the diplomat.

"*Candide*," she replied with an air of mock self-importance.

"Isn't it a little early in the morning for Voltaire? Besides, you always struck me as more of a *Harper's Bazaar* type."

"What's the matter, Frankie? Can't wrap your brain around the concept that a beautiful woman can be an intelligent woman, too?"

"If you know one, introduce her to me. Got any coffee?"

Vivian frowned and made her lipstick-shellacked mouth pouty. She let the old volume she was holding drop with a resounding thud on the counter and pushed off the stool. She wrapped her well-cherished crimson nails around a paper cup and poured something hot and dark into it. I glanced down at the freshly delivered *Honolulu*

Advertiser near the register. The weather was right up front, next to some uninteresting headline about some impending longshoremen's strike; these days, it seemed, all longshoremen's strikes were "impending." The paper said 89 degrees and 90 per cent humidity. A week of kona weather. Gid once told me kona roughly meant "south" in Hawaiian, which was fully appropriate in this case. My day just went kona and it was just starting. There was also the usual coverage on the front page about how the peace talks at Panmunjom were progressing—or not progressing—as it were.

"Where are you off to so early?" Vivian asked.

"Work," I replied. I sipped my coffee.

"What kind of a plainclothes cop goes to work at five in the morning? I thought you told me you have a desk job at the station."

"I do, but on occasion I'm required to get some air and take in the sights."

"Quit teasing, Frankie," she said, genuinely curious. "What do you really do?"

"You ever heard of Missing Persons, Viv?"

"That's your job?"

"No. I'm the guy that deals with the ones that get found."

Her jaw hit the counter. I reached into my pocket and fished out a dime. I flipped it at her, partly to get her to snap out of her shock.

"Think fast," I said.

Vivian snatched it out of the air without so much as blinking, her stare still fixed on my coffee and me. The reflexes of a drum majorette are a thing to behold. Then, flashing a wide, dazzling grin, she flipped the coin back at me.

"Keep your dime and enjoy your coffee, Mr. Policeman Yoshikawa," she said.

"Are you sure? Your uncle is likely to tack ten cents on to this month's rent if he finds out."

"Who says it's free? I'm every bit the pake my uncle is. You'll just owe me."

She gave me a look that stayed with me until I rounded the apartment building and jumped into my Cadillac Eldorado convertible. The Eldorado was the most memorable thing to come out of 1953 besides Walt Disney's *Peter Pan.* Both were meant to make you feel like you could fly. I was one of the first in Hawaii to own one, but nobody gave me a bouquet of flowers or a ticker tape parade. All I got was a greasy handshake from the guy at Schuman Carriage and bank-breaking monthly payments. But the engine was quiet and most of all the seats were comfortable. And that was a good thing because, as I eased the Eldorado out onto a nearly empty Waialae Avenue, I was pretty certain that what awaited me at the morgue was a pain in the ass.

The Honolulu Medical Examiner's Office was a clean and empty place with whitewashed walls and cold, hard green linoleum on the floor. The wide empty corridors were illuminated with hanging stainless steel fixtures that emphasized the frigid feel of the place. The air conditioner was turned down to what felt like ten degrees less than the average office. The whole place smelled of formaldehyde with a faint charnel undertone. It definitely wouldn't be the first place I'd choose to enjoy a sandwich. The medical examiner's realm was Cocytus, the ninth and lowest level of the *Inferno*, where Lucifer's own wings flapped and flapped to create an icy breeze. Just smelling the faint, cold death made my stomach churn like loose limu near the shoreline.

By the time I got there, Gid and the medical examiner were already standing next to the steel table that the body lay on, partially shrouded by clean white linen, which ironically reminded me of a restaurant tablecloth. Both of them were sipping coffee from paper cups and looking down at the cadaver. They appeared to have gotten a head start on the autopsy; I had been ten minutes early, but the cutting had been going on for at least a couple of hours. Gid had suitcases under his eyes.

"Morning, Sheik. Donut?" asked Gid. He hadn't even bothered to turn his head, eyes fixed on the bloated mass on the table.

"No thanks. I had toothpaste for breakfast. I thought about having a stick of gum, but I decided to eat light this morning."

"No time for a quick bite?"

"Some chipper Detective Lieutenant told me he needed me right away." Gid made one of his crooked half-grins at me, where he literally used only half his mouth. That was as chipper as he ever got.

The medical examiner gave us the run-down: Oriental female, sixteen to thirty but probably in her mid-twenties, cause of death drowning, but not before she took some blunt trauma to the rear of the head. It was done with some wicked force, not enough to kill her, but more than enough to put her out for a while. Most likely she was so far gone she didn't even know she was drowning when it happened. The blow was delivered with something heavy and cylindrical, probably some pipe. Whatever it was, it was smaller in circumference than a baseball bat. A preliminary guess, but probably a fairly accurate one, was that she was sapped a couple of hours before she drowned to death, and that she had enough cranial damage so that she was probably practically dead at that point anyway. She drowned about a week ago, probably a couple of days more than a week. She wasn't raped.

Her last night was a night on the town. Last supper: lobster tail and a small amount of marbled beef—filet mignon—and a fair amount of alcohol in the blood. Contents looked like light wine. Champagne, anyone?

Gid looked at the rim of his paper coffee cup where he had been biting it. He sipped more coffee at the chewed place on the cup. "We've got dentals to run now," he said, "and we're going to cross-reference missing persons for any close match. We should have something by lunchtime."

"What about the dress and shoes? They were pretty waterlogged, but they didn't look cheap," I said. My hand in my pocket closed tightly around the handkerchief with the bracelet in it.

"Chanel," said Gid.

"I didn't know you were a connoisseur of women's fashion, Lieutenant."

"I'm not. It's what's on the label."

"Oh."

"I do know enough about Chanel to know that our girl had very expensive taste, though. Daddy must have deep pockets."

"Daddy or someone," I said. "You don't know the half of how deep."

"Tell me."

I drew the handkerchief out of my pocket and unwrapped it slowly while Gid leaned in and stared. A little drama and tension will do that, just like a striptease, but I wasn't purposely trying to build anticipation. I was being damned careful with several thousands of dollars.

When the final corner of cloth was pulled away to reveal the brilliance of the bracelet, Gid let out a low whistle. For several seconds it got so quiet in the examination room that I thought the girl would sit up and demand her property back. Finally, Gid found his voice again.

"Where the hell did *that* come from?" he asked, slack-jawed.

"The deck of the *Hinalea*, the tug tied up next to where we pulled her out," I replied.

"How come the patrol guys that boarded the boat didn't find it before?"

"Because they weren't searching the boat, Gid. They were canvassing for witnesses. You can't fault them for that. Why would anyone look for evidence on a boat that comes and goes? It's not really part of the scene, not any more than my Cadillac, just because it was there a week later."

“Then how come *you* searched the boat?” asked Gid. He looked sideways at me.

“Because a wise man told me to follow my na‘au,” I said. Gid smiled. I continued. “I suppose you could call it a hunch, but it really wasn’t. The wino at Pier 23 told me that nobody drives in or out at night. The harbormaster locks up the place to vehicular traffic at sundown and comes back to open up the gate in the morning. Mr. Mooney—that’s the wino—said he didn’t see any vehicles at night over the last couple of weeks, and he would know because he’s always there. He did say that boats come and go at night, though, including the *Hinalea*. I don’t think anyone bringing in a bundle like that is going to chance doing so in broad daylight.”

“Yeah, agreed,” said Gid, “but what does this have to do with the tug?”

“If you can’t bring a hundred-pound woman into a fenced-off pier by automobile, how else are you going to do it? Are you going to throw her over the eight-foot fence?”

Gid and the medical examiner were looking at me, having finally taken their eyes off the bracelet. Neither of them opened their mouths, not even for coffee, so I continued.

“Or how about bringing her over the water? Because the *Hinalea* is usually berthed there and comes and goes, why not start there, even though it could have been any small craft that regularly comes to fuel. This little bauble turned up on her deck near the stern. Nobody bothered to pick it up and keep it or remove it from her wrist before dumping her. They must’ve been in a hurry. How do we know the bracelet is even related to the incident? We don’t. But it seems like it goes better with a Chanel dress than anything a tugboat crew might wear.”

“Who’s the women’s fashion connoisseur now?” said Gid.

“Still, it could be a coincidence,” I said.

Gid shook his head. “Na‘au, Sheik. What does it tell you?”

The medical examiner looked up from his éclair and stared at me expectantly. He had been taking bites out of it while he paced the length of the steel table, but he had been listening to our exchange with interest.

"My naʻau feels like it's going to jump out of my mouth any second now. It tells me that coincidences are rare and beautiful things, but this isn't one of them. There's nothing rare or beautiful about something that makes too much sense," I said.

"There you go," said Gid, almost like a proud father. "You know what? This is why I call *you* on Sunday mornings, Sheik. You're a thinking man." Again, the thinking man. This thinking man was thinking that he'd rather be one of the other guys for a change, the guys who got the easier stuff. Stuff where there were already suspects. Those guys got to sleep until it was actually time to wake up for work.

"Thanks. I think."

I looked down at the flaccid corpse and thought about all the girls who wore Chanel dresses and diamond bracelets and had filet mignon and lobster and champagne for dinner and how none of them imagined they'd end up with a dent in the brain in the murky green water under Pier 23. Who does?

I made my way to the coffee pot and paper cups and pink box of glazed donuts that were laid out on an unused cadaver examining table like a spread at a church social. The coffee was bitter and cheap. But it was nice and hot in an examination room that was freezing, like all meat lockers are supposed to be. I sipped my coffee and looked again at the ruined flesh that used to be a girl in the prime of her life and wondered what she did to get herself on that steel table. Gid's investigative grand prize, the elusive "why," began to gnaw at my consciousness from behind its heavy veil. Though I had already handled a number of cases in my short time in Homicide, the girl on the table was my first Oriental female victim. Looking at her filled me with an emptiness that wasn't there when I looked at the others. I didn't know why. Maybe it was because that could've been one of my sisters on that steel table. But I couldn't imagine what they might do or say to make someone go through the trouble of hitting them on the back of the head and dumping them into the harbor. It was my job to imagine it, though, and so far I wasn't having a decent go at it.

"Anything else?" asked Gid, turning back to the medical examiner. Gid had been playing with the loose change in his pocket. The metallic jingling was the only sound in the room. He shook the coins rhythmically in a morbid dirge.

"Negative, unless you boys want to watch me close her up," he replied.

Gid shook his head. "So young," he said. "She was someone's pride and joy, and probably someone else's sweetheart."

"All of them are," I said indifferently.

"Okay," said Gid, "that's that for now. We'll be in touch. Let's go downtown, Sheik. We'll start some digging on that bauble you got there and see if we can put a name to that . . . uh . . . face." We looked back at the puffy visage that was bloated beyond recognition as a human being. Pride and joy and someone's sweetheart turned into wet Saloon Pilot crackers in a moment's work. We were all only a step away from losing everything and ending up in the harbor as crab food. It was the sort of little island paradise we lived in; when you knew people too well, they really got under your skin and made you crazy. No getting away from them. When people get too close for comfort, bad things sometimes happen.

"Right," I said, glad to be getting out of the icebox. The one thing I could never stand about the examining rooms was how damned cold they were. I shuddered as I looked at the bloated girl one last time. Dante was right. The lowest hell wasn't a furnace. It was a freezer. Looking at corpses ceased to send a chill down my spine some time ago, but the morgue's air conditioning never stopped doing it.

4

The Honolulu Police Department's Station in downtown Honolulu, the Walter Murray Gibson Building, stood at the corner of Merchant and Bethel Streets and was done in the Spanish Art Deco style so prevalent in Honolulu buildings erected in the 1920s and early 1930s. The corner entrance with its huge doors was framed in red stone quarried in Waianae and looked like the entry to some conquistador's manor. The stairs in the foyer were inlaid with hand-glazed ceramic tile with the receiving desk covered with it. The roof was exposed mahogany timber from the Philippines painted with geometric designs, and there was French marble everywhere in the interior.

A stew of wretched humanity crammed the receiving desk area. It included uniformed cops holding paper cups full of terrible coffee; tired old hookers whose pimps had neglected to come to their rescue and post bail; winos reeking of cheap booze and urine and worse; haole military toughs who went on a bender and forgot to pay the tab; a skinny young punk who rolled a drunk for the ten bucks in his wallet near Kekaulike Street; a couple of pool hall warriors who just got through beating the shit out of each other with cue sticks; and the lowest form of life of all—the shyster in the cheap suit looking for a quick retainer to keep the lights on in his Hotel Street office. Lost souls. Charon's fares, straight out of Dante. That included the cops. I knew because I was one of them. The noise and the stink of the place never totally vanished; they just ebbed and surged in a series of ever-present lulls and rushes.

More military types were being brought in for booking as I made my way up the tiled stairs. It seemed that these days, half of the laundry being brought in for cleaning at the receiving desk was G.I., but instead of uniforms, these boys were wearing loud aloha shirts with their dog tags hanging out of them. They'd be thrown in the drunk tank until the MPs or the Shore Patrol came to pick them up. Disturbers of the peace. There were a lot of them around, each one part of the crew of the "unsinkable aircraft carrier" Oahu had become in the Second World War. Now, the island was a major jump-off point for troops and support headed for Korea and the first stop for those lucky gimps returning stateside from the conflict. One big saloon for the last hurrah or welcome back cocktail and roll in the hay with a warm body. Every day the radio and television had something to report on the slow-moving talks at Panmunjom. Those progress reports were becoming as ubiquitous as the Hormel Girls hawking SPAM in their ersatz military uniforms.

The office of the Homicide Detail on the floor above the receiving desk was a Spartan affair with a row of battleship gray desks like some dormant flotilla anchored out in the middle of nowhere. The only time that most of the desks were occupied was in the morning, before all the dicks hit the road to shag their leads or kill time in the courthouse hallways, except maybe one or two wrapping up a report or preparing to testify. The ceiling fans turned with the blinding speed of an old aunt with a shattered hip and provided as much relief to the oppressive heat and humidity as a hot shower.

My desk was third in a row of five. I had a view of Merchant Street and the Yokohama Specie Bank Building. It had the same metal trays, green blotter and black typewriter and telephone as the rest. Only three things really made it different: an old tin can covered with colored yarn by one of my nieces, filled with pencils; To-san's banker's lamp; and a red daruma doll Ka-san gave me when I finished recruit school. It's something of a Japanese good luck charm. The doll is supposed to be the image of the Buddhist monk who founded the Zen sect. The story goes that he meditated so much that his arms and legs fell off. That's why the doll doesn't have any. It's squat and vaguely egg-shaped and is balanced so that it always springs back upright when you push it over. The eyes are big and blank white. Ka-san told me that I should fill in one black pupil when I set a goal and draw in the other when that goal was attained. The eyes were still blank. I guess for the past few years things like goals have eluded my understanding. But one thing I always understood was a blank stare. So many witnesses and suspects looked at me the way the daruma did every day—with empty eyes. No vision, no feeling, no life. Just a lot of nothing.

Gid had taken the bracelet to the lab and had not yet gotten back to his office. His desk was the only one in Homicide separated from the others by a door. It was a good thing because I think that the solitude was necessary for him, especially during his moments of introspection. He sequestered himself so much to concentrate that it wouldn't surprise me at all if *his* arms and legs, like the daruma doll, fell off one day. I could never imagine what Gid was like as a regular dick, trying to deal with all the noise and nonsense that went on in the open office. Homicide dicks were a busy lot, but as a rule eccentric as well. You'd have to be just a little screwed up to work the cases we did.

One of those eccentrics was banging away at his typewriter when I walked in. Detective Sergeant Clancy "Luau" Lewis was finishing up a report on an apparent suicide which turned out to be neither apparent nor a suicide. We called him "Luau" for obvious reasons. He ate copious amounts of food and looked as if he should be pulled out of an imu himself and laid on a bed of ti leaves. That is, if you could find four guys strong enough to do it. I had never seen Luau in a bad mood, but maybe that's because I had never seen him without something to put in his face. In fact, at the moment he had a pink box of malasadas right next to his typewriter, half of the original dozen already tucked away except for the sugar all over his big doughy face and necktie. Luau's blotter was dark with oil stains fresh and stale and littered with enough crumbs to feed an extended family of mice. Judging by the small pellet-like turds under his desk they'd already had their fill. He also had a framed photograph of Marilyn Monroe on the oily blotter with an inscribed obscene message to himself from her. His hat had a crooked brim and had the look of something that had been mistakenly sat upon and straightened out a hundred times. He could never quite do the top button of his shirt and his tie hung perpetually loose and slack about his thick neck. He sweated like twenty pigs.

Luau was one of those haoles who blew in with the post-war economic boom. Jobs were everywhere to be had, from the docks to the road crews to the cane fields. Luau had come as a clerk attached to some naval unit at Pearl and found some night work as a watchman at one of the Bishop Street banks. He ingratiated his way into the City and County ranks and joined the department soon after he got to know some of the commission members who banked with his employer. Luau rose quickly through the ranks of Patrol, trading favors and volunteering to be the bagman for others on his watch when collection time came for the protection money from the gambling dens and brothels of Chinatown. A grateful handful of captains ensured his elevation to the detective ranks, where he could continue making his collection rounds with impunity.

Luau was still a bachelor at age thirty-three, possibly owing to his table manners and hygiene. His appearance and manner belied his aggressively inquisitive nature, which was more or less expended on station politics rather than on actual cases. When it came to chasing down rumors or picking up leaks from the brass, he had no equal. Often, I wondered if he really did any casework at all; Luau never seemed to have a court date, and he never complained of a report backlog the way the rest of us did. He was too busy feeding his florid face and being a permanent fly on the wall in the Chief's office.

When I came into the office, Luau looked up from his typing. Sugar came raining down from his cheeks when the corners of his mouth pulled up in a smile. "What's up, Sheik? Want one?" he asked. He held up the pink box, dark with grease spots on the bottom. The wax paper within crackled as he shook the remaining few in an effort to entice me. The malasada from Leonard's Bakery had taken Honolulu by storm the year before. If it were the Italians instead of the Portuguese who came to work the cane fields, maybe we'd be having zeppolis instead. Malasadas were basically the same thing as zeppolis, just shorter and fatter.

"Thanks, Luau. You just bought me breakfast," I said. I fished one of the oily, sugary donuts out of the box with a thumb and a forefinger. The malasada was already cold, but nothing would have gone better with the lukewarm cup of coffee I was nursing from the autopsy.

"I heard you and the Lieutenant got a hard one," said Luau. He looked away but I could hear the little grin in his voice. He helped himself to another malasada. The things that gave him a thrill—hot gossip and cold malasadas. Thank God I had a life outside the office. Not much of one, but enough not to care about other people's cases like they were the World Series. "Everybody's talking about it," he said between bites. "I heard about it from the girls in Records."

Records? This one traveled faster than the usual body-in-the-cane-field. I might get feedback on one of those from Records just before the girls knocked off for the day; first thing in the morning was a little too soon for my taste. Luau sat there like a dog begging for table scraps. He licked the sugar off his sausage-like fingers, waiting. Wouldn't he love to know? The ceiling fans turned at the speed of molasses and we both looked at each other, sweating. I didn't want to come across as a jerk about it but being pumped by Luau for information always felt like being hit up for a loan by a financially irresponsible relative. You never knew when his indiscretion was going to drag you down.

"Not much to tell so far," I finally told him. I dusted the malasada sugar off my hands. "All we really know about her is that she had bank-breaking taste."

"Haole?"

"Nope, Oriental. The M.E.'s pretty sure about that."

"Rich girl?"

"Very, or the beneficiary of someone with a lot of money."

"Oh." Luau narrowed his eyes and nodded thoughtfully, curling his lower lip upward. He chewed the remnants of his malasada and folded his arms in front of his chest. Fat beads of sweat clung to his forehead, but then again, they always did, even in the medical examiner's frigid rooms. He ran his pudgy fingers through his limp, wet brown hair and was about to ask another question when Delilah, the Homicide secretary, came into the office, saving me the irritation.

She breezed in through the door, her arms cradling a bundle of files that she promptly unloaded on one of the vacant desks up front. Delilah threw a nylon-clad leg forward and thrust her head back, fanning her neck rapidly with one of the thinner files she'd brought in, her other hand resting casually on the curve of her hip. Luau stared and broke into a leer. His attention was suitably commandeered and I was relieved of his company.

Gid came shuffling through the door as Delilah started her filing. His limp and the perpetual wince he wore always made it look like the act of walking gave him pain, though he had assured me repeatedly that this was not the case. Gid told me that it wasn't the walking itself that gave him the pained expression. It was the thought of where he'd end up once he stopped walking. He pretty much looked that way all the time. Every destination was a nuisance. Sometimes I knew just how he felt.

Gid stopped at my desk and gave the daruma a poke. It dipped and sprung back up on my blotter. He picked up the newspaper Delilah had left on my desk and looked at it. "They're having an orchid show at the Pali Honpa Hongwanji. Free admission. But I bet the orchids aren't free," Gid said. He looked at everything in the paper and shared what he read with us but not the obvious stuff like headlines. He liked making us aware of the odd trivial bits of minutiae that lurked in tiny column inches around bigger articles.

"What would I do at an orchid show, Gid?"

"I don't know. Maybe you like flowers. Maybe you'd like to take your mom. Maybe not. But now you know about it and you have a choice. Knowledge is options, Sheik." He went back to the paper and took it into his office with him, reading as he shuffled slowly. I blew air out of the side of my mouth and turned back toward my desk. *Knowledge is options.* Where did he come up with shit like that?

I sat down at my desk and went through some pink message slips from Friday afternoon. Office of the Prosecuting Attorney—another testimony review. One of To-san's old friends from the plantation trying to get me to buy life insurance from his son. My sister Pansy, probably calling about nothing important. I just saw her the day before and she never mentioned that she had called, which meant that she forgot what the whole thing was about. Typical.

The telephone rang in Gid's office. He lifted the receiver, grunted into it a few times, and then threw it back on the cradle.

"Sheik," he said. "Come in and sit down."

I went into his office and sat down. The only time Gid ever invited anyone into his office to sit down it was to say something they didn't want to hear.

He said something I didn't want to hear.

5

"I think we have our girl's identity, or at least I'd say I'm ninety percent certain that we do," said Gid. "It's just left to the next of kin to confirm and the M.E. to make it official. Missing Persons has a few-days-old report on a Mildred Miyasaki, twenty-eight years old. She's a secretary at the Territorial Attorney General's Office and lives with her parents in the Sheridan Tract." I moved in my seat enough to make it scratch the linoleum. I felt like I had jumped ten feet out of it.

Mildred Miyasaki. Millie. My erstwhile high school sweetheart. We lost our virginity to each other in To-san's old pick-up truck parked behind a warehouse on Ilaniwai Street in a muddled, messy, and painful coupling. Throughout our short-lived young romance, I was angst-ridden by her aloof, detached demeanor. Right then, I felt like I was sinking into the cracked faux leather cushion of the chair Gid kept across his desk for unwilling participants in his come-in-and-sit-down conferences. My high school sweetheart—that soggy mess on the morgue's steel table? I always felt that I'd see her again, but not like that. The face I had kissed was now a waterlogged, bloated bag of rotten flesh. An anguished shout tried to escape the confines of my dry mouth, but I held it until absorbed by my entrails, poisoning every corner of my consciousness with black disgust.

"Something wrong?" Gid asked, right eyebrow arched up, as he took in my barely concealed shock.

"I . . . knew her. From McKinley. I . . . we went out for a little while." I tried to make it come out more nonchalantly. I choked it out.

Gid raised both eyebrows while he looked down at his blotter. It was his way of softening his expression.

"I'm sorry, Sheik. I didn't know," he said. He drummed his fingers on his blotter in the silence that followed, just to fill it up. "Are you okay? We can give this one to someone else. Let you catch up on some of those reports."

"It's fine. I'm okay. I'll do this one," I told him, recovering. It wasn't exactly true, but in that moment, I decided that the alternative would have been unbearable—to watch from the sidelines and ask questions like Luau trying to run down gossip. He was probably sitting at his desk licking his fingers, craning his neck surreptitiously in an attempt to catch what he could of our conversation inside Gid's office. "I haven't seen her for years, anyway," I added. I swallowed the last of my cold coffee. It went down like thumbtacks. "That was a quick identification. What makes you so sure it's her, Gid?"

"Na'au. She's the only Oriental female we've had a report on for months and fits the physical." As far as I knew, Gid's feeling was never wrong. Never. It's what made him a legend as a detective. It's also what gave him heartburn. It was giving *me* heartburn. His foresight was both blessing and curse. Being all-knowing came at a price. Gid once shared with me that it was a gift that rarely made him happy.

"Can't argue with that. If you're right, though, we've got a long day ahead of us."

"How so?"

"A lot of questions need to be answered. She had expensive taste for a Territorial office worker and I can't think of a single millionaire that lives in the Sheridan Tract. Last I checked her folks hadn't exactly won any quiz shows."

Gid smiled. It was a weary smile, but it was warm and genuine. "There's the thinking man I know. I knew I called the right guy yesterday."

"Don't crown me the right guy yet. This thing is far from figured out."

"You'll do it," said Gid. "You always do."

"Maybe not this time. There's a first time for everything."

Gid let that comment pass with a dissenting half-smile and a slow shake of his head. "Did you know her folks?" he asked.

"Sure. As much as anyone could get to know a couple of stoic, old Japanese people from Sheridan Tract." Gid looked at me. I cringed. I knew I had just stepped into something I didn't want and couldn't get out of.

"Good," he said.

Shit, I thought.

The unsavory job of calling on the Miyasakis of Sheridan Tract fell to me because not only was it nominally my case, I was also the only Japanese dick in Homicide at the time and I knew them. A call from the M.E. came in while I was sitting in Gid's office; there was a positive dental match for Millie. Everyone, from Gid all the way up to the Chief, felt that bad news would sound best to the folks coming from one of their own, and one of their own who was already acquainted with them was just the icing on the shit-flavored cake.

That goes to show you how much they all knew about Japanese folks. Bad news was bad news no matter who the messenger was, but being Japanese would just make it more awkward, uncomfortable, and embarrassing than the talk already would be. Knowing them made it infinitely worse. A kanaka or Pake or Portuguese delivering the news could be forgiven as "just doing his job" and the shame of reacting emotionally would be less; a haole doing it would at least provide some consolation that the matter was important. The Japanese guy, on the other hand, would not only be expected to be sympathetic, he'd have to be ashamed as well, almost as if the whole thing were his fault. The problem with me, contrary to expectations, I was neither ashamed nor full of fault after recovering from the initial shock of learning her identity and searching my nonexistent feelings for her. That is, not until I saw her poor folks again for the first time in years.

Sheridan Tract and Moiliili were the other two Japanese ghettos in Honolulu. Only a handful of blocks really separated Sheridan Tract from Kakaako, and the largest of those blocks housed McKinley High School or "Tokyo High" owing to its large Japanese enrollment. My sisters and I all went to McKinley, as did almost every Japanese kid from either neighborhood. My best friend Wally Yoshida was from Sheridan Tract and the Makiki Christian Church where my family went to services was also near it. But I hadn't really seen Wally that often since he lost his leg in Italy then left for law school on the G.I. Bill, and I hadn't sat in the pews of Makiki Christian since I was in high school. Sheridan Tract was just as alien to me as the taro farms on the windward side of the island where Gid's family land was, and I had been over to Gid's for dinner far more often than I had occasion to visit Sheridan Tract. In the end, the brass had no idea that they were sending me into a place that was as unfamiliar to me as it was to them, though they thought the opposite because it was full of Japanese folks. That goes to show you how much they all knew about Japanese folks.

The white house on Rycroft Street was not unlike the pink house on Kawaiahao Street that I grew up in except that it was white instead of pink and in place of a big lychee tree in front there stood an anemic guava sapling amid a well-manicured lawn. Also, no automobile mechanic shop had been attached to it, which was probably one of those things people who lived in Sheridan Tract liked about Sheridan Tract. The neighborhood was indeed considerably quieter than Kakaako; I could hear the buzz of an insect and some kid's bicycle bell from down the block. Next door, the grating of metal on metal drifted over the hedge as an old man worked his shears over it. These were sounds that would be lost in Kakaako, buried beneath the whine of an electric saw or the roar of a large delivery truck. The faces were the same, though, most of them weathered and lined and bronzed by years of merciless sun in the cane fields and full of the weight of a lifetime of backbreaking labor and pent-up resentment. They were faces like the worn tires on the old cars in the streets and the cracked leather seats in their parlors.

I got out of my Cadillac and killed my cigarette on the rapidly heating asphalt of Rycroft Street. I crossed the familiar small front yard and went up the concrete steps to the lanai. On a day when the trades blew, the lanai was a pleasant place to sit when there had been a bench there. In kona weather, though, it was just another forgotten corner of the island-wide steam room. The old bench where I had sat next to Millie holding her hand in the dark was gone. Now she was gone, too.

In accordance with the brass's wishes, I made the call alone. After I knocked on the frame of the screen door and called out a tentative-sounding hello, a frail-looking woman in a white smock over a flowered housedress took the rusty hook out of the eye latch on the inside and opened the door. She seemed even more breakable without the screen between us. Eyes small and watery, you could almost hear them blink. Her pale skin was stretched over her skull and looked like crumpled tissue paper that some thrifty housewife tried to smooth out and reuse. She was a full foot shorter than I was and her hands wrung a dry dishtowel as if trying to squeeze a drop of blood from it. The hands were calloused and spotted and nervous. She looked a lot older than I had remembered, and she was old even back then, I thought. I suddenly felt nauseated and light-headed. This was not going to be easy.

"Miyasaki-san," I said. I bowed slightly with my eyes down, staring at the bristly welcome mat at my feet on the lanai. "Hisashiburi. It's been a long time. It's me. Francis Yoshikawa, from McKinley. I am a Detective Sergeant with the Honolulu Police Department now. I am sorry to bother you at your home and show up this way unannounced, but I have an important matter to discuss with you. Is Mr. Miyasaki at home, too?"

I stood there with my head still bowed and my badge and credentials held open with both hands slightly raised. After a long while, Mrs. Miyasaki finally said, "Come inside." I removed my shoes and followed her into the dark, warm parlor.

"How's your mom?" she asked over her shoulder.

"She's well, thank you."

The room was typical of the kind of folks the Miyasakis were. It hadn't changed since the last time I was there. The low mahogany coffee table was dust-free and covered with a large white hand-crocheted doily, and on the doily stood a heavy wooden bear with a large fish in its mouth. The Miyasakis had not yet gotten around to getting a television set like almost every other family in the Tract. Strange, considering their daughter wore diamonds and Chanel. Or maybe it was the diamonds and Chanel that were strange. An old cathedral radio sat atop a lacquered credenza and calligraphy banners hung by faded silk cords on the whitewashed tongue-and-groove walls. The place hadn't changed at all since I had last been there. Next to the credenza there was a phonograph softly playing a scratchy Japanese pop tune. On the shelf in the corner was a small Buddhist altar with a fresh tangerine next to a senko burner. The smell of the senko permeated the room, making it feel sad and old, like a Buddhist temple during a funeral. How ironically appropriate, I thought, and fought to keep the malasadas and cold coffee from coming up. Senko always made me want to wretch. My childhood memories of the smell were always associated with looking at gruesome, dried-out corpses of old relatives. I had seen many corpses since, but the ones I looked at as a child always unsettled me.

I sat on a low koa-framed sofa with anthuriums carved on the armrest posts with my porkpie hat in my hands. Somewhere in another room a grandfather clock started bonging away. Or maybe it was next door. The houses were all pretty close together in the Tract. I looked at the radio on the credenza and let my eyes wander to the right. There in a silver frame on another hand-crocheted doily was a recent photograph of Millie in studio make-up with lustrous black hair and nice, straight white teeth. Her mouth was small and delicate with soft-edged lips. She was cute in a wholesome way as she had always been, but it was the eyes that haunted me as they hadn't when we were together. When my own eyes met them, the hairs on the back of my neck stood up as if they returned my gaze, photograph though it was. Who the hell dumped you into the harbor, Millie?

I sat there with my hat in my hands listening to the faint wail of the record and smelling the senko, impatient to end my business and get out of that house. I glanced toward the hallway that led to Millie's bedroom door. I thought about the nights I climbed through her bedroom window and had her after she got the gift she requested of me: new white gloves, perfume, or Elizabeth Arden Victory Red lipstick. What the hell was Victory Red, and how was it different from any other kind of red?

My collar was soaked with perspiration. I had broken the bad news to the next of kin before, but never to anybody I knew. After a couple of minutes that seemed like an hour, frail Mrs. Miyasaki emerged from the kitchen with a lacquered tray holding three floral-etched glasses of iced tea. She moved slowly and deliberately and shivered like she was cold in the sweltering room. Her eyes were dull with fear. Her husband, an old man in horn-rimmed glasses, a sweat-stained undershirt, and gray flannel trousers followed her into the parlor. An irascible, ill-tempered son of a bitch when provoked, he scared me shitless when I was a teenager dating Millie but, at the moment, he looked unmistakably scared. They were both terrified of what I was going to tell them. And, being Japanese, the old lady went through the trouble of fixing me something to drink anyway. That hospitality-at-all-costs mentality only made me want to get the hell out even more.

The two of them reminded me of the insipid souls at the shores of the Acheron in the *Inferno*, chasing a blank banner and being stung by insects. Such was the fate envisioned by Dante of those who would not commit in life to one side or another. Had they committed to anything besides turning a blind eye to their daughter's less-than-proper behavior? If they had, maybe I wouldn't be sitting in their warm, sour parlor waiting to show them the way to their own personal hell. They chose instead to take a dip in the Lethe, the river that brought forgetfulness. Shikata ga nai. There was nothing for it. That ship had sailed. Or sunk, as it were.

I rose with some effort from the low sofa; my legs had inexplicably stiffened though I could not have sat there for more than five minutes. I greeted Tadao Miyasaki and showed him my badge in pretty much the same onegaishimasu fashion I had with his wife, Ayako, at the front door. We exchanged pleasantries, me in obsequious small talk and flattery, he in grunts and nods. I took my beverage from the old woman, nodded my thanks and took a sip of the iced tea she had labored to prepare. It burned going down as it met my bile coming up. That feeling in my stomach. It never failed to tell you the shitstorm was coming. I let the feeling pass and I steeled myself for the ugly task to come.

The next few minutes were a strange blur in my memory, like a stupid, destructive act committed during a drunken binge when someone else picked up the tab. I have some vague recollection of telling the old couple that the department believed it may have found their missing daughter and that they needed to go to the Medical Examiner's Office. I believe I offered condolences and some expression of deepest regret, though I can't remember if the speech was in English or Japanese or both. The only thing I remember with any amount of clarity is the way the pathetic folks looked as I talked. Tadao Miyasaki just sat there not looking at me, staring off into the distance at nothing through his glasses, still as a statue. Ayako sat gazing at me with her weak, watery eyes, as intent on looking at me as her husband was on not looking at me, but just as eerily and uncomfortably silent. I ka ʻōlelo no ka make. *In words there is death.* I had a vague impression of rising from the sofa again and bowing low and deeply. I think they thanked me for my trouble. If I were them I would have punched me in the face.

When the whole messy business was over, I tripped my way out the screen door into my wingtips, nearly stumbling and planting my face in the lawn trying to get off the lanai as quickly as I could because I didn't want to prolong my unwanted visit by stopping to tie my laces. When I got back to my car, I heard a sickening, heart-rending wail that so deeply agitated me that I leaned over my door and vomited. The last time a human voice sickened me that way was when Wally Yoshida looked down to discover that a grenade had taken off his left leg. There was blood everywhere. My ears were ringing and bleeding from the blast, but I could still hear Wally screaming like a dying animal in a slaughterhouse. Ayako Miyasaki's mournful voice and Wally's merged in my head until I couldn't tell the difference. It was just one long siren bringing images back of the dirty tourniquet I made, Wally's blood all over my hands. For one harrowing moment, I was back in that goddamned bunker, shivering violently. I crossed my arms in attempt to close myself off from the outside world and shut my eyes tightly. It worked sometimes. Not this time.

Wally and I had been discussing the merits of the local girls, the good and the bad of the Italian women in the village and examining how they stacked up against the girls back home. Haole girls with black hair, something exotic we didn't see much of back home. One run scored for Italy. Pretty faces and nice figures, but more hair in their armpits than we had. One run for Hawaii. One straw-covered bottle of wine and a pair of nylons got Gina, the grocer's daughter, into bed with you; you pretty much had to date Polly Yamanaka for half a year before she even let you hold her hand. Four runs for Italy! That was a bases-loaded, genuine grand slam. Wally and I laughed ourselves stupid. We were just a couple of McKinley High School infielders talking about broads over a split Hershey's bar in a bunker with hot death raining down all around us.

Gina, the grocer's daughter, didn't speak much English, so if she was complaining about why you never took her anywhere nice, you didn't know it. And Italian sounded sexy. One run, *Italia*. Polly Yamanaka could tell you in English how much she liked your mom's tsukemono and she could tell your mom in Japanese. One run, Hawaii. Polly Yamanaka took a bath every night. Two runs for Hawaii!

Hawaii was down two runs in the fourth and Gina was once again at bat for Italy when Wally and I finished the Hershey's bar. I got up to get more candy from our rations behind a pile of spare sandbags when all hell broke loose. We had been laughing too hard to notice the metallic clink of the grenade landing on the bunker floor. Though the roar must have been deafening beyond imagining, I could recall nothing of the sound. What I do remember—what I can't forget—was the blinding flash. After that, the rest was an angry red blur. Then Wally's wail.

The shakes came again along with the tearless sobs. Saved only because I was closest to the rations. Saved because I wanted more chocolate. I wiped my clammy forehead with my handkerchief. I pulled the hip flask from the glove compartment and took a long drink, mostly to get the taste of vomit out of my mouth. The fire slipped down my throat and the world stopped rocking. I looked down at the asphalt for no reason at all and saw a couple of mismatched tire marks, long and arching, left by a car trying to get the hell out of Sheridan Tract as fast as it could. I made like that car and did the same.

6

I returned to the station to report to Gid, who would report to the brass, that the dirty deed of breaking the news to the next of kin had been done in somewhat less than picture perfect form. All hell was breaking loose with the press. The receiving desk area was crammed with haole newspapermen and the chief was talking strategy with the commissioner on the telephone, with all the brass standing around his office like a bunch of nervous mommies at a piano recital. My sister Iris was right. Things were changing. A few years ago, a dead Japanese girl wouldn't have aroused more press interest than a drunk getting rolled in Aala Park. Now it wasn't just the *Hawaii Hochi* hanging around the station. The *Star-Bulletin* and the *Advertiser* had reporters and photographers there. When a bunch of Japanese workers went on strike and shut the islands down, a girl like Millie Miyasaki suddenly became worth the ink. The brass had experience dealing with the political headache that came with haole victims but were ill-prepared to handle the quiet, vexing scrutiny of two out of every five people in the Territory.

I stepped lightly from the foyer to the tiled stairs leading up to the detectives' offices on the second floor, careful not to arouse the attention of the suits and hats and flashbulbs facing the receiving desk. When I got past the landing, I became aware of the rapid, light steps from behind and an alluring floral scent. I turned around and came face-to-face with a pair of glasses.

The glasses had big round frames that were slightly pointed at the hinges. They sat on a girl's face. It was a clear, fair face with delicate brows and pretty dark eyes like cold black coffee. Her hair was darker still, like a Stygian moonless night on the ocean a thousand miles from anywhere. She wore it up in a neat little bun, which exposed the nape of a supple white neck that disappeared into a short-sleeved cream-colored cashmere sweater and was adorned with a string of pearls as white as her teeth. Her attractive contour invited second looks as long as she was seen before she was heard. A pair of legs as fair as her neck came out from beneath her dark skirt, calves curving gracefully down into a smart pair of shiny pumps.

The girl's face had a cute little mouth that opened and said, "Detective?"

"Who, me? I'm the janitor, darling. Just making my rounds." She didn't look convinced.

"A janitor who wears a .38 under his tailor-made jacket. What's the hurry? Overflowing wastebasket?" Fantastic. I was trapped in the stairwell with her. The little notepad and pencil in her hand said she was press. Either that or some secretary lost her way across the street from Hawaiian Dredging.

"Paper or radio?" I sighed, resigned. The large window above the landing flooded the stairwell with sunlight and caught her hair and made it glow with a deep, silken luster. I could hear the general din of the crowd downstairs shouting questions at some poor captain who got roped into an impromptu conference. I just got roped into an impromptu conference of my own.

"*Honolulu Record*," she said. She shot her free hand out. "I'm Ellen Park." I took her hand and shook it. It was nice and warm. Her voice was a touch too loud for conversation. Loud voices were usually the hallmark of people to avoid, but it was somehow cute on her. Just like her sweater.

"Francis Yoshikawa."

"Detail?"

"Vice. I wouldn't stand too close if I were you. I enjoy a hands-on approach to my work," I said with a humorless smirk. I thought I could hear the ticks on my wristwatch actually slow down.

"You're not Vice. You're Homicide. Vice doesn't carry *those* out of habit." She pointed at the three Partagas cigars peeking out of my breast pocket. If it weren't for the racket at the desk downstairs, the scraping sound of my eyes rolling could have probably been heard.

"Look, Miss Park, it was really swell making your acquaintance, but I've got to run. I have some casework and I'm sure you're busy with the Smith Act dog and pony show going on down the street. You *are* with the *Record*, aren't you?" Koji Ariyoshi, activist and student of Mao Tse Tung, established the *Honolulu Record* as a paper for the common man. Ariyoshi was one of the "Hawaii Seven" who were on trial for alleged Smith Act violations. The *Record* came out every Thursday and my sister Iris read it religiously for its "true" reporting and commentary. I liked the pictures of the girls that turned up occasionally on page three.

Ellen Park smiled a triumphant smile. "Yes, Detective, I *am* with the *Record*, and almost all of my colleagues are down the street covering the dog and pony show. Some of them *are* the show. That's why I'm here. There's nobody else to do the Police Beat. And I just caught the biggest fish of all—the detective assigned to the case everyone downstairs is asking about. All those clever haoles and not a single brain among them." She smiled again. Wider, I thought.

"How do you know it's *my* case?"

"You're Japanese."

"Brilliant. I've often wondered about that." She let it pass.

"Don't you think that's the smartest thing the department can do—put their only Japanese homicide detective on a case where the victim is Oriental? I've done my homework, Detective Sergeant Yoshikawa. You *are* the only Japanese homicide detective."

"That's giving the department enough credit, to believe that they'd do the smartest thing. You don't know the department." She stood there, both shiny, tiny shoes rooted on the Spanish tiled stair. She looked as convinced as Ka-san did when I told her I had a stomachache on church mornings. "You're not going to let me get back to work, are you, Miss Park?"

"Of course I am, Detective. I'm going to make a hero out of you. Orientals are watching and I think that one of their own—one of *our* own—bringing the culprit down is an inspiring story. I'm going to chronicle your quest for justice."

Quest for justice. Do people really say things like that? "That's nice," I said, though I was thinking it really wasn't. The smart, cute little reporter prattled on, telling me more about myself.

"I'll bet you went to McKinley, Detective, although you sound more like Punahou, and I'll bet you were a big man on campus." She started laying on the sugar for my futile attempt to shake her.

"End and First Base. All-Territory as a senior in both sports," I said, stepping right into it.

"Then at UH, too?"

"Columbia."

"Ivy Leaguer? I *am* impressed."

"Don't be. G.I. Bill."

"War hero, too?"

"Hardly, compared to some."

I sprinkled some sugar of my own.

"What about you, Miss Park? Farrington, I'm guessing. Homecoming Queen and Student Body Secretary. Then journalism major at UH, where you worked on the paper."

"Prom Queen Runner-Up and Student Body Treasurer. I was an economics major, but yes, I was on the paper. I was its editor-in-chief, as a matter of fact. But you're close enough for a prize."

I saw a way out. "I guess *you* win the prize. Give me a minute and I'll check with my Lieutenant to see if you can tag along with me for a bit. Will you wait here for me?"

"Yes!" she replied, exultantly. I opened the door to the Homicide Detail and closed it behind me. I went straight to the window beside my desk and opened it. I threw a leg over the sill.

"What are you doing, Sheik?" squeaked Delilah. Gid shambled out of his office to watch.

"Shortcut to Merchant Street," I said. I lowered myself over the sidewalk, holding on to the sill by my fingertips. I let go after counting to three and made the additional six-foot drop without twisting an ankle. I sprinted down Merchant as fast as my wingtips would allow me to my car. The last thing I needed was a spunky tag-along reporter who knew everything about everything getting in the way.

When I got to my Eldorado near the corner of Merchant and Kaahumanu, a cool, elegant voice like a Paul Desmond solo behind me said, "Nice car." I turned to see Ruth Prentiss. The silky brunette who had come to Ka-san's the day before to drop off a check for my sister. She was wearing a European-looking jacket and skirt in emerald green with a matching pillbox hat and white gloves. She stepped toward me in fluid movements. She blinked a couple of times and smiled.

"Thanks," I said, "though I can't really think of it as nice until it's all paid for. Do you work around here?"

"Just around the corner. How about you?"

"I'm back on the last block."

"Whom do you work for?"

"I have a government job."

"Lucky you."

"Sure, lucky me. If being a round-the-clock civil servant is lucky."

She flashed a brief smile. It stirred something primal inside me and tied my tongue.

"I won't hold you up. It was nice seeing you again." She blinked and moved down Merchant Street toward Bishop. I watched her move for a few seconds then got into my car. I thought for a second to call after her and get a telephone number but by the time I had looked back down Merchant Street she had disappeared. Oh, well. What can you do? Story of my life.

I figured my next stop should be Millie's place of employment. The midmorning traffic on Merchant Street going Diamond Head wasn't too bad so I ended up at the Territorial Office Building in less time than anticipated.

The 1920s-built Territorial Office Building was done in the Classic Revival style, had a set of Greek columns running up the face of its four-story tower. A stained-glass dome with the Territory seal and Hawaiian motto graced the roof of the open-air lobby at the top of the steps leading down to King Street. The secretarial pool of the Office of the Attorney General was behind a door to the right side of the lobby. The Attorney General himself had a regal office in Iolani Palace, but his support staff couldn't all fit in there with him, so they camped out across King Street along with some other agencies in the Office Building.

The Attorney General's secretarial pool was a hive of queen bees in cashmere sweaters and bright lipstick, buzzing from file cabinet to file cabinet. Though the supervisors looked for the most part to be stern haole or Portuguese women with hair tinted in unnatural shades, the vast majority of the girls looked Oriental. A stocky Portuguese lady with bifocals on a faux pearl chain saw me standing at the counter and approached me before I hit the bell next to the painted sign that read "RING BELL FOR SERVICE. MAHALO." She had the sad, big, wet eyes of a cow and was probably drop-dead gorgeous twenty years and six children ago. She smelled like my sisters' dressers—powder, perfume, and a hint of dust.

"Good morning," she said, trying to hide the Liliha matron with an Eleanor Roosevelt impersonation. "Can I help you, sir?"

"Good morning, ma'am," I said, trying to hide the Kakaako punk with my best Cary Grant. "I'm Detective Sergeant Francis Yoshikawa of the Honolulu Police Department." I showed her my badge. "I was wondering if I might have a word with someone about an employee, a Miss Mildred Miyasaki."

Her eyes went wide and she lost the Eleanor Roosevelt. "Uh, yah," she grunted, pure Kuakini Street, "come wit' me." I followed her to a room behind a wall of steel file cabinets. It had pale green walls with white crown molding and baseboards, just like the rest of the office. A window overlooked Punchbowl Street with Kawaiahao Church and its graveyard visible to the side. She poured a cup of coffee for me and pulled a cigarette out of a neat little silver box that she produced from her purse; her chubby hands shook as she lifted it to her lips. I popped the lid on a chrome-plated Zippo, the twin of the one Gid owned. He had given it to me as a Christmas gift. I held it up for her, and she grabbed my hand with moist, clammy fingers as she puffed.

The woman introduced herself as Gladys Jean Souza, one of the supervisors of the Attorney General's secretarial pool. She looked at me with her head dipped like a frightened child and whispered, "Did you find Millie, Sergeant?"

"Yes, ma'am," I said, with sufficient grimness.

"Call me Gladys," she said.

"I believe we found her yesterday, Gladys. Her parents have been notified and they should be, uh, identifying her this morning. I'm sorry."

She crossed herself and tears rolled down her plump, rouged cheeks. She pulled a handkerchief from her purse and dabbed her eyes.

"Was it an accident?" she asked, voice breaking.

"No, I'm afraid not. I'm a Homicide detective."

"My God," she breathed, "who would want to hurt her? She made cookies and stuff for everybody and brought in manju. Everybody loved her."

"Not everybody." Though I thought I did once upon a time.

The next few tortuous minutes were filled with Gladys's babbling about a hard-working and obedient girl who was generous and nice and clean. And not very well known. I picked up on this about twenty seconds into her monologue on nice Japanese girls who don't talk back and don't try to foist their work off on others. What I needed was to talk to someone who knew her better than her supervisor did, which was not well at all. I lit a cigarette and looked out of the window past Gladys at the Kawaiahao graveyard behind the coral wall and wrought iron fence across Punchbowl Street. A lot of famous people lay there moldering in the ground. I'd bet none of them got there via the harbor with an anchor hitched to them. When Gladys finally had to stop talking long enough to inhale, I took the opportunity to cut in and ask her who knew Millie best at the office. She lined up a parade of young office girls all teary-eyed and full of glowing eulogy for their fallen comrade. They didn't seem to know Millie any better than Gladys. One of them finally said she knew Millie had a boyfriend and had met him once or twice, but didn't think very highly of him. His name was Albert Ishida and he worked at a place called Robert's Tire on Queen Street.

Albert Ishida. *Are you sure, Miss?*

Pencilneck Ishida. He was a tough-talking punk at McKinley High who was always trying to get next to Millie and probably hated my guts back then for managing to land her as my steady. He'd needle me about anything he thought he could get away with then took off when my patience wore thin, to avoid a beating. He didn't enlist after graduation and bragged he'd have all the girls to himself when suckers like Wally and me shipped off to get a bayonet in the gut. He was probably just a coward, but he wasn't alone by a long shot. He bragged that he'd finally get Millie when I left. He didn't know she had already dumped me by the time I was on my way to training camp. It looked like his peskiness finally paid off. The thought of Ishida's clammy hands on the same skin I touched all those nights in her bedroom made me sick to my stomach. Simmer down, Sheik. Millie's bedroom was a long time ago. And it wasn't that great.

After I had listened to my fill of office girl declarations of grief punctuated by their button noses being blown into embroidered handkerchiefs, I asked them to show me the desk that had been Millie's, which was as unremarkable as my own but for the fact it was crammed with dishes and jars of candy and Japanese snacks like senbei and arare. A handwritten card in a feminine script in front of the jars urged the reader to "help yourself." From the look of the waistlines of Gladys and the other office ladies, they probably did just that several times throughout the day. The rest of the desk was sufficiently girly with a miniature fake Ming vase and a stapler and sharpened pencils lined up like troopers on the right-hand side of the blotter.

On the blotter in the middle was a banker's box. I removed the lid and surveyed the contents. There was a kokeshi doll, a folded fan of rice paper, a lipstick tube that looked expensive, an old Waterman pen with a bent nib, a pincushion made to look like a tomato full of pins, and various other knickknacks sentimental and mundane that were the sum of the short life of a young office girl. A photograph of Millie and Albert in an ebony frame lay beneath all the junk. He had his hair slicked back with pomade and wore what was probably one of his father's ties. He looked pretty much the same as I remembered him, except he had a drawn face with sunken eyes that looked a little wild. I felt a twinge of jealousy but let it pass. Millie was beyond our reach.

There was a stack of envelopes and folded papers wedged between the photo frame and the side of the box. I pulled the stack out of the box and examined each piece, one by one. The first few were unremarkable:

a six-month-old utility bill for her parents' place in Sheridan Tract, clippings of *Star-Bulletin* and *Advertiser* ads from The Liberty House, some telephone message slips—mostly calls from home—and a couple to call Albert Ishida, a blank message slip with a handwritten notation on the back that read "D.C. 20%?" and pages of various issues of *Harper's Bazaar* with advertisements for dresses, perfume, and the like, marked with paper clips.

Then came something unusual: an engraved invitation to a charity ball at the Royal Hawaiian Hotel, which happened to be the following evening. An organization, the Roman Holiday Foundation, appeared to be the ball's sponsor. I never heard of it, though the movie with Audrey Hepburn and Gregory Peck would soon be in Honolulu theaters. The blank envelope of the invitation had not been addressed to anyone. I slipped the invitation into my coat pocket.

I thanked Gladys and the weepy young ladies of the Attorney General's secretarial pool and left for Robert's Tire. A shady boyfriend is usually the beginning and the end of a homicide investigation involving a young lady. I had a notion of foolish hope that Albert Ishida would be the beginning and the end of this investigation.

7

Robert's, a dirty little tire place just off Queen Street a couple of blocks away from the Territorial Office Building and about four blocks away from Ka-san's pink house in the opposite direction, had a fenced-in yard piled high with tires old and new. Pushed off to the side, a single dying coconut palm in an oil drum looked as if it were used to block the driveway after closing time. A mean little shop. Because it looked like shit, one might go there for a better deal on a set of whitewalls, but later find out that the grubby little proprietor was a drunk who would take every opportunity to gouge you for every penny.

I parked across the street and tread cautiously past the sorry palm and over the grease-stained concrete to the shack with plywood walls and a corrugated tin roof. The hand-painted plaque on the shabby door said "OFFICE," as if to say, yeah, you've come to the right place, even though it looks like a condemned tool shed. At least the sign was spelled correctly.

I knocked and heard a cough and some unpleasant hacking before a voice said, "Come in." It sounded like someone was dying. I opened the door and was immediately hit by the odor of rotgut rye and stale, cold sweat like a jacket that hadn't seen a cleaner in five years. A hint of reefer smoke and something rotten I couldn't identify also lingered in the air.

A hunchbacked old haole man in a grubby work shirt sat at a desk piled high with carbon invoices and dog-eared catalogues from various tire manufacturers. His open work shirt revealed a yellowed undershirt damp with sweat and a dull Saint Christopher medal dangling from a cheap chain. He looked as if he hadn't shaved or bathed in three days and was intently studying an order form under the sick yellow light of an army surplus desk lamp while taking sips of rye-spiked coffee from a dirty mug.

"Yeah," he grunted without looking at me. The "office" sweltered like the gym locker room at McKinley—only ten times hotter and without the smell of soap. Perspiration began to pour down the side of my face.

"Are you the Robert of Robert's Tire?"

"It's what my mother named me, yeah. Do you want some tires? A rotation? We do those, too, but only on Wednesdays when the part-time boys come in." Robert put his mug down and stood slowly, careful not to knock the tiny, droning fan off his desk, which was about as helpful at cooling the shed down as the crack in the windowpane.

"Is that your Caddy out there?" he asked as he peered through the dirty window, sudden life in his haggard voice, "Wanna set of whitewalls? Sure would look nice."

"Thanks, but I'm here on business." I flashed the badge and his eyes shot out of their sockets.

"Hey look, I told that lady there wasn't no refunds on the set. All sales final. I told her and she said yeah, like she knew what I said."

"I'm not here about that."

"Well, shit, then I don't know where the part-time boys get their reefers from, but I told them if I caught them smoking that shit around here they're all fired. All of them."

"I'm not here about that, either."

"I didn't know the girl was only sixteen. Shit, you know those Japs—they all look so goddamned young, anyway . . ."

"Not this Jap. This Jap is growing older with every misdemeanor you insist on confessing. I'm not here to talk to you, Robert. I want to talk to Albert Ishida. Is he here?"

"Albert? My bookkeeper? Yeah, he's out back doing inventory. I'll take you."

Robert smiled that goofy, irrepressible grin and let out that involuntary chuckle that were the hallmarks of a guy off the hook. He led me out of his sweltering office through the covered shop and into the rear stock area of his lot.

"Albert," he said, still giddy with relief, "this man wants to talk to you. Take a break."

A sullen Japanese male in his late twenties raised a narrow head of black hair slick with pomade and flipped a cowlick out of his wild, unblinking eyes. About five foot seven and thin as a rail, he wore a sweat-soaked white dress shirt a size too large for him tucked into a pair of grubby flannels. Dirt and dust from Robert's tiny stockyard covered Albert's loafers and tire rubber blackened his hands. Something about him was different from when I had last seen him in high school. He looked wild. He looked even wilder than his photograph with Millie. He had one foot in disturbed and the other in deranged.

He looked at me with his crazed eyes, dark circles around them. He jerked his chin up, acknowledging me, flipping his cowlick once more. He squinted at me for a bit and then recognition ignited in his wild eyes. "Mr. Homerun," he said derisively. "Long time no see."

"Yeah, long time no see, Albert. You're looking top shelf." I didn't sneer but my voice did. I flashed my gold shield. "This is a business call, Albert. I need to talk to you about Millie Miyasaki."

He launched into a rapid-fire verbal tirade before I got any questions out.

"Cop now, huh? Good for you, Mr. Homerun. Millie? Haven't seen her. Not in a while. Always giving me the run-around! Always getting me to buy stuff for her! I took her out but she never wanted to put out. I took her to Lau Yee Chai for dinner. And then I bought her that black dress at The Liberty House. I'm getting sick of it! I really don't care that we don't go out any more. Her folks told me she wasn't there. But I know they lie for her! I don't care. I'm sick of it! I bet you were sick of it too!"

That cut, but I held my tongue. He stood there after his barrage, hyperventilating, his chest heaving up and down. He wiped the sweat off his forehead with a bare hand, leaving a smudge of black rubber across it. The black stain made him look like the maniac he sounded like. I could almost hear the hammering of his heart from four feet away.

A gray blur caught the corner of my eye and I moved before the tire iron Albert Ishida held in his right hand could open my skull. The momentum of the swing turned his body and I gave him a swift blow to his upper arm, causing him to drop the iron and lose his balance. He reeled into a stack of old whitewalls, toppling them and planting his face in the dirt. I put my hands on him and dragged him up by the collar, throwing him with no insignificant force into the side of the plywood shack. Ishida let out a muffled whimper and a couple of bloody teeth fell out of his torn mouth into the dust. Clutching him by the neck and pinning him to the wall, I turned his trouser pockets inside out with my free hand. Benzedrine tablets rained down to settle in the dust next to his teeth.

"Fuck!" I shouted. Adrenaline coursed through me. "Did you hit her when you were all hopped up like this? Did you?" I slammed his head into the plywood, released my grip on his neck, balled up a fist, and let it fly for all I was worth. I connected with his nose and he crumpled with a bloody face on a heap of old tires. All the rage of years past, all the years of not being able to beat the shit out of him after all his jealous taunting was in that punch. It demolished him. I felt damned good to finally do it.

"Why the hell did you dump her in the harbor, Albert? Did she deserve that for not putting out after lobster and champagne? Did she deserve to die because you didn't get a return on your investment?" I hit him again just for the hell of it.

Ishida looked up at me, eyes white and wild through the scarlet mess. He whispered mushily through swollen lips, "She's dead?" A long silence ensued as I caught my breath and de-escalated. For an eternity, I stood there looking down at him, lungs on fire. His eyes wouldn't meet mine. Then Ishida started to cry. Wracked with sobs, his skinny frame shook uncontrollably. "I thought she went to France with him," he bawled, barely understandable through the mouth I'd damaged.

"What do you mean 'France' and who's 'him'?" I asked.

"She always said someone would take her to Paris. She said it when we . . . argued. She said it to make me jealous, make me mad and feel like shit. Make me spend more money on her. I . . . I thought it was all talk. Just shit to make me feel bad. A couple of weeks ago we . . . argued . . . about how come I only took her somewhere nice to eat only one time. She said she had it with me, that I didn't really love her 'cause I didn't treat her special. She said she was going to Paris with someone who thought she was special. Then she was gone. I didn't go to her office and I only went by her house once. Her folks said she wasn't home. I bugged them about it a couple of times on the telephone. After that I stopped. I figured she really went."

His last few words were bitter, like the losing quarterback trying to explain the interception he threw. Tears and snot ran down his sweaty, grimy, bloody face over his half open mouth. I noticed I had split his lip; it probably stung like hell. I suddenly started to feel bad for Albert Ishida, assault on a patrolman with a deadly weapon notwithstanding. I helped him up and sat him down on a thick plank laid across some cinder blocks, no doubt Robert's idea of a thrifty waiting room. I didn't sit next to him; the plank looked like it couldn't support the weight of more than one adult and would put a number of splinters in my ass.

"Millie didn't go to France," I told him, ironically unwilling to hurt his feelings after turning his face into pulp. "Someone knocked her senseless and dumped her into the harbor. I'm a homicide detective, Albert. Let's start with the dress. When we found her yesterday, she was wearing a ritzy black velvet Chanel and had eaten some lobster for dinner. This happened a week ago. Do you think that was the dress you bought her?"

"I don't know. Could be."

"What do you mean, you don't know? You don't remember what it looked like? Especially after it cost you, what, like a week's pay from this dump?"

"I never even saw the damn thing. Millie just told me that she had an account at The Liberty House and that she needed me to feed fifty bucks into it so she could get the black dress she wanted."

I looked at Ishida, sitting on the bench like some lost child. Tears were streaming down his dirty cheeks and he wasn't making any effort to stop his nose from bleeding.

"Something tells me that you don't know anything about the lobster dinner, either," I said.

"No," Ishida choked, and then started sobbing loudly, "I never took her for no damn lobster."

"I guess that would be the 'him' who was supposed to take her to Paris?"

"I guess."

"Who is he, Albert?"

He wiped his eyes then blew his bloody nose on his dirty shirtsleeve in the crook of his elbow. I offered him my handkerchief and he put it to his nose to stanch the flow of blood. I pulled a couple of cigarettes out of the crumpled pack in my coat pocket and offered him one. When we were both lit up, Ishida finally spoke.

"I don't know who he is. She never said any names. I still kind of think she made him up. I never saw him. She said it's somebody rich with class who treats her the way she deserves. She always bragged about how he wants to take her here and there and that she only stays with me because we were together a long time and I'm her first. You know, stuff like that."

He took a deep drag and let out a huge white cloud that dissipated slowly in the burning, humid mid-morning air. Both of us started breathing more slowly and sweating like chopped onion in a cast iron skillet. I felt like chopped onion and probably smelled like it.

"I figure he's haole," Ishida continued, "because she'd say he was going to take her to the Navigators Club for dinner and stuff one day and he didn't care she was Japanese."

I looked at Albert Ishida, sitting on the plank bench, face soaked with sweat, blood, and snot, looking blankly out at the sweltering Kakaako morning through his greasy cowlick. I stomped on the Benzedrine tablets that had fallen from Ishida's pocket and tossed him what was left of my Lucky Strikes. He absently nodded his thanks and continued to look at nothing. He was a ruined man with nothing left to look forward to except his tiny paycheck and more hop from his underground pharmacist. I didn't really have to guide him to his personal hell. He was already there. All I did was turn on the lights and let him see it for himself.

"Thanks for the smokes, Mr. Homerun," he said in a monotone.

"Thanks for the exercise. See you around, Albert."

I tucked in my shirt, grabbed my hat off the stack of tires and walked away. As I passed the dying coconut palm, Robert poked his haggard head out of his shack and rasped at me, "Still want some whitewalls? I'll give you a damn good price."

"White*walls*?" I said. I looked down at my bloodied cuffs. "Right now I could use a new white *shirt*." I shuffled back to my Cadillac, got in, and left a cloud of dust in my wake.

8

I stopped at Ka-san's house to wash up a little and change my shirt; she had gone shopping so there was thankfully no need to explain all the blood. The morning paper was lying on the kitchen table next to a bowl of tangerines from my sister Pansy's tree. Pansy was frugal to the point of embarrassment. She made a *gift* of them to Ka-san on Sundays as her *contribution* to the evening meal. Lucky for me, her husband Eldred stopped off at Liliha Bakery and bought a coconut cake to give in addition to the tangerines. Eldred and Pansy's house was full of stuff that Pansy managed to get for free, like calendars from chop suey houses or oven mitts with the name of some mom-and-pop store stamped on them. Their poor children were forced to wear shirts and blouses she had sewn for them using the cloth from old rice bags.

I sat down, peeled myself one of the tangerines, and picked up the paper. The front page featured a large photograph of Harcourt Billings, Sr. of The Billings Trust in a light-colored suit and a shiny hard hat that looked a size too small for his head. He was grasping a shovel handle with the Lieutenant Governor of the Territory at the groundbreaking of some new building somewhere. It must be nice to have that kind of money. Even his hard hat looked like it came from Tiffany's on Fifth Avenue.

The Billings Trust had been a fixture in the islands for over half a century. Old Jeremiah Billings, one of those characters with a handlebar moustache and mutton-chop sideburns like some Civil War general in a high school textbook, made his fortune as a railroad baron in the American West and came to Hawaii by personal invitation from his friend, Sanford B. Dole, President of the Republic of Hawaii after he robbed Queen Liliuokalani of her throne and palace. Shortly after Dole became the first Governor of the United States Territory, Billings, like all haole moneymen from the outside, set deep roots down by sinking a good part of his rail fortune into sugar, then local shipping, and marrying into an old missionary family. By the time he passed on and left the running of the Trust to his son, Harcourt, Sr., the entity had become a household name from Hilo to Lihue. The Billings Trust may not have been one of the Big Five, but it was certainly Number Seven and could make a case for being Number Six. Though Harcourt, Sr. was every bit the shrewd businessman Jeremiah had been, his offspring had more talent for spending money than making it.

Harcourt, Jr. was a notorious playboy with a taste for Oriental waitresses and Hotel Street strippers. He whiled away his mornings on the golf course and his afternoons at the Navigators Club and showed his face at a weekly board meeting at the Billings Trust Building on Bishop Street. He was a charmer, though, by all accounts a loveable lush who was just as often having tea on the verandah of Washington Place as he was draining a martini on the lanai of the family estate house in Manoa. His younger sister, Peg, was an athletic looker with a rebellious streak. Her politics ran decidedly left and clashed with those of her family's. She was the smarter of the two Billings kids and kept her own office in the Trust Building, but mostly ran what kamaaina haole society would call "communist plots" out of it. There were rumors that she had supported food drives for striking stevedores' families out of her own pocket back in '49 when she was fresh out of Bryn Mawr.

I dribbled tangerine juice all over the picture of Harcourt, Sr. by accident and threw the paper in the wastebasket next to the sink. Ka-san had some daikon lying around on the counter looking like fat white seals on some far-off arctic shore near the sink where I ran my hands under the faucet and rinsed the sticky juice off them.

After drying my hands, I made my way back to the to the front door and slipped back into my wingtips. I laced them up, closed the door, and lit a cigarette from an extra pack I had found earlier in my Cadillac's glove box. I lingered on the lanai, leaning against the doorframe and watching the smoke; I exhaled and watched it dissipate slowly in the heavy, stifling late-morning air. I looked out across the street at Mr. Fujita's house and the warehouse next to it and thought about the Miyasakis of Sheridan Tract and the gruesome task ahead of having to enter their home once more and search Millie's room and her possessions. God, if they knew I had already been in that bedroom. Several times. That could only make it worse. Fortunately, decorum dictated that this task should wait for another day; they just went to identify the body that morning. Millie's poor mom would probably break in half and blow away at the thought of me going through her not-so-freshly deceased daughter's underwear drawer and diary on the same morning I came to drop the worst news she ever received in her lifetime. I'm sure the brass would've understood if I naturally deferred the task until at least the following day. And if they didn't then the hell with them.

I had some other leads in the meantime. My visit with Albert Ishida revealed more about the character of the girl I used to know, a girl of modest means and not-so-modest taste. It was obvious that Albert did not buy or otherwise acquire the diamond bracelet on the *Hinalea* for her. He probably didn't know anything about it, either. He deposited some cash into an account at The Liberty House for her to buy the Chanel dress; Ishida made no mention of her shoes. A grudge-holding cheapskate like Albert Ishida would have been sure to mention the shoes too, if he paid for them. The new mystery man in Millie's life probably had some answers. If he could take her to Paris, could he also buy her some bracelet worth thousands? Just how many guys on the island could *that* be?

My cigarette had burned down to an inch-long stub and I decided that at that point I needed to know more about Millie. Her boss didn't know a whole hell of a lot about her and neither did Albert. Her coworkers only ate the food she brought in and praised her ability to not talk back. And I had serious doubts that her parents knew her any better than any of them. Now, after she was gone, I'd have to get to know her better than I ever did if I was to learn Gid Hanohano's elusive *why* of the whole matter.

I decided to drop in at The Liberty House and make some inquiries into Millie's account. It seemed logical and it was on my way back to the station. I got into the Eldorado and headed ewa, toward the station, stopping a block or so shy of it. I parked on Merchant and walked over to Fort Street and into Honolulu's ritziest shop. Anything fine could be found there and if they didn't have it, they'd reach clear around the world to New York or Paris to get it for you, all in less than three months' time.

As soon as you pushed your way through the glass doors, you could smell the new and expensive that it was practically in the air conditioning. The cool air made me feel like some coolie farmer coming into a palace to beg from his betters. One of those betters caught my eye from behind a display case full of silk scarves. She was a pretty hapa girl who looked a lot like Lana Turner with brown hair and wore Chanel—outfit and perfume. I strode up to the display case as if I were approaching the on-deck circle in the Ivy League Championship Series with the bases loaded, pretending I wasn't sweating like a pig under my jacket.

"Good morning, sir," said the Chanel Girl, in a voice as cool and luxurious as the air conditioning, "looking for something special for someone special?" I thought I caught the slightest hint of Waipahu or somewhere farther in her greeting.

"You could say that, though I should probably look for the some*one* special first, but I'm sure you hear that all the time, especially from men who don't know anything about silk scarves." That won the tiniest smile, and what I thought was the slightest blush.

"I'd be happy to show you the entire line. We have stock that's not on display, if you don't see anything you like."

"Oh, I see something I like. A lot." The tiniest smile turned into a full, unabashed grin. "But what I'd *really* like to see is something that's not on display, now that you mention it."

"What color did you have in mind?"

"What color do your account books usually come in?"

"What?" said the Chanel Girl, the Waipahu accent announcing its presence before she quickly recomposed the façade. "I'm sorry, sir. I beg your pardon?"

"Your account books. The ledgers where your regular customers have their account balances and transactions recorded."

"And you would need this, why? Mister, uh . . ."

"Detective Sergeant Yoshikawa." I flipped the leather open and showed her my shield.

Chanel Girl took off toward the rear of the store as fast as her high heels would let her. I glanced down at the scarves. They were as brilliant as prize-winning koi. I casually leaned against the glass scarf display case and played with an unlit cigarette. I was finally beginning to cool down and dry out and feel like I belonged a little more in the grand atrium of The Liberty House. An old Chinese lady in a black silk cheong sam and enough jade to break an elephant's back strolled down the aisle in front of me with her Filipino house girl. The crone shot me a disapproving look and shook her blue coif at me. Maybe I hadn't dried out after all.

Chanel Girl came clicking back with a fat haole man in a European-cut suit in tow. He had a black leather volume under his hammy left arm and was dabbing sweat off his enormous forehead with a monogrammed handkerchief. It turned out he was the floor manager and was most compliant in letting me examine the books.

I found the Miyasaki account without much of a problem; it had been open for less than a year. An initial payment of twenty dollars to establish the account was made by Millie herself about ten months prior, then another twenty went in a month later, again paid by Millie herself. A string of purchases followed: perfume, a summer hat, and a handbag, all imported. Her tastes ran way above Sheridan Tract and a Territorial worker's salary. I tried to imagine my sister Pansy seeing the price of the hat and blanching; she could probably feed and clothe her family for a couple of months for the price of one straw hat made in France. A similar pattern of twenty-dollar deposits and accessory purchases went on until about two months prior when I found Ishida's deposit for fifty dollars and his name in the ledger next to the payment. Cash, of course, like all of Millie's own deposits had been. Then came the first big-ticket purchase: the black velvet Chanel cocktail dress that brought the account almost to zero. There was no activity on the account for a couple of weeks. Then I saw trouble. About two days before Millie had her last supper, I saw a deposit by special draft for a hundred dollars, a purchase of a pair of black patent leather pumps for twenty dollars and a name next to the deposit that deflated my spirit for breaking the case.

I snapped the big book shut and tucked it under my arm.

"The Honolulu Police Department thanks you and The Liberty House for your cooperation, sir," I said mechanically, sounding like one of the hundreds of form letters signed by the Chief. I put my hat back on top of my head and left the cool of the department store for the steam room of Fort Street. The heat ceased to matter to me, though. My blood had run cold as soon as I read the last deposit name on the ledger.

9

I didn't bother jumping into my car to get to the station; I walked the two blocks or so and left my vehicle parked on Fort Street. The station was still crawling with a second shift of newspapermen and I probably couldn't have parked much closer, anyway. I made three quick steps from the station foyer to the staircase, then went up to Homicide.

Gid came out of his office when he heard me enter Homicide. He stood there with his fists on his hips and a cigarette hanging out of his mouth. "You almost gave Delilah a heart attack," he said. He glanced at the window I had jumped out of earlier. "She thought you died."

"Maybe I would've if I went down head first. I'm beginning to feel like I should've."

"The girl from the *Record* you left out in the hallway was pretty mad. When Delilah opened the door for her, she started yelling at Delilah. When she found I was the lieutenant you were supposed to talk to, she started yelling at me."

"Why?"

"Because you didn't talk to me like you said you would."

"How did she know I didn't?"

"I told her."

"Why?"

"Because you didn't."

"What else did you tell her?"

"I said you jumped out the window."

"Why?"

"Because you did."

Gid broke into smile. It had just a shadow of wryness, but it was there. I guess I couldn't expect him to be anything but himself. He peered out the window past me at the Yokohama Specie Bank Building across the street with calm eyes, but I knew he was laughing inside. He reached into his pocket and pulled out a little card. "She told me to give you this," he said. He smiled an actual smile this time. I took the card. Ellen Park. Reporter. *Honolulu Record.* 811 Sheridan Street. Telephone number. I turned the card over. There was a handwritten note: "*You're the story of the year and I'm going to get tell it. I DON'T give up. E.P.*" Swell. She had ugly handwriting for a girl.

I looked up and saw Luau and Jack Morris, who had returned from court that morning. Jack had drifted to the islands because of the war and stuck around after it was over. He was tall and thin with a balding scalp as tight as a Spalding baseball and about the same color. Jack had been a New York Police Department flatfoot, walking the beat somewhere in the Bronx before enlisting and finding his way to Fort Shafter as an MP. After mustering out, Jack decided he liked the weather and the women here too much to go back to the Bronx so he joined HPD and snagged himself a small white house and mango tree in Kapahulu. He also managed to snag himself a hula dancer at the Royal Hawaiian who became Mrs. Jack Morris. Jack and I hit it off immediately as I had actually lived in New York City while going to college and was a diehard Yankees fan like him.

"You went to Columbia?" I remember him asking on the day we were introduced.

"Sure did."

"You do anything there besides live in the library?

"I played ball."

"No shit?"

"No shit. It was Ivy League ball, but it was still ball. I had Gehrig's locker."

"Get the hell outta here! No shit?"

"No shit."

We were friends ever since. Jack liked coming over to Ka-san's every now and then for some miso soup and tofu. He loved the food of his new home; Gid had gone out earlier and returned with a box of manapua he picked up in nearby Chinatown. When I came into the office, Jack and Luau were in the middle of tearing into the sweet barbecue pork-filled buns and washing it down with Delilah's horrible coffee.

"Look what the cat dragged in!" Jack had exclaimed. He set his coffee down.

"Looks like you're eating the cat," I shot back. I jerked my chin at the manapua he held.

"Meow," said Jack. He took a huge bite of the white steamed bun revealing the bright red chopped char siu meat within.

"How was court, Jack?" I helped myself to one of the infamous *cat* buns of Chinatown.

"Ah, you know. Sit around, smoke a pack. Drink some shitty coffee from a paper cup then answer all the questions with 'yes' or 'no,' just the way the prosecutor wants you to. Then have another shitty cup of coffee until the bailiff calls you for the next round of 'yes' and 'no.' The coffee was almost as bad as Delilah's. That was my morning. What's the word on our girl in the harbor, Sheik?"

I peeled the wax paper square off the bottom of my manapua and took a bite. Best stray cat this side of River Street. Gid sure knew how to pick 'em.

"The word is probably 'case closed' by the end of the day," I said, without any cheer in my voice.

"Damn, you're good, Sheik! What is that, twenty-four hours?

That's got to be a record—even for you," Jack said. He slapped me amiably on the back.

"That's not what I meant. I think we're going to get the shutdown on this one. Fast."

"Shutdown?" asked Luau. He suddenly perked up. I could almost see his ears go straight in the air like a cartoon dog stalking his prey. Elmer Fudd's faithful hound. "Didn't you guys just drag her out yesterday? Why would this get shut down?" Luau played it coy, but there was no masking his blatant desire for a whiff of business that wasn't his. He could sense a juicy bit of gossip about to show its pretty face. They all stood there gaping at me. Jack carelessly let the long ash from his cigarette drop to the linoleum. Gid shuffled his way between Jack and Luau, his immense frame filling the space and eclipsing the light coming through the window.

"Come on, Sheik. Spill it. What'd you find?" Jack stared at me and gestured wildly with his hands, as if physically trying to pull a response out of my throat.

I let out a long sigh until my shoulders felt like they sagged to the floor. "Millie Miyasaki was having her tab at The Liberty House paid by Harcourt Billings, Jr." I opened the ledger and showed them.

"Whoa. Tough break, Sheik," said Luau. He meant to make it sound as if he were consoling me, but he could barely conceal his excitement at hearing something so broadcast-worthy. He didn't even bother keeping a straight face.

"The Billings of the Billings Trust?" asked Jack. The question hung in the dead space in the room.

"If you know about another less well-connected Harcourt Billings, Jr., now would be the time to tell me about it."

Fat chance. Who else could drop a hundred bucks by special deposit into the account of some Japanese office girl? It didn't necessarily implicate him, but the investigation would have to go through him and at this point it wouldn't. The Billings Trust lawyers would squash this like an armyworm on the lanai. Harcourt Billings, Jr. was off limits, especially for a Japanese dick from Kakaako, even one with a Purple Heart and a Columbia sheepskin. Can't do a damn thing about it. Move on. There was plenty of other shit in my life that needed my attention.

The problem was my gut feeling wouldn't say shikata ga nai along with my head. My na'au told me that if I let the killer of a girl from Sheridan Tract walk because she was mixed up with someone influential and haole then I got shot at in Europe for nothing. And Wally Yoshida lost his leg for nothing because I was too scared to be anything but an indentured peon who bowed and smiled gratefully when the luna handed him his pennies. I thought about Millie lying on the medical examiner's steel table, bloated and flaccid and totally unrecognizable as the girl I kissed in high school. Maybe my pride wasn't worth much, but it was worth more than that. Harcourt Billings, Jr. took a year off to improve his golf swing between Punahou and Yale while I froze in some foxhole waiting for a German bullet to end my misery. Whiskey was his plaything. It was my medicine. I put my neck on the line in the war for more than protecting the likes of the Billings Trust.

"What the hell," I finally said. "If he did it, I'm bringing him in." And I meant it, even if I didn't believe it. Luau looked up from his typewriter with wide eyes. His blood was buzzing with new gossip to spread.

Jack smiled and said, "I know you will, Sheik."

Good old Jack. Ever the optimist. He was the guy who rallied us when we were down by four runs in the eighth to the Fire Department guys; he acted like this setback with Junior Billings was less than those four runs. For the record, we only made up two of those runs but Jack bought beer for everyone and made us feel like we won the game.

Jack was from the Bronx and never really acquired an affinity with the haole elite of Hawaii. He was the son of Irish immigrants who toiled away for the Astors and Cabots and Lodges and found he had more in common with guys like me than with the Manoa set. In fact, he was always much harder on local haole suspects and witnesses than he was on Hawaiians, Portuguese, or Orientals. Jack hated old money. Old money never gave a shit about Jack Morris. Old money gave his mom a bad back and sent his dad to an early grave. Taking Junior Billings down was just his cup of tea.

Gid looked up at me with sad, tired eyes and shrugged. He smiled a very slight smile and without looking at me he said, "It's up to you. It's your case, Sheik. Take Coach Morris with you if you like. For what it's worth, the folks identified the body earlier. They even gave me a couple of these." Gid handed me a black-and-white photograph of Millie, a miniature version of the one that had been in the frame in the Miyasaki's parlor.

I looked at Jack, who looked back at me expectantly. I said, "Let's take a shot at Junior. Let's hold his pedicured feet to the fire and see what we can get before his attorneys put a lid on everything."

Jack broke into a huge grin, ecstatic to be included in the case of the year. He locked my neck in the crook of his elbow and messed up my hair with his free hand. "Me and the Sheik!" he shouted, and then kissed me on the forehead. Luau side-eyed us with feigned disinterest. Jack then released me, ran to the coat rack, and tossed me my hat. "Junior should be on the back nine at the Nuuanu Country Club right now. You drive, Sheik. I always wanted to ride shotgun in that Eldorado of yours." I opened the manapua box for another one, but there was nothing in there but soggy wax paper squares with bun crumbs stuck to them. Luau sure did a number on the box. Having finished the manapua, he was already on his phone, cupping his hands to the receiver and whispering furiously into it while his eyes darted about. He might as well have been on the corner of King and Bishop shouting at the top of his lungs: Extra, extra! The Sheik hits a snag.

I was glad to have Jack along for the ride that afternoon. The truth of the matter is I needed him along. A Jap like me couldn't get past the first tee at the Nuuanu Country Club—even with a badge—unless he was toting some haole's clubs and scorecard. He might, though, if he was with a haole who also had a badge.

The Nuuanu Country Club was a lush, rolling, verdant blanket nestled up against a deep emerald wall of the Koolau range. Jack and I made a beeline up Pali Highway in the Eldorado and turned right at the little road leading up to the club. We were allowed in at the gate after flashing our badges and I drove up to the clubhouse and parked near the service entrance to the kitchen. The sun was almost directly overhead but shrouded by a thin veil of clouds. The mountains behind the golf course were perpetually green and a glance behind at Nuuanu Valley's other wall revealed the many silver waterfalls cascading in thin veins. They reminded me of the waters that Dante warned of in his ascent to the First Heaven in *Paradiso*. I always thought that the First Heaven should look more like Nuuanu Valley than the moon.

A fifty-cent piece, a gift to the old Japanese groundskeeper, got us Junior's location; he was on the fifteenth hole with a caddy named Yasu. Jack and I walked the paths along the emerald expanse, uphill and downhill until we reached the green on the fifteenth where an old Japanese man in knickers and a sleeveless argyle sweater stood bent under the weight of an enormous bag of clubs, muttering advice to the jaunty heir to the Billings Trust Empire. Behind them far downhill beyond the green was a fringe of trees, then the blocky buildings of the downtown Honolulu skyline and the vast blue of the Pacific beyond the harbor.

Harcourt Billings, Jr. had wavy light brown hair and blue eyes and a thin moustache that made him look a little like Errol Flynn. He was crouched like a carnivorous primate with his face scrunched up in concentration as he eyed the pin in the hole, absorbing all of the old caddy's advice, putter clutched in his hands like there was a bayonet affixed to its end. When the old man stopped muttering, Junior stood up, pulled a flask out of his knickers, and took a long drink. He offered the flask to his caddy. The old man declined with a grunt. It was then that they looked up to see us standing on the edge of the green. Junior's face broke out in a friendly smile as he raised his flask in a greeting.

"Good morning, gentlemen," he said, oozing charm and charisma, "or is it afternoon? I've quite lost track of the time. Yasu says it's what happens when the game takes over. Isn't that right, Yasu?" The old man grunted and nodded. Junior put the flask in his pocket and continued. "What can I do for you?"

Jack took the lead and responded, "We're detectives with the Honolulu Police Department, Mr. Billings. I'm Detective Sergeant John Morris and this is Detective Sergeant Francis Yoshikawa." We took our badges out and held them up for Junior to see as we started walking toward him across the green. Junior Billings smiled a little wider.

"Francis Yoshikawa? Are you the same as the Frankie Yoshikawa who played first base at Columbia? When I was at Yale I kept hearing about a guy from Hawaii who homered off Harvard's hotshot reliever. Was that you?"

I hesitated a bit before saying, "Yeah, it was. Ages ago. I haven't homered off anybody lately." Junior walked toward us and met us halfway on the green, his hand extended. I shook his hand and said, "We're sorry to interrupt your game, Mr. Billings. Detective Sergeant Morris and I are with Homicide and we have a few questions we'd like to ask you."

"Homicide?" he said in a voice that only betrayed mild curiosity as he shook Jack's hand, "Dear God. That sounds important. Yasu, why don't you go back to the clubhouse and get yourself a Coca-Cola or a martini or something and come back? Put it on my account and leave the bag."

“Thank you, Mr. Billings,” the old man muttered. He unshouldered his burden and made for the clubhouse.

Junior pulled the flask out of his pocket and took a long pull. He raised the flask slightly toward each of us in a silent offer. A trickle of sweat rolled down the side of my face as I suppressed the urge to reach out for the flask. We shook our heads and waved our hands in declination.

We watched the caddy disappear over a hill before Jack began to speak.

“Where were you the Friday night before last, Mr. Billings?”

“I was at the Navigators Club and quite in my cups, I might add.”

“All night?”

“All night.”

“Is there anyone who can corroborate your presence there . . . all night?”

“There are several. What’s this all about, Detective?” Junior asked Jack with an indulgent smile. “Am I a suspect of some kind?” He really was a cool customer. Junior Billings remained charming and pleasant through Jack’s hard act. Jack continued to drill Junior about his evening in meticulous fashion and Junior answered every question without so much as a blink. Jack had really been laying into him. Junior Billings was establishment haole and Jack hated establishment haole, which meant he was enjoying this shit. He once told me how he hated other mainland guys who tried to ingratiate themselves with that set and marry into it. Jack drilled some more. I cut in.

“We don’t have any suspects yet, Mr. Billings,” I said in a conciliatory tone. “Right now, we’re trying to gather information. What you tell us may be critical in identifying an individual or individuals who may be responsible.”

“Understood, Detectives. By all means, fire away,” he said. His smile was the smile of someone who has had enough to drink to think he was the life of the party. Junior Billings probably smiled that way all the time, even without the booze.

"Were you acquainted with a Miss Mildred Miyasaki of Rycroft Street? Her friends called her Millie."

"Sorry, doesn't ring a bell." I pulled the photograph out of my pocket and handed it to Junior. He continued smiling as he stared at it.

"She's a looker, Detective," he said, eyes still on the picture. "I don't think I'd soon forget a face this pretty. But it's hard to say. I meet a lot of girls, usually at night and usually with a few cocktails in me. Did she work in a Japanese bar on River Street?"

"No," I told him, "she worked at the Territory Attorney General's. She was found yesterday in the water under Pier 23 chained to an anchor."

"No shit?" Junior said. He raised his eyebrows.

"No shit," said Jack, snatching the photograph from his hand and giving it back to me.

Junior Billings looked at us, his face a mask of charming, drunken politeness. He leaned on his putter like Mr. Peanut leaned on his walking stick.

"Why ask me about this unfortunate young lady?" Junior asked. His eyes moved from me to Jack and back to me.

"It seems that her account at The Liberty House was being generously supported by you at the time of her untimely death," I said. I watched his face carefully.

"Was it? That's news to me." His smile hadn't changed.

"The people at the store told me today. I examined their books."

"Interesting," Junior replied. "I don't recall ever doing such a thing."

"Then why would your name be in their ledger?" asked Jack, evenly but firmly.

"I haven't the foggiest, Detective. I promise to have my people look into it, though, first thing tomorrow morning. But here comes Old

Yasu now, back from the clubhouse. He was in the middle of explaining the break on this green to me and I'm eager to get the rest of his lecture on it. So, if you'll excuse me, I need to finish this game out before teatime at the Moana. I'm meeting my father there. I'm not really keen on going, but what choice do I have? Anyway, I bid you gentlemen good day. Stop off at the clubhouse and have a drink on me if you like on the way out." Junior reached into his pocket, pulled an engraved business card out of his cigarette case and handed it to me. On the card was the name of someone whose title was attorney-at-law and whose address was the Billings Trust.

"This is for you, Detective, should you have any more questions regarding this matter. Give him a call. He's a nice guy—for a lawyer." Junior broke out into a soft laugh. He smiled a lethal smile, a smile like barbed wire daring you to cross it with bare hands and bare feet.

"Thanks," I said, not really meaning it. Jack and I turned toward the clubhouse and began walking uphill.

"Hey, Detective Yoshikawa," Junior called out to me as we trudged our way back to the clubhouse, "I really wished I could've seen your homerun back in college. It must've really been something."

"It wasn't really," I said over my shoulder. I kept walking. "The reliever's arm was tired."

"So's mine," said Junior with a laugh, putter raised in salute. "So's mine."

Sometimes all you can do is get the hell out without making a scene. It took everything I had not to start shouting. To-san would have approved. But I think the effort cost me a burst vein in the forehead.

10

I dropped Jack off at his car near the station; he was going to head over to the Navigators Club to check on Junior's alibi. Having a haole partner came in handy for stuff like that, like it had at the Nuuanu Country Club; if it were me, I might have been able to interview the help there at the service entrance. Maybe.

The next couple of hours were a blur. I found a tuna sandwich and a bottle of cola on Fort Street and tried to enjoy them on a bench while I watched the parade of people and cars. It wasn't working. Food was the last thing in the world I wanted at the moment. I ended up giving the pigeons most of my sandwich so I rounded out my lunch with a couple of Lucky Strikes. Albert Ishida's parents and neighbors had alibied him for the evening of Millie's death; since their "unofficial" breakup, Ishida had become something of a homebody, sulking around his parents' Sheridan Tract parlor and doing the neighbor's books out of the goodness of his hopped-up heart. I guess his breakup with Millie became "official" when she was dropped into the harbor. Ishida was all but eliminated in my mind as a suspect. He was mined for every shred of useful information that morning after my altercation with him. It wasn't much.

Gid's inquiries into the diamond bracelet so far turned up nothing, confirming our initial suspicion that the thing wasn't purchased here. All the jewelers locally capable of putting something like that together or acquiring something like it said that all such pieces—

and there weren't many—were accounted for and that none of their owners had made a complaint that their piece had gone missing. No insurance claims for such an item had been made and no theft reports. This development, though, was more intriguing to Gid than it was frustrating. Often, he told me, the absence of information is just as relevant as the presence of it, and that many missing diamonds was one such instance. As always, Gid left me with something to think about.

I drove makai to Kewalo Basin where I brought a morning extra of the *Advertiser*. I had just been on Fort Street with a cola and tuna sandwich. I didn't have much of an appetite when I fed the birds earlier, but nothing will give you more of an appetite than trying to pry information out of the likes of Junior Billings. I managed to stop at an okazuya and get another lunch.

To-san used to take me to Kewalo Basin to watch the fishing boats come and go when I was a kid. Sometimes he'd even rescue me from Sunday school to do so, when the girls would dutifully sit in the sweltering Makiki classroom next to the church and learn all about how and why Jesus loves us so. Maybe that's why they still spent all of their Sunday mornings there while I still saw the sampans with their Oriental sails, mostly with closed eyelids from the comfort of my bed, awash in the warm embrace of bourbon.

Seeing the boats and feeding the fish breadcrumbs and rice was my special time with To-san, time when I had him all to myself. Time that wasn't spent with him foraging for kiawe logs and branches out on the scorching Nanakuli coast or scrubbing the furo or helping him change the oil in some old car. Boat time at Kewalo was pure goofing off time and my mind would wander back to Kewalo Basin when I was pinned down by German machine gun fire in some cold, damp bunker in France or, after the war, trying to cram all of the strange-sounding stanzas of Chaucer into my brain in my tiny dorm room in Morningside Heights. It also made me think of Wally's dad. He was a fisherman and had a sampan just like the ones at Kewalo. Mr. Yoshida was sent to Jerome, Arkansas during the war because fishermen were thought to be likely Japanese spies. Wally was able to get him home early by writing a letter saying he just lost a leg for America. If America couldn't give him his leg back, could it at least give him his dad back? It worked. Sometimes things do. Sometimes they don't—like with To-san. He was supposed to go to Jerome, too, along with Wally's dad, but he caught pneumonia in that tent colony on Sand Island and died while he was waiting for the boat. All because he taught calligraphy in the evenings at the Moiliili Language School. I never told Wally that the real reason I enlisted was because I was scared shitless that they'd take Ka-san or Violet in To-san's place if I didn't. But I was too late to save him.

I wasn't too late, though, to do the right thing for Millie. Not yet. And I felt that I owed her the effort somehow, despite our thorough lack of genuine affection for each other when we were together. It wasn't for lack of trying. Maybe now I could show her I cared by figuring this thing out and bringing it to its proper conclusion. I grimly chuckled at the irony. Millie was dead—killed in the most gruesome way—and I was still trying to impress her somehow.

I went to the Basin when I needed a break. After twenty-four hours of the girl in the harbor, I needed a break. Most of my appetite was back, probably because I was feeling the pint of bourbon I had picked up at a Queen Street liquor store. I parked right alongside the pier and got out with my paper, booze, sandwich, and a couple of pieces of mochi the old man at the okazuya threw in for free with the sandwich. That's what being a cop around here gets you—two free rice cakes to ease the headache.

I sat down on a bench under a tin awning. I took a long pull from the pint and surveyed the wooden hulls bobbing up and down in a row—traditional sampans with their pine masts sticking up in legion like a bare winter forest. Pigeons congregated in front of the awning, but in a more *laissez-faire* fashion than they had on Fort Street. Fort Street pigeons were bill collectors. At Kewalo Basin, they were more like the guy whose job it was to cut the grass at a city park when there wasn't any grass to cut.

After finishing the sandwich, I unwrapped the two pieces of mochi—colorful little lumps of momentary happiness in twisted wax paper. Powdery, sweet and sticky at the same time, there's nothing in the world quite like it. Maybe the perks of being a cop in Honolulu weren't so bad after all. When the mochi was gone, I took up the *Advertiser.* Reading the newspaper cover to cover was a habit Gid Hanohano had instilled in me. He did it every day and said it was a critical part of being a good investigator. No part of the paper was insignificant, he told me, not even the advertisements. One never knows when any of that information will turn out to be relevant to an investigation. Gid called it the "lay of the land" and told me that any investigator who didn't have a feel for it was flying blind. *Knowledge is options*. Everything from the war in Korea to an orchid show at the Hongwanji. Leave nothing out.

It seems the newspapermen wasted no time in getting the commission-approved release to press. A physical description of the victim was in the article, but not her identification. Doubtlessly, that would be tomorrow's headline. I thought about the Miyasakis and how their quiet little world had turned into a veritable canto out of the *Inferno* and was about to get even worse. The poor folks didn't even have Virgil to guide them through the hellish twists and turns of the strange, hostile place the world had become with the violent death of their daughter.

I went through the rest of the paper, something I had not done at Ka-san's, with the pre-extra morning edition. Of course, under the blatant headline of the girl in the harbor, Harcourt Billings, Sr.'s groundbreaking ceremony and short article was there, along with the photograph of him in a very shiny hard hat. The peace talks at

Panmunjom were moving at a snail's pace but they were moving. The talk between the UN guys and the communist Koreans north of the 38th Parallel was now about prisoners of war and repatriating them. I checked out the latest Schuman Carriage advertisements and skimmed over some piece about a Democratic Party fundraiser being attended by the rebellious Peg Billings, Harcourt, Jr.'s kid sister. Peg's flirtations with the local element ran deeper than Junior's baser, fun-loving association with them. It was rumored along with the story of helping stevedore families during the strike of '49, that Peg regularly made donations to the Longshoremen's Union and was frequently seen talking to Oriental labor and education leaders in public places.

My sister Iris, the high school math teacher and self-styled activist, had mentioned that she met Peg Billings at a couple of Democratic Party functions. Iris said Peg was pretty, friendly, and had a "dirty mouth." Peg, or "Red Peg" as she was sometimes billed, was pretty much in the newspapers all the time and there were rumors that her antics caught the attention of the HUAC. I wondered if she had the same attorney as her brother with the same stack of his engraved business cards and I wondered if that attorney had done something about the HUAC for her. There was no mention about Junior in the paper. There never was. While the newshounds thought it good copy to harass Red Peg, her brother's carnal adventures were curiously of no interest to them.

I moved on to the sports section and perused the National and American League box scores and finished the last page of the last section before folding the whole thing up and chucking it in a wire trash basket covered with bird shit. I drained the rest of the pint and tossed it on top of the paper. I stood and watched one last fishing sampan cast off in its quest for ahi and dragged myself back into the driver's seat of the Eldorado, which was as hot as an oven. It was time to go back to work. I had almost sufficiently anesthetized myself for the task. Almost. Ending my little break was like waking up from a bad dream only to realize you were living the bad dream and the sleep didn't do you any good. I didn't want to do this. I wanted to do something else. Anything else. I wanted a vacation. I wanted a raise. I wanted true love in my life and justice in the world. I wanted a hell of a lot of things. Most of all I wanted another drink. I couldn't get any of those things at the moment. All I could do was get was back to the station so I pointed my Cadillac toward it and pressed the gas pedal.

11

By the time I got back to the station it was already almost four o'clock. No more press feeding frenzy, at least for the moment. From the desk sergeant, I heard a solitary wino receive a lecture on hygiene. I don't believe that an epiphany resulted. Words of wisdom. I shuffled my wingtips up the tiled steps to the second floor and opened the door to Homicide.

Delilah was on her way out. She had her hat on and her purse slung over her shoulder and white gloves on her hands. She looked at me like I was a bunion on her left foot. "It's about time. You have a visitor, *Detective*," she said, with an extra squeak in her voice. It got that way when she was angry. Or in the throes of passion, so I'd heard. She didn't look very amorous so I could only assume she was mad as hell. She confirmed the assumption by pushing her way past me out the door and nearly knocking me back down the stairs. I looked at my desk through the doorway to find the source of Delilah's irritation.

Ellen Park was sitting in my chair, reading one of my reports and poking the daruma absently with a red fingernail. Her eyes behind those big lenses took in the words I had hammered into the carbon.

"Hey! Put that down! It's confidential!" I croaked, my throat whiskey-dry.

"Not bad," she said, clearly ignoring my request. "You have a split infinitive here and you seem to have some trouble with subject-verb agreement, but overall your writing has a lyrical, almost poetic quality to it. '*She proceeded to bludgeon him with his own wrench in a frenzied, reckless state of mind.*' That's powerful. You have a way with words, Detective."

I bristled. The first girl to tell me I had a way with words was on a slab in the morgue. I stalked up to the desk, snatched the report out of her hand, and threw it back in the metal tray.

"What are you doing here?"

"You have a short memory, Detective. I told you I was going to cover your quest for justice for Mildred Miyasaki, and you told me I could tag along."

"I was joking and . . . hey, how do you know her . . . uh . . . the victim's name?" It was jarring to hear it spoken again although it had been in my head all day.

"Where have *you* been? Your Chief released it to the press about three hours ago. *You* may have been joking but *I* wasn't. Didn't you get my note?"

"Yeah. You didn't win any prizes for penmanship. What do you want from me, Miss Park?"

She looked up at me through those big glasses of hers. Her dark eyes were earnest, or looked like they were. They didn't move me. "I want your story," she said. "It's important. Important for the workers on the docks and plantations to know that one of their own is fighting for one of their own. Important for their children to know that a cop who looks like them is on the big case."

"I've heard a lot of sales pitches for a lot of things I've never bought, but I've got to admit this is the first that tried to sell *me* to me. Nice try." Ellen Park shot out of my chair and looked up at me through those huge lenses. She clasped her hands together in a pleading gesture.

"Come on! I won't get in your way. And I don't just take—I give, too."

"What could you possibly give that I'd be interested in?"

"I was at the Territorial Attorney General's today. After you were there, of course. I had to endure all the nauseating tittering from those girls about the tall, handsome detective with the movie star moustache. But I played along and got a goldmine of information on Millie."

"I already know about Albert Ishida. I already talked to Albert Ishida. You're going to have to do better than that." I almost added that I already *knew* Albert Ishida.

"I wasn't talking about Albert, silly. I was talking about *Paris*." I looked at her. She looked back with eyes exaggeratedly wide.

"Tell me," I said.

"No."

"No?"

"No."

She sat back down with her lips pursed and started poking the daruma again. I watched it dip and spring back about five times before an idea wormed its way into my head. Maka'ala ke kanaka kāhea manu. *Be alert and get the bird.* I thought one just walked into the snare. I bit the proverbial bullet and said, "Look, I'm sorry about this morning. Why don't we have dinner and talk about this case then? I mean, to the extent that I can talk about it."

"Don't tease me," she said. She continued to poke the daruma.

"I'm not teasing. How about I get you at seven thirty or so?"

"Are you asking me for a date, Detective?" She tilted her head and looked at me sideways.

"No. This is business, Miss Park. A date implies enjoyment." She smiled big at me, a smile that said *I'll ignore that last crack because I'm above it.* She held the martyr's grin for a couple of beats more before her gaze softened.

"You don't look so well," she said. "Are you okay, Detective?"

"It's been a long day. And I'm sorry about the cracks. This hasn't been an easy thing, Miss Park."

"No need to apologize. And it's Ellen, Detective. Pick me up at seven thirty." She wrote her address on my blotter.

"It's Frankie, Ellen. I'll see you at seven thirty." She got up and walked past me in crisp, choppy steps toward the door, where she stopped and turned around.

"Please do me a favor when you come to get me. My father runs a roulette game in the back of the store. Don't tell my folks you're a cop."

"My lips are sealed. Besides, his games are the concern of a different division." She smiled and waved and I listened to the echo of her pumps on the tiled stairs fade. Gid came shuffling out of his office with army duffels under his eyes. He smiled an exhausted looking smile like it took his last ounce of strength to pull the corners of his mouth up a fraction of an inch. At that moment, I knew just how that felt.

"Hell of a way to get a date," he said.

"It's not a date."

"If you say so. The University Florist has a special on red roses. Two dollars and fifty cents for a dozen with long stems."

"It's not a date, Gid."

"If you say so. I'm just letting you know, that's all."

"Yeah. Knowledge is options, right?"

"That's what I like about you. You're a fast learner. I'll see you tomorrow, Sheik." He put his big brown fedora on and shambled past me to the door, pausing to lay his paw of a hand on my shoulder. "Have fun," he added with a small, crooked grin. I rolled my eyes.

"See you tomorrow, Lieutenant." I grabbed my hat and turned off the ceiling fans and headed down the stairs myself. I got into my car and I pointed it home.

As soon as I got into Kaimuki, I found my ass on a red leather padded stool at the neighborhood bar and grill on Waialae Avenue. I had about three hours before it was time to pick Miss Cashmere Sweater up for our dinner discussion and I needed another drink.

The old man behind the bar knew how I liked it set up: a finger of Four Roses bourbon in a heavy, big-mouthed old fashioned glass, no ice, on my right and a clean ashtray on my left. Sometimes there was a fried aku bone or some such other glorified kitchen scraps.

There was a Red Sox–Yankees game on the radio and the usual crowd of three old guys in shirtsleeves with nothing better to do sat in a booth contentedly gnawing away on their complimentary aku bones in silence and draining bottles of Primo. When someone was announced to have gotten a base hit, the short one with the missing teeth would shout, "Son of a gun!" This was the extent of their conversation.

The whiskey was spicy and went down like fire. Did Junior Billings really have a relationship with Millie? If he did, he might have had good reason to lie to Jack and me about knowing her. Did he dump her into the harbor or maybe pay someone to do it? Why? What makes anyone that angry or desperate? That's even if Junior was remotely involved in this. One thing was for sure. This was a premeditated and calculated act.

Crimes of passion end in some cane field beyond Wahiawa and, if the perpetrator's lucky, the unfortunate victim gets consumed in the big pre-harvest burn. In most cases, we usually end up finding the body because the perpetrator himself confesses and points us in the right direction. *No, Detective, I didn't mean to kill her. She made me mad and the trigger just kind of pulled itself. I loved her. Really. I'm so sorry. Yes, I'll take you to her.* He hangs his head in shame, tearful as the cuffs are put on. Then comes the long, quiet ride out to the middle of nowhere and the grisly discovery. The medical examiner's boys pack up the stiff and take it downtown while we take Mr. Perpetrator back to the cellblock. Reports with carbons. Sit down with the brass and brief them so they can brief the press. Case closed.

This case wasn't going to be like that.

I finished the drink and tossed a shiny quarter on the bar. I'd settle up the tab at the end of the week. Good ol' Policeman Yoshikawa.

He's always good for it. And he'll keep coming back. I pulled my hat on, snapped the brim in the front down and walked toward the door past the three old guys listening to the game. It wasn't live, of course. It never was out here in the middle of the ocean. It was the bottom of the seventh and Mickey Mantle was stepping up to the plate. It's funny how a bunch of grown men would bite their nails over a game that was already won or lost hours ago. If I couldn't see it live, just show me the box score. I wished, and not for the first time that day, that this case could be like that. Just show me the box score. The problem was it was live and I was at bat. So far, I fouled one back. Strike one. Everyone was watching. Everyone wanted The Sheik to hit one out of the park. All I could do was stand there and wait for the next pitch.

I stepped out onto Waialae Avenue and squinted as the sun and the humidity hit my face. Wavy lines were still coming off the blacktop and my collar was immediately soaked. It was time for a shower. Where the hell was I going to take Miss Ellen Park for our little dinner conversation? That's when it smacked me in the face. Where would Millie have had her last supper? If I was a Japanese girl working in a Territorial office with a penchant for lobster and champagne and had some filthy rich beau who could afford to take me there, there's only one place I'd really want to be. Especially dressed in Chanel.

When I got back into my sweatbox apartment, I picked up the telephone and asked the operator to put me through to the place I was thinking of. Miss Ellen Park was in for a singular treat and if my hunch was on the money, I'd get some answers.

12

Three cigarettes, two cups of self-percolated Maxwell House, and a twenty-minute cold shower were enough to get me out of the Four Roses haze and into a clean shirt and suit. I slapped on some Guerlain Impériale from the ornate glass bottle that had been To-san's, the one he saved for special occasions. I figured that if I were going to go through with the illusion that I was on a dinner date I might as well smell the part.

I took Beretania Street all the way to Kalihi, making a quick stop at University Florist to pick up a dozen roses. I thought they'd be a nice touch and maybe make her more amenable to sharing what she knew about Millie and Paris. Knowledge is options. Thanks a lot, Lieutenant. Park's Grocery stood with its produce still on display out front just off Kapalama Canal. Termites flitted energetically around the naked bulbs that illuminated the little store. Korean and American canned goods and big jars of kimchee filled the plywood shelves crammed so close together that even the rats would've died if the place caught fire.

A kindly woman in gold-rimmed spectacles and a white apron stopped chatting in Korean with a customer when I walked in. Garlic and dried fish in the air. Chili peppers and cabbage in wooden produce boxes. It wasn't Kansas and it wasn't Kakaako.

"Can I help you, sir?" she said in a heavily accented shout that was every bit as smooth as the Four Roses I was imbibing earlier.

"Thank you, ma'am. I'm here to see Ellen."

"AERAN! AERAN!" she bellowed with about as much effort as it took her to breathe. She grinned at me with a mouthful of crooked teeth. "I'm Aeran mama," she said, in a slightly less thunderous tone. Volume ran in the family.

"Pleased to meet you, ma'am. I'm Francis Yoshikawa."

"You like some tea? Korean tea. It's good."

"I'm sure, but thank you, no. We have reservations."

"We do?" A clear, cheerful voice cut in. "I guess this must be a special occasion and I'm lucky to be invited."

Ellen was wearing a smart white dress printed with blue flowers and a dark shawl. Her hair was still up in the neat little bun and her eyelashes looked like they might have been touched up a little through the big lenses.

"I told you I wasn't pulling your leg," I said. I held the bouquet of roses out for her to take.

"I thought you said this wasn't a date," Ellen said with a smirk.

"I thought *you* said it wasn't supposed to be," I said. I took a long look at her dress. She cleaned up nice.

"I'm not the one who brought me these beautiful flowers," she said. The smirk softened into a shy smile.

"They're just to say thanks for coming and talking to me. Don't ever say I never gave you anything." Ellen took the bouquet and brought the roses up against her face, closing her eyes as she took in their scent.

"Thank you," she said, "they're beautiful."

"Well, we'd better get going or they'll give our table away." Ellen thanked me with a chaste little kiss on the cheek. She stood on her toes and steadied herself by placing her hands on my shoulders. Good thing I shaved.

"Where are we going?" Ellen asked. She tugged at my tie, straightening the hurried knot I had made and giving my shoulders and lapels quick brushes with her gloved hands.

"A little place I know of," I told her.

We got out of Kalihi and not a moment too soon. A group of men, some Korean and some who weren't, started trickling into the store. Tough customers by the looks of their hands and faces, all there to participate in the activities Ellen's dad had set up in the back, no doubt. They filed in one by one, some in undershirts, all with unlit cigarettes hanging from their lower lips, just hanging in the still air waiting to be ignited. The motley parade nodded their greetings to Mrs. Park and disappeared behind a faded silk curtain hanging over an open doorway in the back.

I took King Street toward Waikiki. The evening was warm and the air was pregnant with sultry moisture. The moon hung heavy and low over the Koolaus, bathing the ridges in an eerie glow. I had the top down, so Ellen pulled a smart-looking blue silk scarf from her bag and draped it over her coiffure, knotting it efficiently under her chin with precision. Probably nothing this woman ever did in her life was sloppy. Except for her handwriting.

We talked as we rolled toward Waikiki, cigarettes glowing like the fireflies near Camp Shelby where I did my basic training before shipping out to Europe. Ellen held her cigarette daintily between her index and middle fingers.

Before Ellen thought to ask where we were going, we were already on King Kalakaua Avenue, right in front of the red-jacketed Filipino valet boy. Ellen looked up at the A-frame with wide dark eyes.

"Sternwood's? We're going to *Sternwood's*?"

Ellen stepped out of the Cadillac when the valet held the door open for her. I joined her on the walkway leading up to the restaurant. Gas torches, their orange flames rippling lazily skyward, illuminated the concrete path. She undid the scarf around her head and moonlight and torchlight danced on her black hair up in its little bun.

"You sure know how to impress a girl, Detective," she said.

The steep pointed roof loomed up in front of the moonlit sky like the temple of hedonistic delights it was. Sternwood's opened shortly after the war and quickly became the culinary epicenter of the islands. Every haole executive on Bishop Street took his wife there for her birthday and his mistress there for Friday evening cocktails. A Japanese civil servant like me takes a girl there to impress her and, if he's lucky, interviews a witness or two. If my guess was right, Millie had her steak and lobster here.

A slender hapa haole girl in a peach kimono and auburn hair full of shiny pins gave us the red-carpet treatment at the podium. She addressed me as "Mister" Yoshikawa and pulled a couple of long green leather-covered menus from behind a potted palm. She cradled them in her left forearm in a manner that made me think of Moses bringing the Ten Commandments down from Mount Sinai.

We started to follow our kimonoed hostess out of the foyer and past an interior moss rock wall hung with a hundred orchids illuminated by floodlights from below. The hostess led us to a small table hidden in the shadow of a pillar and a large potted ficus where we were seated with all the faux-Oriental flourishes that came with the geisha suit. Our hostess turned and gave us a deep, authentic-looking Japanese bow that would have made Ka-san proud. She looked relieved to be rid of the huge green menus that may as well have been stone tablets.

The lights were dim in the temple of fine dining but the whole room was aglow with the shimmer of professionally teased coiffures and the sparkle of thousand-dollar baubles. Ellen illuminated our own humble table with her smile, which I noticed for the first time. It was genuine and adorable and full of sweetness and light, things the tired mind sees without lingering over them too much. I sent our waitress off to the bar to fetch a Tom Collins for Ellen and a Johnnie Walker Black Label for me while Ellen excused herself to powder her nose. I took the opportunity to dash back to the podium in the foyer and have a quick chat with the hostess who seated us.

"Can I help you, Mr. Yoshikawa?" she asked, looking up from the giant reservation ledger. She was wearing a pair of bifocals that she promptly removed and stuck into her large kimono sleeve.

"I sure hope so," I said. I took the photograph of Millie out of my pocket and held it up for her to see in the dim light of the foyer. She took her bifocals out again and focused. Her eyes widened then narrowed and her voice became a shade less smooth than it had been a moment before.

"I don't understand," she said, trying hard to sound perplexed but not doing a very good job. It came out a little too quickly and loudly.

"Have you seen her? Two weeks ago?"

She stared at me. I stared back. She looked down. I continued to stare back. When she brought her eyes back up, she looked defeated and afraid.

"Why do you want to know, Mr. Yoshikawa?"

"It's Detective Sergeant Yoshikawa," I said, showing her the shield. "It's important, Red. You'll read about this girl in tomorrow's paper. I need to know if you saw her here."

She nodded her auburn head silently, then hefted the reservation book open and turned a few pages. I stepped behind her and looked over her shoulder as she pointed to an entry. I could just make out the penciled scrawl under the faint glow of the podium's thin yellow bulb. *Billings, 2.* I did a quick mental calculation on the date. Two weeks before last Friday. That put us in the ballpark of the autopsy timetable.

"Thanks, Red," I said, tucking a five-dollar bill in her kimono sleeve. "I didn't hear it from you. Who waited on them?"

"Alice," she said. "Alice Honda."

"Is Miss Honda here tonight?"

"She's waiting on you, Detective."

"Great. Thanks," I said. I love coincidences. They're so much rarer than happy endings and always more useful.

I stepped lively back to our table and sat back down. Ellen had fortunately not yet returned. Our waitress had come back from the bar. She wore her hair up geisha-style with a handful of dangling silver pins and sported a pale pink kimono. She was cute in a demure, Japanese, Makiki-Church-bake-sale way. She glided gracefully up to the table, her kimono barely moving. A couple of cocktail napkins came out of nowhere and our drinks were delicately placed on them. A small, pale hand tipped with candy-pink nails reached for the ashtray in front of me and replaced it with a clean one.

"Will that be all, sir, or can I do something else for you?"

"You sure can, Alice."

"Excuse me? How do you know . . . ?"

"Or Miss Honda if you prefer, but I try not to stand on ceremony when I'm supposed to be off-duty. My name is Frankie Yoshikawa and I'm a Honolulu Police Department Detective." I took the badge out for the one-hundred-and-first time that day. I was beginning to feel like I should just pin it to my forehead. Alice Honda froze.

"Relax," I told her, "you didn't do anything but you may have seen something. Did you wait on Harcourt Billings, Jr. a little over a week ago?"

Alice nodded mutely, still in shock.

"Did he dine with someone?"

Another mute nod. I pulled Millie Miyasaki's photograph out and showed it to her. Alice stared at it for a moment then looked away and nodded.

"Did they fight?"

"No," came her small voice after what seemed like ages, "they sat very close together and spoke to each other very quietly."

"Did he bring her here before?"

"Only a couple of times. Mr. Billings always wanted this table because I think it's really dark here and he usually comes in through the kitchen. I suppose he thought nobody would recognize him. I guess being with a Japanese girl and all. I guess . . ."

She blushed so furiously I could see her red cheeks, even in the poor light.

"Did they stay long?"

"Dinner and dessert, then they left. They couldn't have been here for more than two hours."

I decided to take a shot for the grand prize, just for the hell of it. Just because I was there. "Was she wearing a diamond bracelet? You wouldn't have missed it. The thing would've lit up even this corner."

"No," she said, "but . . ." Then she shook her head and fell silent.

"But what, Alice?"

"Nothing. I was going to say she wasn't wearing anything like that, but . . . *he* might have been. But I guess that's silly. It was maybe a fancy watch or a cufflink or something that would peek out from under his sleeve every now and then. It was really bright." I tried to recall Junior Billings' wrist from earlier that day at the Oahu Country Club and if he had some gaudy watch on. It didn't seem that he did.

At that moment, I sensed the presence of Ellen hovering to the side of the table.

"Thank you, Alice. That will be all for now."

"Very good, sir."

And she went gliding away across the crowded dining floor with her empty round tray.

Ellen stood there with her arms crossed, smirking in the candlelight.

"On a first-name basis with the help, Detective? She's cute. Were you flirting with her while I was freshening up and looking at the koi in the pond?"

"Flirting? No. That would be one sure way to get your steak spit on."

Ellen smiled sardonically and slid effortlessly into the chair I pulled out for her. I snapped the Zippo open as she fitted a cigarette into a holder and that's when I really took a good look at her hands. They were pretty and graceful and everything she did with them seemed to turn out perfect. Blue smoke passed from her lips like the haze over the Koolaus.

"Tell me what you learned about Millie," I said.

"She was an interesting character," Ellen began. She paused to take a quick drag of her cigarette. "Most of the girls at work saw her as a nice girl who had a lot of snacks on her desk and never talked back to the pool supervisors or the attorneys. I'm sure you got that in your brief conversations with them this morning. But some of them also had some conversations with her over lunch, where she'd tell them things they didn't expect to hear from such a reserved girl."

"What kinds of things?"

"Things like her ambition to go to Paris—I'll get more into that later—and how she thought this place was so backwards and people here have no taste or class or sense of what is really good."

"Do you agree with that assessment?"

"Some of it," she said. She tapped the end of her cigarette daintily and a small bit of ash fell into the ebony ashtray. "I think Millie was generally right about the way most men are here: self-absorbed, no manners, no sense of the world beyond this place."

"Yeah, I talked with Albert Ishida today."

"Can you blame her?"

"With *that* as a yardstick? Hardly. But you agree we're all like that?" I winced inwardly. Was I one of Millie's ignorant hicks, too?

"*We*?" Ellen slapped my shoulder playfully and smiled, "Don't tell me *you* ever considered yourself in the same class with the likes of Albert Ishida, *Detective*." She said "*Detective*" with that added emphasis that could have been either flirtatious or sarcastic as only the cleverest women could. I had to give her that: she *was* clever. Irritatingly so.

"It doesn't matter what *I* think *about* me. What do *you* think? *Are* we all alike?"

She sat there and looked at me with her head tilted to the right like a bird. She narrowed her eyes, scrutinizing my face in the dim candlelight.

"You're different," she said. "You're smart and you're eloquent, but probably not as smart as you think you are and too eloquent for your own good. You're handsome and you know it, which can make you insufferable company at times. You think that your cynicism protects you from pain and ridicule but all it really does is inflict it on others. Yes, you're different, Frankie Yoshikawa. You're as different as they come."

I didn't know if I was just complimented or insulted. She had a way of doing that. It was starting to drive me crazy. It was the kind of thing that made me want to call it an evening and make her walk back home. Or pull up her dress and give her a dirty spanking.

"You really have me pegged, don't you?" I said. "I'm flattered that you don't think I'm one of the brutes and yokels that Millie Miyasaki seemed to think this island churns out by the dozens but you make me sound like I'm just a different species of vermin." Ellen threw her head back and laughed. It was a pleasant laugh, a falling stream of silver that was warm and cool at the same time.

"You're funny, too," she said.

"So go ahead and laugh at me. What else was wrong with this place besides the men, according to Millie and to her office mates?" I felt like after all these years, I was finally beginning to get to know the girl I erroneously called my first love.

"Mostly she'd complain about things in general. I guess it wasn't just the men here that really bothered her. It was the way most things are here. The girls said there was a word that she always used to describe this island. Provincial."

"Like how nobody here knows which fork is the salad fork? Or whether red or white wine goes with a particular dish? Or the difference between *baroque* and *rococo*?"

Ellen smiled. "Exactly."

"I suppose she never left the island." I thought about Millie's folks' limited means. They were about as limited as my folks. I saw the world thanks to the war. Millie had no such opportunity.

"You think so? You'd think she had been all over the world to every cultured place, the way she put Hawaii down."

"I know because I've been to those places and once you're there, you begin to realize that things aren't better there, just different. Sure, in Europe they still dress for dinner, even in the poorest house, and there's wine with every meal. But they don't bathe every day. And that includes the rich people."

Ellen made a face and giggled. "I'll bet you've acquired some knowledge during your time away."

"Only enough to impress the girls at home."

"Okay, Detective. Impress me. Say something sophisticated and worldly."

"Chianti—the red wine in the straw-covered bottle—is named for the region in Tuscany that produces it. About twenty years ago, the district was re-drawn and subdivided into seven distinct districts of production: *Classico*, *Colli Aretini*, *Colli Fiorentini*, *Colline Pisane*, *Colli Senesi*, *Montalbano*, and *Rùfina*. These are the names that appear on the labels—when there are labels."

"Not bad. You'd have to do more than *tell* me about it, though. But you get high marks for culture."

"I'm not all that cultured. I couldn't tell you for the life of me if red or white wine goes with my mother's nishime."

Ellen laughed with her chin tilted up, exposing her throat, pale golden in the pulsating candlelight and fragrant with her perfume. "I'll bet Millie would have really liked you. It seems like you were just her type."

"I wouldn't be so sure," I said. I thought back to my time with Millie in high school and how our conversations wouldn't have filled a chewing gum wrapper despite the fact that we rutted in the humid dark of her bedroom for as many times as I brought her a gift. "I've had the *pâté de foie gras*-stuffed pastry of Strasbourg with champagne and still prefer the manapua from that dirty little place in Chinatown. Besides, I have a nasty tendency to mock self-important people."

"It didn't seem to me that she was self-important. After all, most of the girls remembered her as 'nice.' I think she was genuine in her dissatisfaction with Hawaii only because she wanted so badly to see the world beyond it. One of the girls said that Millie told her that as a little girl, she wanted to see California, where all the picture shows were made. Then she wanted to see the skyscrapers in New York and the big department stores there. I heard that Macy's and Gimbels and Lord & Taylor make The Liberty House look like a country store. Is that true?"

"I don't know about *that*. I've been to all three and I think they're just like The Liberty House, only with more of the same stuff over more floors. So what was it you heard about Paris?"

She answered the question with another question, and one that wasn't related to the question I asked. "I take it you don't have any suspects yet?"

"I don't know if I should be sharing that with you. There is a matter of case confidentiality. You're with the press."

"Well, what if I was, say, your girlfriend, and you were just sharing your thoughts on the matter after a long day at work?"

"Is that what you are?" I laughed.

"I could be, in theory. Then you could talk to me about all your troubles and you wouldn't have to worry about . . . confidentiality. I'd keep all your secrets." Ellen crossed her heart with a crimson fingernail.

I thought just for a second it would have been nice to be that fingernail. Then I remembered what she was: a distraction.

"Believe me," I told her, "I could tell you all my troubles and none of them have anything to do with my cases. Theoretical girlfriend or not."

"I'll get it out of you. The night's still young. Unless you do a pretty good job of distracting me," she said, "but don't get any ideas. I'm not cheap or easy."

"Neither am I."

"At least you have nice manners for a cop. They must've been something you picked up in Europe."

"Don't speak too soon. My 'European' table manners consist of opening a can of rations and drinking Chianti straight out of the bottle."

Ellen laughed her silvery laugh again, and it fluttered up to the teak rafters. "Well, let's hope you show me your Columbia University table manners instead, then."

"I was planning to, but it's only fair to warn you that in New York City they were fairly impressed with my Kakaako table manners." I listened to her from across the white linen. It was curious, her laugh. As loud as *she* was, it should have sounded like a braying donkey. But it didn't. It was soft and clear like a little Christmas bell.

"Paris," I said.

"Oh, yes," she said. Her smile changed from warm to business and suddenly it was difficult to see the eyes beyond the big lenses. She changed her demeanor like socks. I wondered if it was even possible to get close to a girl like her, but I didn't wonder too much. "The girls who ate lunch with her said she talked about how she was going to be taking vacation time at what would have been the end of this week to go to Paris. They thought she was lying just to impress them. Nobody believed that she'd be able to afford a trip like that and why not? She and her folks weren't exactly Rockefellers. But she would get peeved when they accused her of making it up. She also said her admirer made all the arrangements and all she had to do was get a passport and pack a bag. She even said that she'd bring some perfume back for a few of them."

"Albert Ishida had doubts about those plans and then thought she might have gone when she disappeared. Any mention of this admirer's name?"

"No," said Ellen. She toyed with the straw in her drink then looked at me with her head tilted sideways as I had seen her do before when sizing me up. "But I think *you* have an idea, don't you?"

"Why would I ask you if I did?"

"Come on, Frankie! Play fair! I told you what you wanted to know; now it's your turn. Why do you think I came out tonight?"

"It wasn't for the free dinner?" As if on cue, the food arrived and she momentarily dropped the subject to admire the meal because there was a lot to be admired about it. It wasn't something the dog wouldn't eat.

The T-bone steak was just about the best thing I had ever eaten in my life to that point, not counting Ka-san's pickles or Saloon Pilot crackers. Ellen had scallops and another Tom Collins. She ate in neat, dainty bites and dabbed her red lips with her napkin after almost every one. It had been a long time since I had eaten with a girl. It was nice just to watch her use a fork and knife with her pretty, perfect little hands. It made me feel like dinner wasn't just to line my stomach before I assaulted it with booze. Before the Baked Alaska arrived, Ellen excused herself for more nose powdering and I had another cigarette. She returned after a few minutes all smiles at the sight of the dessert and we talked a little about the drudgery of our daily routines over good coffee, which is about as rare on this island as a diamond bracelet on the deck of a rusty tugboat.

After I took care of the check we made our way out of Sternwood's to pick up the car. I winked at both the auburn-haired hostess and Alice Honda on the way out and got uncomfortable, forced smiles in response. It was nice to be appreciated.

I drove Ellen back to the store on the canal and walked her to the door. The lights were off in the front but the raucous laughter of men about to lose their money came drifting to the street from the back. Ellen and I stood for a moment looking at each other.

"Thanks for your help," I told her.

"Thank you for dinner. It was really nice."

Moonlight caught her dark eyes and they illuminated every derelict corner of the night. They turned up at me and pulled me in. Without knowing how it happened, I was standing closer to her and I found my hands on her soft shoulders. She looked up at me and I felt my face being drawn down toward hers. She closed her eyes. Her lips parted and said, "Harcourt Billings, Jr."

"*What*?" It was worse than a bucket of ice water down the front of my trousers.

"Harcourt Billings, Jr. I got up and talked to our waitress before dessert. I knew you weren't just flirting with her. Why didn't you just tell me what you found out?"

"Confidentiality. I can't give away every shred of my investigation. Not to a reporter. Not even if she is my theoretical girlfriend."

Ellen turned on her heel, took three choppy steps toward the door and turned suddenly to face me again. She brought her hand up to her face dripping with mock affection and blew me a slow kiss. "That's your theoretical good night kiss."

"Don't flatter yourself, darling. I wasn't going to kiss you."

"The hell you weren't. And I never kiss on the first date."

"This wasn't a date, remember?"

"Vividly," she said. She stomped petulantly into the store and slammed the door. I made a face at the door and got back into my car, nearly broke the key in the ignition starting it and yanked it into gear.

"Theoretical good night kiss," I muttered and tore away along the canal.

I drove back to Kaimuki dumping whiskey from my hip flask onto the Baked Alaska in my stomach. Gid told me to always trust my gut feeling, but at the moment it was really irritating me. My head told me that Ellen Park was a silly little girl with a silly little agenda who hid her inherent silliness behind a smart mouth. My gut feeling disagreed. And worse, so did something south of it.

Old Chang's building was dark when I got back. The bird shit was white on his Packard's hood and it glowed in the Kaimuki moonlight. I knew his screams would wake me before the alarm clock. I let myself into my apartment. I took a cold shower and lay in the humid dark of my bedroom. I let myself descend into that place between consciousness and oblivion where it felt just like a second drink.

13

In the morning I dragged myself into the Homicide Detail Office feeling like the peanut shells under the bleachers at the stadium. Surprisingly, Jack was already there, playing with a bright yellow yo-yo with a cigarette hanging out of his face. Delilah was buffing her nails at her desk. Luau was licking his fat fingers between bites of a guava Danish. Gid was sequestered in his office, going through his morning routine of examining the paper cover to cover; he was getting his lay of the land. Everyone was doing what everyone did.

"How'd it go at the Navigators Club yesterday? Did you already tell everybody?" I asked Jack, cutting to the proverbial chase while pouring myself a cup of Delilah's coffee. It was as fragrant as a sewer and every bit as elegant.

"Aw, hell, Sheik," said Jack. He let the yo-yo descend. "I was waiting 'til you came in to start telling it, but there isn't much to tell."

"Tell me anyway."

"I got there just in time for high tea," Jack said. He took a drag from his cigarette and exhaled a puff of grey, adding to the haze in the office. The yo-yo went up and down. "Of course, I was none too welcome in my off-the-rack suit and even less so after flashing my buzzer at the manager. He wouldn't have let me in but a suggestion that I could make a call to the press to join me did the trick. Everybody I talked to remembers Junior being there at the club all evening."

"He couldn't have been," I said, incredulous. "I have witnesses at Sternwood's who say he was dining with Millie Miyasaki a couple of hours before she died."

"You do? The stiff white bodies over at the Navigators Club have him all alibied up."

For a moment, the office was quiet enough to hear the ceiling fans buffet the cigarette smoke around.

"Trust money will buy an alibi," I said.

"Not this one," said Jack tonelessly. "A permanent fixture at the club named Colonel Whitman and his brother-in-law from the mainland caught him behind the kitchen out back in a hot tangle-up with the help. He was kissing one of the handsome young Japanese busboys. I guess his taste isn't limited to Club Ginza girls. The Colonel nearly had a heart attack." Jack let out a chuckle he couldn't suppress but his eyes didn't chuckle along with his mouth. "Junior would rather have been caught throwing that girl in the harbor—trust me—at least Harcourt Senior would pony up for a defense. If Senior found out about the busboy, though, he'd cut Junior off without a cent. Even the kanaka valet and the bartender corroborated his presence at the club and confirmed his departure just after 11:30 p.m. Just about every old haole playing canasta or sucking a martini heard about Junior's hot kiss and gawked at him as he left the club."

"Shit," I mumbled into my coffee, which was getting colder and fouler by the second.

"He has enough pull to get one or two witnesses to perjure themselves," Jack said, "but the whole damn Navigators Club? They're clannish but they're not *that* clannish. And that buzzard Colonel Whitman is so uptight that he couldn't have possibly made up that story of Junior and the busboy."

"Didn't you just hear me, Jack? Last night I talked to a waitress at Sternwood's and she confirmed she waited on Junior and Millie. The reservation is still in the big book, for crying out loud."

"I heard you, Sheik. I'm not saying you didn't hear what you heard. I'm just telling you what I heard, that's all."

"Just say it. What's the word of a couple of Jap girls against twenty haoles?"

"Aw, Sheik. Don't be like that." Jack put the yo-yo back in his pocket and stared at his shoes. He was embarrassed but he didn't have any reason to be. It's one of the things I liked about him.

"Shit, Jack. What now?" The question was rhetorical; I don't think I've ever had any response to that one other than a shrug. I was out of answers and I wasn't expecting any from Jack. He gave me one anyway.

"Let's go to the boat at the pier."

"The *Hinalea*?"

"Yeah."

"Why? It's been a couple of weeks and we're not even sure the bracelet was . . . the victim's." I almost said her name. Almost.

"It's a good guess. Time to test your theory about the diamonds. And stuff might still be there, even two weeks later, especially if nobody thought about it. Except you, of course."

"Why the hell not? I don't have anything better to do," I grumbled. It seemed like an exercise in futility, a field trip Jack concocted just to make me feel better. *Let's get some air, Sheik. Things will work out, Sheik.* He probably didn't believe it any more than I did, but he expected me to.

I felt a large, calloused hand settle on my shoulder. Gid Hanohano's hand. The other one came to rest on Jack's shoulder. He had somehow managed to sneak up on us during our exchanged unnoticed—another rare talent for a big man. He frowned thoughtfully and spoke without looking at either of us.

"They're supposed to be doing some paving today on Route 92 in Iwilei. That means you'll get no interruptions at the pier." Gid had just dropped one of his little nuggets of knowledge from his cover-to-cover read of the newspaper.

"Any more orchid shows or church bazaars?" I cracked. My mood was quickly sliding down the toilet with my investigative prospects and all the ideas I had that I thought were good about the case.

"Not until this weekend. There are a couple in Aiea. Church bazaars, not orchid shows. The next orchid show isn't for another month, but it'll be a big one at the Civic Auditorium. Lots of dendrobiums," he said earnestly. Gid knew I was being sarcastic but he answered me anyway. I had to laugh a little.

He gave us both one final pat on the shoulder before shuffling back into the dark solitude of his office like the proverbial groundhog retreating back down its hole after seeing its shadow. We didn't have any groundhogs in Hawaii but we did have Gid Hanohano, whose infrequent emergences from the shadows to impart wisdom were regarded as omens.

"Come on, Sheik. You heard the man. No interruptions. Let's go."

I grabbed my hat and we walked out of the office. Gid had seen his shadow. Maybe there would be a change in luck.

We got into the Eldorado and I drove back to the pier.

The *Hinalea* looked the same as it had on Sunday. Even the mooring lines were wrapped around the cleat in the same manner. The pier was deserted; not even the old wino could be found. I eyed up the tug with barely concealed distaste, took off my coat and threw it in the back seat of the Eldorado.

I looked back at the *Hinalea* silently rising and falling with the gentle ripples of the harbor. The air was oppressively moist and hot and a fly buzzed near my ear. This case had taken me from the cool, dark interior of Sternwood's in the company of a pretty little smart-mouthed reporter back to the hot fish reek of a tug pier. All in less than twelve hours. Millie made the same trip in a fraction of the time but ended up in worse shape. I guess I shouldn't complain.

"What's wrong, Sheik?" asked Jack.

"This boat kind of gives me the creeps. I suspect this is how the body was brought to the pier, even though I haven't done any of the research on the vessel itself yet."

"Yeah, well, it kind of gives me the creeps, too. Let me ask you something. What makes you think it was this particular boat? I mean, it could've been any small boat."

"Just a feeling I guess. Besides, this is where I found the diamond bracelet, remember? The girl at Sternwood's said Junior was wearing something flashy near his wrist, and a load of diamonds at the scene seems to be too much of a coincidence, don't you think?"

"No argument from me. Shall we?" Jack bowed like a royal carriage footman and gestured toward the gangplank with a flourish.

"Yeah," I said. I tried to fight down the bile and panic rising in my throat. I knew that vengeful spirits occupied that rust bucket. Or rats.

Jack and I climbed aboard the old tug. It was only a little after nine in the morning but the sun was already beating down on the back of my neck like an open blast furnace. The stink of industrial grease and fish guts hung heavy in the morning air. Jack headed straight for the rusty metal door to the galley. I followed him somewhat reluctantly. Inside, large, soft spots of muted blue exploded in my peripheral vision as my eyes adjusted from the blinding white sun to the warm, filthy darkness of the galley. When I could finally make shapes out in the gloom, I saw Jack in a crouch with a small chrome flashlight, the kind boy scouts take with them on camping trips. He was running the beam slowly around the deck near the galley portal when he stopped the beam and waddled in his crouch stance forward.

"Bingo."

"What, Jack? Talk to me."

"Right here, Sheik. See that? It's blood." He pointed to a minute dark spot on the deck. There's some hair, too. Looks black and long—Oriental? Could be our girl's."

Jack stood up to stretch out and I bear-hugged him from behind.

"Nice work, Jackie! Let's get the lab guys down here." Jack and I continued to find stray hairs and small spatters. We traced the trail of droplets and hair out to the deck.

It was difficult to follow the blood through all of the tangled lines and trash that littered the deck. It hadn't rained in the last couple of weeks, which helped a great deal. We managed to move aft in the general direction of the stern when I saw it. A rusted bolt on the rail. Something small and dark clung to the jagged, oxidized edges of the bolt's head.

"Black velvet," I said. I took Jack's magnifying glass and examined the small black stuff. I had been vindicated. The *Hinalea* had been Millie's last ride.

14

Pier 23 soon turned into the chaotic mess it was when we first brought Millie out of the water. This time it was almost a dozen bodies, some in police olive drab, some in shirtsleeves combing the decks, holds, and everywhere else on the *Hinalea.* The lab guys arrived shortly after.

We left them to it. We stopped by a Nuuanu Avenue okazuya to pick up some treats for lunch before going back to the office to fill Gid in. The old groundhog had seen his shadow again and he deserved some tempura. I watched Jack's eyes light up as he looked at the oily Japanese fare in the glass case under the cash register at the okazuya.

John James Morris of Pelham Bay, New York. He was one of those peculiar haoles with a taste for the pedestrian, local stuff whether it was furikake-crusted musubis and hash patties from a little okazuya on Nuuanu or the parade of brown-eyed waitresses at every cocktail lounge on King Street. Jack didn't go in much for the "tropical" drinks or the steel guitar music that had lately caught on with the tourists off the *Lurline* who littered Waikiki Beach with their oil-covered pink forms. Jack liked things "real," which meant strange colors, smells, and tongues. If he couldn't read the menu, he was sure to like the fare.

When we got back to the station, we put the spread out on Gid's desk, for once sitting in there without him telling us something we didn't want to hear.

Halfway through our feast, Delilah appeared in the doorframe of Gid's office, one hand on her hip and the other clutching a crumpled pink piece of paper and glaring at me.

"Hey, Miss Dee," said Jack amiably. "Help yourself to a musubi or some of this other stuff . . ."

"No thank you, Jack," she said. Then she turned to me and said, "You have a message, Detective Sergeant Yoshikawa. From a *girl*." She thrust a pink piece of paper in my face. Ellen Park. About an hour before we got back with the food.

I walked over to my desk, lifted the telephone receiver, and dialed the exchange on the slip. After a few clicks and rings a voice came through the receiver as softly as a Louis Armstrong trumpet solo.

"*Honolulu Record*, Miss Park speaking."

"I didn't know you were still talking to me. I thought that notion died last night on your doorstep."

"Oh, forget it, Frankie. I'm not mad. I know you were just being you."

"What's *that* supposed to mean? Wait. You know what? Never mind. Don't answer that. I don't want to know. I'm tired and I'm frustrated and I'm full of no whiskey. What can I do for you?"

"Relax," she said, "I called earlier to tell you that I can actually do something for *you*."

"What would that be?"

"Take me to lunch and I'll tell you all about it. Don't worry. It's worth it."

Against my better judgment I was behind the wheel of my Cadillac five minutes later. It was getting to be a habit, doing things against my better judgment. Maybe I never really had any to begin with.

I drove through the Sheridan Tract about two blocks past the Miyasaki place to Sheridan Street where the *Honolulu Record* maintained its hand-fed press and small offices. Ellen Park was waiting out front in a pale green dress with a smart little leopard print hat tilted at an angle on her shiny black hair, which was packed up in its neat little bun. Her eyes smiled at me through the big lenses of her glasses. I was thinking that it wasn't so difficult looking at her; it's what happens when you don't get enough sleep.

"What do you feel like for lunch?" I asked, holding the passenger door open for her.

"I'm a girl of simple tastes. Buy me a tuna sandwich and I'm yours." She got into the car and smoothed her dress out at the thighs. I shut her door and got back behind the wheel.

"I wish I knew this before last night. Scallops and Baked Alaska at Sternwood's got me a door in the face."

"I'm sorry. Was it that bad?"

"I'm still pulling splinters from my nose."

The lunch counter at the Fort Street Kress was teeming with office girls of all makes and models: Japanese girls in starched blouses who lived up the street from Ka-san and worked in some Territorial stenography pool; Hawaiian girls with big flowers in their hair like Delilah who danced hula in some Waikiki show after a day of answering telephones; haole girls in expensive dresses who took dictation for the cigar chewers who grabbed their asses with impunity; Filipino girls with bright faces and lace collars who filed away endless stacks of paper for chump change.

I sat in the middle of this aviary with Ellen, admittedly a rare bird in her own right. We split a tuna sandwich with a dill pickle and shared a Green River from the fountain. I really only had a cone sushi and a Coca-Cola from our celebratory okazuya feast, so half a tuna sandwich fit the bill. The young Hawaiian soda jerk in the clean white shirt and matching smile put two straws in the glass. We looked at the straws, then at each other, shrugged, and drank.

"How did a man of letters like you end up being a cop?" Ellen asked.

"What else was I going to do? Go to school for six more years and put kids to sleep with lectures on Dante and Chaucer? I guess you fared better. You're actually a reporter."

"If you can call drawing a hundred dollars a month salary being 'actually a reporter.' It's not exactly the *Star-Bulletin* or the *Advertiser.* I still help out at my parents' store when I'm not at the *Record*. But at least I have a clear conscience knowing I'm doing my part to make this a better place for a lot of people. I think that you're in the perfect place to help the same people." She sounded like my sister Iris.

"How's that? I think I'm barely in a position to help myself."

"Come on, Frankie. You're a war hero and an Ivy League-educated son of Kakaako. You made detective in just two years after becoming a police officer and you're now in a unique position to make sure the killer of an Oriental girl from Sheridan Tract is brought to justice. You, Frankie Yoshikawa. Not some haole commissioner who's only interested in making the noise go away."

"You really make me sound like I'm some prize. Do you believe it, or is it part of your craft to sell me to the huddled masses?"

"Of course I believe it. I just wish you would, too." I thought I heard something in her voice that I hadn't heard in anyone's for a long time: sincerity. Maybe I wasn't just a lot of ink to her after all. Or maybe she was just that good at setting the trap. She was just that good at a lot of things.

"What makes you drive so hard?" I asked her. "What makes you do what you do for a hundred bucks a month instead of something else for more? Why do you care if I break this case or not?"

"Eddie," she said.

"Old boyfriend?" I asked. She shook her head. "*Current* boyfriend?" I asked.

"No, silly. Eddie was my little brother. He enlisted with the 5th as soon as hostilities broke out in Korea. Naturally, they took him in a heartbeat. Korean linguists were in short supply. He was captured at a place they called Heartbreak Ridge and they put him in a Chinese prison camp at Pyoktong. My mom got a letter from his commanding officer last year saying he died of starvation."

"I'm sorry," I said. I took another sip of the Green River. Ellen's eyes were suddenly distant and wet and a little obscure, like rain moving out over the ocean. I asked the next question cautiously. "Why would that make you want to take on the establishment when communists killed your brother?"

"Oh, Frankie. Communists didn't kill Eddie. The *war* did. The craven haoles who sat in their mansions in Manoa killed him. They were willing to offer up my brother and his friends as sacrificial lambs while they sent their own sons off to college on the mainland. Did you know that Hawaiians and Orientals from Hawaii have suffered five times the casualty rate as all the men from the entire U.S.? Do you have any idea what that *really* means?" Her voice was at its full volume and burned.

"Yeah," I said quietly. "I think I have an idea."

"Oh," she said, suddenly hushed. "Oh, Frankie. I'm so sorry. Of course you do."

"Forget it," I told her. I smiled a little. "Yes, I lost friends like Eddie. Lots of them. Too many of them. And yes, it wasn't at all fair. But how do you think my case is going to bring your brother back?"

"It won't. But if you find the killer of an Oriental girl and bring him to justice you'd be telling the world she mattered. That *we* matter. That my brother and boys like him matter and that their lives aren't any cheaper than the lives of those haoles whose money bought them a way out. Show them we all matter, Frankie. Show them they can't sweep Millie Miyasaki under the rug. Or you."

"They should have had you write those propaganda leaflets they dropped from the sky during the war. I'm not the shining example you're making me out to be. When we left Sternwood's last night, I was certain that Junior Billings was there with her just a couple of hours before she died. After I found out that he was making deposits into her account at The Liberty House, Jack and I braced him while he was playing golf yesterday and he acted like he didn't know what the hell we were talking about. Then Jack went to the Navigators Club and found that just about everyone there alibied him for the entire evening. I'm not sure where Junior was. Maybe you'd better write someone else into your feature." I took a drag off my cigarette and looked at the linoleum on the floor. Ellen moved in closer until our knees were touching and she slapped me on the upper arm.

"Don't be so down on yourself. You'll figure it out. That reminds me. I called you because I've got another lead for you. For *us*, really. I spent the morning over at the Territorial AG's office again. I got the Portuguese lady to tell me something I think you might find interesting."

"Gladys Jean Souza? She hardly knew Millie to hear her tell it. She only liked the food on her desk."

"How long did *you* spend talking to her? Five minutes? I told her that I'd put her picture in the *Record*. A *nice* picture of her, right next to her interview. Gladys Jean wants to be famous. Didn't you get that?"

"Sure. She can talk just like Eleanor Roosevelt when she has to. But the only pictures of her *I* could have promised would have a number under her chin. What did she tell you?"

"She thought that Millie had *two* boyfriends."

"Albert Ishida and Junior Billings?"

"No. Albert and someone else who called a couple of times for her when she was out of the office about a week before she disappeared. I got her to give me the name and telephone exchange." Ellen opened her purse and pulled out a notepad. She flipped through the pages and looked thoughtfully at each one until finding the notation she was looking for. She put the notepad down on the lunch counter and pointed to the name she wrote down with the telephone exchange. Mr. Cadiz. Her handwriting was so terrible on the telephone exchange I had to ask her if a particular character was a 3 or an 8. I excused myself and walked to the end of the counter where I showed the soda jerk my badge and asked to use the telephone. I dialed Homicide and asked Delilah to shag the number for me. I thought I could hear her filing her nails before she even cracked the reverse directory open. When she finally came back and gave me the party, I had to ask her if she was sure. She said she was sure, that she wasn't stupid, and hung up hard.

I walked back along the counter and took my stool. Ellen looked at me with expectant eyes through her big lenses. "Well?" she asked.

"The number comes back to the longshoremen's union hall."

"Really? That's interesting. I wonder if Mr. Cadiz is Danny Boy Cadiz. I interviewed him a couple of months ago."

"Danilo Cadiz? The organizer?"

"The same."

Danny Boy Cadiz. His name was in the papers lately quite a bit, and most especially in the pro-labor *Record* where Ellen worked. Danny Boy Cadiz gained some notoriety as an aggressive organizer of the Filipino membership during the strike of '49. He wasn't just muscle. Danny Boy had class and charisma. He supposedly had a haole girlfriend and rumor had it he was eyeing up a Territorial Legislature seat in the following year's elections. Then I thought back to the day before, when I was at Millie's old desk going through her things. The handwritten note: "D.C.—20%?" Without stopping to think why I shouldn't, I told Ellen about the sudden epiphany.

Ellen smiled broadly and brilliantly. "Very impressive, Frankie Yoshikawa! You see? You *are* the stuff of heroism, even if you may not think so yourself." Our knees were touching again. It suddenly became hot at the lunch counter. A half-dozen dolled-up office girls waited for our stools, fanning themselves with their high heels dug into the linoleum. They were about to release the parking brake on their patience. A couple of them looked at their little gold wristwatches and clicked their little tongues and sighed huffily. Ellen paid them about as much attention as she would a sea cucumber on a reef.

"Shall we call on Mr. Cadiz?" I asked. I guess I owed her that much for the lead.

"Let's go!" She grabbed my hand and pulled me off the stool. The little leopard hat was halfway out the door before I even dropped my coins on the counter. Her energy and enthusiasm may have started to rub off on me. Or maybe it was her perfume that did. I took hurried steps after her out the door toward my car.

15

The brand-new longshoremen's union hall stood just a couple of blocks outside of Waikiki on the ewa side of the Ala Wai Canal. A striking modern structure four stories tall, it housed the offices of the local's leadership. Ellen, acquainted with the building, had access to its offices because she was with the *Record*, which received support from the local. I pulled up in front of the edifice and got out to open Ellen's door on the passenger side. The sun beat down mercilessly on the asphalt fronting the building and coconut fronds hung dead still in the lack of breeze. My shirt was wet and plastered to my back under my coat. Ellen fanned her neck with her hand in a white glove. It was just a little after noon and I felt like a piece of mullet in a bamboo steamer.

The glass doors opened and spit out a couple of dark, burly men in work shirts accompanied by one not so dark or burly in a suit. The suit waved to Ellen. She waved back. We went into the new building and its new air conditioning. In the lobby, a newly painted mural dominated the wall behind the staircase leading up to the offices on the upper floors. The mural was done in earth and nautical tones depicting the mostly brown working people of Hawaii. It reminded me of the work of Diego Rivera. I stood transfixed for a moment admiring the mural when Ellen's voice brought me back.

"Come on," she said. "The organizers' offices are upstairs." I followed her up the staircase to the offices on the second floor. The hallway still had the smell of a new building. The carpet still clung to the odor of a showroom though it had been trod on countless times since being installed and the paint on the walls still smelled fresh. We stopped at a door at the far end of the hall. Ellen told me it might be better if I waited for her while she talked to the secretary.

"I'll wait," I said. She opened the door and went in. A few seconds went by in the quiet, new-smelling corridor when a door down the hall opened near the staircase. A feminine silhouette in russet brown came out of the door. It was the profile of Ruth Prentiss, my sister's financier. She walked hurriedly down the staircase. I found myself breaking into a half-run to try to catch up with her. But I didn't try too hard. If it were two days before, I would have collapsed a lung trying to catch up with her. It was somehow different at that moment. Maybe I was too tired or distracted or worse—the little reporter was growing on me. Like algae or bread mold.

I settled for hurrying to the top of the staircase and watching Ruth exit the lobby and walk a few yards out of sight. Then I saw the white Mercury Coupe glide past the glass doors and disappear. I walked back down to the end of the hall and lit a cigarette. After a few drags, the door opened and Ellen's laughter came ringing out into the hallway as she said goodbye to the secretary with a dainty wave of her gloved hand. She closed the door behind her.

"Danny Boy isn't here right now. He's out on the docks somewhere talking to stevedores about some back-pay issue. We can leave a note on his desk, though." I followed the little leopard hat and pale green dress down the hall toward the staircase. She stopped at the door I had seen Ruth come out of. She knocked and a gruff "come in" pushed its way through the wood in response. Ellen turned the knob and opened the door.

The office was sizeable for a room with just two desks. One desk was empty and clean with a brand-new blotter and ebony pens with gold caps mounted on a name plaque that said "DANILO C. CADIZ."

There was a bottle of Johnnie Walker Black Label and four cut crystal tumblers on an antique silver tray next to the name plaque. On the other side of the plaque there stood a law dictionary, a book on accounting principles, and a King James Bible between two silver bookends shaped like naked cherubs. The chair, a big padded leather number in oxblood with brass studs on the armrests, looked more like a banker's chair than a union organizer's.

The other desk, messy with papers and carbons, held a black typewriter on a war-scarred blotter. On it, an overflowing porcelain ashtray shaped like a pineapple on a stack of papers and a mug from the Kau Kau Korner half full of cold coffee sat in front of the typewriter. A squeaky green chair behind the desk held a man whose head was as large as a stockpot and, on that head, a quart of pomade slicked back his black hair. He had a wide shiny face and beady, rodent-like eyes. His stocky torso was covered in a brown tapa-print aloha shirt with the sleeves rolled up. He wore a cigarette tucked behind his ear and a gold pinky ring with a red stone as big as a Buick's taillight on his right hand. His hand looked empty without a cue stick in it. Or a blackjack. He chewed tobacco like a dirt farmer from some Steinbeck novel made into a movie and spit into a gray metal wastebasket. He was Japanese—a typical Kakaako warubozu—the kind who stole candy and cigarettes from the little mom-and-pop stores on Queen Street and terrorized the girls walking home from school on Kapiolani Boulevard, but grown up. There was no name plaque on his desk but if there were it would've read GOON. He looked up at us and leered at Ellen, taking her form in slowly with his rat's eyes. I didn't like the way he did it.

Ellen said, "Hi. We just want to leave a note on Danny Boy's desk."

"Go ahead. It's a free country," he said through a mouthful of brown juice. "You're the girl from the *Record*, aren't you?"

"Ellen Park. Do you work with Danny Boy?"

"Yeah. Or at least *I* work while he's out there selling himself. Why don't you ask *me* some questions? I can show you a better time. Come sit on my knee." He patted his knee and laughed deeply but humorlessly. He turned his big round head to finally look at me. His beady eyes sized me up; there was challenge in them. "Who's the tailored suit? Your bodyguard? Why don't you tell him to take a break so we can have a good time," he said to Ellen. He laughed raucously. A thin trickle of tobacco juice escaped his mouth and ran down his chin.

"That's right. I'm her bodyguard," I said. "But it's only a part-time job. I'm a full-time charm school instructor. Looks like you could use a couple of lessons."

The laughter stopped. The man clenched his hammy fists and got out of his chair.

"You're really funny, you know that?" he said. The head breathed heavily and its beady eyes pierced me.

"I just call them as I see them," I said. Leading with his big round head, he lunged forward. Ellen quickly wrapped her arms around me and pushed me toward the door.

"I left a note for Danny Boy," she said, voice high and loud and a little edgy. "If you see him could you tell him I stopped by? Thanks." Ellen hustled me toward the door. The head halted its lunge.

"Sure," said the head. "Better teach your boyfriend to be more careful, baby. He might end up with some bumps on his pretty head."

"Only if you hit me with your mouth," I said. "It's your biggest and strongest part." Ellen shoved me out of the door into the hallway. She was strong for a little Korean girl. She grabbed me by the hand and pulled me down the hallway to the staircase walking rapidly.

"You didn't have to be so hard on him. I can take care of myself, you know. Weren't you ever taught to turn the other cheek?"

"My cheek-turning days ended when a bullet found its way to my shoulder in France. I didn't like the way he talked to you. Or looked at you."

Ellen stopped and smiled a two-hundred-watt smile. "Do you care about me so much, Frankie Yoshikawa?" I felt blood rush to my face. I coughed and the cigarette dropped out of my mouth onto the linoleum.

"I didn't like his manner, that's all." I yanked the pack of Lucky Strikes out of my pocket and lit up another, just to give my hands and mouth something to do. We walked out of the building back into the heat.

"Whatever you say, *Detective*." Her smile got brighter. "Are you going to go back to the station now?"

"No. I need to go back to Millie's parents' house and search her bedroom. It's only a couple of blocks from the *Record*, so I'll drop you off before I call on the folks."

"I don't have to be back just yet." Ellen looked at me expectantly.

"No," I said.

"*Please*?"

"No." She sat down in my car and I closed the door for her after she pulled her dress in. I got in on the driver's side and put the key in the ignition and turned it.

"So, you're going to go over to her grieving parents' place and suggest to them that you need to go through her underwear and most intimate possessions? *You*? A *man*? That's going to go over well. But what do *I* know? I'm just a girl who gets an idea once in a while. You're so much smarter than me so I'm sure *you'll* figure out a way to pull it off. Why, the case is practically closed . . ."

"Stop it! You know what I can't understand? I could fit you into the glove compartment of this Cadillac but it would take a couple of cattle cars to hold the headache you're giving me." Ellen had a point, and it bothered me to acknowledge it. "All right. You are to remain somber and professional and for the love of God you will let me do the talking to the folks, okay?"

"Cross my heart." Ellen beamed. I shook my head. We got onto Kapiolani Boulevard and headed ewa to Sheridan Tract. We were there in five minutes.

There were more cars on the street parked around the house than there were the day before. Ellen and I crossed the lawn, passed the sickly guava sapling, and went up the stairs to the lanai. The lanai deck was full of shoes and many soft voices from within came drifting through the old screen door. I knocked on the screen door frame. We waited for what seemed like an eternity without looking at each other. The discomfort of being there hung between us like a chaperone.

Millie's mother at last emerged from the gloom behind the screen like a ghost, soundless save for the soft flapping of her straw house slippers. Her red, watery eyes made it look as if she had been up all night crying.

"Good afternoon, Miyasaki-san," I said. I showed her the badge and bowed once again. "I am sorry to bother you again. This is Miss Ellen Park, with the *Honolulu Record*. She has come to accompany me in searching Millie's room and possessions. If it is your wish, she will not solicit any comment from you. I am sorry to have to intrude this way, especially when you have company. Might we come in to take a brief look?"

The frail woman nodded and unhooked the rusty hook that held the screen door closed.

"Daddy," she announced to her husband, "police. Frankie Yoshikawa."

In the dark parlor, I could see Tadao Miyasaki sitting in a koa framed chair in a white shirt and dark tie with a glass in his hand. He looked up over his bifocals to grunt a greeting and continued to sit. The floor had been cleared and the furniture pushed against the walls for people to kneel and offer Buddhist prayers. The prayers were momentarily done and standing people filled the space. Older relatives and a few closer to my age were all dressed in somber colors. A Buddhist priest in his dark kimono and brocaded purple sash about his shoulders was conversing with some ancient-looking characters with bent backs—another cluster of lost souls waiting for the boat at the shores of the Acheron. The burning smell from the senko's urn was overpowering.

"Come in," she said. We removed our shoes and entered the house. Millie's photograph in the silver frame was now adorned with black velvet ribbons, which disturbingly reminded me of the waterlogged Chanel dress that clung to her corpse. Ellen and I nodded and half bowed and half smiled silent greetings to the praying visitors. Ayako Miyasaki led us through the parlor into a dark hallway. We walked toward the front of the house, where she opened a door.

"Thank you," I told her. She bowed and walked back down the hallway.

Millie Miyasaki's bedroom was neat and clean. It hadn't changed at all, though I wasn't used to seeing it in daylight. The bed sheet was floral and a sheer canopy hung over four dark wood posts. A teddy bear with a pink bow around its neck remained nestled between two large pillows. I resisted the unnatural urge to sit on the bed and see if it still retained its springiness.

The room itself was light and airy on nights when the tradewinds blew. That day, hot and stuffy, the canopy hung limply from the bedposts without moving. It felt like the last night I was in there, the last night I had her, the last night so many years ago. I looked down at the floor and avoided looking at Ellen, fearing she could see right through me to the thoughts that knotted me inside.

Millie's small writing desk and wooden chair near the window still looked out into the front yard. I crossed over to the window and looked at the whitewashed sill. There were thin scuffmarks on the white paint, thin enough to have been made by a fancy pair of heels. I opened the window and looked down at the grass below, which looked flattened and broken compared to the other patches of grass around the house. Millie was still making surreptitious entrances and exits through this window, probably still late at night. The thought of it made me sick for reasons I couldn't understand. It wasn't as if I still had feelings for her. Those vanished with the beginnings of wisdom so long ago. It was probably the disturbing thought that someone who had done as I did may have been responsible for her violent end.

The desk held some girly stationery and some pilfered office supplies. No recent correspondence, no address book with names and telephone exchanges remained on the desk. No secret love letters. A dresser held neatly folded underwear, sleepwear, and some casual clothing and nothing else.

"Well," I said to Ellen, "is this the room you imagined after interviewing all those office girls?"

"Something doesn't seem right . . . all the nice things she was supposed to have . . . there isn't really a trace of any of it . . . how about the closet, Frankie? Did you look in the closet?"

"No. Shall we?"

The door was locked, and neither Ellen nor I could find a key elsewhere in the room. I took a switchblade out of my pocket and tried to pick the lock without much success.

"Let me," said Ellen. She deftly took a bobby pin from her coiffure and inserted it into the keyhole. A few seconds later, a click sounded and a tiny spring twanged.

"Not bad," I said. "Maybe you *are* good for something." Ellen rolled her eyes at me. I opened the closet door and found a daisy-chained metal cord dangling just inside the top of the frame and pulled. The single naked bulb illuminated the small closet. What was within was something.

"Chanel, Christian Dior—these are all from France and all very expensive," gasped Ellen. She looked through the dresses on the hangers. The whole closet was a shrine to all things *Parisienne*. Millie had tacked to the inside of the door photographs of cafés, street scenes, and the Eiffel Tower, which had been cut out from magazine pages. She also had color postcards of Renoir and Toulouse-Lautrec paintings on her closet door. Three very expensive looking pairs of shoes and a high school French language textbook lay on the floor. On the shelf were five hatboxes and none of them looked cheap. I took them down and Ellen and I opened them one by one. As expected, they all contained hats as elegant and costly looking as their boxes would suggest.

"Frankie," said Ellen. She peered into the last Christian Dior hatbox after removing a stunning red felt hat. "Look at this."

She tipped the box to show me a letter-sized manila envelope within. I reached in and pulled out an unsealed and unlabeled envelope and spread its contents out on the bed: airplane tickets to Los Angeles, then New York, then Paris. Pan American and TWA. There was also a brand-new United States passport in the name of Mildred Toyoko Miyasaki, issued a week before her untimely death. The tickets were for two weeks after her last supper at Sternwood's. They were cut about the same time her passport was issued. I mused to myself that had she lived, she might have just reached Paris that day. There were also five photographs: one of the outside of what looked like a warehouse with a hand-painted sign above the door "DHM 3" and the rest of the interior of a warehouse with shipping pallets stacked with large sacks, one a close-up showing that the sacks were rice bags. The date signature on the photographs read "AUG 12 1949."

"Do you think Danny Boy Cadiz was Millie's secret boyfriend and Paris traveling companion?" asked Ellen. She stared dumbfounded at the tickets.

"I doubt it. A union organizer might be better compensated than the average stevedore, but not *that* much better."

I took the envelope with the tickets, the passport, and the strange photographs; Ellen and I replaced the rest of the closet contents and exited the sad little room. I stopped briefly to inquire about the tickets and the passport with her parents, who not surprisingly knew nothing about them. Millie's mother was still in the process laying out more food in the kitchen. Stuff like kombu maki or oden without meat in it. Funeral food. I never touched the stuff. Ever since I was a kid I couldn't bring myself to eat while senko hung in the air and people were crying. She offered some to us and we thanked her but respectfully declined, as I needed to get Miss Park back to work. Then we bid them a good afternoon and left.

Paris wasn't just a pipedream for Millie. She was really going to go. Junior Billings was the only pocket deep enough I could think of that Millie had been associated with to set up something like that. Something told me that Billings cash bought those tickets, but it also told me that Junior had really been at the Navigators Club the night of Millie's death despite the presence of witnesses that placed him at Sternwood's; it also told me that Junior had not lied on the 15th green of the Nuuanu Country Club. It made no sense. It bothered me.

After two short blocks, we were back on Sheridan Street in front of the *Honolulu Record*. I got out of the car and opened the passenger door for Ellen. She took my hand and pulled herself out of the Cadillac and stood facing me on the sidewalk, looking at me through those big glasses of hers. The little leopard hat had not moved all afternoon.

"Thanks for the sandwich and the fun. I'm going to do my interview with Gladys Jean Souza now. Are you going back to the station?"

"No, I've got to do some legwork on that tugboat. I'm pretty sure that's how the body got to Pier 23," I said. Then I added, "It *was* fun. Thanks for tagging along."

"Call me anytime you're stuck with a hard case. I'll always give you a hand," she said, smiling. She turned and walked into the *Record*'s front door. I watched her walk and stood there for a moment. I lit up another cigarette and got back behind the wheel of the Eldorado. It was hot. This is how it must have felt like in First Ring of the Seventh Circle of the *Inferno*, where the violent were condemned to suffer for all time in a boiling river of blood. I wondered what violence *I* had committed to be consigned there. Maybe it was my violence against common sense; I was murdering it. I drove out of Sheridan Tract back toward town.

I never thought I'd ever set foot in that bedroom again. Millie's ghost clung to the comforter on her bed. It followed me out and had a seat in my head. I pulled my hip flask out of my coat pocket and took a long drink to chase it out. She had made me a locker room celebrity and I supplied her with trinkets her folks never would have bought for her. A fair trade at the highest level in the twisted world of high school.

That didn't mean she deserved what happened to her or that I didn't care. Ironically, I cared more about her at that moment than I ever did when we were supposed to be in love. I had to give her justice, but not because of Ellen's lofty pronouncements about lifting Orientals out of the shadows of oppression. I had to do it because Millie's ghost would hang around and continue to haunt me like those obake stories my folks told me until I finished this thing.

I took another long drink and got back to the business of trying to finish this thing.

16

Contrary to what most people believe from reading pulp novels or watching picture shows or even catching just a glimpse of an entire case by reading some reporter's summary in a newspaper, most of detective work is not made up of interviewing sobbing witnesses or chasing confronted suspects in dramatic fashion through crowded public places. A good fifty percent of a dick's time is spent doing research of the nature I was doing on the *Hinalea*. Another forty-five percent is spent typing reports and killing time at the courthouse before taking the stand and answering "yes" or "no" to attorneys' short questions like Jack did on the prior day. That leaves just five percent for sobbing witnesses and fleeing suspects, and even at that witnesses rarely sobbed and the suspects even more rarely attempted to flee. Most of the time they kind of just stood there with their heads down. Sometimes they sobbed, too, and far more often than any witness I've interviewed. If anything, it's the opposite. It's the witnesses who bolt and run. Or at least they want to when they find out that they're in for a half hour or more of my company.

My afternoon was a headache-filled nightmare of poorly lit and poorly ventilated file storage areas, first at the U.S. Coast Guard Station at Pier 4 and then at the Territorial Business Registration Office. The whole goose chase for information lasted three and a half hours and at the end of it my shirt was soaked through with grubby cuffs and collar. I guess boxes of paper don't need air conditioning or light or comfortable seating the way people do. When the occasional unfortunate sap like me needs to take a look at them, he steps into the world of forgotten records, a hideous place of heat, dust, and discomfort—and on a kona winds day, the vaults where they bury those things are that much worse. Still, one might say that the information I recovered was worth the effort, though it really only firmly put me back in the position I was in earlier that day.

My research at the Coast Guard told me that the *Hinalea* was originally christened the *Mackenzie* thirty years before and was first the property of the Western Maritime Services Corporation in San Francisco. Her keel was laid in a Brooklyn shipyard and she was brought west when Western Maritime acquired a handful of vessels at fire sale prices when the original party that ordered the tugs from the Brooklyn shipyard filed for bankruptcy. Two decades later, Western Maritime modernized its fleet with brand new tugs and they sold the *Mackenzie* to something called the Kewalo Group based in Honolulu along with two other tugs, the *Cortez* and the *Anne Marie*. The Kewalo Group appears to have been some kind of marine assets acquisition firm that resold the three vessels a couple of months later to local entities. The Maui Tug and Barge Company acquired the *Cortez* and *Anne Marie* from the Kewalo Group and the ships remained in that company's Kahului-based fleet until they were sold six years later to a company in Singapore.

Diamond Head Marine, a company I never heard of, purchased the *Mackenzie* from the Kewalo Group. She was rechristened the *Hinalea* and that's where the trail stopped at the Coast Guard. And not a moment too soon—I was about to pass out from oxygen deprivation. Who knows how long my bones would have lain in that dust-covered room before some unlucky clerk discovered them?

I thanked the young ensign in charge of the records section and drove a handful of blocks mauka to the Territorial Business Registration Office. My foray into their records holding area could hardly be called more pleasurable than my experience at the Coast Guard. The room turned out to be less musty than the Coast Guard's records vault, but it was twice as hot. I left my coat and my hat in the car as neither of them had any pressing business in a stuffy Territorial file room.

A homely Japanese girl with a ton of makeup meant to hide a multitude of acne scars and not doing a very good job of it, led me to the section I wanted. All records older than a decade were filed by "number" instead of alphabetically by registration or trade name. Fantastic. I was probably going to be there, sweating, until they decided to make Hawaii a state. Armed with only a master "list" of file numbers and corresponding file dates, I rolled up my perspiration-soaked sleeves and got to the dirty business of looking through manila folder after manila folder, taking a best-guess stab at the registration dates based on what I knew from the Coast Guard vessel registration dates, which didn't help me a whole hell of a lot; all that knowledge really only gave me a starting point to work backwards from. I thought I was going to go blind squinting at the typewritten trade names in the poor light of a handful of naked bulbs hanging from pre-war cords. Our property tax dollars at work.

Fifty-five minutes, three paper cuts, and a sore neck later, I found the file I was looking for. TH-36-1165 belonged to Diamond Head Marine, A Territory of Hawaii Corporation and wholly owned subsidiary of the Billings Shipping Corporation, which in turn was owned by the Billings Trust. Diamond Head Marine. DHM. I looked at the photographs again from Millie's hatbox. DHM 3.

Great. Just another lead that pointed to a guy who was extremely well connected and had the apparent ability to be in two places at once. I let out a loud, pained yell when I discovered that the tug was owned by the Billings Trust and kicked a metal cabinet. Nobody noticed. Why would they? It was like yelling in a mausoleum and then expecting all of the corpses in the cemetery to sit up and shush you. I sat on a banker's box, took out my handkerchief, and wiped my forehead in a futile gesture. I felt like Dorothy in *The Wizard of Oz*, who risked life and limb only to find out at the very end of the journey that she had the power all along to get home on her own. Only if I could tap these particular ruby slippers together, they'd just take me back to the Homicide office and a cup of cold, bad coffee and the stark realization that I had a doomed case. I found myself wondering if Junior Billings ever got anything out of his caddy Yasu's lecture on the break of the green on the fifteenth hole, because he was likely to continue to spend his mornings at the Nuuanu Country Club for the foreseeable future despite the fact that his family owned the vessel used in a homicide to transport a victim that he likely knew. Again, I yelled. Again, nobody noticed.

I thanked Miss Pockmarks on the way out from the file area and back into the air-conditioned office, then left the temporary relief of the artificially chilled air and staggered out into the sunlight to my waiting convertible. The black leather seats had been baking in the afternoon sun, just right for scorching the palms of my bare hands and making my ass perspire through my boxers. The joys of sunny Hawaii.

I took the hip flask of bourbon out of the glove compartment, feeling brave for having done so without oven mitts. I took a long, agonizing pull from the warm flask. The bourbon burned going down and would've made for a cheery fireside libation in another place and time. On a torrid afternoon in downtown Honolulu, though, it tasted like something a house painter forgot in a jar on someone's lanai. I chased it with a handful of Sen-Sen mints to cover the poison on my breath. I started the car and headed back to the station.

There was little parking around the intersection of Merchant and Bethel Streets. I ended up a couple of blocks farther away. The afternoon sun was a little behind the buildings on the makai side of Merchant, causing them to cast long blue-gray shadows across the street. The shade brought little relief in the wet, stifling heat. I loosened my tie and undid the top button of my shirt. I got out of the car after killing the engine and looked up to see a russet brown dress floating down Merchant Street and turning the corner onto Bishop. I ran to the corner and caught a glimpse of the dress disappearing into a large sand-colored building. The Billings Trust Building.

I took my handkerchief out of my breast pocket and wiped the back of my neck. Ruth Prentiss had told me she worked around the corner. I didn't think she meant literally. I chewed on the coincidence, but not too long. My shirt was getting wetter and I could feel the steam in the crown of my hat building up. I dragged my feet back up to Merchant and started the three-block trudge back to the station.

When I got back to the office, Delilah and most of the dicks had gone for the day. Gid was still in his office going over his endless stack of files with his goofy little bifocals resting at the end of his monument of a nose. It's not that his nose was noticeably large; Gid's entire head was enormous, so everything on it was too. Jack was playing with the yellow yo-yo again, staring out of the window through the blinds at the traffic below.

I came in with my coat slung over my shoulder and my hat tilted back high on my head with my tie loosened and hanging limply from around my neck. I must have looked about as peppy as the Lucky Strike dangling unlit from the corner of my mouth. Jack heard my footsteps, turned around, and jerked a lighter out of nowhere. I had the Lucky Strike going in a couple of puffs.

"We found more hair—some Oriental, most likely our girl's, and some something else—Hawaiian or Samoan, the M.E. thinks. Could be the regular operator of the tug," said Jack, still working his bright yellow yo-yo up and down. "We had the lab guys dust for prints, too, all over the vessel—just in case. How'd it go with you, Sheik?"

"She was going to go to Paris this week. She had tickets and everything. It wasn't just a brag or wishful thinking. Some union man named Cadiz was sniffing around the AG's office for her before she disappeared. I stopped by the union hall but he wasn't in. I'll catch up with him tomorrow."

Jack let the yo-yo go slack and stood staring at me. I told him about the strange photographs and the weird invitation to the Roman Holiday Foundation ball in her work desk. Then I told him about all the digging I had done on the *Hinalea*'s ownership and who it all pointed to.

Jack stood there puffing away and wound the yo-yo back up. Gid had shuffled out of his office to hear the latest. We went over the latest and I bid them both aloha. Time to get home because I wasn't getting anywhere else.

I found myself at the bar and grill instead, back on the same red leather barstool I warmed with my ass the day before and the same setup in front of me. The three old guys in the booth were even more silent than they were on the previous day. There was no ballgame on the radio. I wasted no time in building that magical haze around me that only whiskey could make. I felt a little better about myself as I killed off drink after drink.

Wally Yoshida's voice came floating back from half a world away.

"You know what I miss most, Frankie?" he asked. He was lying in a cot in a hospital tent, waiting to go back stateside to some hospital there. A pretty haole nurse with red hair and freckles had just changed the dressing on his stump. They amputated what was left of his leg just above the knee.

"Polly Yamanaka?"

"Besides Polly. Maybe *more* than Polly."

"I give up. What *do* you miss most?"

"Rice."

"*Rice*? I never would've guessed *that*. You could miss so many other things about home. I know I do. Why rice?"

"I don't know. I guess it's the simplest thing there is, and it's the simplest things I miss most. When I get home, I'm going to eat a whole pot full. I won't even put anything on it. No gravy, no shoyu, no furikake, not even my mom's tsukemono. Just plain, hot rice," he said. I laughed. Wally was going to go home and get his big pot of rice. He was missing a leg, but he kept the rest of him. I was still intact but I could lose a lot more than that by sticking around. Not for the first time I wished I could've traded places with him, missing leg and all.

Rice was a big deal to a lot of folks. During the strike of '49 it was such a hot commodity that folks were willing to pony up half their salary to make sure their families had enough to see them through it. I came back from Columbia in the midst of the strike and found Ka-san and my sisters in a terror-stricken state. Iris alone seemed determined to defend the striking dockworkers, her "comrades in arms." What if there was no rice? How would we live? Wally was ironically at Harvard Law School when all that was happening. He didn't have rice there, either, except the hard, dry stuff they had at chop suey places in Cambridge. Such a lot of fuss over the simplest thing.

I looked at my empty glass and thought about having another, then decided against it. Somewhere, there was always another drink waiting to be had. It wasn't as if I'd never see another shot of whiskey again.

I stood up, stretched my legs and looked out of the plate glass window of the bar and grill at Waialae Avenue. A bevy of colorful automobiles paraded uphill and downhill: black, white, silver, pale blue, forest green, custard yellow, Christmas ornament red. It was like one of those reefs in any bay on Oahu when the water was pristine and a rainbow display of colorful fish could be seen hovering brilliantly over the jagged coral.

The three old guys sat in their booth in front of the window, drinking their Primos and picking at their Neptune's Platter, not saying a single word to one another. Japs. Always so quiet in each other's company. Haoles think it's because we're philosophical and mysterious, each one of us a Zen monk in shirtsleeves. I just think it's because we'd already figured each other out a long time ago so there's nothing left to be said.

17

When I got back to my apartment I poured a finger of Haig and Haig Pinch into a rocks glass and dragged out the white dinner jacket, black tie, and pearl studs and cufflinks that I hadn't used in some time. I drank about half of my drink and got into the shower. After drying off, I finished the other half of my drink, brushed my teeth, and got dressed. The Roman Holiday Foundation ball was about a half-hour away. I went downstairs and got into my car and took a leisurely drive into Waikiki, approaching it from the Diamond Head end.

They didn't call the Royal Hawaiian Hotel the Pink Palace for nothing. The 400-room Spanish-style edifice was pink outside and in. Its lobbies, halls, and ballrooms were all illuminated with art deco indirect lighting that made the walls and ceilings glow fuzzily like the sky of a sunset beyond the Waianae Mountains on an overcast day. Even the lush gardens on the grounds were strung with pink Chinese paper lanterns that bobbed like benign specters in the darkness on nights when the trades blew in gently from over the Koolaus. The lack of breeze caused the pink spheres to hang motionless like so many tapioca beads suspended in a thick black pudding.

I pulled the Eldorado right up under the portico and turned it over to a white-jacketed valet. The Roman Holiday function was in the main ballroom and was already crowded by the time I arrived.

I hadn't worn a white dinner jacket since my sister Pansy's wedding. The black bowtie chafed, but I remembered from those team dinners in college that the bowtie's advantage over the necktie was that it never ended up in your soup. I felt like a waiter in the strange, restrictive outfit. When I got to the ballroom, it became apparent to me that this was actually a longshoreman's union function. I made a couple of discreet inquiries and found that the Roman Holiday Foundation was a front for a body of Hollywood actors, writers, and directors who supported labor; it was named for what would become the hit movie of the year, the last screen credit for writer Dalton Trumbo, one of the "Hollywood Ten" who were blacklisted. The movie would be coming soon to theaters so the name didn't raise any eyebrows. The Roman Holiday Foundation secured the venue for them and provided a little glitz. The rumor was that Humphrey Bogart himself made the call to the hotel. A few years before, there would be no way a labor union would have been able to hold a function of any kind at the Royal Hawaiian, once a bastion of moneyed kamaʻaina haole society. But make no mistake, the tuxedoes in the ballroom weren't only filled with the burly bodies of stevedores or leg-breaking union goons whose calling cards said "organizer" below their names. In attendance were the upstart elites, the new faces of Territorial politics and chic local celebrity: recently-arrived haole agitators from as far afield as Detroit, Chicago, New York, and, of course, San Francisco; kanaka actors and musicians who managed to land bit parts in big Hollywood pictures and returned home with new politics and new money; young local Oriental lawyers, professors, and business owners sick of being disenfranchised despite their growing numbers; a couple of celebrity mainland-types who were dragged before the House Un-American Activities Committee in attendance to lend their star-power and some propaganda to the proceedings.

Even a couple of big Hollywood stars made brief appearances while ostensibly on "vacation" in the islands. There was, of course, the presence of the most influential and important union leaders despite the absence of the regular rank-and-file membership. A couple of those who were in the midst of standing trial for alleged Smith Act violations were in attendance and lauded as heroes and martyrs. All this was above my head, though. I was not so much star-struck as I was curious as to what a Territorial office girl like Millie Miyasaki had in common with any of these people.

I grabbed a coupe of champagne off a tray of a circulating waiter and took a sip. It was fairly good stuff. I looked at the ballroom entrance just in time to catch a dream blowing in. It was a girl. A girl to make you sit up straight and chew the brim of your hat. She had lustrous black hair down to her shoulders and lips as crimson as the apple that put Snow White into a coma. The red didn't end there. Her whole stunning self was encased in it. Even her shoes were the same lipstick hue. The red dress curved dramatically with the contours beneath. All of that nonsense in Dante about gentle hearts being set on fire was the stuff of utter silliness until I laid eyes on her that hot, languid night in Waikiki. She made me want to run home and crack open my *Divina Commedia* and read it again. Our eyes met and she smiled and walked straight toward me.

"Good evening, *Detective*."

"*Ellen*? Ellen Park?"

"Didn't recognize me without the glasses, did you?" She threw her head back and laughed that laugh and her identity was clearly unmistakable.

"Sure," I lied. "But I've got to say you clean up nice."

"You do, too." She reached out and tugged at the satin lapel of my dinner jacket.

"I feel like an organ grinder's monkey."

"You look dashing, Frankie Yoshikawa. It's nice to know that you know how to dress for the occasion."

"You *are* the occasion." I couldn't take my eyes off of her. That's why I was completely taken unawares by what happened next. Ellen and

I stood there gawking at each other like a couple of teenagers when a familiar voice from behind my back said, "Ellen! Hi, Ellen!"

Ellen tilted her head and looked past my shoulder and said hello. I turned around and came face-to-face with the familiar voice.

"Hey, Frankie!" said the voice. "This is a pleasant surprise! I didn't know you supported any cause more important than yourself. Isn't this something, Chester?"

"Iris. Chester," I said to my sister and brother-in-law. Ellen looked at Iris then at me with interest.

"You two have met?" Ellen asked me.

"We go way back," I said. "We met when I was born. Iris is my sister."

Ellen's perfect little red mouth had formed itself into an astonished grin. "That's amazing! I never would have guessed!"

Marvelous. A wrench in the works I never saw coming.

"Have you known my baby brother for long, Ellen?" Iris asked, beaming. I winced. Baby Brother. She was just getting started with her line of questioning. Chester grabbed a new coupe of champagne from a passing tray and put an empty one into the vacancy he created. I sensed the train coming and opened my mouth to step in front of it, but Ellen, quick as ever, responded.

"Frankie and I haven't known each other for very long. We met through his work."

"So you two are here . . . *together*?" my sister asked, smiling like the Cheshire Cat.

"No," I said as Ellen said "Yes."

"Yes," I said as Ellen said "No."

"It's work related," I said.

"I'm covering one of your brother's cases," said Ellen.

"Here?" asked Iris. "At tonight's function?"

"Well, we decided to discuss my findings and there wasn't really time to do it during the day. It's kind of like killing two birds with one stone." Smooth, Sheik. Like sandpaper.

"It's so much nicer than doing it in some stuffy office," said Ellen. "I think Frankie was brilliant for suggesting it. We can go over the specifics over champagne instead of cold coffee in paper cups." She had come to my rescue in convincing fashion. She was clever and quick and, as it finally occurred to me, drop-dead gorgeous when she wanted to be.

"Oh," said my sister.

Then suddenly Iris and Ellen broke into a frenzied conversation that left Chester and me to talk about more relevant things, like baseball. As we chatted about recent trades in both the National and American Leagues, I cast my glance furtively about the ballroom looking for anything significant. It wasn't easy. I had no idea what I was looking for.

Iris stopped in the middle of the story she was telling Ellen when her eye caught someone on the lanai at the opposite end of the ballroom. She quickly apologized to Ellen and told her that she needed to take me to see someone very quickly and promised to be back in a minute. She asked Chester to keep Ellen company while we were gone. Then she grabbed my sleeve and we were off to the races, dodging couples doing the mambo on the dance floor and red-faced power brokers slapping each other's backs and waving champagne coupes and cigarettes around in hazardous fashion.

Halfway across the dance floor, Iris was hailed by a booming voice that shouted over the orchestra: "Hey, Iris!" It was the pumpkin-headed goon from the union hall who shared an office with Danny Boy Cadiz. He had already undone his bowtie and was twirling some frizzy-haired girl in a rhinestone-studded skirt.

We stopped. Iris said, "Hey, Kaz! This is my brother Frankie. Frankie—Kazuhiro Sekiguchi. He's with the union. He raises a *ton* of money."

"We met," I said. Kaz Sekiguchi eyed me up with his beady little eyes.

"Yeah," he said, surprised. "I didn't know you were Iris Imada's brother."

He extended his hand. I shook it. There was posture and menace in his handshake. It was more of a threat than a greeting. His hand was wet with perspiration and champagne. I fought the urge to wipe my hand off right away. That was the second time someone had found it surprising that Iris Imada was my sister. I was beginning to feel like some guy who sold life insurance who turned out to be heir to the British throne. We left him and Frizzy to finish the mambo as Iris continued to drag me along. I said, "That's not who you wanted me to meet?"

"Who, Kaz? No. I'm going to introduce you to somebody who *gives* a lot of money, not raises it." I could imagine what Kaz Sekiguchi's technique was for fundraising. A lot of arms were probably twisted until they reached their wallets and opened them.

In a matter of seconds, my sister had pulled me clear across the main ballroom of the Royal Hawaiian to the lanai on the opposite side. The warm, moist air hit me in the face and I could taste the salt on the sluggish, barely existent breeze coming off the water as we stepped outside. The moon made a shimmering path on the black ocean and the slow surf could be heard lapping against the sand between the Latin notes of the orchestra playing "Perfidia." Politicos talked shop on the crowded lanai in the cigarette haze they generated. I found myself face-to-face with an attractive, expensive-looking blonde I recognized but had never met in an indigo sequined evening gown over her athletic frame. She had pretty blue eyes but a severe, squared jaw that gave her an intimidating air. Standing next to her was a serene brunette in a beige silk gown with a big bow in the back above her ass. This one I had met before. The blonde broke into a smile upon seeing Iris.

"Hi, Iris! I thought you'd be here tonight. Where's Chester?"

"He's inside enjoying the refreshments, but you'll see him a little later. I want to introduce you to my baby brother. Frankie, this is Peg Billings. She's been so helpful in financing our efforts to start a teachers union. Peg, this is my brother Frankie Yoshikawa. He works for HPD."

The hairs on the back of my neck stood up and I felt bile rise in the back of my throat. Na'au. Dumbstruck, I extended my hand. Peg Billings gripped it like a longshoreman and shook it. Standing beside Red Peg with her arms folded across her chest and watching me with cold, hard eyes was Ruth Prentiss. She had gone from sophisticated dream to guard dog in no time flat. Her smile hung by a thread.

"Pleased to meet you," I finally managed to say, still stunned by the coincidence that didn't feel like a coincidence.

"HPD, huh?" said Peg. "Which division are you assigned to?"

"Homicide Detail," I said truthfully, not being in any position to evaluate my responses before they left my mouth. Surprise will do that to you.

"That must be an interesting assignment," said Peg, taking a sip of champagne. "Oh, forgive me. This is my personal secretary, Mrs. Ruth Prentiss."

"We've met," I said. I extended my hand to Ruth. "It's nice to see you again so soon."

Ruth blinked as she shook my hand in the same dainty fashion she had on Sunday at Ka-san's house but this time it felt like a dead fish. "Likewise," she said. She smiled thinly and watched me warily. So, she *did* work in the Billings Trust Building. Behind Ruth, a tall man with an undone bowtie took a sip from his drink and made eye contact with me for an instant before fading back toward the ballroom.

"Well, you must be very busy lately," said Peg, turning her attention back to me, "if the *Star-Bulletin* and *Advertiser* are any indicators."

"As must you," I said, having finally recovered from the initial shock of our meeting. "Actually, the cases I'm working on now really aren't the kind of stuff that makes the papers," I lied. I kept my fingers mentally crossed that Iris wouldn't blurt out something about the girl in the harbor. If Peg had talked to her brother at all, she might know that I interviewed him the day before at the Nuuanu Country Club. The conversation was quickly going down a road leading to a bad neighborhood. Time to get off the bus.

Ruth Prentiss finally spoke, changing the subject for me, but not in a direction that I would have liked. "How did you come to receive an invitation to this function, Detective? Are you politically active like your sister?" Her voice was calm and soft but had a hint of something stronger beneath it, hiding. Like an inquisitor, hiding a red-hot poker behind his robes, talking about the grace of God.

Think fast, Sheik. "The extent of my politics is making sure my address is current on the registration rolls. Iris is the real activist in our family. I vote the way she tells me to. My lieutenant, Gideon Hanohano, is related to about half the people on the island and he knows the other half anyway. I believe the invitation came to him through a cousin or someone in the union leadership. I apologize—the person's name escapes me. Gid isn't much for these functions, so he asked me if I'd be interested in going in his place. So here I am. Besides, I don't think there's a tuxedo in all the islands large enough for Detective Lieutenant Hanohano."

The women laughed all around. It was time for me to exit, stage left. And fast. I said, "It was a pleasure talking with both of you, Miss Billings, Mrs. Prentiss. Thank you both so much for all of the help you've given to my sister. I'm sure you have some important things to discuss, so I'll leave you to it."

"On the contrary," said Peg, "I'd like to hear a little about your work . . ."

"There you are, Frankie Yoshikawa." It was Ellen. She appeared unexpectedly at my sister's side. "I agreed to get all dressed up and be your date for this function and you up and leave me for the company of a couple of beautiful women. Some date you are." Everyone laughed. Peg apologized to Ellen for detaining me and introductions were made all around. She had saved me again. Peg Billings and Ruth Prentiss were display-room beautiful but that night they had nothing on this resourceful little reporter in her red dress.

I shook hands again with both women and Iris assured me that she'd be along to join us again in a couple of minutes then launched into some pitch to Peg and Ruth about possible recruitment numbers at schools on the windward side of the island and other such stuff while they listened indulgently. I was thankfully forgotten at that point and took the opportunity to surreptitiously disappear. I looked back at Ruth Prentiss and wondered about her visit to the Union Hall. What was she doing there? She was also at the Royal Hawaiian, and so were Kaz Sekiguchi and a bunch of other union men. I suppose it made sense if she was running errands for Peg, who was an ardent union supporter.

As I made my way back in the ballroom, I became aware that I was being followed. I led Ellen back to Chester and asked him to keep her company while I went to the men's room. I skirted the edge of the ballroom and headed out into the lobby, walking briskly toward the men's room. My tail—the tall, dark fellow in a white dinner jacket and undone bowtie whom I had seen on the lanai behind Ruth Prentiss—followed. He was a handsome specimen with slick black hair. I entered the men's room and sought out a urinal at the far end past the old Filipino washroom attendant standing dutifully by his tray of colognes and folded hand towels.

As I stood relieving myself, the man who followed me from the lanai whispered something in what was probably Ilocano to the washroom attendant and placed a folded bill in his hand. The attendant nodded silently and exited the men's room, leaving the two of us alone. Tall, Dark, and Handsome sauntered over to the urinal next to mine and proceeded to use it despite the fact that every other urinal was available for his use. I squeezed my upper arm down on my .38 beneath my dinner jacket for reassurance. Being crowded in that fashion while taking a leak really disconcerted me. The staccato of urine hitting porcelain was the only sound.

After a few heartbeats, he spoke to me while staring straight at the wall in front of him.

"Good evening, Detective Yoshikawa. Are you enjoying the event?"

"I was until someone followed me into the men's room and insisted on keeping me exclusive company while I pissed."

The man laughed. "I apologize, Detective, but this was the only way I could be sure to speak to you without being observed."

"Then by all means, speak."

"I'm Danilo Cadiz. I'm with the Local."

"Forgive me if I don't shake hands 'til we've washed them, Mr. Cadiz. I know who you are. They call you Danny Boy."

"I couldn't help overhearing your conversation out on the lanai. Please forgive me. I believe you are the detective assigned to the case of the poor girl they fished out of the harbor?"

"If you were eavesdropping, then you must've heard the part where I told the ladies out there I don't handle big-time cases."

"You're being modest, Detective. I have a cousin at HPD who works in dispatch. She says you're the Man of the Hour—the great Gideon Hanohano's protégé."

"So?"

"We need to talk about the dead girl and what she knew."

"So talk." I shook the last drops off and put myself back into my trousers.

"Not here," Cadiz almost whispered, his tone becoming very serious. "This place is full of eyes and ears and I have something to show you. Do you know the Freitas Meats place where they make the sausage near the Kapalama Military Reservation?"

"Yeah."

"Meet me behind the warehouse there at midnight. I'll be sitting in a silver Buick Roadmaster."

I heard Danny Boy zip up and flush the urinal. He walked away toward the marble basins to wash his hands.

"Give me a minute before you exit the men's room," he said. He dried his hands on a white linen towel. He threw it in the large wicker basket next to the attendant's cologne caddy when he was done. "I'll take a rain check on that handshake 'til midnight."

"Sure," I told him. "Do I need an escort?"

"Relax, Detective," Danny Boy said as he exited the men's room without turning around. "I'm your friend."

I stood there for a moment thinking of what just transpired and walked over to the marble basins to wash my hands. I looked in the large mirror and stared at the Man of the Hour. He didn't look so impressive to me. I splashed some water on the Man of the Hour's face, dried off with a linen towel, then chucked the towel in the basket and exited the men's room.

I found the washroom attendant leaning up against the pink lobby wall smoking a cigarette and looking at nothing. I flipped him two bits.

"All's clear," I told him. "Carry on." I made my way back to the ballroom. I needed a drink.

18

I returned to the ballroom to find Chester and Ellen laughing about something and drinking champagne and smoking; Iris was still circulating about glad-handing labor leaders and political hopefuls. I grabbed two coupes off a passing tray, downed one, and then sipped from the other.

"Thanks for keeping company with Ellen," I said.

Chester was still chuckling as he took another sip of champagne. "It was my pleasure, Frankie. Ellen and I were just talking about a boring accounting professor we both had at UH."

Ellen smiled. "He was always putting people to sleep," she said, and then took another drag through her ebony cigarette holder. That night, everything she did with her hands and mouth was elegant and ethereal and effective. I was beginning to think that even her handwriting would have been nice if she picked up a pen.

"I guess I'd better get over there and join your sister or I'll never hear the end of it," said Chester.

"Tell Iris that I'll see you folks at Ka-san's on Sunday. Ellen and I need to get going. Thanks again, Ches."

My brother-in-law nodded goodbye and disappeared into the roiling mix of tuxedoes and evening gowns. I took Ellen's hand and gently pulled her in the direction of the lobby. When we were out of the ballroom and the blare of the orchestra was made softer by the heavy double doors which closed behind us, Ellen stopped and asked, "Are we leaving because you managed to get what you came for on your case?" Nothing ever escaped her attention.

"I think I did. I've got a meeting with Danny Boy Cadiz at midnight in Kalihi."

"I didn't see him. I thought for sure I'd run into him and get a chance to ask a few questions. You found him?"

"He found *me*. He's keeping a low profile. I don't think he's here anymore."

"I figured you were here in connection with the case. This seems more your sister's speed than yours. How did you get an invitation to this ball, anyway? Was it through Iris?"

"No. I took Millie Miyasaki's. It was among her personal effects at the AG's office. How did you get here tonight?" Her eyes widened at the mention of Millie's name.

"I took a cab," she said. "So, what's your meeting with Cadiz about?"

"Not here. Let's take a ride. I'll take you home after."

We drove along the shoreline past the *Beaux-Arts* War Memorial arch of the Natatorium and parked on a cliff on the slopes of Diamond Head overlooking the ocean. The long glowing path of reflected moonlight shimmering on the dark water threw a faint and ghostly light on the coconut palms lining the shore. Waikiki was sunny, vibrant, and bursting with a legion of colors by day and alluring and sensual by night, adorned with the jewelry of a plethora of little brilliant lights.

"Danny Boy sought me out in the men's room," I told Ellen. "He mentioned Millie and said we needed to talk about what she knew. He wouldn't say any more. Too many eyes and ears. I'm supposed to meet him in the back of a sausage factory in Kalihi."

"Take me with you."

"No."

"Come on, Frankie. We've been through this before. I *know*

Cadiz. I've interviewed him before. I haven't gotten in the way so far. In fact, I've *helped* your investigation. I think my being there gives you a better chance."

"You're probably right. So far you always have been. But you're not coming with me."

"Why not?"

"It's dangerous. Something could go wrong and I don't want you to get hurt."

Ellen looked at me with the moon in her eyes then looked away, down at the floor mats. She smiled demurely and said in an uncharacteristically soft voice, "You *do* care about me, Frankie Yoshikawa."

"Of course I do."

She was beautiful in the moonlight, more than anyone under the moon ever was. I put a finger under her chin and lifted it so I could see her eyes. They glistened with the beginnings of tears. Without thinking and before I could ruin the moment by doing so, I leaned in toward her and kissed her. Her hands came up to cradle my face and her lips parted and the world was hot and silent.

"I told you," she said huskily, "I don't kiss on the first date." She bit my lips and my tongue gently.

"It's okay. This isn't a date, remember?"

I threw my arms around her and pulled her into my lap and we continued frantically under a silken, cloudless sky littered with a million tiny stars. Her weight and her heat felt exquisite and her perfume filled my head.

In the back of my head I knew, though, that eventually the clock would strike twelve and I'd find myself behind a sausage factory talking to Danny Boy Cadiz in his silver Buick Roadmaster.

It was Ellen who finally said, "Look at the time," and I noted with satisfaction that she did so with an obvious note of disappointment in her voice.

"I know," I said. Then, without really thinking before opening my mouth, "Would you give me just a few minutes more before we go? I'd like to tell you something."

"Sure."

"I knew her."

"Knew who?"

"Millie. Millie Miyasaki. She was my high school girlfriend." I wasn't sure how well it would go over, and the timing for this confession may have been lousy. To my surprise, Ellen threw her arms around me and pulled me close.

"I'm so sorry, Frankie. No wonder you were reluctant to discuss it with me."

"Don't be sorry, darling. You couldn't have known. For the record, anything I felt for her ended a long time ago, when I was still a kid. I don't know why I'm telling you this now."

"It's okay. If anything, it's even more important that you catch whoever's responsible for this. And don't worry, I won't mention your past connection to her in my piece."

I wanted to tell her more. I wanted to tell her everything. I wanted to pour out my soul about the memories haunting me, to see this thing to the finish, to exorcise the specters of a muddy past. I wanted to tell her that the moment I kissed her that evening I stopped thinking about Millie and Junior Billings and the wretched heat and humidity for the first time that week. It was the first time a kiss made me forget everything and it was better than whiskey, and I wanted to tell her so more than anything else. All that came out, though, was "Yeah."

I drove Ellen home with her head on my shoulder, breathing softly and contentedly as we made our way back through town to Kalihi and her parents' store on the Kapalama Canal. Even that sluggish trench of still water seemed to have all the charm of the ocean off Diamond Head just because I held her, dizzy with her nearness.

I glanced down and caught a glimpse of my watch. Eleven-fifty. Just enough time to get to the sausage factory, which lay about eight or so big blocks due makai of where we stood.

"Good night, darling," I told Ellen. I was extremely unwilling to go. "You'd better get inside before I turn into a pumpkin. I'll call you tomorrow morning."

"You'd better. And be careful, Frankie Yoshikawa."

I got one last kiss before she disappeared into the darkened storefront. I stood there for a heartbeat then moved back to my car with heat on my mouth and in my pants.

It took me less than five minutes to get there from the Parks' store at just about midnight. As soon as I pulled into the back of the gray corrugated tin structure I was hit by the charnel odor. It was the smell of burnt hair, old blood, shit, and death. Slaughterhouse smell. Dead animals. Nothing in the world smelled worse except a battlefield. I was reminded of Wally's septic stump where his leg had once been and the awful smell of the infirmary tent where I had visited him before they shipped him stateside. We'd play cards as I sat on an empty ammunition can next to his cot. We didn't talk about girls anymore—the subject always made him cry. "Who's gonna want me, Frankie?" he'd ask. I told him leg or no leg he was still better looking than Mits Kuroda and a better dancer, too. Wally laughed, but I think it was more to make *me* feel better and less guilty.

The silver Buick Roadmaster was parked with its lights off just where Cadiz said it would be. I could see him sitting behind the wheel. Cautiously, I scanned the back lot visually and couldn't make out any movement; the place was littered with worn shipping pallets and partially rusted oil drums with one word painted in white on them: "INEDIBLE."

I took the hip flask out of the glove compartment and had a quick drink. It had cooled down considerably since the afternoon, but the liquor still tasted like turpentine. I lit a cigarette and got out of my car. The air was still and warm and my neck started sweating as soon as I shut the door. There was an eerie silence except for the buzzing of flies in the oil drums. I approached the Roadmaster with my hand in my jacket resting on the butt of the .38.

"Danny Boy?" I called out in an attempt to get Cadiz's attention.

Cadiz ignored me. I walked right up to the open driver's window and was about to speak again when I saw the dark stain on the passenger's side on the white leather upholstery. Danny Boy Cadiz's handsome face was tilted up and his eyes stared blankly at his windshield. His mouth hung half open. A burnt hole graced his left temple; his right was gone, splattered no doubt all over the Roadmaster's interior.

"Shit," I said.

I made my way back to the Cadillac with leaden feet and reached for the radio. Then I stood in the yellowish floodlight of the parking area adjacent to the small, empty stockyard. I saw a pair of mismatched tire tracks that looked like the ones I saw in Sheridan Tract in front of the Miyasaki place. They led away from the empty space next to the Roadmaster toward the street. There wasn't much else except for the stench of dead things. Twenty minutes must have passed before the first prowler arrived; I went through three cigarettes and nearly emptied my flask of paint stripper waiting around. In an hour, the place was crawling with olive drab police uniforms. Gid Hanohano and Jack Morris were the last attendees to arrive at Danny Boy Cadiz's going away party. It didn't matter. I was the first one to get there and I was late myself. Danny Boy had already shoved off with Charon to cross the Acheron and nobody was there to say bon voyage except the one who pulled the trigger and put him on the ferry.

Gid shuffled up to me with the same apparent lack of urgency with which he did everything. It really wasn't that he moved slowly. He just looked as if he did. It was probably that way with all large objects. The earth completes an entire rotation in a mere twenty-four hours, but often the day seems to drag.

He stopped a few paces in front of me and handed me a cigar.

"It's not one of your fancy Cubans, but it's better than smelling *this*. This whole place stinks like about twenty kills or more."

"Thanks," I told him, "I think it's more like fifty or more, but the other forty-nine were pigs and they're now in your morning Portuguese sausage. The one in the Buick was my informant."

"Oh?" said Gid. I could almost hear his eyebrow rise as he said it.

I puffed away and told Gid and Jack about what had transpired at the Royal Hawaiian. Both of them listened thoughtfully.

"Interesting," was all Gid said, pondering again.

"I just had Freitas Sausage this morning with my eggs," said Jack. "I don't think I'll be having it tomorrow morning."

"It's tomorrow morning right now," I said wearily.

Gid blinked and rubbed his forehead. "Long night," he said to me.

"Yeah, long night."

"What do you think Danny Boy was going to show you?"

I raised my tired eyes without thinking to look through the chain link fence that separated the sausage factory lot from the warehouse lot next door.

Holy shit. There it was.

"That," I told Gid, and pointed to the warehouse next door, a large nondescript, tin-covered box with a hand painted sign above the door reading "DHM 3."

19

Gid, Jack, and I surreptitiously drifted away from the bustle of the sausage factory scene into the lot next door. Jack picked the padlock on a rusty chain and we pushed the tin door aside about a foot or so, just enough for us to squeeze in. Two of us, anyway. Gid stood outside peering into the breach, unwilling to put any more effort than was necessary to get a look. Jack turned on his chrome boy scout flashlight and swept the place. It was full of pallets piled high with white sacks of rice. Lots of rice. Enough to feed an army.

That's all there was: rice. Jack scratched his bald scalp and squeezed back outside through the crack. I lit up a Lucky Strike, took one last strained glance around by the light of my Zippo flame and squeezed out after him. We re-did the padlock and wandered back to the scene to wrap up. I pondered what about a warehouse full of rice was so important that a man got a bullet in the head for almost showing it to me.

I drove back to Kaimuki with a splitting headache. When I got home, I undressed and flopped into bed just in time to hear Old Chang dragging the tin garbage cans out to the curb. Four-thirty a.m. No wonder he was grouchy most of the time. Who wouldn't be if you started your day before five in the morning?

I tried to sleep but couldn't. This had gotten a lot bigger in the last few hours. First it was Millie in the harbor and my guess would have been that the motive was something personal and confined to her and the party who did her in. Now a union man had known she knew something and wanted to tell me and literally lost his head over it. I went through five cigarettes lying on my back in bed, sweating on my futon. I rolled over and had a couple of drinks out of the bottle of scotch on my nightstand. Because nobody was watching, I didn't bother to pour it in a glass. Between drinks, I sucked the limp Kaimuki air through my mouth and felt as if the wet miasma would choke me. The sun crept up into the room and killed whatever lingering illusion of cool the night created. I sweated. I lay in bed, smoking and drinking more and thinking about pretty girls with bloated faces and handsome guys with half their skulls missing. I was unfortunately cognizant enough to set my alarm just in case I fell asleep.

The two brass bells rattled annoyingly. It was seven o'clock.

After a cold shower and a terrible shave, I headed downstairs to grab some coffee for the road. Vivian Chang was minding the counter, face buried in her Voltaire. Her hair was in a ponytail that morning like some junior high service club girl. I bid her good morning. She looked up from her book and her jaw unhinged.

"Frankie! My God!"

"That's what all the girls call me. Will you be a sweetheart and give me three cups of coffee for the road? And a couple of those nine-layer rice cakes, too. Yeah, I know. I look like your uncle should've put me out with the rest of the trash at four-thirty."

"Rough night?" she asked. She filled three paper cups with coffee and put them in a box, then put two rice cakes in a brown paper sack lined with wax paper and stuck the sack in the box. The sack had once held vegetables from Oahu Market. It even had bits of ong choy leaves at the bottom.

"I'll live." I fished four dimes out of my pocket and dropped them on the counter. I watched them roll about until they wobbled to a halt near the register. I'd live, all right, but I wouldn't be happy about it that morning.

"You didn't put any cream and sugar in here, did you, Viv?" I asked. I looked down in the box at the three cups.

"Of course not. I know how you take your coffee. Black. Just like your heart." She stuck her tongue out at me and continued her reading. I walked out and waved at her without looking back. I got into the Eldorado and looked at my haggard eyes in the rearview mirror. I lit up a Lucky Strike. The smoke tasted like topsoil. I felt like something the cat spit up on the rug. I put the car into gear and pulled out onto Waialae Avenue.

I dragged myself through the station receiving desk area once again crammed with newspapermen. Word had gotten out on the Cadiz job. I cast my eyes about looking for Ellen. She was near the desk with her little black pad and pen out. Her hair was back in its cute little bun and her big glasses were back on her face. She was still as beautiful as she was under the moon in that red dress. She was transformed that night and I'd never look at her the same way. I caught her eye and she gasped. I put a finger over my lips and motioned for her to take the elevator up and meet me on the second floor. She nodded and broke away from the crowd. I moved to the staircase with ease. None of the haole newsmen noticed me. They probably thought I was a wino waiting to be booked; my eyes were bloodshot and my hair was barely combed.

When I made it to the second floor, the brass elevator door opened and Ellen got out. She was wearing powder blue and looked fresh and clean and lovely. I probably looked just the opposite. Despite that, she ran into my arms and held me tight.

"What happened, Frankie?"

"Danny Boy couldn't stay awake for our meeting. Somebody got to him first. He was dead when I got there, right after I left you last night. I was on time. Someone came early. Someone who must've known he was going to meet me and followed him from the Royal Hawaiian." Her face was horror-stricken.

"You look terrible. Did you sleep at all?" She stood on the tips of her toes and gave me a kiss and pushed some of my hair back behind my ear.

"No."

"What are you going to do now?"

"The Lieutenant and I will probably follow up on the *Hinalea*. I know that's how Millie's body got to Pier 23. She wasn't assaulted there initially. I can't have you tag along on this. It may get rough. I'll come and get you for lunch, though," I said, changing my tone and putting a smile on my face, however weak. "It'll be a real date. How about it?"

"Okay," she said, almost shyly. Her mouth smiled but her eyes looked worried. "I need to finish up my initial article for press tomorrow morning. Then I'm going to go to the union hall and look into Danny Boy's associates there."

"Ellen, don't," I said. "It's getting ugly now."

"I'll be okay. You just make sure you get me in time for our 'first date' at noon." Before I could say anything, she tiptoed and kissed me once more and made her way down the tiled stairs back to the media throng at the receiving desk. I listened to the echo of her heels until it was swallowed up by the shouts and questions of the rabid pack.

When I got into to the Homicide Detail office, Jack and Luau had already hit the road. They were meeting with the prosecutor on another case. I found it unbelievable that Luau actually *had* a case to talk to the prosecutor about. I found Gid sitting behind his desk finishing his cover-to-cover read of the paper, wearing the same suit he had worn a few hours before at the Freitas Meats scene. He looked about as peppy as he always does, which is not at all. Gid always looked the same. He looked up and took his silly little glasses off.

"Times Supermarket is having a sale on sliced white bread. Twenty cents a loaf," he said, straight-faced and surreptitiously, as if he were passing on military secrets.

"Is *that* what's going on out there right under our noses? Thanks for the hot tip, Gid."

"Are you ready?" he asked.

"For what?"

"We're going to see the harbormaster."

"You sure you want to do this, Gid? You look like you've been here all night."

"You look like you've been up, too. Let's go." He stood up slowly and arched his back, unleashing crackling noises as he did. He buttoned his top button and tightened the knot on his tie. I handed him his hat.

"I'll drive," I said.

"Good."

We could have walked. Aloha Tower, the harbormaster's control center, was only about three blocks away from the station. We were both too tired, though, and knew we had a lot more day ahead of us. Best to save the steps for when we really needed them. It took me almost ten minutes to go those three blocks and find a place to park. During that time Gid was mostly silent until I killed the engine. He made no effort to get out of his seat on the passenger side until he said what he had to say.

"When we get up there, you let me handle it and watch the door if I tell you to. I hope it's not going to come to that, but I've been getting the run-around from Pinky."

"Okay, Gid. But why would Pinky give you a hard time? You guys go back a way."

"Going back a way doesn't always mean you're going to get it straight from somebody. Especially if that somebody was always a little on the shady side. He didn't return my calls yesterday. That's why we're going to call this morning."

"Surprise visit?"

"Best not to let him see it coming." He finally opened the door and lifted his mass out of the car. The car must have risen about six inches. I heard the shock absorbers sigh with relief. We walked to the tower.

Wilton "Pinky" Davis was Honolulu's harbormaster. He worked his way up through the Republican Party patronage system under the Territorial legislators who pulled strings for those who played ball with them and went from being a port pilot to the office in Aloha Tower in less than twenty years. Pinky was one of those haoles with a chip on his shoulder. His father was in the merchant marine and couldn't afford to send him to Punahou, so he went to Roosevelt High School, the "Poor Man's Punahou." Roosevelt is an English Standard school, which means a lot of Japanese kids can't get in because their command of the language's nuances isn't haole enough to pass the oral "exam" for entrance. Pinky, like almost everybody, married one of Gid's thousand cousins. He was called Pinky for obvious reasons; he was practically magenta under his messy head of red hair. He was one of those friendly blowhards who pissed and moaned about everything from the condition of the roads in Iwilei to rising property taxes. His enormous gut told the story of a hundred cases of Primo downed at a hundred baby luaus.

Gid and I took the stairs all the way up to Pinky's lofty perch, the elevator broken. The same "under repair" sign hadn't moved since the last time I went up to Pinky's office, when I was still a flatfoot in a new blue uniform. How Pinky hauled his bulk up and down those stairs every day was beyond me. Gid and I caught our breath when we reached the harbormaster's floor. We lit a Lucky Strike apiece and Gid nodded and opened the door. We went in.

Pinky was leaning on his secretary's desk with his tie loosened, telling her some bawdy joke she must've heard ten times before. He held a coffee mug like it was a martini glass and his cigarette wagged up and down in his lips as he talked. The secretary, who could have passed for Delilah's younger sister, stopped her sycophantic laughter when she saw Gid and me enter the office. Pinky turned around to face us.

"Hey, Gid! I was just telling Phyllis the one about the priest . . ."

"Pinky," Gid said, quietly but with frosty menace. "You never called back."

"I got busy. Hell, you know what it's like to get busy."

"Ten minutes of looking in your books. A five-minute telephone call. How busy *were* you?" Gid's voice remained level, low, and dangerous.

"Aw, for Christ's sake, Gid! That's a *Billings* boat you're sniffing around. I gotta cover my ass. You know the position I'm in here."

"You mean I know *how* you got the position you're in." He turned to me and said whisper-soft, "Sheik. Take this pretty young lady for a walk downstairs and buy her a cup of coffee on the pier, okay? I'll catch up."

"Okay, Gid." I turned to the girl behind the desk. She smiled nervously. I said, "Will you come with me, Miss?" She nodded and stood up and grabbed her hat and purse as quickly as a shortstop. I held the door open for her. The volcano was about to go active. I knew it and the girl knew it. So did Pinky Davis. His eyes were big and white and brittle with fear. I hurried after the secretary down the stairs. She was flying. When Kilauea blows it's best to get the hell out and go as far away as you can. As I rounded the first bend in the staircase down, I heard furniture break. I cringed for Pinky but I felt a little lighter knowing that someone was finally having a worse morning than I was.

I bought the girl a cup of coffee like I promised I would and we strolled along Piers 13 and 14 where the *Lurline* usually tied up. The passenger liner wasn't there that morning so we could see the tugs and fireboats across the still green water at Pier 15. Once Phyllis relaxed, she opened up to me about how uncouth Pinky was and how he was always slapping her okole. I got about twenty minutes worth of stories about Pinky making passes at her and buying her presents after she got sore about it, when I saw the mountain in his fedora shuffle toward us from the makai end of the pier. The volcano was dormant again, as if the eruption never happened. Gid thanked Phyllis for her patience and apologized for the inconvenience and urged her to go back up the tower and help Pinky "clean up." She said goodbye and strolled away at a leisurely pace.

Gid looked about the same as he had before we went up the tower, except that he had a pocket handkerchief wrapped around his knuckles.

"That must've been some conversation," I said. I looked at his hand.

"The chairs are solid koa," he remarked indifferently. He lit a new cigarette, puffed slowly, and trotted out the fruits of his labor. "The *Hinalea* hasn't left the harbor in a month," he said. "She berths at Pier 23 or Pier 36 depending on the space available at 36. Sometimes barges unlade at 36 so the *Hinalea* has to move to 23. She has a regular crew of three. One is already alibied—the engineer is merchant marine trained and splits his time between the *Hinalea* and the *Lihue Princess*, one of Billings' larger cargo vessels. He's been at sea for nearly a month with the *Princess*. Here's the other two. I called Delilah and had her look up their records." His non-wrapped hand held a slip of paper torn from his notepad. In Gid's crisp, even, machine-like handwriting were written two names and addresses.

"Thanks, Gid," I said. I put a Lucky Strike in my mouth and looked at the names. Woodrow Kalani Tyler, 58 years old, was the *Hinalea*'s skipper. Tyler lived on Date Street in Moiliili and had spent thirty years in the employ of the Billings Trust's various maritime concerns. He had a clean record but according to Pinky, Tyler had a fondness for drink and had run a vessel aground on a reef about ten years ago. Billings Shipping had retained him, though, and he hadn't had an incident since.

The other name I recognized. Samson Kainoa Makuakane was two years older than me and was once a halfback on one of McKinley's near-championship teams. He ran with a tough crowd but was good to his teammates. I was one of them. Sam Makuakane was the *Hinalea*'s mate and he had a rap sheet as long as Jack's inseam, though mostly misdemeanors like petty theft, drunk and disorderly, and disturbing the peace. Sam once did a six-month stretch at Territorial Prison for misdemeanor assault, probably the most serious of his charges. The court reduced his sentence from a year for good behavior. If my memory served me correctly, on the playing field, Sam's idea of good behavior was spitting in an opposing defender's face instead of punching it. Though this earned him the coach's wrath, it endeared him to his teammates—me included. Sam sent a Punahou linebacker to the hospital for a late hit on me out of bounds. I broke my arm, but the Punahou guy got a lot worse. Coach said it cost us the game and the championship; I couldn't play after my injury and the referee ejected Sam so we were two men short in the final quarter. But the incident solidified Sam Makuakane as a hero in my mind and those of my teammates. Sam also supplied our booze in high school. I remembered the taste of the gin from his dad's liquor cabinet those nights I used to sneak into Millie's bedroom window. Sam lived in Papakolea, no doubt in the same house he grew up in or very close to it.

I lit the Lucky Strike hanging from my mouth. Gid was staring out over the water at the fireboats. The air hung heavy and moist and hot around us and smelled like a tide pool with a barrel of crude oil dumped into it.

"What did you do to Pinky?" I asked, more out of curiosity than out of concern for the harbormaster.

"Nothing," he said. He continued to stare at the fireboats with his cowboy squint. "I messed up his office a little and gave him a friendly reminder."

"About what?"

"About conflict of interest. He's a duly appointed official of the Territory of Hawaii and he's also on the Billings Shipping payroll. That's

Federal time. Alcatraz. No Primo or pretty girls with flowers in their hair on *that* rock."

"So he gave the two names."

"He didn't like it, but he gave." Gid smiled a little smile under his fedora brim. Then he added, "I also reminded him to tell my cousin Ethel and my Aunty Hoku that I had some stuff from our lo'i patch for them and that I'd bring it by on Sunday."

"If you can't count on family, whom can you count on? Shall we go visiting?" I held the pad page up with the two names on it.

"Coffee first," said Gid.

20

After stopping at the Nuuanu Avenue okazuya for a couple of paper cups of black coffee and some wax paper-wrapped cone sushi for breakfast on the run, we arrived at the Moiliili home of Woodrow Kalani Tyler, skipper of the *Hinalea*. The heat was already beginning to rise and ducking into the shade of the tiny front lanai was a welcome relief. A plump and pleasant Hawaiian woman in her fifties with long black hair shot through with silver answered the screen door of the small white house. Gid and I identified ourselves and she smiled and invited us in.

The woman introduced herself as Tyler's wife, Momi, and asked us to have a seat in the parlor while she fetched "Woody" for us; a plate of fresh-baked sugar cookies and hot coffee appeared a couple of minutes before the skipper of the *Hinalea* hobbled into the parlor with the aid of his wife.

Woody Tyler's left foot was heavily bandaged and he lowered himself into a moss green armchair with no small effort. He was an enormously fat man whose gout had been acting up over the last month. In fact, Tyler had actually been housebound for the past two weeks. His doctor, some general practitioner named Elias Chun Hoon, had been making daily house calls to check on his foot.

House calls. I almost asked Tyler for the good doctor's telephone number. Who the hell made house calls anymore?

Gid and I looked at each other. Obviously, Tyler was not our man. Gid asked him how long the *Hinalea* had been tied up at Pier 23.

Pier 23? Tyler said Sam must've moved it because the barge wasn't due at Pier 36 for another week or so. Shit.

Sam Makuakane. Over a hundred yards, two touchdowns, and a vicious retaliatory jaw breaking hit on an opposing linebacker in a one-point loss to Punahou. That cost us the championship. Sam's wrapping a chain around Millie and dumping her into the harbor was likely to cost him a lot more than that. I hoped it wasn't so.

I tried to tell myself we were just dropping in on Sam Makuakane to ask some routine questions, questions that may get us closer. But I couldn't shake the feeling that we might be walking into something else. I couldn't believe that Sam was Millie's killer. Why the hell would he do that? He probably remembered her as my high school girlfriend, but I couldn't see them moving in the same social circles at all. Millie had something of an ugly disdain for kanakas. She feared them. It was a point of contention between us; many of my friends, including Sam, were Hawaiian.

On the drive to Papakolea, Gid got on the radio then ate the last cone sushi. There were a couple of grains of rice suck to his face near the corner of his mouth. He said, "I told dispatch we were headed for Makuakane's house in Papakolea and gave them the address. Luau and Jack will be swinging by after they finish up at the prosecutor's office."

"Why the back-up, Gid? It's just an interview." He felt it, too. I tried to play it off, but Gid was more responsible than that.

"I don't know. It's the na'au, Sheik. If your ideas are right, this guy probably has something to do with the victim ending up where we found her. I just want a couple more of our own. Just to be safe."

"Okay, Gid." When Gideon Hanohano's gut told him something, it was usually wise not to ignore the impulse.

"Why not just turn around right now and get a warrant?" I asked, a gnawing nervousness building inside me.

"You're feeling it, too," said Gid, reading my mind. "But you know we're not there yet. We only just found out that he was most likely the one who's had access to the boat, that's all." Suddenly his face softened and he said, "Sheik, I know Makuakane is a friend of yours. If you like, we can turn around and get Jack to do the interview with me."

"It's okay," I told him. "Anyhow, Sam might be more willing to open up to an old teammate. We lost a championship together, remember?"

"I remember. I was at that game doing crowd control for extra cash when I was in Patrol. It was raining and all you kids were covered with mud."

"Yeah," I said, remembering. "Mud."

I made a right on Ward Avenue and the Eldorado climbed the side of Punchbowl Crater. I glanced up at the coconut palms randomly dispersed across the residential landscape like stray whiskers left over from a terrible shave with a dull razor. None of their leaves were moving. The fronds hung listless and still in the moist, thick air. My hair became damp under my hat and my collar was soaked. Gid, however, being Gid, didn't even break a sweat. He looked for all the world like it was autumn in Central Park and he hadn't uttered a word since we started our ascent up Ward Avenue.

Gid was usually silent on rides like this, but he rarely looked bothered. The frown he wore wasn't the frown of intense concentration I was used to seeing; it was the furrowed brow of worry. It made me nervous. I knew better than to ask him what was wrong, though. I knew him well enough to know all I would get out of him would be a terse "nothing" in response. It was best not to attempt any small talk when Gid was in one of his moods. I had done it before and ended up listening to my own voice get swallowed up in the long awkward silence.

We followed the contour of Punchbowl into Papakolea. The Hawaiian neighborhood was alive with activity. Shirtless boys, still too young for school, played football in the streets or threw rotten mangoes at each other or at passing cars. I hoped mine wouldn't be one of them; I just got it washed on Saturday. And I had the top down. The boys' mothers were out hanging laundry on near-invisible lines strung between mango trees; the sheets and blouses they clipped up hung motionless in the humid morning air, as starkly still as the pink paper lanterns had been the night before at the Royal Hawaiian.

Every face in the area, from the football boys to their wash-hanging moms to our own was scrunched up with irritation. The heat and humidity and the smell of overripe mangoes got into everyone's clothes and heads. All of Papakolea seemed soaked in perspiration and only the flies were having fun.

Sam Makuakane's house turned out to be a small one-bedroom cottage on the lot behind the main house that belonged to his aging aunt and uncle. The cottage might have been mistaken for a tool shed without its windows and porch. A rusted Ford truck was parked next to the cottage, its bed full of dead leaves and rotten mangoes that had fallen from an enormous tree above it. Large black flies swarmed everywhere, attracted by the sticky pungent-sweet odor of the fruit.

I parked on the street in front of the aunt and uncle's place, and Gid and I followed the two worn dirt tracks in the rough grass made by the rusted truck's tires. Though only a few yards recessed from the street, the area around the back cottage and the giant mango tree was eerily quiet, a forgotten corner of a forgotten district on a forgotten island. The sounds of the playing boys and the occasional passing automobile seemed strangely muted and very far away, as if Gid and I took some ancient footpath up the slopes of Punchbowl to some isolated heiau and we weren't twenty steps from the street. The faint buzzing of flies and mosquitoes and the occasional mynah song were really the only immediate sounds until we mounted the two board steps leading up to the tiny porch. They creaked mournfully under our weight then we could hear the faint, scratchy sound of an old radio playing Bing Crosby drifting through the screen door. The interior of the little parlor was too dark to be seen through the screen.

Gid knocked on the frame and called out, "Hello? Hello? Anybody home?"

A voice came from within, slurred: "Go away. No money. I can't buy nothing."

"We're not selling," I said. "We're looking for Sam Makuakane."

"Who're you?"

"HPD, Sam. We need to ask a few questions."

A silence of a few heartbeats followed as Bing sang about being a pig with dirt on his face. At the moment, I felt like one. The voice said, "Come inside, then. Door's open. No need take off your shoes."

Gid pushed the rickety screen door inwards. The parlor within was small and dirty. A sink and a small stove and an icebox at the far end made up a kitchen of sorts, with a doorway beyond that presumably led to a bedroom and maybe a toilet. In the space in front of the "kitchen," a plywood board supported by two overturned mandarin orange crates served as both dining and coffee table. There were a couple of small stools and an old office chair scattered about the makeshift table. A battered bookcase near the front door held bottles of cheap rye whiskey, most of them near empty; an old football trophy; and an ancient cathedral radio, the source of Bing Crosby. The trophy made me smile in spite of the strange tension in my gut.

A dirty brown sofa with several worn holes, where stuffing and a stray spring here and there burst out, sat on the opposite side of the box-and-board table against the wall. On the sofa sat a dark, muscular man in a pair of worn blue overalls and no shirt underneath. He hadn't shaved in a couple of days and his face was lined and beaten by the sun and a few intervening years, but he still looked like the halfback I played ball with all those years ago. And he still looked just as tough to tackle.

He rose from the sofa to his full height, just a couple of inches shorter than Gid. We showed him our badges and Gid introduced us. "Good Morning, Mr. Makuakane. I'm Detective Lieutenant Gideon Hanohano and this is Detective Sergeant Francis Yoshikawa."

Sam Makuakane squinted at me upon hearing my name and said, "Frankie? Frankie Yoshikawa from McKinley?"

"Yeah," I said, smiling. "How are you, Sammy? You're looking good."

Sam Makuakane extended a large, calloused hand and smiled, revealing a mouthful of crooked, chipped yellow teeth. He gripped my hand firmly and shook it enthusiastically.

"How're you, Frankie? Long time no see," he said.

"Can't complain," I told him. "What you up to these days, Sammy?"

"Ah, you know. Work when I can get it. I'm the mate on a tug. It's okay. Pay's not bad when there's work." An empty fifth on the floor near the sofa told the story of Sam's breath and his unfocused eyes.

"We just need to ask you a few questions about where you were the Friday before last."

"I was working, I think. Down at Pier 36." Sam swayed and jammed his hands in his overall pockets and widened his stance slightly to help himself keep his balance. Sweat glistened on his bare shoulders and on his forehead. The air thick was with fear. Sam's fear. And mine.

"What about at night?" I asked.

"I was here, I think."

"Were you with somebody?"

"No. Just me. Just by myself."

Gid produced Millie Miyasaki's photograph and handed it to Sam. Sam pulled his left hand out of his pocket and took the photograph with it. His thick wavy hair now looked like someone had doused it with a fire pail. Sam stared at the photograph and sniffed loudly and wetly.

I could hear him breathe through his mouth like an injured dog—or maybe it was me. A fly buzzed and hit a dirty glass pane.

"Do you know this young lady, Mr. Makuakane?" asked Gid. He watched Sam quietly. A few more heartbeats thundered in my head as Peggy Lee sang something with a vaguely Latin beat on the old radio. Sam stared at the photograph in silence but without scrutiny. He stared like the daruma on my desk. A look full of nothing.

"Yeah," he finally said. "Isn't this your girlfriend from McKinley, Frankie?"

"Yeah," I said.

Sam closed his eyes for half a lifetime and rocked back and forth like the *Hinalea* silently bobbing on the minute ripples on that windless Sunday morning. Then his eyes snapped open and he extended his hand to give Gid the photograph back, but his hand shook so badly he dropped it on the floor before Gid could grasp it. Gid slowly and painfully started kneeling to pick up the dropped photograph and said, "I'm sorry, Mr. Makuakane. Did you say you knew her or not?"

What happened next took only three seconds but strangely unfolded so slowly that the images are still clear in my mind. Sam pulled his right hand out of the pocket where it had been residing since he got off the sofa and in a deliberate motion punched it forward toward Gid with a small revolver in it. The gun roared and belched a tongue of sharp red fire from its muzzle and I saw Gid collapse sickeningly onto the makeshift table, the weight of his body knocking the board off the two crates. I felt my hand go inside my jacket and grasp the butt of the .38. It somehow came free of the shoulder holster and found its way out into the open, pointed at Sam Makuakane's broad chest. I heard Sam say, "Frankie?" and three claps of thunder ripped the thick air in the stifling, dirty parlor. Three crimson explosions from Sam's bare back sprayed the whitewashed tongue-and-groove wall behind him with gore and he was thrown back onto the sofa. The revolver fell out of his hand and went spinning across the floor toward the front door.

My heart beat in my head like thunder and my ears rang.

After what seemed like a lifetime I moved toward Sam splayed on the old brown sofa, my .38 leading the way. He was panting rapidly in short, shallow breaths. There were tears running down the sides of his face into his ears. I moved a little closer.

Sam said, "Frankie. I fucked up. Tell Lei I'm sorry I screwed up. Tell her, okay? Tell her I'm sorry."

I said, "Sam, did you dump Millie into the harbor?"

"Yeah," he gurgled. More tears.

"Who told you to do it, Sam? Who?"

"I had to do it. Please, Frankie. Tell Lei I'm sorry."

"Why, Sammy? Why did you have to do it? Who told you to do it? I know someone told you to . . ." But all Sam did was stare back at me blankly through tear-swollen eyes. The daruma's eyes. This one wouldn't spring back up, though. Sam Makuakane was down behind the line of scrimmage. Time to punt. No more answers.

I took a couple of breaths. It was hot and stuffy in that little cottage. The sharp, burnt smell of gunpowder and the metallic tang of fresh blood filled my nostrils, masking momentarily the scent of rotting mangoes and damp dirt outside the window.

Then my heart rose to my throat. "Shit," I mumbled to myself, "Gid."

I turned around.

21

I saw Gid lying on his side where the makeshift table used to be. His coat was soaked with blood. I dropped to my knees next to him and put my fingers on his thick neck. There was a pulse and he was breathing. Alive. Thank God.

Frantically, I opened his coat and looked for the wound. His shirt was warm and red, but the single source of blood appeared to be a wound to the right shoulder. The round had passed through, tearing a hole in his coat. Gid had been in the process of kneeling to pick up the photograph. Had he been standing, he may have been dead. I took my handkerchief out and applied pressure to the wound. Gid was mercifully unconscious. It could have been the shock or the pain or the blood loss, but most likely things went black for him when his head struck the plywood board that had been the surface of Sam Makuakane's little table. I cradled Gid's huge head in my left arm while continuing to apply pressure to the wound with my right hand.

My mentor lay bleeding on the dirty floor of a Papakolea shack. Gid's hunch had been right. It always was. As if on cue during that thought, I heard footsteps on the porch outside and looked up through the screen door. Jack and Luau. "Get in here!" I yelled.

The whole time from Sam pulling his revolver to Jack and Luau's arrival I seemed to be trapped in a surreal, fuzzy-hued world where every sound was distorted and muffled. Things snapped back into sharp focus and every sound became three times louder as soon as Jack burst in through the screen door with Luau on his heels. They took a second to survey the carnage in the small room and their eyes went wide when they rested on Gid's flaccid, bloody form. Jack crossed himself. Luau said, "Shit." Jack started crying.

"Gid's been shot," I yelled, hoarse with grief and shock. "He's alive but he needs help! Now! One of you get on the radio and get help!"

Luau took off and sprinted off the porch back toward the street. He was amazingly athletic and agile for a fat man. Jack gave me a hand with Gid. We moved him into a more natural position on the floor and took turns applying pressure to his wound. In a few minutes, the wail of sirens came through the screen door, piercing the thick, wet Papakolea air. The distant noise of a crowd began to build and surge beyond the front house.

Eventually, the ambulance arrived and a couple of burly young men in white uniforms stabilized Gid and took him away to the Emergency Hospital. As I watched the stretcher move to the street where the ambulance was, I could see Luau directing the chaos that ensued as a result of his radio calls. The outside street had become a zoo of prowlers, olive drab uniforms, and every resident of Papakolea standing around craning their necks.

Jack and I stood on the front porch of the dingy little cottage. The thousands of leaves on the big mango tree drooped silently, motionless in the lack of wind. We lit a couple of Lucky Strikes up and I gratefully took a couple of gulps from his hip flask. I told him what had happened that morning starting from our visit to the harbormaster to the moment he and Luau came through the screen door. When I was finished talking Jack looked at me, astonished.

"Shit," he said. "You did it, Sheik. You made the big case. You got the killer. You know what? You're not just the best dick I know. You're the best damn dick I ever heard of."

"No, Jack. It's not over."

Jack stared at me, incredulous. "Why the hell not, Sheik? Didn't the M.E. say the cause of death was drowning? You just got a deathbed confession from the guy who dumped her into the harbor. I'd say you got your man. Case closed."

"I don't think Sam Makuakane knew Millie Miyasaki very well. Someone directed him to do it. Yes, he technically killed her by dumping her unconscious body under the pier, but where's his motive? And what about Danny Boy Cadiz?"

"I don't know, Sheik. Maybe Millie looked at him the wrong way. Maybe she looked at him the right way. Maybe he was so drunk he didn't know what the hell he was doing. Who cares? Does it *really* matter, Sheik? You got his confession; you gave him justice. There won't even be a *trial*. Just your report. This is where the girl's sad story ends and you did a damn fine job, Detective."

"Someone else is responsible for this, Jack. Cadiz was trying to tell me something and died trying, and I'm pretty sure he wasn't going to tell me that Sam was the mastermind behind all this. Is that justice? Shit, Jack. All I got is a dead witness. A third one, if you count Millie and Danny Boy Cadiz. Sam could've told us who told him to throw the girl in the harbor. But he can't now. I killed him."

"Come on, Sheik. This may be as good as it gets. If you think Junior Billings was remotely within reach before this happened, now we can't touch him. We got the girl's confessed killer and possibly the only man on earth who could've fingered Junior Billings and now he can't talk. For the love of God, Sheik, put this big feather in your cap and let it lie. You deserve it." Jack looked at me with confused eyes that were a little sad, too. He patted me on the back and left me on the porch to join the mayhem on the street.

A little later, some of the brass arrived at the scene. It was a couple of majors and the assistant chief. They made me tell everything from the start, again and again. After I had finished the story for the third time, the assistant chief said, "You did good, Yoshikawa. Real good. There will be a commendation. You're a hero, Detective. We're all very proud."

I nodded numbly and managed a smile of appreciation. I excused myself and wandered into the street to my car. The paper bag that held our okazuya breakfast was still on the front seat, right where Gid had left it. All around olive drab uniforms and dicks in dark suits swarmed about like flies on the rotten mangoes in the bed of Sam Makuakane's old truck. The onlookers had settled in for the long haul, some setting up chairs in their front lawns and sipping coffee or beer like some Fourth of July picnic, the fireworks about to start. I wanted to tell them they just missed them, the show's over. What the hell was wrong with people?

I got into my Cadillac, started it up, and hit the horn twice to clear a navigable path through the sea of teeming humanity. I heard some of the olive shirts applaud as I pulled away. There he goes. Frankie "The Sheik" Yoshikawa, legendary homicide detective. He put down the man who shot his lieutenant and saved the day for all the station brass and the newspapermen and okazuya owners of the world. Let's give him a medal and free mochi.

And he still never caught the one who was really responsible for slaying his high school sweetheart and throwing her into the harbor. But who cares? Three cheers for The Sheik. Another piece of bronze to go with his Purple Heart. His picture in the papers—not just Ellen's *Record* or the *Hochi*, but the *Star-Bulletin* and *Advertiser*. The spiffy young man in his olive drab uniform shaking hands with the Governor. A dozen plumeria and carnation leis around his neck like the winner of the Kentucky Derby. He is blinded by the flashbulbs.

Isn't life just wonderful for me? I had braved the turbulent waters to get to the First Heaven. I should've been thrilled. I should've felt vindicated and validated and excited to be alive.

I felt like cutting my own throat.

All this backslapping and glad-handing for me while Gid lay on a gurney bleeding. I got Millie's Charon but not the one who put her on the ferry. There was a hole in the middle of me a hundred times bigger than the ones I'd made in Sam Makuakane, a hole so big that a hundred fifths of Four Roses couldn't fill it and a hundred medals couldn't cover it up.

Was this the way of things, To-san? You would say, "Shikata ga nai." It can't be helped. Bear the good and the bad with dignity. Take your commendation with gratitude and set a good example for all the warubozus in Kakaako. There is no shame in being gracious, Hide-kun.

My na'au was rising again and threatening to spill my breakfast on my lap. It was telling me that Millie deserved more from me than the tubes of Elizabeth Arden Victory Red and a half-assed excuse of an investigation. Danny Boy Cadiz deserved more for the bullet he took to the head though I barely knew him. And Gideon Hanohano, my friend and gentle teacher, deserved a hell of a lot more. If I rested on these false laurels, I'd be doing nothing more than looking the other way.

I stopped looking the other way the day that grenade found its way into our bunker. It was because I looked the other way that Wally Yoshida lost his leg. I wasn't going to have another friend lose something else because I chose to look the other way.

Na'au. I smiled a grim smile. Thanks a lot, Lieutenant.

I drove to the Emergency Hospital to look in on Gid. The doctors told me that Gid would make it once he was stabilized and that he needed to rest more than anything. They told me that as soon as they were able, they would be moving him to the Queen's Hospital that was ironically just downhill from the bloody scene of his wounding in the shadow of Punchbowl.

I got back behind the wheel and I pointed the Eldorado Diamond Head down King Street, and drove to the Sheridan Tract. It was almost one o'clock. It had been the longest morning of my life, and I was late for a lunch date.

I got out of my car and into the door of the *Honolulu Record*. A middle-aged Japanese lady in a white blouse and gray skirt sat at a black typewriter clacking away. I cleared my throat and she looked up from her typing. She looked horrified. I glanced down and saw Gid's blood all over my shirt. Oops. Sorry, ma'am. It had been that kind of a morning.

I smiled weakly at her. "Is Miss Park in?" I asked. She nodded without a word and disappeared back into the office.

About a minute later, Ellen came out front looking like a dream in her pale blue dress though her face was darkened with annoyance. "This is not the way to start a first date, Frankie Yoshikawa. An hour late is just as good as being stood up."

"Sorry, darling," I said. I opened my coat to show her the blood on my shirt. "I was delayed."

When she saw my shirt, she turned pale, her hands coming up to her mouth.

"Frankie!" she gasped. "Oh, my God! Are you okay?"

"Gid's been shot," I said.

Ellen threw her arms around me and pulled me close, rubbing my back and whispering in my ear, "Thank God you're safe. What happened?" I took in the sweet, comforting scent of her hair and perfume. I only shook my head in response. She looked up and brushed my hair at the temples with her thumbs. "Can you wait for me just a minute?" she asked. I nodded and she disappeared back into the office.

I looked out of the window next to the counter and gazed out at Sheridan Street. Beyond the whitewashed houses crowded together, beyond Tokyo High and Kakaako and Iolani Palace, Gid lay with his eyes shut, numbed into blackness by elephantine doses of morphine. I nearly lost him. I was congratulated by the brass and praised for saving Gid's life. The truth was that he really saved mine by taking that first bullet. He saved us both. Without that extra time, I could have never reacted and shot Sam Makuakane. My heart broke for Sam, too. He was my friend. I was sickened that I had to take his life. What the hell had he meant when he told me he "had to do it"?

Ellen returned with her purse, a typewriter in a brown leather case, and a cute little straw hat.

"Are you doing a little better?" she asked.

I nodded.

"Let's go," she said.

"Go where?" I asked.

"Home," she said, "first mine and then yours. I took the rest of the day off. I'm going to take care of you, Frankie Yoshikawa."

Tenderly, she slipped her hand in mine and guided me out the door and to the curb. We got into my car and drove off to the little market on the canal in Kalihi. Ellen had me come into the store and wait for her while she gathered a few things. I had a cup of tea with her mother. The tea was mild and soothing and had a floral taste.

When Ellen reappeared, she was wearing a blue sleeveless gingham blouse with white capri pants and white espadrilles. She was carrying a large basket and a small overnight bag. She said something to her mother in Korean then looked at me and said, "Let's go."

I said goodbye to Mrs. Park and thanked her for the tea. If she noticed the blood on my shirt, she hadn't said anything. Maybe she was used to the sight of blood with the occasional dispute arising out of her husband's backroom events. Maybe she was just polite. There are such people.

We took King Street all the way to Kaimuki where it became Waialae Avenue. Ellen said that she was looking forward to seeing where I lived. I offered to take her to see my desk at the station so she amended her statement and said she needed to see where I slept. Again, I offered to show her my desk at the station. Ellen laughed, then clung to my right arm and rested her head on my shoulder.

Everything had happened so suddenly that day that I had not had the opportunity to get my place cleaned up. I made a mental note to invite my sisters over. That would usually do the trick. They'd take one look at the place and kick me out while they went to work. Two Four Roses and an aku bone later, I'd return to find the Presidential Suite at the Waldorf-Astoria, minus the President. Violet once told me that what my place needed was a woman's touch—some flowers on the table or someone special's photograph in a silver frame. I think what she really meant was an empty ashtray and no socks on the floor. And nothing says, "Hey, ladies, I'm available," like a half-empty fifth of whiskey on the nightstand.

On Waialae Avenue, Ellen looked about with awe. "It's so nice here. All the houses are so new and white," she said.

"They sure are," I agreed. "Too bad I don't live in one of them."

When we arrived at my apartment, Ellen immediately took charge. She ordered me to get into the shower at once and took my bloodstained clothing away and she told me to take my time and get nice and clean because she had a lot to do. The warm water was soothing and I felt as though I could stay in there forever with it running over my head and down my back. When I felt I was sufficiently cleansed of the morning's carnage, I stepped out of the shower to find a fresh towel and a clean set of casual clothing waiting for me atop the toilet tank, the only horizontal surface in Old Chang's tiny bathroom. I dried off and pulled on the red madras plaid shirt and khakis Ellen picked out for me. I combed my hair, shaved, and brushed my teeth.

I emerged from the bathroom to find my apartment transformed. It wasn't changed in any significant way, but little touches announced that it wasn't the same place I woke up in. There were no shirts or ties hanging from the backs of dining chairs and the *Life* magazines were placed in a tidy stack near the window. In the middle of it all was a beautiful, fresh-faced Ellen with a white apron over her blue gingham blouse, sitting at my little dining table. She had prepared a couple of chicken salad sandwiches with a sliced apple and two glasses of cold milk.

Ellen complimented my apartment as we ate; she called it "modern," and I asked her if "modern" was her euphemism for "tiny." She laughed and wiped my face with a napkin every so often. I told her that she made the best chicken salad sandwich. She gave me the other half of her own sandwich and got up to wash our plates.

I stole behind her and put my arms around her. She leaned back into me. I slipped a hand into her blouse between buttons and under the silky cup of her brassiere, feeling at last her bare, sublime flesh. I kissed the nape of her exposed neck, filling my head with the scent of her. Then she turned to face me and our mouths met. She gently bit my lips. Her wet, soapy hands reached up to caress my face.

I said, "Thank you. I think I love you."

She bit my lip again and said, "I think I love you, too." I ka ʻōlelo no ke ola. *In words there is life.* We made love that was deliriously perfect. We said things to each other in short, choppy half-phrases in distorted voices. We made other less articulate sounds.

When we were finished, the effects of a sleepless night and an armed confrontation descended on me like a falling anvil from the sky. I fell into warm waters as dark and as fragrant as Ellen's tresses and settled gently at the bottom.

22

I awoke a couple of hours later to the sound of pots and pans on the stove. I wandered out of the bedroom to find Ellen dressed again, apron and all, busily preparing something that smelled spicy. I pulled on my clothes from the neat folded pile on the dining chair and lit a cigarette. Ellen walked over from the stove, took the cigarette out of my mouth, and kissed me gently. She took a drag herself and put it back in my mouth.

"You look a little more like yourself. That's good," she said.

"Thanks to you." She stood in the kitchen amid the steam from the pots hanging still and lazy in the thick kona air. She looked at me with the impossible all-consuming hope of a child under the 60-watt light of my mean little kitchen.

I drew her into me, drowning in her essence. "I guess I have a girlfriend, and not just in theory," I said into her hair.

"After what we did today, I'd better be more than just your girlfriend," she said.

"You're my goddess," I told her. "What about the part where I could tell you all my troubles? Did you really want me to do that?"

"Yes."

I sat her down on the sofa and proceeded to tell her everything, confidentiality notwithstanding. We shared a cigarette while I gave her all of the case from the start—from the Sunday morning call from Gid to my barging in to the *Record* in a bloody shirt. Ellen lay against me and listened thoughtfully. I left nothing out. I even told her about my stilted high school romance with Millie. It didn't bother me like I thought it would. What I felt for Millie in high school had nothing on what I was feeling for Ellen. It wasn't even close.

When I was done, we stayed on the sofa holding each other in silence for a moment. Then she looked up at me and shook her head.

"You've been through so much. You're so smart to have figured out everything."

"I'm not that smart. And I haven't figured out everything."

"You got the man who killed Millie. That's something, Frankie."

"Sam *technically* killed her, yes. But I think that he thought she was already dead when he threw her body in the water." We sat down to the intricate Korean meal she had been preparing for us while I napped. I learned all of the names of the various red-hot pickles and the few that didn't make you break out in a sweat. There were short ribs and soup and colorful rice cakes. It was better than the steak I had at Sternwood's and I told her so. We talked some more over dinner.

"I went back to the union hall this morning," she said between sips of the same floral tea her mother had offered me. "Everybody there was very tight-lipped. Cadiz's office mate, Kaz Sekiguchi, was particularly rude to me and stormed out when I started talking to him. He called me all kinds of nasty names and said I should just let Danny Boy rest in peace."

"Didn't I say he could use a charm school?" I sipped some tea myself, which had a curious cooling effect on the palate. "Do you think he sounded like he'd have a good reason to not want to talk about Danny Boy?" I asked.

"You mean do I think he might have been responsible? I don't know. He was so insistent on not saying anything that it may be possible. He was very upset. Then again, nobody else at the union hall would really say anything to me either. I did manage to get something out of the secretary, though."

"Oh?" I had some more kimchee and rice and washed it down with more of the floral tea. "What would that be?"

"Danny Boy has a younger brother. He's at the family house in Waipahu with an injury. Romeo Cadiz. They call him Romy. The secretary said he and Danny Boy were very close. They practically went everywhere together."

"I guess it's less than an hour to Waipahu at this time."

"You're not going anywhere, Detective. Not tonight. You rest while I finish my article. Have a drink and relax and try to forget about everything that happened today."

"Everything?" I leaned in and kissed her neck.

"Well, of course not *that*." She blushed. I did as she commanded and poured myself a drink from my diminishing bottle of Haig and Haig Pinch and sat on the sofa while she did the dishes. The air in the room was thick with humidity and her perfume and the remnants of garlic and kochoojang from our dinner. I sipped my Haig and Haig and let its warmth spread in my chest. It all happened so suddenly with her. The last person I said "I love you" to had been To-san as he lay shivering with his eyes closed in a dirty little tent on Sand Island. And he couldn't hear me. He caught pneumonia waiting in that miserable camp for his boat to California so he could begin his "relocation" at Jerome along with all the other "dangerous" Japs in Hawaii.

The crank and clack of her typewriter filled the room. She typed rhythmically and steadily. I drifted slowly and sweetly into a soft, fuzzy sleep.

Ellen shook me gently and took the glass from my hand. She was wearing one of my pajama shirts and looking at me sideways, the way she did when she was trying to read me. There wasn't much in me to read. I had dozed off. She had finished her article. She told me I could read it over breakfast and insisted I brush my teeth and shower and get into some appropriate sleepwear. I was a child again. It was nice. She had become my Beatrice, my guide in *Paradiso*, a place I was heretofore totally unfamiliar with.

While I did as I was ordered, Ellen got on the telephone and called home and said a lot of things in Korean to her mother. It sounded angry. Then again, Korean always sounded angry to me, much in the same way that Japanese always sounded worried. When she hung up, she told me that everything was fine. Ellen told her mother that she would be staying the night to watch over me and there was nothing for her to worry about. I called the Queen's Hospital and was assured by a doctor that Gid was stable and that no visitors would be allowed outside his immediate family and that he was resting. We climbed into my bed and she put her head down on me. A black wave of exhaustion engulfed me.

In the morning, I drove Ellen to the *Record*, then I began my descent into publicity hell. I found parking a couple of blocks away from the station on Nuuanu Avenue and walked into the main entrance, glancing up at the lintel as I did. It read "HONOLULU POLICE STATION" but it might as well have been inscribed with "*ABANDON ALL HOPE, YE WHO ENTER HERE*." Right. If I had *really* remembered my Dante, I would've taken the back entrance straight up to *Purgatorio*.

The whole station had become a zoo with braying creatures of all stripes released from their cages at the newspaper and radio offices. While Ellen and I were barricaded from the outside world and playing house in my apartment the day before, the brass lost no time in putting a press release together proclaiming the Miyasaki case resolved and releasing it. The desk sergeant was trying to placate them all by saying repeatedly that neither he nor anyone else had any knowledge about the case. I used his bluster as cover to sneak my way past the throng to the stairs that led to the Homicide Detail office. I pulled my hat low over my face and dared not make eye contact with anyone and moved at a brisk walk. Ellen wasn't there. She didn't have to be. She already got her exclusive the night before and was busy getting it to press for the Thursday weekly.

After making it into the Detail undetected, I was greeted by applause and backslaps. Almost all of the Department's dicks were there. Delilah threw a lei around my neck and planted a sloppy kiss on my cheek. All of them pressed me for my tale of the day before, though they had already been regaled by Jack and Luau's version. My re-telling of the shooting was brief and wooden. Jack chided me for being modest, but I felt somehow that the impromptu little hero's feast they had all planned for me was inappropriate. Gid was in the hospital and the matter, so far as I was concerned, was far from being resolved. I put a happy face on for them anyway and had a large slice of my favorite coconut cake with a steaming cup of Delilah's dirt-like coffee.

If I considered the matter to be unfinished, it was clear that the brass disagreed. One of the dicks left a morning paper on my desk. The *Advertiser* headline, based on the press release, read:

SHOOTOUT IN PAPAKOLEA; HPD GETS DROWNING VICTIM'S KILLER

Great. I was Wyatt Earp. Why the hell did newspaper guys use terms like "shootout" anyway? Nothing very Gene Autry about what had happened in that cramped, hot little parlor. No bravado or drama. Just three men scared shitless and the horrible smell of death. Jack complained that the haoles at the paper had "gypped" me by not mentioning me by name in the article; I thought it was merciful that both Gid and I were identified only as "HPD detectives." I didn't want the island knowing that the Miyasaki case was mine when I knew work still had to be done on it. I was haunted by the thought of reporters swarming Gid's bedside at Queen's. For all I knew, it was already happening and the thought sickened me. But I had read Ellen's feature piece on me while she cleaned up after breakfast and she made me seem like some kind of folk hero. Like Paul Bunyan or Momotaro or Maui the Trickster, guys who did impossible things and changed their worlds irrevocably with their deeds. When the *Record* got out that morning, I'd loom large enough. A big shadow over Kakaako. It was enough to make me drive the Eldorado through a guardrail into the harbor.

A photograph of Sam Makuakane's little cottage with the big old mango tree and the rusted Ford truck next to it accompanied the article. The photographer did a brilliant job with the late afternoon lighting. The gray-toned scene looked almost homey, like a Norman Rockwell painting minus the red-cheeked haoles, except for the cordon and the uniformed cops standing around on the porch. And a photograph could never convey the bouquet of rotting mangoes, gunpowder, and blood.

I folded the newspaper and tossed it into the wastebasket.

I smiled, nodded, and joked mechanically with the rest of the dicks during our little party with the same zeal usually reserved for telling relatives you don't see all that often what you've been up to for the past ten years. I had Gid on my mind as I ate my coconut cake, and I could tell that he was on Jack's and everyone else's, too.

I begged off hanging around any longer than I had to in the office by saying that I needed to research a few things before starting my report on the Sam Makuakane matter and that I would be dropping in on Gid before lunch. I thanked all of them for the cake and the laughs and I slipped out of the station using a side exit.

I drove back up to Papakolea to Sam Makuakane's place. I hadn't poked around the day before after the shooting. I didn't think there was a need at the time. Now that Sam was gone, I needed to try to find some answers, answers he could no longer give me. When I got there, the neighborhood had for the most part settled back into its lazy pre-incident routine, with only a few shirtless and barefoot little boys in rolled-up dungarees. They were gathered near the sidewalk watching patrolmen and lab guys move in and out of the little shack.

I walked toward the cottage, carefully dodging the over-ripe mangoes strewn about the rough lawn. In the shelter of the big tree, one extraordinarily huge purple and red mango teemed with black flies. It was almost the size of a regulation football. Just for the hell of it, I kicked it with the heel of my shoe and watched the flies scatter in a thick cloud. How thoughtless of me. All they were doing was minding their own business.

I ducked under the cordon and nodded good morning to the uniforms hanging around on the porch. They were drinking coffee out of paper cups and eating malasadas out of a pink cardboard box balanced precariously on the railing. I guess the smell of the place didn't bother them. I took a deep breath and opened the screen door.

Inside, the small dirty parlor now smelled worse than the Freitas Meats back lot had. I took the last of the Partagas cigars out of my coat pocket, bit off the end cap and lit up. The room was just as we left it the day before, thankfully minus Sam Makuakane. The old sofa where he had expired was soaked with congealed blood and the flies had taken to it like the mango I kicked outside. The wall behind the sofa was splattered with gore. I looked at my feet and saw blood on the floorboards and on the piece of plywood that was once a tabletop. More blood. Gid's blood. I thought of Bruyères and the little brick-and-plaster cottages stained the same way, though the autumn chill had made the smell somewhat less revolting. I stepped away into the back and pulled my hip flask out of my pocket and put it to my lips. The emptiness was there again, the desolation inside like all the souls of the unfaithful being whipped about in the *Inferno*. The warming salve slid down into my soul and beat back the image of Sam's resigned look just before I shot him. I choked back a sob and drowned it with another sip.

I conferred with the lab guys and the sergeant in charge of the scene, and they confirmed that there was nothing of much interest in Makuakane's rude little dwelling. The hefty Portuguese sergeant was smoking a cigar in Sam's bedroom. He complimented the pleasant smell of my Partagas and I apologized for not having one to give him. I looked down at the crate Sam had used as a nightstand. There was a full ashtray on it with a worn Bible and an old yellowing photograph in a dime store frame of two children—a dark, shirtless boy hugging a fat little girl with fair skin and dark eyes. I instantly recognized the boy as Sam by his wide grin and I remembered the girl as well, though when I knew her, she was older. Sam's younger sister. Then I remembered her name was Leilani. Lei. *Tell Lei I'm sorry*. I made a mental note to seek her out when the matter was finally put to rest and keep my promise to an old teammate and friend.

The sergeant told me that the evidence gatherers had found some hair and blood in the bed of the old pickup outside and that the lab guys would be testing the samples. I already knew they'd find it was Millie's. I thanked the sergeant and the lab guys and made my way out of Sam's cottage. I walked toward the old truck. The smell of rotting mangoes and rust were a welcome change from the carrion odor of the parlor. My Partagas was out so I stood by the truck and put a cigarette in my mouth. As I fumbled around in my pockets for the Zippo, I looked down at the leaf-strewn dirt under the mango tree. I walked closer to the bare spot that had caught my eye and kicked a few of the yellow and brown leaves aside. Tracks. Tire tracks. A familiar looking pair. The same two mismatched tires that had made a getaway arc in front of the Miyasaki house on Rycroft Street and marked the slaughterhouse lot at Freitas Meats.

The flies buzzed about in careless, airy patterns with no breeze to hinder their flight. I was already sweating under my hat and collar although it was only a little past nine in the morning. I walked to my Cadillac and started it and headed for the hospital.

White and sterile on the inside, the Queen's Hospital smelled strongly of antiseptic and faintly of the septic. It reminded me a little of the hallways at the medical examiner's office but not as cold or lifeless. After all, this wasn't the house of the dead. It was the house of the dying.

For Gid's sake, I tried not to think of that as I wandered into the little shop in the lobby that they had for folks like me who thought to visit their loved ones but didn't think to bring them anything. There were lots of folks like me, so this little shop made a killing. A tired old battle-ax of a Portuguese matron sat behind the register with blue hair and a little pair of spectacles on a faux pearl string balanced on her big red nose. She wore an engraved nametag that said AGNES and showed that she worked for The Queen's Hospital.

Agnes was flipping through the pages of a *Life* magazine and shoveling pastel Jordan almonds into her mouth like they were coal needed to get the Union Pacific from Chicago to Portland.

I looked about at the various toys, knick-knacks, candy, and bouquets in the little shop. I picked up a fluffy brown teddy bear with a pink ribbon around its neck bearing the legend: IT'S A GIRL. The bear stared expectantly at me with its little button eyes. Sorry. It just wasn't Gid. I put the bear back down and found a small white wicker basket full of yellow daisies. I gave Agnes the dollar that the little price tag on the basket said it was worth and a dime more for a pack of Wrigley's chewing gum and a Hershey's bar.

"Mahalo for your business, sir," said Agnes in a monotone. She didn't even look up from her *Life* between mouthfuls of almonds.

"Mahalo yourself," I said. I raised the sunny little basket in a salute of gratitude that went unseen.

Gid was on the second floor in a ward where the patients were demanding and the nurses tired. They dragged themselves about from room to room, making their rounds, white nylons the only things holding them up. I found Gid in a private room looking makai toward town and the harbor beyond. He was lying in a Spartan-looking bed with his enormous shoulder swaddled in bandages. Gid looked up and smiled weakly at me.

"Hi," he said. He sounded like he had been wandering around in the Mojave Desert looking for a glass of water.

"How're you doing, Gid?" I asked.

"I've been better."

"Yeah, you'll be fine. It'll take more than a pea-sized slug to bring down a mountain like you." Gid laughed his wheezing laugh that turned into hacking that wracked his body violently.

"Sorry," he rasped. "Laughing makes the damn shoulder hurt like hell."

"Then you'd better not review any of Luau's reports until it's better."

"What reports?"

It was my turn to laugh. Gid smiled and said, "Well, I guess we can close the books on the Miyasaki case. I heard you got a dying confession out of Makuakane."

"He said he threw her in the water, yeah."

"And the M.E. said cause of death was drowning, remember?"

"I remember. But . . ."

"Sheik," he said, almost tenderly, "let it go. I know all the stuff you dug up. If you dig some more, you'll only give yourself—and me—a big pain in the ass. You *know* how these things go."

"What about trusting my gut, Gid? What about *that*? How can I let it go?" I stared down at the linoleum tiles at my feet. They were white with light gray speckles, like some small bird's egg. Or like Millie's pale, mottled, bloated face. I shut my eyes for a second then opened them and looked up at Gid. He was smiling. Probably bigger than I had ever seen him smile.

"Then don't. I was just trying to give you a break. I should've known better," he said, voice like gravel in a driveway under slow moving tires.

"Here's some daisies to add to the botanical garden you're growing next to your bed." I cocked my head toward the massive collection of flowers on a table near the window, anthuriums and roses and a rainbow of fragrant blooms of all sorts from the brass and Homicide and Gid's ten thousand relatives. I set my humble offering down in the colorful jungle. I walked back to the side of the bed and held out my hand. Gid grasped it with his huge paw of a left hand and squeezed so hard it almost hurt. He was going to be fine.

"Rest up," I said. Gid lay there with a crooked smile, blinks getting longer. He forced his eyes open with some effort.

"You're the best, Sheik. The best damn detective I ever trained. The best damn detective I ever worked with. You don't have a thing to prove."

"I had the best teacher."

Gid smiled and closed his eyes.

Quietly, I made my way out of the room as the morphine claimed him once again. I walked down the hall past the tables of folded linen and the tired nurses. It was time to tie up the Millie Miyasaki matter the right way and get to the Danny Boy Cadiz matter. Taking care of one would take care of the other. Or so the na'au told me. Thanks a lot, Lieutenant.

As I traversed the lobby walking past the little store where I had bought Gid's flower basket, I saw Ruth Prentiss get into an elevator. She was wearing an expensive floral print dress with white gloves and carrying a wicker picnic hamper. She glanced at me and smiled demurely, nodding a greeting. I nodded back, forcing a smile in return. It was like seeing a ghost, one who would haunt me as long as I didn't finish this thing.

23

When I got back to the Homicide office, nobody was there. Delilah had gone down to records and everyone else hit the road. There was still half a pot of her shitty coffee now as cold as death and two slices of the coconut cake left over from the morning's little party. Gid's office was dark and lonely. I walked in and looked at the old chair and its worn leather and his desk full of files. The old green blotter on his desk was full of ink scars and little absent doodles, pictures of grotesque little cartoony faces with their eyes bugging out and their teeth gritted and their wiry hair sticking straight up. He must have drawn those little faces while he was on the telephone with the chief, listening to his inane, moronic instruction. It was his way of pulling his hair out and screaming. That was Gid, always the dormant volcano, always the serene, placid facade with a thousand emotions roiling just beneath the surface. He was cursed by having to work for men stupider than him. There weren't a lot of guys in the world with that problem but Gid would always have that problem. As long as I worked for Gideon Hanohano, I'd never have that problem.

I walked out of his office and back to my desk. Gid's office had begun to feel like the *Hinalea* or Millie Miyasaki's bedroom, and I felt sick and scared just standing in there. I tried to put it out of my head; the doctors said he would be fine. I guess it was probably seeing his blood again at Sam Makuakane's place, then seeing him lying in that bed all drugged up that brought me down. If only I were faster. If only

I had seen it coming. He'd be sitting right there in that squeaky chair reading the paper cover to cover and telling me that Liliha Bakery had custard pie again or that Alfred Apaka was going to be on national television sometime in September. I took the hip flask out of my pocket and tried to wash the feeling away.

I gave the daruma on my desk a poke and watched him spring back up and rock for a bit. I felt as empty as his eyes. Then I saw the pink message slip on my blotter. In Delilah's girly hand it said that Herb Cooper of Schuman Carriage had called while I was out. What the hell was *that* all about? I sat down and picked up the receiver and dialed the exchange. A girl with one of those clipped, metallic voices answered the phone at Schuman Carriage. She sounded like she was probably one of those pretty kanaka girls whose mom sent her to charm school in the hopes of landing a show business career, who got no closer to Hollywood than the switchboard at an automobile dealership. She probably had a lot of mascara on her lashes behind a pair of rhinestone-studded cat eye frames. She probably thought she had better things to do than talk to the likes of me and she was probably right. I asked to speak to Herb Cooper and she put me through.

Herb Cooper had a radio announcer's voice. He was not the salesman who sold me the Eldorado. "I'm the manager," he said. Booming and cheerful, he sounded as if he were giving me the exciting news about some cleanser that got stubborn stains out of the basin better than the leading brand. I cut to the chase.

"What's this about, Mr. Cooper? I'm current on my payments."

"Well, sir, I'm pleased to tell you that you won't have to worry about *that* anymore. From now on there won't be any more payments!"

"I'm sorry. What?"

"This morning your 1953 Cadillac Eldorado has been paid off."

"*Paid off*? Paid off by whom? I sure didn't. There must be some mistake . . ."

"Oh, there's no mistake, sir. Please hold the line for a moment and I'll get the message that went along with the payment."

"Sure." I lit up a Lucky Strike while I waited. During the war and in my time in HPD I had seen a good many shocking things but nothing that absolutely dumfounded me like this. I poked the daruma a couple of times and it wobbled about erratically then settled back upright. Then Cooper's booming voice came back.

"Mr. Yoshikawa? Are you there?" I said I was. He continued. "Your Cadillac was paid for in full this morning with this accompanying message: 'Thank you for a job well done. The people of the beautiful city of Honolulu are grateful and none more than myself. Your efforts have made our paradise on earth safer and we will all rest easier knowing there is one less villain out there. Harcourt Billings, Sr.'"

The Lucky Strike dropped out of my slack mouth and made a smoldering hole in my blotter. I felt disoriented and distant.

"Hello? Mr. Yoshikawa? Are you there, sir?"

"Yes . . . yes, I am," I said, recovering. "Thanks for your trouble, Mr. Cooper. But I was right. There has been a mistake." I put the receiver back in the cradle as Cooper's booming voice continued talking. The office was quiet again save for the sound of traffic filtering up from Merchant Street through the windows and the slow beating of the ceiling fan blades.

I got up and grabbed the big directory off Delilah's desk and brought it back to mine. I leafed through its pages and I picked up the receiver and dialed. I reached the Billings Trust switchboard and after five minutes or so of being bounced by the switchboard ladies from one department to another and identifying myself a dozen times I was finally put through to Harcourt Billings, Sr.'s secretary. She had a voice like the head librarian at Columbia, the one who sent out arrears notices on fees for overdue books.

"May I ask who's calling?" she said for a second time, as if she couldn't believe what she heard the first time I said it.

"Yoshikawa. Y-O-S-H-I-K-A-W-A. Francis. That's with the common spelling. I am a detective with the Honolulu Police Department."

"Is Mr. Billings expecting your call, Detective?"

"Well, not really. This is concerning . . ."

She cut me off abruptly. "I'll be happy to take a message for Mr. Billings, Detective. Could you spell your name again for me please?"

"Y-O-S . . ."

She cut me off again. "Hold the line, please." I held the line. A few seconds later a different voice came back. It was a dark, heavy voice full of authority and hidden menace. It was as silky and black and rich as the sunless depths of the ocean. It was the voice that resonated in the empty frigidity of the Ninth Circle of Hell, the voice that spoke clearly and forcefully from three mouths though they gnawed on the bodies of legendary traitors. It was the voice of Lucifer himself.

The voice said to me, "Good morning, Detective Yoshikawa. What can I do for you?"

"Good morning, Mr. Billings. You've done quite a lot for me this morning but nothing I deserve." The devil's voice laughed like distant thunder rolling in the void of death as deep and as cold as his realm.

"Hardly, Detective. You've done us all a great service."

"All the same, I can't accept your generosity. It's too much."

"Why don't we talk about this over coffee? I maintain a suite at the Blaisdell Hotel for private meetings. It's on the top floor. It's the corner suite overlooking Fort and Beretania. Could you be there in twenty minutes, Detective?"

"Sure," I said, and hung up. My stomach tightened. I pulled out the .38 and opened up the cylinder to make sure it was loaded. Not for any reason, really, except that I was scared. I had just gotten off the telephone with Lucifer and he had summoned me for an audience in Cocytus. Who wouldn't shit himself on the spot?

I grabbed my hat, went down the back stairs, and walked down Merchant Street toward Fort Street. I decided to leave the Cadillac where it was and take the stroll to the hotel. It gave me the creeps knowing that my car was tainted by Harcourt Billings, Sr.'s long touch when he reached out and paid it off. I passed all the bodies on the sidewalk as if they were ethereal specters haunting the gardens of Limbo, souls of the unenlightened. I nearly moved right through a couple of them. I stuck a cigarette in my mouth then changed my mind about it and put it in my breast pocket.

I finally reached the Blaisdell Hotel and nearly ran into Luau's massive bulk as he exited the lobby. He was stuffing the remnants of a custard tart into his face and carrying the familiar collection valise. I always suspected this is what he did with his time when he hit the road. It sure wasn't to work cases.

"I didn't know you had rounds here, too, Sheik," he said with a full mouth. "I thought I knew all the girls who worked the Blaisdell. They're all class, aren't they? Can't tell 'em from real ladies."

"Sure," I said. "I guess they feed you, too."

"What's not to love about 'em? They pay up in cash on demand and they'll do special favors as a tip." He leered and moved his hips obscenely. "Well, I got three more collections on Fort Street before Chinatown. Busy morning. Have fun collecting, Sheik." He grabbed his crotch and winked at me as he sauntered out onto the sidewalk.

"Sure," I said. If Luau wanted to believe I was a bagman for some of the brass like him, I couldn't care less. I was strangely grateful for the quick, amusing encounter with him because it took a little edge off my nerves. Not as good as a drink would have, but enough to get me to set foot in the lobby.

I made my way to its elevator. An old Japanese man with a white walrus moustache in a red drum major's jacket with black piping and brass buttons and white gloves closed the cage door and said, "Floor?"

"Four," I said, and we began our ascent, which felt a lot more like a descent, deeper into the realm of the damned. The elevator operator let me out on the top floor. I walked down the hall to the mauka end and knocked at the door.

"Come in," said the icy voice from the telephone. "It's open."

The suite was bigger and airier than I imagined it would be. Through the windows I saw the lush green wall of the Koolau Mountains, capped with low-hanging pewter clouds. The room was furnished with the same Edwardian-style furniture that had probably graced the hotel's rooms when it opened in 1912 and had probably been re-upholstered and cared for with kid gloves. The rosewood legs of the chairs and sofa shone with a deep, smoldering luster. The wallpaper was an antique gold and ivory and a genuine Tiffany lamp glowed softly on a credenza near a door that no doubt led to an adjoining bedroom. On the walls were gilt-framed photographs of Jeremiah Billings with King David Kalakaua and Queen Liliuokalani and various sugar mills and ships from four-mast schooners to four-stacked steamers.

On a high-backed chair sat a pale man with ice-blue eyes and silver hair. He was wearing a dark suit with a silk tie that must have cost as much as my car. I had seen his picture in the paper on Monday morning when he had been wearing a gleaming hard hat and was throwing a ceremonial spade of earth to the side for the camera. He smiled a frigid smile and rose from his chair, extending his pale hand. I shook it. It was cold. Not the cold of a corpse or the cold of a fish but the cold of steel like the barrel of my service rifle after it sat propped against a plaster wall in the chilly October air of Bruyères. The hand gripped like steel, too.

"Detective Sergeant Yoshikawa," he said, like a judge addressing a man condemned to the gallows. "It is an honor to make your acquaintance."

"Likewise," I responded. He motioned for me to take the other high-backed chair. The chairs were separated by a low small round table on which a silver service and two china cups and saucers sat on a tray. I sat.

"Coffee?" rumbled the low thunder.

"No thank you."

"Please don't mind if I do." He poured himself a cup from the silver pot. It smelled warm and seductive like a sultan's harem piled high with silk cushions and soft nude forms. He took a ponderous sip and looked at me.

"Both of my children have made your acquaintance this week and they both tell me you have a very impressive bearing, Detective. I can see they are correct."

"Thank you, Mr. Billings, and thank you for your . . . gesture . . . with Schuman Carriage. It was most generous and unexpected but I'm afraid I can't accept it." The cold blue eyes burned with sinister, frigid flame.

"It's not a bribe, Detective, if that's what you're thinking. It's a gift of gratitude from one citizen to another for a job well done. You see, Samson Makuakane was in my employ and I don't suppose you could imagine how very ashamed we all were to learn that one of our charges was responsible for something so heinous. It's like a bad nightmare but it's over now thanks to you." Charges. Bad children at the orphanage. That's all Sam was to him. That's all *we* were to him.

"I still can't accept it."

"Can't you? I thought your people consider it an insult to refuse a gift. Please don't insult me, Detective."

"My 'people' aren't accustomed to accepting payment for unfinished jobs. I'll make my own car payments, thank you." I rose from my seat, though it took all my strength in both legs.

"*Unfinished*? What's that supposed to mean, Detective?" I thought I caught a note of concern in his voice. It was barely noticeable, but it was there.

"It means exactly what it sounds like, Mr. Billings. I haven't completed work on that particular job. Sam Makuakane's death didn't end my investigation. It was the beginning."

The ice-blue eyes pierced me with daggers of frigid steel. He rose from his chair like the dorsal fin of a shark emerging an arm's length from your flimsy raft. Then he threw his head back and he laughed. It was a loud and evil laugh to chill your blood to freezing. The cruel winds of Cocytus blew with that laugh. He looked back at me and smiled.

"Have it your way, Detective. I don't know what more you think there is to find. Make your own payments if you wish. But if you ever change your mind, call me. We'll sit down again in this very suite and we'll have some coffee and we'll talk some more. I'll pay off that Cadillac of yours. I may buy you another, too, if that's what you want. All we need to do is understand each other."

"Sorry, Mr. Billings," I said. I put my hat back on my head and snapped the brim down in front. "My *people* are notoriously bad at understanding. You know that."

"Well," he said, extending his hand. "I have a plane to catch. Thank you for this . . . illuminating . . . discussion, Detective. I'll be seeing you."

I shook his hand. It felt even more rigid than before. "Yes," I told him. "I'll be seeing you." I walked to the door of the suite and opened it then said over my shoulder, "Have a safe trip."

"You, too," said the devil. "Stay safe and be careful. And Detective?"

"Mr. Billings?" I replied without turning to face him.

"I understand you had quite the pretty young lady in your company at the Royal Hawaiian event. Good for you. I know if I were young and had a girl like that, I'd want the very best for her. At your age, it's all about making the right decisions for your future, seeing you don't jeopardize it. Believe me, I've seen it all. One day you're on top of the world, the next . . . well . . . you're a smart guy, I can tell. I know you'll do right by yourself and the ones you love."

I didn't respond. Those last words hung like icicles in the still kona air. I shut the door behind me and went down the hall and called the elevator. I pulled my hip flask out of my pocket and nearly drained the thing. The liquor sped through my blood and my breathing slowed. What was I doing? Harcourt Billings, Sr. was in the business of many things, but making idle threats wasn't one of them.

Ellen.

What *was* I doing?

In a couple of minutes, the cage came rattling up with its operator in his monkey suit. He opened the cage door and I got in. He closed the door.

"Did you enjoy your stay?" he asked as the cage grinded its way down to the ground floor and Fort Street.

"Sure," I said. I flipped him two bits. "It was a barrel of laughs."

24

I ran for my car and made a beeline for the *Record*. I was guilty of no less than five moving violations trying to get from downtown to Sheridan Street. I didn't even bother cutting the engine when I pulled up in front of the little newspaper's offices. I burst in through the front door.

"Ellen! Ellen Park! Where is she?" I was yelling but didn't know it until I saw the reaction from the secretary sitting at the desk behind the front counter. Her eyes were big the way eyes often got when they beheld madness.

"She was supposed to be back a half hour ago," said the secretary. Then, as if to fray my nerves even more: "It's not like her to be late."

"Where . . . did . . . she . . . go?" I asked, trying to keep my voice even and level, but sounding like I was fighting off a seizure.

"I think she went to the Union Hall . . ."

I didn't stay to hear her finish; I bolted back to my car and tore down Sheridan to Kapiolani Boulevard and sped toward the Union Hall on Atkinson. My head was swimming. Though it was totally irrational, I cursed myself for letting her out of my sight that day. The three minutes it took me to get down Kapiolani to the Union Hall on Atkinson seemed like three hours. When I got there, I ran up the stairs bellowing her name. A secretary told me she had just left—some dark sedan picked her up in front of the building. The secretary said Ellen seemed surprised but got in with some hesitation. Was she headed back for the *Record*? Yes, she thought she was.

I jumped back into the Eldorado and took off back down Kapiolani for the *Record*. When I turned up Sheridan, I could see the rear end of a black Ford pull away from the curb in front of the little office building. I nearly took off after the Ford, but in a rare moment of lucidity, I thought to myself, if Ellen were in that vehicle against her will, why would it have stopped in front of her workplace?

I pulled in front of the office to catch Ellen opening the front door.

"Ellen!" I yelled. I jumped out of the Cadillac and rushed toward her.

"Frankie?"

I grabbed her and held her close. "Ellen," I said.

"Nice to see you, too," she quipped with a playfully sarcastic edge, letting me squeeze the breath out of her. Then her face went straight. "What's wrong? You're shaking."

"Who was that? The dark car?"

"That was Harriet, one of the union attorneys. She said she was headed back to her office and said she'd drop me off on the way."

"You're all right, thank God. Take the rest of the day off. Please." I felt my heart rate slow back to normal and I started sweating as I caught my breath.

"Um, okay . . . what's this about?"

I looked around, suddenly self-conscious. I forced a smile. "I'll tell you over lunch."

We got into my car and I drove Diamond Head on King Street to Moiliili. I turned right on Hausten Street and pulled up in front of The Willows, a charming little open-air restaurant of the kind where they served cocktails in tall skinny glasses with frosted plumerias etched on them and had a girl at the front who sold cigarettes and chewing gum and always wore a pikake lei like it was perpetually her birthday. I handed my keys to a bored valet and we entered the little garden of the restaurant. Strains of "Beyond the Reef" sung by a trio of big ladies in matching muumuus and white carnation leis came drifting through the lauhala fronds. We were seated in the large verandah overlooking the pond. The water was as still as glass and the pearl white and fire-orange fish slowly meandered back and forth in the shade of the awning as if purposely displaying themselves for us, urging us to buy something, like street peddlers flaunting their colorful wares in the ruined streets of Belvedere, Italy. Whenever I saw koi, I thought of Wally wading into his family pond with his little scoop net capturing all the dead bamboo leaves that had fallen in. Maybe he'd just have to get a net with a longer handle these days.

I made small talk, telling Ellen about the mob atmosphere at the receiving desk that morning and my visit with Gid and how his condition was improving. I dropped some chicken curry on my lapel and Ellen immediately bolted to the bar for a glass of seltzer. She dipped her linen napkin into the glass and made the stain go away. As she did so, I got to thinking that I could really use a girl full of little magic tricks like that to make my world a sunnier place. I was tired of turning to a bottle of scotch to do the same thing because it wasn't really doing the same thing. Then I shuddered, thinking about how I almost lost her before I really had her.

When my lapel had been sufficiently restored to its pre-curry condition, Ellen came back to what she called my "bizarre behavior" when I collected her in front of the *Record.* I told her about my morning meeting with Harcourt Billings, Sr. at the Blaisdell Hotel and his last words.

"It's over, darling," I said. "I'm dropping the matter right now."

"No! You can't!" she retorted, indignant. "I won't let you."

"I won't put you in danger. I can't. I love you."

Ellen threw her arms around me and kissed me gently on the cheek. "I love you, too. But you can't stop now, Frankie Yoshikawa. If you do, we're through."

"I won't risk you just so you can get your story."

"This isn't about my story. It's about you. I *know* you. I've known you from the start. You can't walk away from this. That's who you really are, Frankie. Even if you tell the world you don't care. I know you do, and it will destroy you if you let this go. That's why I fell for you."

"Really?"

"Well, that, and I'm a sucker for the moustache. It makes you look like Clark Gable when you smile."

"And because I'm so charming, too?"

"Don't push your luck, Detective."

I thought about what she had just said, but I didn't think too long. She was right. I had to finish this thing. If I didn't, she'd never respect me. And I wouldn't respect me, either. If she knew me from the start, then I knew her, too. From the start. That stubborn little reporter in the stairwell who wouldn't quit. Why the hell had I ever thought that she'd let me quit?

"Okay, darling. But you do as I say until it's over. I will not have you cavorting about town as an easy target for Billings' hired friends. You will do your interviews by telephone from a safe place. You will not show yourself unless it's in my company. Agreed?"

Ellen made a face. "I have a job to do, *Detective*, just like you. You can't keep me caged up just because Harcourt Billings, Sr. made some veiled threats. I'm not afraid."

"I am."

"Of *what*?" Ellen's voice was strained. She thought I was ordering her about.

"Of losing you. I thought I lost you today and I didn't want to live."

"Oh," she said, suddenly subdued. She smiled a little under her bowed head.

"Are we agreed, then?"

"Yes."

We finished our lunch and she told me about her morning. She got her story to press and got herself a handsome raise to $125 a month, which was a big deal considering the *Record*'s meager budget. By the time she left for the Union Hall, she had already taken calls from as far away as Waialua about me. I figured that this gave me a day more of working the matter and the Cadiz case before the whole island knew who I was.

Our waiter, a low-key Filipino with pomaded hair and a sufficiently obsequious personality, came around after our post-dessert cigarette with the check. Ellen and I had developed a habit of sharing each other's dishes, which I think secretly annoyed him. I left him a large tip and a full ashtray.

As I drove back toward downtown, I thought of Gid lying in his hospital bed with nothing to do but lie there. Something was wrong with *that* picture. He wouldn't just lie there. Not Gid. He'd do what he could. Read the paper. Cover to cover. Then I laughed quietly to myself. Knowledge is options. He was still guiding the case even from his back. I asked Ellen if she was still familiar with the photograph morgues at the *Advertiser* where she started her newspaper career.

"Like the back of my hand," she said. "Who do you think put all those pictures back after everybody pulled them out of the files?"

"How would you like to visit your old stomping grounds and show me around those files?"

"Looking for something specific?"

"Society photographs."

"What for?"

"Some of the guests at the Roman Holiday Foundation ball at the Royal Hawaiian. Do you have the time? I was hoping to catch Cadiz and someone in a picture there."

"Let's go," she said.

I pulled up in front of the *Advertiser*'s building on Kapiolani Boulevard. The old green edifice housed the newspaper's offices and their enormous printing presses. We went up the short flight of concrete stairs past the potted palms into the building. Ellen led me straight to the archives where the photograph morgue was housed and we went to work poring over some glossies.

The Advertiser archives were at least air conditioned and well lit. There were only two other people in the photograph morgue that morning—a naval officer in a khaki uniform looking at old Pearl Harbor stuff and a spinsterish Pake lady in a starched blouse and severe skirt. Her hair was pulled back so tightly it looked like it was painted onto her skull. She was probably the self-appointed historian in some local Chinese society on Vineyard Boulevard. Both seemed engrossed in their own tasks and neither acknowledged us as we entered.

The files we settled down with came out of the society section. These were party and opening night snapshots of local kanaka performers and the occasional Hollywood type—I counted one of John Wayne, one of Frank Sinatra, and two of Jane Russell. The photographs were of these people on the beach or sitting in director's chairs on the set of some motion picture or getting off some airplane with big fat carnation lei around their necks, with a scattering of pictures of local politicians in happy-go-lucky poses with their wives all martinied up in pillbox hats.

Then we started finding the pictures of the Billings family: Harcourt Billings, Sr. with the Governor of the Territory at some ship's christening; Harcourt, Sr. and Harcourt, Jr. at some charity golf tournament at the Nuuanu Country Club, Senior with his arm around Junior, both of them wearing big, fake smiles and those sleeveless, V-neck golf sweaters with goofy designs on them; another of Senior, Junior, and Peg at some admiral's daughter's wedding reception. One happy family. The photographs of the Roman Holiday Foundation attendees turned out to be useless; they only featured mainland celebrities and no stray people in the background.

"Frankie," Ellen whispered. Her eyes were big behind her big lenses. "You have to see this."

She handed me a picture of Red Peg shaking hands with Jack Hall, the labor leader and one of the "Hawaii Seven" defendants. When I looked at Peg's hand grasping Hall's, I thought of her stevedore-like grip from the other night at the Royal Hawaiian. I looked at the hands more closely. It hit me like a sledgehammer to the face. There, around Peg's wrist, her hand engulfed by Hall's, was a bracelet chock full of diamonds. The photograph was about a year old.

Junior wasn't Millie's last date.

Peg was.

25

I asked Ellen if she had somewhere safe I could take her until I could get her for dinner after I did the things I suddenly needed to do. She told me to take her home, to her parents' Kapalama store. I took her there.

"Are you sure? It's the first place Billings' thugs will look if they don't find you at the *Record*."

"Daddy keeps a loaded automatic behind the counter under the register. And I know how to use it."

"Pardon me, Annie Oakley. Home it is, then. And remember, don't you set foot outside until I come to get you."

"Cross my heart, Detective."

I lingered for a moment as she moved toward the door.

"What are you waiting for?" she asked. "We both have a lot of work to do."

"Aren't you going to kiss me?"

"This is technically our first date, Frankie Yoshikawa. I told you I never kiss on the first date."

"What about last night? And the night before?"

"Those weren't dates, remember?" She ran to the door of the house and opened it then turned and blew me a kiss. "Don't worry. You can take me to dinner tonight and that will be our second date. You'll get your kiss—and my own investigative findings—then." She hurried inside and left me on the sidewalk, sweating. I got into my car and drove back toward town again.

I knew where Millie Miyasaki had died. Sam Makuakane was just an accomplice who got rid of the evidence but in fact ended up inadvertently killing her. I needed to think about *where* her would-be killer thought she had died. If she was alive and well when she departed Sternwood's and was incapacitated by the time she was taken to the *Hinalea* at Pier 36 for her final journey to Pier 23, then she received her blow to the head somewhere between the two. I thought about something I had seen at the Sheridan Tract house. Something I had also seen outside of Sam Makuakane's shack in Papakolea and at the sausage factory where Danny Boy Cadiz had bought it. It was time to enlist some help from the family.

I drove down Punchbowl Street makai from the hospital and hung a right on Queen Street into Kakaako. I pulled up in front of the Konishi Radiator Shop on Halekauwila Street. It was a small, cramped dirt lot filled with automobiles of all kinds awaiting work. A large work area under a corrugated tin roof housed three vehicles that were currently being worked on, hoods up like dental patients with their mouths open waiting for the drill. The work area was immediately adjacent to a once white house, its walls long gray with soot and grime. Two young, skinny Japanese guys in oily blue coveralls with dirty red bandanas hanging out of their rear pockets leaned idly against one of the vehicles, smoking. I got out of my car and walked up to them.

"Morning Jimmy, Howard. Where's Masa?"

The two of them smiled and waved and pointed to the back of the shop. I walked past the cars with their open hoods and found my brother-in-law Masaichi Konishi's feet under a stripped-down '32 Ford. I called to him and he came sliding out from under his coveted Deuce Coupe. He sat up and showed me a white, toothy grin in his near-black-with-grime face.

"Did you come to arrest those two vagrants in front?"

"Come on, Masa. You work those guys too hard. I almost never see them get a break."

Masa laughed and wiped his forehead with his own blackened bandana. "Don't tell me you're already having problems with that brand-new Cadillac of yours."

"The car's still okay for now. I actually came to see if I could borrow your bookkeeper for a little while this morning."

"You'd be doing me a favor. Your sister's been on me all morning long to get those jobs out and quit working on my Deuce Coupe. I already told her I've got to get it ready for racing on Saturday. Go on inside. She's doing invoices, but I'm warning you, she's not in a good mood."

I smiled and nodded sympathetically to my brother-in-law, then went up the steps leading to the side door to the kitchen. I took my shoes off and pushed the screen door open to find Violet sitting at the dining table with her bifocals balanced on her nose, sorting out several carbons into neat stacks by date and client. Old Grouchy Face. She looked up at me and said without smiling, "Oh, hi."

"Take a break, Vi. Come ride with me. I need your help."

My eldest sister looked at me over her glasses like I was some outer space invader out of Buck Rogers and said, "*What*?"

"I said I need you to come with me. I need your help. We won't be gone long."

"Help with what, Frankie? I'm busy here. Was this Masa's idea? He's going to get it. He'd better be working on jobs for paying customers and not his hot rod. What was he doing out there?"

"I don't know," I lied. "Come on, Vi. This isn't a joke. This is work stuff. *Please*?"

My sister let out a long, guilt-inducing sigh and said, "Okay, but I have to be back in an hour. Where are we going?"

"Sheridan Tract. Let's go."

"Wait. I can't go like *this*." Violet was wearing a frumpy housedress with a pink cardigan sweater. She got "chilly" in the morning and evening, even in kona weather. I rolled my eyes.

"You look fine, Vi. I just need you to take a look at something. We're not going to see anybody."

"We'd better not, stupid."

"I promise."

Twenty minutes later, after my sister's "couple of minutes" to fix herself up, we got into my car. Masa gave me a surreptitious look that said *keep her out as long as you can* and told us to have a nice time. I passed a few warehouses heading mauka until I hit Kapiolani Boulevard and hung a right before my sister started speaking.

"Nice car. First time *I* get to ride in it. The kids said it was nice."

"Well, you're always welcome to come along for our Sunday evening spin. Even Ka-san can come if she wants."

"Oh."

Violet sat there and looked out at the passing warehouses and storefronts on Kapiolani. She wore the same stern look, frozen from the time we were kids. I referred to her as Old Grouchy Face behind her back, but never to her face. Old Grouchy Face was the enforcer growing up when To-san and Ka-san were in the shop, too busy to deal with my antics. She was only nine years older than me but was more of a parent to me growing up than a sibling. My other sisters and I fought like cats and dogs, but not with Old Grouchy Face. In a lot of ways, I feared her scolding and lectures in English more than I feared the stern, spare, shame-inducing admonishments in Japanese from my parents. Violet was a lot louder and a lot scarier. And she hit. Hard.

The sky was mottled with scattered clouds and the breeze was somewhere on the other side of the world. On the streets of Sheridan Tract, steamy air hung about the lanai and front yards like a shroud. I pulled up in front of the house next door to the Miyasaki place and we got out of the Eldorado. Violet had her arms crossed in front of her chest and her chin tucked into her lace collar, like she was standing on a glacier. She even shivered a little.

"Come on, Vi," I snarled through gritted teeth. My sister looked about the neighborhood, self-conscious, as if some newspaper photographer was going to jump out of a mock orange hedge and snap a few pictures of her when her hair wasn't cooperating. I shook my head and grabbed her by the wrist and pulled her to the spot where I parked on Monday when I first came to call on the Miyasakis.

There they were. The skid marks I had seen while sitting in my car listening to Ayako Miyasaki wail and thinking of Wally. The same tracks that were in the dirt near the mango tree next to Sam's little cottage in Papakolea and in the back lot of Freitas Meats in Kalihi. I pulled Violet to the spot near the curb and pointed at the dark track.

"See that, Vi?"

"What, the mark?"

"Yeah."

"You dragged me over here to look at a mark on the road?"

"Come on, Vi. Nobody knows more than you about this stuff. What kind of tire left that mark?"

My sister squatted on her haunches the way Ka-san used to when she pulled weeds out of her little vegetable garden. She pulled her bifocals out and looked. She stood up after two seconds had gone by.

"Goodyear."

I smiled. I knew my big sister would come through. "What kind of car was it?"

"What do you mean 'what kind of car?' Lots of cars have this kind of tire. I can't tell by just one track."

"You mean you could tell if there were two?"

"There's another one? Why didn't you say so, stupid?"

I pointed it out to her. Violet demanded a tape measure, so I went back to the Eldorado and got one out of the glove compartment. She took a couple of measurements and told me to write down the numbers.

"Hmm," mumbled my sister.

"What?"

"The other tire is a B.F. Goodrich. And it's almost bald."

"Well?" I asked in anticipation.

"Well what? I have to take this back and look up the numbers. How important is this?"

"Very."

"Call me tonight after dinner. I'll get Masa to help, too."

"You know what, Vi? You're my favorite sister." I hugged Violet.

"I know," she said. Old Grouchy Face had an invisible smile that hovered behind her scowl.

I dropped my sister off at her shop and pulled away to the sound of her yelling at her husband. I would've stuck around to defend Masa, but I had other places to go before it got too late.

A quick visit to the travel agency confirmed that Ruth Prentiss had booked the Paris round trip for Peg Billings and Millie Miyasaki. Then I returned to the station. I took a side entrance and elevator up to the second floor to avoid the swarm of newspapermen. Undoubtedly, they had all seen Ellen's article in the *Record* and now knew to be on the lookout for a Japanese plainclothesman heading up the stairs. When I reached the Detail office, Jack was already there. He was standing at his desk, playing with the yellow yo-yo and puffing away on a cigarette like a steam locomotive.

Jack looked up and said, "The Sheik comes home to roost. Did you finish your report on the Miyasaki girl?"

"Not yet. There's still more. Junior Billings doesn't have the talent of being in two places at once. He wasn't Millie's mysterious rich haole boyfriend. Peg was."

Jack looked sideways at me. "Red Peg Billings is in the eyebrow-raising business, that's for sure. You think Peg has something to do with the girl's death?" He had let the yo-yo hang at his side.

"Possibly. She was Millie's date at Sternwood's while Junior was with the busboy at the Navigators Club. She bought Millie a trip to Paris and it was her bracelet that was on the deck of the *Hinalea*."

"That's something," said Jack. "Are you sure you want to take on the Billings Trust?"

"I have to."

"It's your career, Sheik. The case is closed. Think about it."

I thought about it. I thought about Gid lying in the hospital with his shoulder wrapped up. I thought about Millie and how she never saw the end coming. I thought about the Miyasakis in their funeral-home-like parlor with the bottom out of their already empty lives. I thought about Sam Makuakane, loyal to his last breath to someone who was really responsible for the death of a girl. I thought about Danny Boy Cadiz and his desperate attempt to get information to me in his last hours. I thought about Wally Yoshida bleeding in a bunker in Italy, screaming. I thought about my father shivering under an army blanket in a tent on Sand Island waiting to die. To-san bore it with dignity to the end. I wouldn't. I'd go down swinging. Maybe the Billings Trust would lay me out for the count, but not before I gave it a black eye. Shikata ga nai? Not this time, To-san.

And I thought about a girl who wrote an article about some Japanese dick from Kakaako who made the world right by pursuing to conclusion a dead-end case that nobody was really supposed to care about. A girl who really believed I had the ability to see the right thing done. I couldn't make a liar of her.

"The time for thinking is over. There's only *doing* now," I told Jack.

"And what *are* you doing, Sheik?"

"Taking a drive out to Waipahu, to start."

"Waipahu?"

"Danny Boy Cadiz had a younger brother he was close to." Jack wound the string of his yo-yo up and started playing with it again.

"Okay, Sheik," he said. He was watching his yo-yo go down and up. "You go out to Waipahu and lean on Danny Boy's kid brother. I'll use my haole face and see what I can scare up from Red Peg herself. She's at the yacht club at some charity dinner for crippled kids. Yeah, I know. Gid taught me how to read the paper cover to cover, too. Then I'll check out that Diamond Head Marine warehouse on the sly."

"You don't have to do this, Jack." I felt like throwing my arms around him.

"Yeah, I do. For Gid. You were right, Sheik. It's not over."

"Thanks, Coach. I'll buy you breakfast tomorrow morning."

"Sternwood's?" He batted his eyelashes at me and puckered up.

"Fat chance. Try the Kau Kau Korner."

"Thanks, Big Spender."

We left the office and headed to our cars.

26

I headed out to Waipahu. The sky continued to be tinted a dull, threatening gray and the air was oppressively still and heavy. I had thrown a shotgun into the trunk to hedge my bets with some upcoming interviews. Stevedores didn't always play nice when backed into corners. I had gone through what remained of my pack of Lucky Strikes and I was sweating like Sidney Greenstreet. After getting through the initial crush of automobiles in town and wearing out my brake pads in Iwilei, the going became smooth after getting on Kamehameha Highway going out toward the ewa side of the island. I had the top down again and flew through tall green waves of sugarcane and past the occasional rusted and rotted skeleton of some long-abandoned horse cart. I listened to Sinatra on the radio then some commentary about the possible agreement between the UN and the communists about prisoners of war at Panmunjom. I thought about Ellen's brother Eddie and about how he might have been coming home soon if he were alive.

I took a two-minute break on the long drive out to the country to pull over and hack one of the thick purple stalks of sugarcane with an old cane knife of To-san's I kept in the trunk. I whittled the thick outer covering of the stalk with my Swiss Army knife to get to the juicy fiber within and cut pieces to chew. While I gnawed on the sweet cane pieces, I took swigs of lukewarm bourbon out of my pewter hip flask.

I got off Kamehameha Highway and headed into Waipahu Town, the rustic little plantation community I had vague recollections of as a very young kid. The blacktopped smokestack of the Oahu Sugar Company mill, the community's monolith, pointed up toward the dark clouds. Gid once told me that Waipahu was named for a natural spring and that his ali'i ancestors used to visit on day trips from the windward side to swim in and lounge around. When I was a kid, I never did see it. I saw just a sea of cane and the rickety tin-roofed firetraps we all lived in. The sight of the place always made my ankles itch. As a kid, I was mercilessly feasted upon by mosquitoes, just like the Undecided on the shores of the Acheron, running after their white banner. And it was appropriate, I guess. Waipahu for those who worked the cane fields was hell on Earth. We drove past Arakawa Store on Depot Road where To-san used to buy us peppermint sticks and manju. He always bought a couple of peppermint sticks for himself, stowing them in his shirt pocket for later. Arakawa's was in the process of building a huge edifice, the biggest building in Waipahu that wasn't a part of the sugar mill.

I headed into the Filipino village, which was just beyond the old Japanese village where I was born. Shirtless brown men lounged on their small porches with cigarettes hanging out of their mouths, some drinking beer and one or two absently strumming a small guitar. Women with shiny black hair in colorful housedresses hung laundry or plucked chickens and chatted animatedly with one another.

The shack that was the abode of Bonifacio Cadiz and his large family was big for the village. A lychee tree shaded the front porch and tall marunggay bushes heavy with long slender fruit and tiny blue-green leaves lined the lot's edges in a de facto fence. Chickens roamed about freely, bobbing their heads like jerky little clockwork toys and pecking for stray feed in the mushy grass. An old woman with a face as dark and lined as a bomber jacket sat in a wicker chair on the porch, smoking a Toscano. She wore an old black dress and shawl over her silver hair and regarded me with sharp, shiny eyes and smiled a smile of missing teeth when I approached her. I glanced over my shoulder. Folks everywhere were coming out of their houses and small yards to get a look at a Japanese guy in a suit. Kids had come out of nowhere to admire the shiny red Cadillac. I greeted the old lady, introduced myself, and showed her my badge. She smiled and nodded like I just handed her a church pamphlet. I asked for Romy Cadiz and she uttered one word: "Inside." I removed my shoes at the threshold and pushed through the screen door.

The air inside was thick with the pungent aroma of bagoong and green mangoes. A couple of pretty young girls with aprons over their black dresses bustled about, dusting furniture and knick-knacks on a shelf. A big picture of Jesus spreading his robes to reveal a brilliant, burning heart in his chest looked benevolently down on the parlor. It hung over a brand-new television. On a sofa opposite the television lay a lanky young man in an undershirt. His plaster-bound leg was propped up on a low rattan coffee table. He was laughing loudly at Milton Berle on the television as if I hadn't even entered the room.

"Romy Cadiz?" I asked.

"Yeah," the television viewer answered. He didn't remove his eyes from the screen and was still smiling at Berle's last one-liner.

"I'm a police detective, Mr. Cadiz," I said. Romy Cadiz continued to watch the television, but he stopped smiling. I walked over to the television and snapped it off. Romy continued to stare at the screen, watching the little white dot of light on the picture tube get smaller and smaller.

He said without looking at me, "What you like?" The two girls, probably his sisters, made a hasty exit out of the parlor but continued to peer at us surreptitiously through the kitchen door.

"I need to ask you a few questions about your brother."

"Which one? I get four of them."

"The dead one," I said. "I'm a homicide detective." Romy finally looked at me. I took out my badge.

Romy Cadiz blinked once and said, "Go to hell, Cop. I don't know nothing."

I said, "Fine. Have it your way. You can sit here in your father's parlor and answer some questions about Danny Boy or I can drag you downtown where you can sit in a cramped room with no windows, no Milton Berle, and no cigarettes, and think about how much you don't know."

I took my cuffs out. My patience was already hanging by its fingernails. "I'll carry you out so you won't have to use crutches."

"Okay!" he shouted. "What the hell is your problem? You come out here in that fancy red Caddy. You come out here wearing that suit. The whole damn world knows a cop came to see me now. I just want to lay low for a bit. I was going to stay with my sister and her family on Kauai after the funeral but now it's too late. Everybody knows you came to see me!" A brief echo of his shout hung in the heavy air then was swallowed by the humidity. He dropped his head into his hands in a gesture of despair. Something more than frustration rattled in his voice. There was the unmistakable clammy stink of dread in his talk.

A sudden frantic flapping of chicken wings and an errant squawk from outside broke the silence in the room. Romy jerked his head up in response. His eyes moved rapidly from left to right and back again then he relaxed.

"Who're you afraid of, Romy?" I asked.

Romy said nothing.

"Look, Romy," I said, "your brother told me that he needed to tell me something. Something he didn't want anyone else to hear. He told me where to meet him. Alone. When I got there he was dead. I think someone killed him because of what he was going to tell me. I don't know what Danny Boy wanted to say to me. But if you have any idea, we've got a better chance of finding who killed him."

Romy Cadiz stared at me. He took a few short rapid breaths through his mouth. He said to me, "You the cop who was working on the Japanese girl in the harbor?"

"None other."

"I thought you guys got him. The guy who killed her."

"Sort of. We got the guy who dumped her into the harbor. We didn't get who told him to do it. What did Danny Boy know about her, Romy?"

"I don't know. I'm not sure," he said. He stared at his fingernails like he just had them manicured. Then, without looking at me, he said, "He got really upset and scared when the papers talked about her on Tuesday morning. He said he probably should see the police and that he gave her something and that maybe she used what he gave her. He said if she did, they got mad and maybe that's why she's dead."

"Who're *they*, Romy?" I asked.

"I don't know. He mentioned Kaz Sekiguchi. He said Kaz said he was stupid and that he was going to get hurt if he didn't drop it. He said maybe Kaz was right, but it was too late already."

Kazuhiro Sekiguchi. He wouldn't talk to Ellen about Danny Boy. But he'd have to talk to a grand jury. Or to me.

"What happened to your leg, Romy?"

"Cargo net broke and a crate fell on it yesterday."

"A crate named Sekiguchi?"

"Something like that."

"Why?" I asked. Romy had begun to hyperventilate.

"Kaz said he was doing me a favor. He said it was time for me to have a vacation and lay low. If I had a work accident, nobody would ask questions about why I wasn't around for a while. He said things had to settle down after what happened to Danny Boy." Romy fidgeted on the sofa like a six-year-old at church. His usually bushy hair was limp with perspiration. The sharp percussion of knives on a cutting board echoed. I stood near the window and started fanning myself with my hat. I could smell the mud outside under the ti leaves.

"Sounds serious," I said. "You're sure you don't know anything about what your brother gave the girl or what he thought she would do with it?"

"I told you already. I don't know nothing. I don't want to know." Nobody said anything after that for a long time. Romy Cadiz stared at the darkened picture tube of the brand-new television as if he were watching a prizefight he bet his life savings on.

"Okay," I said. "See you around, Romy. Enjoy your vacation."

I headed toward the door. I was almost out when Romy started shouting.

"Wait! You can't just come here in that goddamn red Cadillac like a cop for the whole world to see! They'll kill me now! You gotta help me, Cop!"

"You don't know nothing, remember?" I said, turning slightly. "That means you'll be fine. Good luck with that, Romy." I put my hat on my head with added finality.

"Okay!" he screamed. His voiced cracked in a half sob. "Okay. Danny Boy was trying to get some photographs." I took my hat back off.

"Danny Boy met the girl at some party Peg Billings gave at Lau Yee Chai for the union leaders. He knew the Japanese girl was Peg's new playmate and he knew she had a taste for expensive shit but no money. He was going to give her twenty percent to get some pictures she talked about. Pictures she saw in Peg's office."

My heart started beating faster and harder until its hammering drowned everything else out. "Twenty percent of what, Romy?"

"Danny Boy was going to put the squeeze on the Billings Trust. He was talking about a hundred grand."

There it was. Blackmail. Danny Boy aimed high. Political ambitions fueled by world-class greed. And Millie had signed on for a ride on the gravy train. Peg was no more to her than I had been—a means to something she wanted. Twenty thousand dollars was a far cry from Elizabeth Arden Victory Red, but the concept was the same. I fell for it and I gave. So did Peg. I only hoped for Peg's sake the experience in bed was better.

"And that's it. That's really it. I don't know any more. Now you gotta help me, okay?"

"Who do you think is going to hurt you, Romy?"

"I . . . I don't know. Whoever it was got my brother. Kaz said lay low."

"Don't worry," I told him, "we'll take care of you. First thing tomorrow I'll send a prowler here and it'll take you to the airport. Buy your ticket to Kauai at the counter and go visit your sister for a bit. Our boys will make sure you get on the plane in one piece."

Romy Cadiz sat there. He was one of those witnesses that bled information slowly once punctured. Once they bled, though, they became self-conscious of the mess they made. They tried to stanch the flow and often they could, but the mess was already out there. There was no way to clean it up. He was afraid that someone would see the mess that he made. Maybe with good reason.

I turned and walked out through the screen door. I looked back one more time and saw a deflated balloon of a man lying flaccid on the sofa. "Thanks for the little talk, Romy. It was fun," I said without smiling. One of the girls came out of the kitchen and turned the television back on for him. Milton Berle was still cracking wise. Romy Cadiz shook and brayed but I couldn't tell if he was chuckling or sobbing.

27

The drive back into town from Waipahu was a less idyllic affair than the ride out there had been, my head still full of what Romeo Cadiz had just told me. Millie Miyasaki was as smart and as motivated as I remembered her but not as innocent. A roll in the sack for lipstick was charming in a goofy, juvenile way compared to big-time extortion. Maybe she was more motivated than smart. She bit off more than she could chew and ended up under the pier. Did she get involved in a game she didn't understand the rules of? The stakes were a lot higher than a black velvet dress and a pair of shoes. Had she underestimated the hazards of this place in her disdain for it? Honolulu may not have been the Mecca that was Paris or New York, but its sharks had just as many teeth.

The sun had started to sink and set fire to clouds as thick as mayonnaise in an okazuya tuna sandwich. The humidity asserted itself with a vengeance when I was slowed by the downtown traffic. My Cadillac moved sluggishly down King Street, past the pretty girls and homely girls, the bankers, the lawyers, the accountants, and the insurance salesmen who had all come out of their offices like potato bugs crawling out from under a moss rock when the lawn gets flooded by passing mauka showers. All of the faces were blank with fatigue and yearning to get the hell out of downtown. Exhausted by their climb up Mount Purgatory, they were done climbing for the day. I envied them all. My day wasn't over yet. My climb had many more steps before I could throw in the towel. In a handful of blocks, I was back in familiar territory.

I turned makai on Punchbowl Street and I glanced at the Territorial Office Building where Millie Miyasaki spent her days and wondered if she thought she had some kind of ticket out of her purgatory. Then I hung a left on Queen Street at the corner where a new Territorial building stood across from the old Kawaiahao Church graveyard. Another block and I was in the old neighborhood. Kakaako.

Kaz Sekiguchi lived with his parents in a dark green house with a tin roof on Coral Street. The windows had whitewashed sashes and the lawn was about two shades lighter than the house. There were red and green ti leaves all around the yard. I drove past the front yard and saw a pau hana party just starting up in the carport. I parked my car at the end of the block. I got out of the car and almost got the shotgun out of the trunk but changed my mind about it. It was Kakaako. This may have been his turf, but it was mine, too.

Three stevedore gangs' worth of bodies were crammed into the little space. You could smell the payday cash about to be lost in a craps game. The small tin-roofed space was wall-to-wall undershirts and bottles of Primo. The faces were dark and hard and full of violent mirth. Beer-fueled laughter and shouts of hope and then dismay floated out of the carport and up to the red-gold tinted clouds. A burly kanaka with a cigarette hanging jauntily out of the corner of his mouth picked out an absent tune on a koa ukulele. I strolled up the drive, loose gravel crunching under my shoes. Glistening faces turned in my direction, hot with challenge. The little ukulele song died with a final off-key note. Stevedores. The hardest working men in the islands—bodies knotted and bronzed by the merciless sun on the docks and made dangerous by years of injustice—men who had taken all they could take. They came in a variety of colors—Hawaiian brown, Japanese tan, haole red—but in one size. Large. They all stood frozen, eyes first on me then on Kaz. He finally lifted his huge head and looked at me. The giant head of Kaz Sekiguchi was red and swollen not just with drink but with a savage beating. His eyes were nearly swollen shut and he drooled out of his torn mouth where a cigarette hung, pasted to the pus on his lower lip. Someone had done a vigorous foxtrot on his face. He was pouring okolehao into paper cups for a couple of the more serious revelers. Everyone was sweating.

"What you want?" he asked, in a way that seemed not very much like a question. Someone loosened Kaz's perspiration valve a couple of clicks. His beady little eyes shifted back and forth under the swollen lids. He was breathing like a panting Labrador after a few rounds of fetch.

"I just want a quick word, Kaz," I said.

"This is a private party. On private property."

"Then step out on the street and talk to me if you're not going to invite me in," I said, and then I couldn't resist adding, "unless you're scared." I lit a cigarette and puffed while I watched him seethe.

"Fuck you, Cop," he snarled. He moved forward through the crowd of corded muscle and cigarette haze then stalked down the gravel drive toward me. The one thing I loved about apes like Kaz Sekiguchi is that they were predictable: All you had to do was call him out in front of his playmates and he'd come. I turned on my heel and led him out onto the dust of Coral Street. Crickets were starting to chirp from the grass around the ti leaf plants.

I stopped when we were about one driveway down the block. I continued to puff on my Lucky Strike and looked at him from under the snapped down brim of my porkpie hat. I was getting anxious for no reason I could understand, but I forced myself to act as if I had all the time in the world. It worked, so far as I could tell. Kaz was running out of bluster and he looked about as comfortable as a steel folding chair.

"Okay," he said. The tough in him was making a last stand before turning and running away. "What is this shit?"

"This shit," I said, "is about Danny Boy Cadiz's brains splattered all over the upholstery of his Buick Roadmaster."

"Talk, then," he said with the last drop of nonchalance left in his veins.

"What was Danny Boy Cadiz going to do with the photographs he got from Millie Miyasaki?" I asked. The sweat on Kaz's face went from hot to cold in no time flat; you could almost feel the drop in the temperature.

"I don't know nothing about no photographs," he spat. It was about as convincing as a Hotel Street dance hall girl telling you how handsome you were while eyeing up your roll of tickets.

"One more time, Kaz. Danny Boy Cadiz told me a couple of nights ago he needed to meet with me and talk about the girl in the harbor. She had some photos of the Diamond Head Marine Warehouse Number 3 and a whole lot of rice in it four years ago. The warehouse still has a lot of rice in it. I was to meet Danny Boy at that warehouse that night. I did, but he grew a hole in the head before I got there. I know that you knew something about this. Now do you tell me what you know, or do I cuff you up in front of your friends and drag your ass out of here announcing to them that you're under arrest for the murder of Danny Boy Cadiz?"

"I never kill him!"

"Save your breath for the grand jury. You can scream at them all day long about how you didn't do it. By the way, if your folks are in the house, I'm going to have to tell them I'm arresting you." I took my cuffs out. That was all it took. I found you could play nice or rough with Hawaiians, haoles, Pakes, and Portuguese, but mention you're letting his parents in on the shame and the Japanese tough guy crumbles. Every time.

"Okay. Danny Boy made a deal with Peg Billings' new little girlfriend. He met her at Lau Yee Chai and told her about his plans to run for a Territorial seat. He told her he needed something good he could bring to the press, some kind of scandal to make him look good. He had an idea about what happened in '49 and maybe who was behind it. He was telling me she could get a hold of photos she'd seen in Peg's office and he offered her twenty percent for the pictures."

"A warehouse full of rice during the strike. What did *you* know about it?"

Kaz rocked from side to side like he was holding in a desperate piss. He ran his thumbs over his fingertips at his side and bit his lower lip. I stood stock still watching him squirm. Inside I was smiling, enjoying the show. He sweat some more. The front of his undershirt was not quite as wet as Pearl Harbor.

Finally, he spoke.

"The rice was brought in from offshore by fishing boats. A few of us got paid in secret by Diamond Head Marine to unlade the rice at night at Kewalo Basin then move it in our own trucks under tarps to the warehouse. It was being sold on the black market in Chinatown at eight times the normal price."

I was thunderstruck. I remembered Ka-san and my sisters having to deal with the crooks in Chinatown just so they could have rice. They weren't alone. During the crippling six-month strike in '49, rice and toilet paper were like gold. Every local family needed the stuff to live. The Territory tried to clamp down on gouging, but in the end, it could do little to stop the illicit traffic. The demand was too great and too many were willing to get their rice at whatever the price. I remembered my sisters Violet and Daisy braving the hoodlums prowling the back alleys and gambling dens of Chinatown to rendezvous with the black-market rice dealers to get their precious rice for Ka-san and their own families. I told them not to do it. It was dangerous and expensive. I was too self-righteous to do it for them. I was still on my high horse fresh out of Columbia on the G.I. Bill so they went behind my back. I looked Kaz in the eye and it made me sick to my stomach.

"I ought to go over to the craps game in your garage and tell all your boys how you sold them out during the strike. You brought black market rice in for cash when they were starving for the right to a few more pennies an hour. Is that why you put a bullet through Danny Boy's head? Because he knew you for the piece of shit you are?"

"Don't!" he bawled.

"Why the hell not? I'd rather see them tear your miserable ass apart than throw you in a cell. You deserve as much for what you did to them. And Danny Boy."

"No!" Kaz's voice was hoarse and cracked and battered like his conscience. "No! I didn't kill him! I was his friend! I tried to warn him! I tried to warn his stupid brother, too! He wasn't going to do anything to *me*. He wanted to make a name for himself. If he couldn't get the big campaign money out of the deal, he'd bring them down. Bring down a big haole business. Make the Republicans look bad so he'd get the nod from the Democrats out in Waipahu. The Democrats are the future, he said. Watch. Next year. He wanted to ride that wave."

"What do you mean?"

"Diamond Head Marine got us to make the strike last longer. Longer than it would have. We were set to settle a couple of months in, but they got us to stretch it out while they brought more rice in for the black market. We got some extra money and free rice for our families. Danny Boy was going to put the bite on Diamond Head Marine. They were working with us through Peg Billings. She was telling us to hold out longer and giving us money. Danny Boy was using her dyke Japanese girlfriend to get proof that they were bringing in the rice then trucking it to the black market Pakes in Chinatown. They got him. They got the dyke, too. I told him he was playing with fire. I never told him I was in on it, but I told him I knew about it."

My cigarette fell out of my mouth. Kaz was sobbing. His face was slick.

"*They* got him. *They* got her. *Who* got them, Kaz?"

"I . . . I don't know. Diamond Head Marine. Billings people. Not us. We're all scared. Danny Boy would've brought them down on all of us with his goddamn games."

"And you're sure you didn't shut him up for good?" I asked.

"I didn't!" he shouted emphatically. The ukulele stopped plunking down the street at the Sekiguchi place. A lone gecko chirped a loud and mournful chirp.

"How long were you at the Royal Hawaiian, and what did you do after?"

"We stayed until midnight then we had saimin on John Ena Road before I took my girl home."

"I'll check your alibi, Kaz. If you're lying, I'll hunt you down myself." I took a clean handkerchief out of my pocket and tossed it carelessly at him. He fumbled it nervously and eventually grasped it near his knees.

"Who was the haole girl who left your office the other day before I came with Ellen Park looking for Danny Boy?"

"Ruth. Danny Boy's girlfriend." Kaz couldn't have done a better job of flooring me if he had hit me with one of his hammy fists. Danny Boy really was playing with fire.

"One last thing. Who did this to your face?" I cocked my chin toward his swollen visage.

"Cop," he said. "I thought you came back to finish the job."

"What cop?"

"A haole."

"Sergeant Morris?"

"I don't know his goddamn name."

"When?"

"This afternoon. Caught me coming out of the Union Hall."

"Why?"

"He didn't like my answers, I guess."

"Enjoy the party," I told him. "I'll tell my sister you said hello."

I walked back down Coral Street as the sky turned from red to purple. None of the stevedores in the carport so much as looked our way. The laughter was a little more subdued. Kazuhiro Sekiguchi was more than subdued. He had his own personal anchor, dragging him to the bottom. All their blood was on his hands. Millie Miyasaki's blood. Danny Boy Cadiz's blood. Sam Makuakane's blood. He didn't pull the trigger but his greed helped to bring them all to darkness. I couldn't take him down for it, but I didn't have to. He was already there. Kaz was lying in the mud of the Third Circle of Hell getting rained upon with piss and shit. The fate of the gluttonous for all eternity. He gorged himself on black market rice while his brother stevedores and their families starved to make a better life for all of them. Hypocrite. He'd get his when the Billings Trust got theirs.

Have a nice night, Kaz, if you can. Drink up and to hell with you. You deserved the beating Jack gave you.

The early evening air in Kakaako was as damp and as warm as it was anywhere else on the island but always seemed to be sprinkled with a little extra misery. Black grit went along with the moisture to stick to your face and slowly drive you crazy. There were some loose ends to be tied up, but not many. I got into my car and drove a couple of blocks to my sister's place.

The radiator shop was closed for the day but yellow light spilled out of the windows of the house it was attached to. I parked on Halekauwila Street right in front of the shop. The chain link gate to the shop was closed, but I let myself in a smaller pedestrian gate by the mailbox. A neatly trimmed mock orange hedge ran the perimeter of the yard just inside the chain link fence. It gave off a fresh and fragrant odor that belied its worn-out industrial surroundings. I stepped on the small concrete slabs shaped to look like stones that were set in the grass until I reached the stairs leading up to the front lanai. I climbed the steps and knocked on the screen door frame with the knuckles on the back of my open right hand. A six-year-old girl with her black hair in pigtails came to the screen door. She was wearing a pink dress with a lace collar.

She said, "Hi, Uncle Frankie!"

"Hello, Katie," I said to my niece. She tiptoed up to the hook and undid it with her fingertips while I removed my shoes.

"Mom! Dad! Uncle Frankie's here!" she bellowed at the top of her tiny lungs. Her two older brothers came bounding out of the kitchen in their plaid shirts and dungarees.

"Uncle Frankie!" shouted Nelson, the ten-year-old. "Can we go for a ride tonight?"

"Can we?" echoed his eight-year-old brother Stanford.

"Sorry, guys, not tonight." Their little faces fell. I think I was probably more disappointed than they were. "I came here for work, but I promise we'll go for an extra-long spin on Sunday." I reached in my pocket and pulled out a couple of bubble gum packs with baseball cards. I actually kept a couple on hand because I liked the gum. The boys shouted their thanks and ran off to tear open the wrapper to see whom they got. I found the Hershey's bar I had bought at Queen's that morning and gave it to Katie. Her face lit up and she smiled a jack-o-lantern smile without front teeth. "Better put that in the icebox for a little while," I told her. "I've been driving around all day with it in my pocket."

"Thanks, Uncle Frankie! Look, Mom!" she held the candy up for my sister to see. Violet had come out of the kitchen with her hair up in a scarf. She was holding a long pair of hashi and smelled like vegetable oil.

"I thought you were just going to call," she said.

"I was in the neighborhood. And I need to use your telephone."

"Well, sit down and eat. Masa's just finishing up."

"Thanks, but I've got to run. What did you find out about the car, Vi?"

"It could be a handful of models. Most of them Mercuries."

My blood cooled enough to send an involuntary shudder through my body. "Coupe?" I asked.

"Sure. That's one of them."

I raised my eyebrows and exhaled through my mouth. "Telephone?"

"Yeah." Violet pointed to the black telephone on a doily on a credenza next to their television. I strode over to it and picked up the receiver and dialed. I got Ellen's mother saying something in Korean on the other end. I spoke Ellen's name slowly and loudly and was rewarded by the sound of her voice momentarily.

"Frankie Yoshikawa! I was worried sick. You didn't call all afternoon."

"Sorry, darling. I've been stretched out between town and Waipahu since lunch. Maybe I can come and collect you and you can worry yourself sick sitting with me at some restaurant."

"I'm packed and waiting."

"Packed?" I smiled a smile from down in my trousers.

"Of course. I told my mom you need some looking after. I told her I'd be sleeping on your 'extra bed,' like I did last night. She even insisted that I bring some tea for you."

"That's nice of her. See you in a few minutes."

I returned the receiver to the cradle and turned to see my sister and her daughter standing cross-armed smirking at me.

"Mom says you were talking to your girlfriend, Uncle Frankie. She said she's probably too pretty and too smart to be with *you*."

I rolled my eyes at my sister, then said to my niece, "She's probably right. I'm just lucky."

28

I drove to the Park Grocery on the canal in Kalihi where Ellen was waiting for me in a white blouse through which I could faintly make out the sensuous trace of her brassiere underneath and a blue skirt with a cute little pair of blue heels. She adorned her black hair—up in her neat little business bun—with a blue bow. Her glasses were perched on her little nose. She had an overnight bag and a basket full of tea from her mother and other stuff from the store for my icebox. I lifted her up into my arms and kissed her with vigor I hadn't possessed all day. It was our second date. For the moment my fatigue vanished.

We drove through Chinatown and passed the red and gold storefronts filled with gaudy silks and dried things to be ground into cure-all tea and chickens and ducks hanging from metal hooks. We passed the empty banks and business houses along King Street and the silent Iolani Palace and the courthouse across the street. After Kawaiahao Church faded away, the storefronts became a mix of Japanese and Chinese and Portuguese proprietors of everything from dentistry to chicken feed. We passed Honolulu Stadium where I broke my arm; it was dark and quiet that night. We flew through Moiliili with its mochi stores and okazuyas and laundry hanging on lines that crisscrossed every lanai and alley.

I hadn't really noticed any of it with Ellen snuggled up against me. King Street became Waialae Avenue and before I knew it we were in Kaimuki. I pulled into my usual parking space next to Old Chang's building on 10th Avenue and put the top up on the Eldorado as soon as I was done unloading Ellen's things. I could smell the rain coming. We stowed her bag and basket in my apartment and grabbed an umbrella then we walked out to the corner of 10th and Waialae and crossed the street and strolled uphill a block to a chop suey joint where the waiters wore high mandarin collars on their necks and pomade in their hair. On a Thursday night, we practically had the place to ourselves. The only other party was an old couple with special requests for "soft" food that wouldn't be too hellish on their dentures. They argued with each other in Cantonese, no doubt over the relative "softness" of each dish. Luckily, Ellen and I still had our mouths full of real teeth and we could order anything on the menu with reckless abandon but settled instead for sweet sour something and some noodles smothered with assorted marine life. We sat together on the same side of the table the way people in love do before their relationship descends into that place filled with exhaustion, children, and contempt for one another's bad habits. We sipped black oolong tea out of little porcelain cups and complained about the slippery, blunt ivory-colored chopsticks that Pakes are so fond of. Ellen was accustomed to the slender metal rods that Koreans used and I preferred the Japanese wooden hashi with pointed ends.

Ellen filled me in on her findings. She had made a few calls from behind the register at the Park Grocery. The redhead hostess at Sternwood's confirmed that Ruth, Peg Billings' secretary, made the reservations for the night of Millie's death, not Anita, Junior Billings' secretary.

"In fact," Ellen said, "there was an implication that the staff at Sternwood's actually knew that Peg was dressed up as her brother, complete with fake moustache and all, and simply played along."

"That would certainly explain their reluctance to disclose any of it to me." I thought of Barbara's agony and Alice Honda's reticence. Ellen then told me that she spoke to the floor manager at The Liberty House and he confirmed, too, that it was Ruth, not Junior's secretary, who made the deposit to Millie's account by special draft. Then I told her about my interviews of Romy Cadiz and Kaz Sekiguchi and of the deal Millie struck with Danny Boy for the photographs. I told her that Ruth Prentiss was Danny Boy's haole girlfriend. And I told her about the black-market rice scheme that Diamond Head Marine, a Billings Trust subsidiary, was behind.

Ellen's eyes got that gleam I had grown accustomed to in such a short time. "This is big, Frankie," she said. "Bigger than a dead girl and bigger than a dead guy. You really uncovered something here. Now I know why Kaz Sekiguchi was so nasty and closed-lipped. He's got a lot to lose."

"His fellow longshoremen will crucify him." I put two Lucky Strikes in my mouth, lit them and placed one of them between Ellen's lips.

"Danny Boy may have wanted to get the word out to advance his own career, but I think it was the right thing to do. *Everyone* needs to hear about this."

"Everyone will. And you're going to tell them, darling. But you have to promise me that you'll let me handle getting the hard evidence tomorrow when I end this thing. Even at that, there's no guarantee that I'm going to. Harcourt Billings, Sr. and his daughter will do everything they can to stop us. And their everything is different from our everything. Their everything is bigger and nastier and ends people. This is the stuff that tears down empires. People have died. More may die. I won't have you in harm's way. Let me do this on my own. Promise?"

"I promise," she said. Then her eyes behind her glasses clouded with concern. "But you'd better promise me that you'll stay out of harm's way, too, Frankie Yoshikawa."

"I'll try. I may not be able to and that's the truth. Even if I manage not to get hurt, my career may be in the toilet. But either way you have a hell of a story." I laughed more heartily than I had since before Sunday. Since before we dragged Millie out of the harbor. Since before the world had changed for me by picking up this lead robe of a case and wearing it on my back all the way up Mount Purgatory.

Ellen slapped me playfully on the shoulder with an open palm. "That's not funny, Frankie Yoshikawa," she said, though she wore a tiny smile.

She put her hand on my leg and absently ran it back and forth without saying anything. The old couple slurped their congee noisily but otherwise ate in silence. A pair of the idle waiters had a seat at one of the many vacant tables and started making gau gee in a metal pan, spooning ground pork into wonton wrappers and folding them into little rectangular dumplings.

I finished up the rest of the noodles and had the sweet sour put into an oyster pail for the icebox. I paid the bill and had them throw in a pack of Choward's Violet mints and grabbed a toothpick by the register. We stepped out of the aluminum-framed glass door onto Waialae Avenue. The air was oppressively damp but the sky had yet to tear open.

When we got back, I led her to my bedroom without turning on the lights. For a blissful time, we did not speak about the case. I drifted off to sleep with her voice in my ear and I dreamed a beautiful dream of Ellen and baseball cards and bubble gum and mochi and long, hot baths in the old furo.

It couldn't last. It never does. Ellen's voice called me back from that blissful place to gray, dingy Kaimuki. She was dressed for work in a pink cashmere sweater and gray herringbone skirt. The first hint of light was beginning to filter in through the blinds. I sat bolt upright in my bed. It would all end today. The case would end. Maybe my career would, too. Not to mention my life, if I wasn't damned careful.

Ellen had already prepared breakfast for us and we ate in near silence. Ellen knew. Though apprehensive, she smiled sweetly and sipped her coffee in silence. I put on the tie she had chosen for me and we walked downstairs to the Cadillac. The rain had started and Waialae Avenue was slick like obsidian, and tailfins of a hundred different cars moved in and out of the white-gray mist. The kona storm was finally breaking. We got into the car and joined the general migration into town. More subdued than I had ever thought Ellen capable of being, her boundless energy, though not gone, manifested itself in nervous little gestures and small comments, neutral and unsure. She gripped my hand tightly, wringing all of the essence out of it.

"I need one last thing from you today," I said.

"Anything," she replied, not looking at me.

"Go to the Queen's Hospital this morning and say hello to Gid and tell him I'm ending it today."

"What?"

"Please, darling."

"Okay."

I pulled up in front of the *Record* on Sheridan Street and got out into the rain to open the passenger door. I gave Ellen a hand out of her seat and we hurried under the meager awning. She stopped suddenly and grabbed both of my coat sleeves, pulling me to her. We stood there for some time in an embrace under the poor shelter, oblivious to the rain. She was beautiful in the wet.

"I'll be waiting for you right here when it's all over today," she said in a voice loud and clear over the staccato of the falling drops. "You'd better come back to me in one piece, Frankie Yoshikawa. If you don't, we're through."

"I'll be here."

As I drove away I could see Ellen in my mirror still standing in front of the door in the rain, watching my car until she was swallowed up by the grey, wet gloom.

I hung a left on Punchbowl Street and headed into Kakaako. In a few minutes, I was on Kawaiahao Street in front of the pink house. I got out of the car and ran up to the lanai. Getting the laces off a pair of wet wingtips was a challenge.

I found Ka-san in the kitchen peeling daikon for pickling. I stopped to say hello and told her that I was only passing through. I needed something from my old room for work. She nodded. I went straight to my bedroom and found the volume I wanted in the low bookcase next to my bed. It hadn't been opened in years—my McKinley yearbook from my senior year. I found the page I was looking for and got confirmation of something I strongly suspected but wasn't sure of until I saw it on the page. I put the book back and returned to the parlor.

I peered into the kitchen where Ka-san was still peeling daikon. She finished stripping another one of the large white radishes of its tough skin and threw it into a large water-filled stockpot. I poked my head into the kitchen door.

"Bye, Ka-san. See you Sunday."

"You bringing that girl?"

"What girl?" I asked, feigning ignorance.

"The Korean girl Iris said."

"Oh. *That girl.* Yeah," I told my mother. "I was thinking I would."

My sister sure had a big mouth. All of them did when it came to news about someone else. It was already Friday. I should've known that Ka-san would've known about Ellen by Thursday morning. So much for surprises.

"She eat nishime?"

"Yeah, Ka-san. I'm pretty sure. Her family is from Korea, not Mars."

"Oh. Okay."

All such conversations with my mother went that way. All of her questions were direct and to the point. And most think that the Japanese were a subtle and tactful people. Whoever spread that rumor never met Ka-san.

I left my mother peeling daikon and drove to the station. It was just before eight o'clock. The receiving desk was not as busy as it had been on the previous mornings that week. The tiled floor in the foyer was slick with rainwater from the various shoes that tracked it in from Merchant and Bethel Streets. I didn't even have to hide as I headed straight up the stairs. There were no reporters, no photographers. Millie was yesterday's news. Just a Japanese girl who was dumped into the harbor by a tug operator in a bad mood. What a difference a day makes. Besides, they were all at the Union Hall trying to get more on the Cadiz case.

This time I went all the way to the top floor where I visited Colson Reese, a district magistrate who knew my parents well. Judge Reese was originally from Kentucky, one of those places where important men had last names for first names. Important women, too, for that matter. To-san always worked on his cars, including the big black '42 Cadillac Fleetwood he still drove. Also a circuit judge when they were short, he had the power to give me what I needed that morning. I asked him for a favor and he gave it to me, but not before asking if I really wanted it. I told him I really wanted it and he told me okay, it's my neck. Twenty minutes later, I walked out of his chambers with a warrant. I could feel the envelope, heavy with the weight of my entire career and reputation, drag me back down to the second floor.

I got into the Homicide Detail to find the place empty. I heard no noise except the sluggish ceiling fans. Though still early, where the hell was everyone? Jack? Luau? The telephone on my desk rang. Ellen.

"Gideon says hello and be careful," she said, her voice over the receiver somehow sounding as distant as Paradiso was from the Ninth Circle of Hell. "And Mabel Makuakane is in a coma, on life support. You'll never guess who's footing the bill."

"I have an idea. Thanks, darling. I'll see you soon."

"You'd better, Frankie Yoshikawa."

I put the receiver back in the cradle and sat for a moment, poking the daruma and watching it wobble about on my blotter, wondering what Jack was able to scare up the night before and what caused him to beat the crap out of Kaz Sekiguchi besides Kaz's winning personality. I wondered why Delilah wasn't sitting at her desk doing her nails.

That's when I heard it.

It came over the P.A. in a crackle. I hadn't caught the prior broadcast, which must have come out before I got up to the office.

"The officer down has been identified as Detective Sergeant John J. Morris of Homicide. Repeat: the officer down has been identified as Detective Sergeant John J. Morris of Homicide."

29

I sprinted out of the Homicide Detail office, down the tiled stairs, and nearly slipped and opened my skull on the landing. I recovered and took rapid, choppy steps the rest of the way down to the receiving desk and grabbed the first patrolman I saw by the collar.

"Jack Morris! Down! *Where*?"

The startled young flatfoot stammered, "The beat guys found him in an alley off Kekaulike and King. They thought he was a drunk until they saw the blood. Stabbed in the gut several times. Big knife. He'd been bleeding out for a while. I think they're bringing him in to the Emergency Hospital now."

I released my grip on his collar and dashed down the foyer stairs out onto Bethel Street and ran to the Emergency Hospital receiving area. In the few steps from the station to the hospital I managed to find every sidewalk puddle with my wingtips. The cuffs of my trousers were damp to mid-calf and the rain dripped off the brim of my porkpie hat. I shoved my way through the dark raincoats of the patrolmen clustered in the area and forced my way to the gurney.

"Sir . . ." the doctor started. He held his hands up to keep me at bay.

"It's okay," said a uniformed lieutenant. He slowly eased the doctor back with a forearm. "This is Yoshikawa, his partner."

The doctor nodded and stepped aside. I looked down at the gurney. The white sheet covering it was soaked dark crimson, reeking of the iron tang of a slow, steady bleeding. I could almost taste it hanging on the damp, rainy air. I grabbed the blood-crusted hand that protruded from the sheet and it squeezed back weakly.

Jack's thinning brown hair was damp with rainwater and perspiration. His breathing, rapid and shallow. His green eyes clouded over. A slow, pained smile formed on his crusted lips.

"Sheik? Is that you?" he rasped. "I can't see you but I can smell that fancy French whorehouse lemon cologne of your dad's." He laughed weakly then coughed violently, sending large, dark clots of blood up out of his mouth to slide down his grubby cheek.

"Yeah, it's me, Jack. What the hell happened?"

"He got me, Sheik. They got me. Got me good. Make sure they don't get you, pal." He coughed some more and gagged violently.

"Who? Who did this? Who's 'he,' Jack? Who's 'they'?"

"Should've let this lie, Sheik. I'm not as smart as you. I never saw this coming. I was going to get you and march into the Billings Trust, but he was smarter. They were smarter. Headed me off at the pass."

"Who?"

"One of ours. Luau."

He coughed some more and then his contorted face smoothed and went calm.

"So long, Sheik," he said. "Keep your eye on the ball. Be good."

"Jackie! Don't you go, Coach! Stay with me! *Stay*, Goddamn it!" Jack went still and quiet, and I bawled into his bloody chest. The uniformed lieutenant pulled me gently away after a moment and the doctor pulled the bloody sheet over Jack's face.

"Shit," I blubbered. I shoved the uniforms out of my way and burst back onto the rainy street. I ran out into traffic and nearly ended up on the hood of a Buick. Then I laughed suddenly. Tears. Tears for Jack. I hadn't cried out my lifetime supply after all.

I reached my Cadillac on the other side of the street, fumbled with my keys, opened my trunk, and pulled out a raincoat and the shotgun. Maybe I should've grabbed the umbrella, too, but who needs an umbrella when you've got a hat? I hung my badge from the breast pocket of my suit and pulled on the raincoat though I was already soaked. I pulled my hat low over my face against the warm kona rain. I carried the shotgun as low and as subtly as I possibly could, which was not at all. I was about as inconspicuous as a cockroach on a tray of haupia and I didn't care. Pedestrians moved aside like pigeons fluttering away before an automobile when they saw me. I felt like the Earp Brothers and Doc Holliday taking their stroll through Tombstone to the O. K. Corral but with better fitting clothes and a hell of a lot wetter. I marched down the sidewalk in front of the century-old Melcher Building where Hawaiian Dredging had their offices. Pretty young office girls and sour old bookkeepers came up to the windows to watch me walk by. I gritted my teeth and picked up the pace.

I crossed Kaahumanu Street and walked past the old Bishop Bank Building with its Italianate windows and the brownstone Bishop Estate office next door with its rough-hewn blocks, which were pretty much the same as the ones used to build the museum in Kalihi. I then crossed Fort Street and the pedestrians became thicker, like a bed of limu close to the shore. The umbrellas parted for me like the Red Sea in the Bible. That's the magic of carrying a shotgun on a crowded street. The half block to Bishop Street was interminably long and wet. I moved slowly despite a determined effort to get to my destination as quickly as possible. It was as if I were underwater, which wasn't far from the truth. Warm rain fell vertically from a pale gray sky and water cascaded from the coconut fronds down onto Bishop Street and onto my head.

After what felt like an eternity, I made it at last.

The Billings Trust Building was about a quarter of a century old and stood near the makai foot of Bishop Street, a mere couple of blocks from the harbor and Aloha Tower. It was a large, sand-colored block that looked something like an Egyptian temple without the gigantic statues and the hieroglyphics. All buildings from that time in Honolulu either looked like that or a Spanish mission, and both types were Art Deco monuments. At a distance the edifice had a Ptolemy-like look about it, though as one got closer Chinese design elements became apparent: characters for good luck and long life cast in bronze; Manchu Dynasty–inspired lamps suspended by heavy chains; mosaics of colorful island reef fish rendered in decidedly Oriental style. It was ironic, considering the Trust and the family behind it treated Orientals like slaves on their plantations.

The four-story Art Deco chunk replaced the old coral block Victorian structure that was built during the monarchy and occupied shortly after its fall by Jeremiah Billings. The old building had been a bank of modest size and was deemed too small for the purpose of housing the beating heart of the ever-growing Billings Trust. Harcourt, Sr. had the old bank razed and put the Temple of Ra in its place. It was strangely ostentatious for a man so low-key.

The lobby was a cavernous atrium with inlaid black Belgian tile on the floor in delicate lotus blossom patterns. If the outside of the building was like some huge desert temple of antiquity, the inside was the resplendent throne room of a Ming or Manchu emperor, except that it was filled with the desks of mandarins slaving away at their typewriters and telephones. A huge chandelier that hung in the void reminded me of the Empire State Building, except upside-down. The lobby seemed like the perfect place for a strange altar used to glorify the gods of a millennia-gone era—or human sacrifice. I think it was the effect the architects were trying to achieve.

I stood in the entryway under the colorful tile work, dripping. I tilted my hat up slightly and wiped the water from my face with the back of my free hand. Point of no return, the glass doors my Rubicon. I took a breath—for Gid, for Jack.

I opened the door and stepped in.

In front of all the desks in the atrium, there was a single reception desk where some cute blonde with a ginger or pikake lei around her neck probably sat and made flirty eyes at visiting big shots. She wasn't there; the desk was empty. The low koa booth to the right of it wasn't. It was full of a gorilla in a watchman's uniform. When he saw the shotgun he put down his coffee on the morning crossword puzzle that had his attention a second before. He stood up.

He was an ex-military type: haole, balding, red nose from too much booze the night before, big frame supporting a big gut, and anchors blue with age tattooed on his hairy forearms, like Popeye the Sailor Man. His gray uniform was smartly creased in all the right places with a bright tin badge on his chest and a shiny patent leather gun belt encircling his girth.

He drew himself up to full height, which was about the same as mine. He said, "What's with the artillery? This is a house of business." Then he put his hand on the butt of his revolver.

I said, "Don't. HPD Detective." I looked down at the gold badge hanging from my pocket. I dripped some more on the Belgian tile. Popeye drew his hand away from his belt and held his palms where I could see them. "I know this is a business house," I said. "I have business on the third floor."

"Do you have an appointment?"

"No. Let's call this a walk-in."

"If you don't have an appointment, I'll have to call Mrs. Prentiss upstairs before you're allowed up."

"No, you don't. I have a warrant."

Popeye eyed me disdainfully. "I don't give a shit," he said and picked up the receiver of the black telephone in his booth. He started dialing.

Before he was done, heavy footsteps came up from the side and fat fingers depressed the cradle of the telephone, ending the dialing.

"I don't think that's necessary, friend."

Popeye handed the receiver to the fat hands and they put it back into the cradle. The fat hands were attached to a fat man who looked at me and grinned.

"Luau," I said.

"How's tricks, Sheik? What're you doing here?"

"Serving a warrant and making an arrest. You?"

"You know, taking a break from making the rounds. Coffee here's good. Beats the shit out of Delilah's." He laughed thunderously, filling the atrium with his obscene noise. I watched the dingy shirt stretched over his sloppy belly shake as he did so.

It was splattered with hours-old blood.

Jack's blood.

Luau caught me looking and his hammy hand made a move for his holster. I racked the shotgun and pulled the trigger and hit the floor. The slug tore through him and swung his gun hand high and wide as he pulled the trigger. Popeye caught the bullet meant for me in his forehead.

A thick silence descended on the atrium.

In the space of a couple of heartbeats, two big men had become flaccid mounds of dead flesh on the cold tile. There was blood everywhere. I got up and wiped some of it from my face with a handkerchief. I looked at Luau's lifeless eyes staring up at the painted ceiling.

"That was for Jack, you son of a bitch," I told his bleeding corpse.

Not much time to do what I had to do. Prowlers would be there in twenty minutes, maybe a half hour tops. I got into an elevator.

The elevator was lined with mirrors that made it look like there was an army of me going to pay a call on the third floor. At that moment I thought of Ellen standing in the rain, watching my car disappear and wondering if she'd ever see it drive back to her again. I wondered the same thing.

The elevator stopped without so much as a light jerk and a bell announced my arrival on the third floor. Peg's floor and the executive offices of Diamond Head Marine. It occurred to me that she ran that particular concern of the Billings Trust. I walked down a long hall and nearly got lost in the deep blue carpet before coming to a pair of large koa double doors inlaid with more Chinese clouds and dragons in brass.

I pushed the double doors open and went in.

The reception area of Peg Billing's office was airy and full of light from the many windows along the outer wall and the overhead lamps. The illumination from outside was gray and blurry from the rain. The floor was covered with an old Tabriz carpet that sported intricate geometric patterns in blue and gold on a blood red background. Large Chinese and Korean ceramic pots in each corner housed a veritable jungle of miniature palms. Modern sofas upholstered in off-white shantung silk, and a long koa coffee table dominated the center of the room. The whole place was larger than my entire apartment and smelled like money. Lots of it.

At the opposite end of the room was a large koa desk just to the side of a koa door with a brass plate that read "MARGARET J. BILLINGS." Behind the desk was the cool brunette whom I knew to be Ruth Prentiss. She was wearing a neat Chanel outfit in black with white trim around the collar and cuffs of the jacket. She looked up at me and blinked her long lashes a couple of times.

"Good morning, Detective," she said in a voice as cool as the rain sliding down the outside of the windowpanes. "Good morning, Mrs. Prentiss," I replied. "I'm here to have a word with Miss Billings."

"She's very busy this morning. Perhaps you would like to make an appointment for early next week?"

"I'm afraid my business with her is of a more immediate nature. I'm sure she'll accommodate me." I held the shotgun loosely at waist level. The irony of speaking so politely while I was dripping rainwater and gore would have made me laugh if I could see myself.

"Why don't you join me?" I asked. She stood up slowly and opened the door behind her. I followed her in.

The opulent room looked more like a sultan's entertainment chamber than an office. The walls were lined with plush divan-style seating upholstered deep imperial purple and piled with jewel-toned pillows of silk, velvet, and damask. A Tabriz rug even larger and more ornate than the one in the reception area covered the floor with more potted palms in Korean celadon along one side. Impressively, there was an original Gauguin in a gilt frame on a wall opposite the windows, a Tahitian pastoral scene of women carrying baskets with colorful sarongs around their generous hips and flowers in their hair. Were they doing laundry? I doubted that Peg Billings ever washed anything in her entire life except her own hair. And she probably had people who did *that* for her, too.

Peg was sitting behind a desk that was more a large table than a desk. Her gold hair was up in business-like fashion and she wore a dark suit with a white blouse open at the throat. She barely looked up from the papers she was reviewing when she said, "Good morning, Detective Yoshikawa. Are you soliciting for police charities or is this a social call? Either way, I'm more accustomed to setting appointments for such things." She spoke calmly and evenly. I was no more to her than another salesman asking her to look at his wares or another suitor asking for a date.

"Good morning, Miss Billings. I regret to inform you that this is neither a charity solicitation nor a social call. I'm here on business. Police business."

"Oh?" She arched her eyebrow.

"Miss Billings," I said, "let me come straight to the point."

"By all means, Detective," she said. She hadn't bothered to look up at me. "We're both busy people."

"We are. And we're about to get busier. A few days ago, a young lady by the name of Mildred Miyasaki was found in the harbor. She had been dead for a little over a week before that."

"I know," she said. "I read the papers. I also know the killer was shot by you people and that the matter is now closed."

"Your information is half correct. The man who threw her in the water while she was unconscious was shot two days ago. I know because I shot him. He shot my lieutenant and would've killed him and me if I didn't do it. However, the matter is not yet closed. I'm going to close it. That's what I'm here for this morning."

"I'm afraid I don't understand, Detective." She continued to look at her papers but at this point she was only pretending to read them. I had her full attention despite the fact that she wouldn't look at me.

"You knew Mildred Miyasaki."

"Did I?" The shuffling of papers became ever slightly more rapid and just a touch sloppier. Her blue eyes glazed over and she seemed to fade in her seat.

"You picked up her tab at The Liberty House using your brother's name. You took her to Sternwood's dressed as your brother the night she died. You didn't really fool anybody there, but that's beside the point. You booked a trip to Paris for the both of you." The paper shuffling stopped. Peg's hands dropped to her sides and she sat staring vacantly at a spot on her desk. I watched the steely confidence drain from her face until all that was left was a mask of insecurity. Out of the corner of my eye, I saw Ruth Prentiss stand woodenly by the window, the distorted light through the rain-streaked panes casting an eerie glow on her face.

"I . . . I loved her," came a tiny voice, distant and misty and weighted with futile longing.

"I know."

"I met her at The Liberty House a couple of months ago. It was during lunch hour. She was trying perfumes at the counter and I was picking some up for myself. Chanel Number Five. It smelled like heaven on her. It's what I wear, too. I bought her a bottle on the spot." Peg smiled absently. "She was so fresh and innocent, and fine, beautiful things genuinely delighted her. They made her glow. She was more beautiful than all the beautiful things I ever gave her, inside and out. We met later that day and we talked like we had known each other for all time." It made me flinch involuntarily to hear that; most of my conversations with Millie in high school consisted of me bragging and her nodding. Scintillating it wasn't.

"Why did you use your brother's name to make a deposit to her account at The Liberty House? Why did you pretend to be him at Sternwood's?"

"Come on. I thought you were a *detective*. What rock have you been living under? The papers would have had a field day if they knew I was in love with a woman. My father would disown me and cut me off without a cent."

"You weren't willing to pay the price for true love, then. Is that how it goes?" I took a pack of cigarettes out and offered her one. She took it absently and I held the lighter out for her. Then I lit one up myself.

"My position of privilege is what would have made it possible for us to be together and I couldn't jeopardize it. Then there was the matter of Millie's parents. Do you think *they* would have understood?"

"I knew them. I can't say they would have been thrilled," I conceded.

A solitary tear made its way down Peg's cheek. She still wouldn't look up at me. I let some smoke out and continued to drip on the fancy Tabriz.

I said, "And then there's the bracelet."

"I gave it to her that night after dinner. She always admired it so. I wanted her to have it, to wear it in Paris. In Paris there are a lot of places we could be open about our feelings for each other. They call it the City of Light."

"I know." No wonder Millie hated this place. Provincial. Unenlightened. City of Darkness. Using the salad fork on the entrée and drinking from the finger bowl. Peg's eyes became dreamy and looked out the window at the rain. I said, "I found the bracelet on the deck of an old tug called the *Hinalea*. Samson Makuakane operated the boat and used it to bring her to Pier 23 where he dumped her into the harbor with an anchor chained to her body. Your family trust owns the *Hinalea* and employed Makuakane." I took the envelope out of my inside coat pocket and threw it on her desk. It came down with a sickening smack on the blotter.

"What's that?" she asked.

"It's an arrest warrant."

Peg finally looked up. Her blue eyes were rimmed with red; they were heavy with tragic loss. When she brought them up to meet mine, she did so fiercely and directly. Their intensity unnerved me. She said, "That's very clever, Detective. Millie was the one person in the world who mattered to me. Do you think I would order her death?"

"No," I said. "The warrant's not for you."

30

Ruth Prentiss stood in the fluid, dim light of the wet window with her small hands in her ridiculously large Chanel pockets and her eyes blinking rapidly. I looked Ruth up and down and said, "Chanel. You've done pretty well for yourself, Mrs. Prentiss. It looks good on you."

Ruth just stood there blinking at me, hands in her pockets and shoulders hunched like there was a chill in the room.

"My condolences, Mrs. Prentiss."

"For what?" She blinked again.

"For the murder of your boyfriend. I'm very sorry, but the question is: are *you*? Oh, yeah. You and Danny Boy Cadiz were supposed to be a *secret* item. Sorry, cat's out of the bag. You know those stevedores, such gossips, especially about themselves. Danny Boy hinted at who the haole girl he'd been running around with was, but I practically had to beat it out of Kaz Sekiguchi. So, are you?"

"What?" she asked. Another blink.

"Sorry . . . sorry he's dead. Danny Boy had something important to tell me on Tuesday night at the Royal Hawaiian. He overheard me talking to you and Miss Billings here. You saw him follow me from the lanai to the men's room. I was to meet him in the back lot of a Portuguese sausage factory in Kalihi. He kept the appointment but wasn't in any mood to chat when I got there. But you knew that, didn't you?"

"What are you talking about?"

"Okay. Be coy. It's cute and it goes with your outfit. What about the photographs?"

I took another drag from my cigarette and blew the smoke toward the Gauguin on the wall. It dissipated slowly in the recessed lights in front of the painting and made the Tahitian washerwomen look like they were toting their baskets in a fog. Nobody said anything so I kept talking.

"Let's try this again. Millie Miyasaki got a hold of some photographs. Photographs of Diamond Head Marine's Warehouse Number 3. The pictures were snapped in the midst of the stevedore dock strike of '49 and showed a lot of bags of rice. They were evidence that rice was being brought in during the strike and hauled by secret scabs and being sold on the black market. The scab who told us said Danny Boy had big plans to use those pictures to expose Miss Billings or the Billings Trust, whoever encouraged the union leadership to draw out the strike so more black-market rice could be sold."

"That's a lie!" yelled Peg. Her eyes were now aglow with ferocity. "I really wanted to help the workers! I gave them my own money to help keep their families fed while my aunts and cousins marched in those damn 'broom brigades' with the rest of the haole women! I wasn't making a cent off their suffering!"

"No, you weren't. I believe that you believed you were helping. Your father used you and your convictions to his advantage. Your money bought them a few cups of rice and cans of SPAM that may have tided them over for a week. Some of them. But your father made sure that key players could endure a half-year strike with goods he distributed through the secret scabs. You were the front, Miss Billings, but his real spokes-girl was the good Ruth Prentiss."

"You don't have to take this, Ruth," Peg said. "Tell him, Ruth. Tell him he's lying."

Ruth Prentiss stood rooted to the Tabriz, blinking. She didn't say anything.

"Ruth?" said Peg, all trace of righteous indignation gone from her voice. "Ruth? Tell me he's lying. Please?" Ruth didn't say anything. I took another drag.

"The photographs were found in Millie Miyasaki's bedroom," I said to Peg. "That's what Danny Boy wanted to talk to me about. He was to cut her in for twenty percent of whatever he could get from the Billings Trust for the pictures. Millie had expensive taste and probably wanted to pay at least some of her way through Paris. Whatever free spirit Millie had become since high school, she was still Japanese. Danny Boy would make his play by either getting a hundred grand out of the Trust to inflate his war chest or deliver the scandal to the press and the Democratic Party leadership to make sure he had their endorsement for the Territorial Legislative seat he was eyeing up in next year's elections. I think you didn't know anything about the rice. But Danny Boy didn't know that. He was warned and he was getting scared—especially after Millie ended up dead. He probably had no clue that he was very close to the real facilitator of the scheme and he shared his designs with her, which is how she found out about Millie having lifted the photographs, probably from Ruth's very own office."

Peg was hyperventilating, though quietly. Her eyes were glazed over. I looked back at Ruth. She was a statue. She ceased to be elegant to me in that moment. She was a caged reptile with its throat ballooning up and down.

"Danny Boy was shot at point blank, while he was sitting behind the wheel of his car. The only person who'd be able to get that close to him with his guard down would be his mother or his girlfriend. His mother was on a porch in Waipahu smoking a rolled leaf." The rain continued to beat the windows from outside. The tops of coconut palms drooped in the gloom beyond the glass. I was dripping less. Nobody said anything; nobody even breathed. So I continued. "There were tire tracks in the Freitas Meats lot. One Goodyear and one B.F. Goodrich—almost bald. Those tracks were in front of the Miyasaki residence in Sheridan Tract. They were also in the dirt under the mango tree at Sam Makuakane's place. Millie came home from dinner at Sternwood's by taxi—giddy on champagne with a brand-new bauble from her ladylove. You were already there in the shadows. She didn't even see the pipe that cracked the back of her skull. You thought you killed her, Ruth. You dragged and threw her in the trunk of your Mercury Coupe and got out of there in a hurry, as the tracks suggest. Nobody was awake in Sheridan Tract, but you didn't want to hang around. If we were to go to your car now and have our lab guys look at your trunk, I'd bet my pension that they'd find traces of Millie Miyasaki."

Peg was distraught. "Ruth . . . say you didn't." Her voice was tiny and frail. Nothing on Ruth moved except her eyelids.

I took another drag, let it out, swallowed hard, and continued. "You panicked. You had a body in your car and didn't know what to do. You went to get help from the one person in the world who would always help you, no matter what. But he was so drunk he didn't know she was still alive, either, did he, Lei?" The porcelain doll cracked at the mention of that name. Her chest heaved up and down under her Chanel jacket and her eyes shifted wildly back and forth.

"I thought I recognized you on Sunday morning at my mother's place. You were a lot heavier in high school and your hair was frizzier and you wore glasses. The blinking was the same, though. This morning I had to look at my McKinley yearbook to make sure—I didn't know that your Christian name was Ruth until I saw it. Ruth Leilani Makuakane. You changed your name when you got married and remained Prentiss after you divorced. Sammy's pale, chubby little sister who pulled the haole from your dad's side." I could hear her making strange little whimpering noises under her breath. The blinking was now completely out of control.

"Your brother loved you, Lei. So much so that he took a shot at my lieutenant knowing that one of us would kill him. He made a dying confession and put it all on himself. I knew Sam. He had a quick temper and he was a rotten sportsman but he was no killer. No amount of money would've gotten him to do what he did—what he thought he did—which was get rid of a corpse. Nothing, except the need to protect the little sister he always doted on. You drove to Papakolea in distress. You thought you were a murderer. Sam put the body in his truck and he went to Pier 36 where he loaded it onto the *Hinalea* and took it to Pier 23. He made what appeared to be an ordinary fuel run to Pier 36. Sam was an experienced tug operator. He knew that he could neither leave the harbor nor dump the body en route to Pier 23 without attracting the attention of the Coast Guard. He moved the *Hinalea* a couple of times subsequent to that evening, but he missed the bracelet." Outside, the rain hit the windowpanes with beautiful violence. Inside, I kept talking just to fill the dead air in the room.

"I'm the one who put him down, Lei. It gave me no pleasure but he gave me no choice. Sam was my friend. He protected me. He protected you with his last breath, which incidentally was a message I was supposed to give you. He wanted me to tell you that he was sorry. Sorry for screwing up. He made me promise to tell you, so here I am." At that point, I realized that I wasn't just dripping rainwater or Luau's blood. I was dripping tears. And so was Ruth Prentiss.

She started to chew her lip until it bled through the five-dollar lipstick. Gid Hanohano's voice whispered in my ear from somewhere over the years. I didn't have the answer so I asked. I asked in a voice that was cracked by loss and regret.

"Why, Lei?"

"Stop calling me that!" she shrieked. "There is no Lei anymore! What would *you* do if your mother's life hinged on a hospital bill that was more than your salary could cover? Mr. Billings covered everything as long as I helped and kept things quiet."

There it was. It was brilliant. Peg had given Ruth carte blanche to act on her behalf, so every one of the secret scabs would assume that the generosity—and instructions—came from Peg and her bleeding red heart. Ruth shook like a frond in the trades. She said, "Would you let *your* mother die because you insisted on doing the 'right thing,' Detective? Does that badge allow you to be so cold-blooded and cold-hearted? You knew my brother. You knew he was loyal and he had a good heart but he was totally incapable of caring for our mother. She went from bad to worse. The burden was on me to look after her. I couldn't have that greedy bitch Millie ruin it. Or Danny Boy. It would mean the end of Mom's life support."

I thought about Harcourt Billings, Sr., that smiling rich man in his shiny hard hat with his shiny shovel. The icy devil that tried to buy my complacence with monthly payments on a new Cadillac. He used a desperate girl to reap a huge bonanza from the suffering of thousands like my mother and the many starving, striking stevedores.

"I lost a friend today," I said. "He was a good detective who was doing his job. He came and talked to you last night at the yacht club, didn't he, Miss Billings?"

Peg nodded absently. "He asked a lot of questions about me and Millie. I told him the truth. I was tired of living with it. Your friend was smart. He asked who knew I was out with her at Sternwood's that night and I told him only one other person, so he talked to Ruth."

"The other one must have intervened at that point."

"What do you mean?" asked Peg.

"The other cop," I said. "Your father had Luau Lewis on his payroll. That fat leech would soak up all of our talk about our case in the office and call him to give him updates on our progress. I ran into him at the Blaisdell Hotel when I went to talk to your father. He told me he was making a collection. He was. Just not from the high-class hookers in the lobby. He was getting his salary from the man in the private suite."

"My father has some . . .unusual . . . friends," said Peg, haltingly. "I just thought Detective Lewis was one of them."

"Come on, Miss Billings. Wake up. Harcourt Billings, Sr. doesn't keep company with the likes of a plebian worm like Detective Sergeant Clancy Lewis. He buys them. Luau Lewis could be had at a fire sale price. Your father was there at the yacht club and saw Detective Morris question you and Mrs. Prentiss, so he had his lapdog put a stop to it. Luau followed Jack to the Diamond Head Marine warehouse then gutted him there like he was an animal at the slaughterhouse next door. He dumped Jack in a dirty Chinatown alley. Then he went to see Kaz Sekiguchi to find out if we knew anything about the strike and scam of '49. He worked Kaz over something fierce. Lewis is lying in the atrium downstairs now, so it's only a matter of minutes before this is all over and believe me, I can hardly wait."

The shotgun was beginning to feel heavy and so was my heart. It broke for Peg and the betrayal of her lost love, for Danny Boy and his lost ambitions, for Jack and his lost life. It broke for Sam and his loyalty and for his little sister and their mom in a hospital bed. And for my ruined career as a police officer and for the certain loss of my pension, too. It broke for a lot of things but not for the Billings Trust. So I soldiered on to the inevitable.

"Harcourt Billings, Sr. tried to pay off my Cadillac at Schuman Carriage yesterday. How do you suppose he knew I drove a brand-new Cadillac Eldorado? I ran into Mrs. Prentiss on Monday on Merchant Street near Kaahumanu. 'Nice car,' she said. I told her I was making payments on it. She must've told Old Billings that it was probably a good way to get to me and ensure I'd lay off the whole Miyasaki thing. Sure, his hired gun Luau Lewis could have told him, but I think my version is more romantic. It's the poet in me."

Peg looked at Ruth, aghast. Ruth looked right through her at the wall.

"I'm sorry, Ruth. I really am," I said. "I'm sorry about your mother and I'm sorry about your brother. But I'm going to have to take you in. You're under arrest for the attempted murder of Mildred Miyasaki and for the murder of Danilo Cadiz."

"No," she said.

Then, quick as one of her many blinks, her hand was out of her big pocket and it was full of a gun. I should have remembered that this sort of thing ran in the family. The muzzle of my shotgun remained pointed right at her. She seemed not to notice. She pointed her gun at Peg. She was sobbing and shedding hot, bitter tears but her gun hand was steady as steel.

"Damn you, Peg," she wailed. "You're so blind! She was going to *ruin* you! All that little bitch ever wanted from you were *things*—perfume, dresses, dinners, Paris. *I* had to arrange it all! How sick is *that*?"

"No, no, Ruthie! Millie wasn't like that! She never asked me for anything! I'm the one who gave to her! She never asked!" They were both sobbing now. I shouldered my shotgun and aimed in. I prayed. It was silent and it was in my head but it was a prayer nonetheless. Reverend Takaki would be proud. Please God, I prayed, don't let this thing fuck up.

The wail of sirens could be heard over the din of traffic and rain. Some unfortunate clerk had found the mess in the lobby. The cavalry was coming.

Ruth said, "I was making contact with the union for your father. I started dating Danny Boy so we could get him to start thinking strike again. He was smarter and more ambitious than Kaz. Kaz got cold feet when I floated around talk about a second strike. The photographs were taken by the scabs as proof they did the job so they could collect. I was moving the photos little by little from the DHM offices on this floor so *you* wouldn't get suspicious. Danny Boy would have double-crossed me to get ahead; he would have ruined everything. He and that . . . that . . . girl were going to ruin *you*. I never loved him, anyway. I love *you*, Peg. I've always loved you."

"Oh, Ruthie," Peg cried. "Millie wouldn't do that. She was proud and she wanted to show me she could contribute in Paris. That's all."

"Shut up, Peg! Didn't you hear me? I love you! *Me*! Not her!"

"Ruthie . . . Ruthie . . . I love you, too, but not that way . . ."

"Damn it, Peg! It's all over now and it's all your fault!" She pulled the hammer back. I prayed one more time and held my breath. Then, curiously, she said to me but without taking her eyes off of Peg, "My top left drawer, Detective. You'll find everything you need. Take it and do what you will."

"What?" I asked.

Ruth said, "God damn you, Peg. I love *you*."

Then it happened. Before I could do anything, Ruth had turned her gun hand back toward herself, jammed the shiny revolver's muzzle in her mouth, and pulled the trigger.

"NO!" I yelled. Nobody heard. I was drowned out by a roar. The same roar that was the last thing that Danny Boy Cadiz heard in this world.

31

Sometimes things don't go the way you plan them. In fact, it's been my experience that they rarely do. I was supposed to ask a few questions, establish Ruth Prentiss's motives and get a confession, if I were lucky enough to do so, then serve the warrant, take her back to the station, book her, and sit back and watch the shit fly between the Billings Trust attorneys, the brass, and the press, and my career start its downward swirl toward the sewer.

I got the motive and confession, but Ruth found the ultimate way of avoiding arrest.

There was blood and brains and little bits of skull everywhere. The poor Tabriz carpet had soaked up more than water off my raincoat. Peg Billings wouldn't stop shrieking. She screamed until she was hoarse then she curled up in a ball under her desk. Numb, I went to Ruth's desk in the reception area and opened the top left drawer. There was a large, fat envelope full of documents and photographs detailing the black-market rice scheme and the payoffs made to secret scabs. There were also instructions for the next big strike. The rice we had seen in the warehouse was being hoarded in preparation for the second strike. I tucked the big envelope into my raincoat.

I pulled the hip flask out of my pocket and drank sloppily. I somehow kept my head and my stomach and went down to the atrium to greet the troops.

The whole building was crawling with uniforms and dicks over the next few hours. Lab coats with cameras showed up too. Harcourt, Sr. was out of town and Junior was having drinks at the Nuuanu Country Club. Even with all the bodies and activity, there was a strange, hushed sense about the way everyone conducted their business. Discreet was the watchword. The brass knew what went down at the Billings Trust Building and that a Homicide dick was involved. They wanted no blood in the water for the press sharks to smell.

After an hour or so, the M.E. showed up with the same major who told me I was a hero on Wednesday in Papakolea. I wondered if the major came to tell me that he changed his mind. We went through the paces again, but this time I only had to tell my story a couple of times over. The brass was probably more than a little relieved that nobody in the Billings family had any culpability in the matter. That's not the way I saw it. Harcourt Billings, Sr. bled the island during a strike he opposed in the press but helped to perpetuate under the table. He realized a huge black-market profit. And he put Ruth Prentiss up to the task of helping to run the scheme and hide it. He used her mother to buy her. He tried to use my car to buy me. But nobody cared what I thought. I could feel it coming. This wouldn't just be a cover-up; this was going to be a full-blown secret burial in an unmarked grave. Not if I could help it. I gave the envelope under my arm a squeeze.

Peg's driver showed up to collect her and take her home. She got up out of Ruth's seat and moved from behind Ruth's desk like a phantom, not so much walking as gliding slowly and soundlessly out of a red world of violence and trauma into a clean, quiet snow-white tomb. She paused as they passed me.

"Goodbye, Detective."

"Goodbye, Miss Billings."

She walked down the hall and joined the driver at the elevator. They got in and I watched the brass doors close slowly on a head of golden hair and the saddest of faces. Empty and bleak, the hallway echoed, I thought, with the quiet sound of the elevator doors closing. I walked back down the hall and rejoined the zoo her office had become.

In the end, Ruth did more than avoid a messy trial and sentence. She did what her brother did for her. She protected the one she loved. Her ugly, self-inflicted end assured that Peg would not be subjected to the embarrassing and potentially life-ruining spectacle of having to testify at her trial. Ruth had passed through the Gates of Hell that morning and probably abandoned all hope long before entering. The envelope she brought to my attention may be her ticket up Mount Purgatory. I knew that her brother was already at the summit of *Purgatorio*, maybe even waiting for the waters to take him up to the moon.

A brother and a sister willing to kill for love willingly died for it. And I was caught up in it when all I was doing was my job, a job I might not have for much longer. Strangely, or maybe not strangely, I didn't much care.

I dragged myself back to the station at two-thirty in the afternoon. I was worn out by all of the questions. There wasn't a lot of time spent on Ruth Prentiss's suicide, but a hell of a long time spent on what happened in the atrium. I told them repeatedly tests would show that the older blood on Luau's shirt would be Jack Morris's. There was a lot of frowning and muttering and headshaking over the matter. It would be a public relations black eye for the Department for sure.

I walked back to the station down Merchant Street. The sidewalks weren't as crowded. The rain had washed the gore from my raincoat and I was just another sopping wet pedestrian—with a shotgun.

When I reached the station, every cop at the receiving desk mobbed me, wanting to know what happened. Everyone had listened to his radio. I didn't say much. The brass had told me not to comment, that they'd be releasing their own statement to the Department and to the press. There wasn't a lot to say, in any case. A girl shot herself. I wouldn't be going to court to stand around with their shitty coffee and say "yes" or "no" for the prosecutor; I'd be typing two reports and drinking Delilah's shitty coffee right at my desk. Ten or so pages with carbons. That's all the lives of four people amounted to. Case closed. Jack and Luau and the watchman at the Billings Trust were another matter. I didn't even want to think about it, and I didn't comment on it as instructed. The brass would handle that one.

Eventually, the mob at the receiving desk would lose interest. Just like the rest of the island.

I went upstairs and into the Homicide Detail office and found it just as empty as I left it in the morning. I looked at Jack's desk and at Gid's office and let a couple of tears escape. I opened Jack's top drawer and found his yellow yo-yo. I looked at it for a moment and then dropped it in my pocket. I pulled on my raincoat, grabbed my hat, gave the daruma one last poke, and left the office without looking back. I walked down the tiled stairs and ran my hand along the black wrought-iron railing and walked right past the receiving desk with its chorus of lost souls waiting to book and to be booked. I went down the stairs in the foyer and lit a Lucky Strike and thought about a girl in a silver frame that ended up in the green murk of Honolulu Harbor. A girl I had once thought was the whole world. She went down for her hopes and dreams because they were tainted with want of money.

It starts out small with a pair of gloves or a tube of lipstick then it grows. Paris. Diamonds. Twenty thousand dollars of blood money. When your dreams have a price tag and you try to get someone else to foot the bill you can fool yourself for a very short time thinking you got a deal, but you wind up paying in full with interest.

Charon was the bill collector. He took Millie's payment as his fare and gave her a ride across the Acheron.

Danny Boy Cadiz and Ruth Prentiss were the same as Millie. They got others to finance their mercurial hopes, some altruistic and some avaricious, but they ended up in the same boat as Millie in the end, looking over the bow of Charon's ferry to the far shores of oblivion. It was a hell of a ride from Sheridan Tract or Papakolea or Waipahu and a damn expensive one.

Luau Lewis survived on the scraps that were thrown his way for a lapdog's job. It was one thing to shake down hookers or gambling den owners for payoffs but it's another entirely to take out one of your own. He'd take Judas Iscariot's place in Lucifer's mouth in the very lowest Circle of Hell. Traitor. He couldn't die enough times for what he did to Jack.

Only Sam Makuakane was different. His violence, in the end, had the noblest and purest of motives. It always had, whether it was breaking the arm of an opposing linebacker for a cheap shot on a teammate or shooting the shoulder of a Detective Lieutenant to save a little sister. The irony was that he'd be reviled as a murderer while the others would be thought of as victims. Yet I had no doubt he'd be up there on the moon in the First Heaven looking down at all the rest of them, including his keepers in life, the rotten Billings Trust.

Jack. John James Morris of Pelham Bay. Why he decided to follow me on my idiot's crusade for the truth I'll never know. He was more practical than that, and shedding his mantle of caution cost him his life. I finally exorcised the ghost of Millie by bringing the matter to its bloody conclusion, but the ghost of Jack Morris would haunt me for the rest of my life, always reminding me that the right thing is often not the easy thing. It was something To-san tried to tell me, too. Sometimes the world shits on you and all you can do is grin and bear it, especially when you're doing what's right. It took Jack's ultimate sacrifice, though, to make me see that as long as you're on the straight and narrow it's possible. Keep your eye on the ball. Be good.

I drove to Queen's to visit with Gid. I told him all about my conclusions and about everything that transpired that morning. He had heard about Jack. All he could do was say Jack's name a couple of times and close his eyes. He listened with a thoughtful frown to the rest of it then shook his great big head ruefully.

"The curse of the rich," he said, not without a touch of sadness in his gruff voice.

"What?"

"Terrible stuff like this can happen to just about anyone. But normal folks like you and me—like Millie Miyasaki or Danny Boy Cadiz or Sam Makuakane or his sister—we suffer a little bit then we die. Not the rich. Not Peg Billings or people like her. They suffer, but they live on because that's what their station buys them. Longevity. Perseverance. But they suffer, Sheik. They suffer a long time. That's the curse of the rich."

"Well, it's a damn good thing we'll never be rich, then."

Gid laughed that quiet, wheezing laugh of his. Gideon Hanohano. Always the thinking man. I could do worse than to grow up to be like him. The curse of the rich. How the hell did he come up with shit like that? I shook my head and laughed along with him. He was right, though. He always was.

The doctor stopped by and told me that Gid would be discharged in the next couple of days. The news made my heart lighter. I deserved a little good news, I thought, after everything that had transpired that day.

Gid looked up at me from his pillow. He smiled his slight, tiny smile. "So much blood," he said. "Are you going to be okay?"

"I'll live," I told him. "That's *my* curse, I guess. It's what happens to thinking men."

"Fast learner." Gid laughed that dry, silent wheezing laugh of his.

On my way out, I stopped at the door of Gid's private room. I said, "So long, Lieutenant. We had some good times, didn't we?"

"There'll be more. Go home and take a break. You earned it." I waved and walked out. Take a break. Maybe for good. Maybe the brass would wait until Monday before asking me for my badge. Maybe I could teach some high school English and coach first base. But I didn't think about that for long. The only thing on my mind at that point was driving a few blocks Diamond Head down King Street to Sheridan as quickly as I possibly could. I was thinking of a girl standing in the rain in my rearview mirror.

The rain had not let up all day though at times it was heavier than at others. In about ten minutes I was parked in front of the *Honolulu Record* with its hand-fed press and its little staff, which included a reporter who earned $125 a month, the same reporter who was about to break the biggest scandal in the islands since the Massie case. I got out of the car and pulled my hat low on my face and started toward the door.

I didn't get halfway across the slick sidewalk before Ellen came bursting out the door and flew straight into my arms. She nearly knocked me all the way back to the Cadillac. We kissed. Her face was streaked with rain but I knew that there were tears there, too. She felt so absolutely perfect in my arms that the week's suffering melted away and slipped into the gutter with the downpour.

"You're all right!" she shouted above the hammering rain, elated.

"In one piece, as promised."

I handed her the envelope. "Knock yourself out, darling," I told her. Ellen grasped the envelope and threw her arms around my neck.

"I love you," she said.

"I love you, too." I ka ʻōlelo no ke ola. *In words there is life*. And much more life than you'll ever know when you've been through all of the Circles of Hell and back.

Then it suddenly happened. A gust from the mountains swept down on us and nearly blew the hat off of my head. A chill surged through us and we clung to each other tightly, shivering. I smiled. The trades had come back. Kona winds were finally gone. I looked out from where we stood on the sidewalk on Sheridan Street past the *Record*'s little building at the mist beyond. Diamond Head was completely shrouded by rain.

The turbulent waters bore me away from *Purgatorio* to the First Heaven and my Beatrice was there to guide me. Somewhere in that grayness further than we could see was Paris. But so was Kaimuki.

We got into my car and I drove us there.

Acknowledgements

A detective book from Bamboo Ridge Press, one of the most respected literary presses in the nation. Who would have thought it possible? Not me. Nonetheless, here it is, beyond all logic and expectation. This wonderful accident—which really is no accident—is the result of the support of many exceptional people whom I wish to thank with my deepest appreciation:

Jayson Chun for the initial push to tell a story of this special place that hasn't been told before in my own way all those many evenings ago in Kaimukī; Sarah Mattos, for encouraging me to finish this project, with the belief that I was more than the sum of my paycheck and what I did to earn it; Pat Patterson, who, with Jayson and Sarah, endured the torment of my first draft and invested nearly as much time in reading and commenting as I did in writing; Lillian Nakamura and Tom Hutton, for your patience and for enduring the torment of subsequent drafts and for being kind enough to give me feedback; Steph Cha, a wonderful and talented writer I much admire, for her generosity in my early days of querying and for introducing me to Corey Johnson; Corey Johnson for making the outrageous suggestion (at the time) of submitting a couple of chapters to Bamboo Ridge Press;

Juliet S. Kono Lee, Jean Yamasaki Toyama, Christy Passion, and Ann Inoshita, brilliant poets and literary giants all, for taking a chance on noir and for championing my work; Donald Carreira Ching for all his outstanding work in obtaining the grants which help support the work of Bamboo Ridge Press; Juliet Lee and Jean Toyama for casting their discerning gaze on my manuscript and helping me to shape it into something that impresses even me; beyond that my gratitude to the editorial team I was blessed with—Juliet, Jean, Gail N. Harada, Joy Kobayashi-Cintrón, Normie Salvador, and Ken Tokuno, the most thorough and discerning people I have known; for the breathtaking cover, Tommy Hite, artist, and Jui-Lien Sanderson, book designer, for the outstanding package. If it's true against cliché that a book *can* be judged by its cover, I can only hope my words do your combined work justice.

I would like to thank Steph Cha, Naomi Hirahara, Ed Lin, Rodney Morales, David Mura, Pamela Rotner Sakamoto, and Don Wallace, writers revered by me and countless others, for their generosity in reading and endorsing my work.

For putting my mind at ease, I would like to thank Wing Tek Lum, who showed me how the sausage is made. You are the best at what you do. I would like to thank Eric Chock and Darrell H. Y. Lum for the beacon that is Bamboo Ridge Press. I hope this work will become a worthy part of the legacy you started.

I would like to thank my mother Carol, my stepfather David, my sisters Lori and Kerrie and their families for all of the love and support; and all the Kikkawas, Okumuras, Wards, Amians, and Saos—I am honored to be considered one of you.

Most of all, I would like to thank my wife, Arnie, and my children, Caroline and Cole, for making my life perfect by being perfect.

A product of Hawai'i Kai in East Honolulu, Scott Kikkawa is the author of noir detective stories set in postwar Honolulu featuring Detective Sergeant Francis "Sheik" Yoshikawa. His work has been published in *Bamboo Ridge, Journal of Hawai'i Literature and Arts. Kona Winds* is his first full-length novel. The New York University alumnus is currently a Federal law enforcement officer and lives with his family in Honolulu.